This one is dedicated to every reader who has picked up an Ever After Street book – thank you for joining me on the journey of my first series!

1

'Congratulations! It'll be the very first Ever After Street wedding!' I clap enthusiastically along with the rest of the shop-keepers after our co-workers, and friends, Sadie and Witt have announced their engagement.

There's something wonderful about a wedding announce-ment, but when you're the last one of your friends to still be happily single, there's something awful too – the impending insistence that you cannot attend a wedding alone and must imminently find a 'plus one', usually followed by the kind offer to find one for you if you need any help, and the sudden insight that someone's half-brother's cousin's neighbour's friend works with someone who'd be *perfect* for you.

'The wedding will be on New Year's Eve at the castle. You're all invited, and we won't take no for an answer, of course!' Sadie says. 'And don't forget, plus ones are mandatory! No one can enjoy a wedding alone! Love is supposed to be shared!'

Ah, there it is. The unavoidable assertion that if you haven't found 'the one' yet, you're somehow lacking something, rather than just having standards and not wanting to settle for someone who doesn't set your world alight and make you feel like Disney princesses do when they meet their princes.

We're at what was supposed to be a meeting for the shop-keepers on Ever After Street, but Sadie, who makes beautiful dresses at The Cinderella Shop, and Witt, who owns the castle that looks out over the street from the hills behind, have surprised us all by announcing their engagement and upcoming wedding, and I'm as pleased for them as everyone else, because they're the happiest couple and the most perfect match, but weddings have a way of reminding you that *you* haven't found your perfect match yet and everyone who's happily coupled up feels sorry for you, especially for a wedding on New Year's Eve when you're staring down the barrel of another year of singledom, and the only thing you're likely to kiss at midnight is a tub of leftover Christmas chocolates.

'Don't you just love a wedding?' My best friend Mickey, who runs The Mermaid's Treasure Trove curiosity shop, drops her arm around my shoulders. 'And what a perfect excuse to get back into dating!'

'I don't want to get back into dating. The right man will fall into my life when he's supposed to, and if he doesn't then I'm happier being single than I would be in a relationship that isn't the right fit.'

Even Mickey, my eternal plus one and partner in all things single, met a handsome history teacher over the summer and is now happily coupled up. All my fellow shopkeepers are, actually. Over the years, they've all met their perfect someone, and I'm still alone, working in the museum on the hill that overlooks the street, surrounded by artefacts that have stepped right out of a fairytale, and daydreaming of brave princes and handsome strangers, enchanted forests and hidden beasts, and trying to cling onto my conviction that true love's kiss is out there for everyone, and I'll find my own version of it someday.

Even if that day is unlikely to be before Sadie and Witt's wedding in three months' time.

'Ren knows a couple of single teachers...' Mickey sounds like she's been planning this conversation for a while, but to me, her partner's teenage daughter is looking like my best bet for a plus one, or maybe I could bribe one of my sisters into coming with me...

'And no, you can't take Ava.' My best friend can clearly read my mind. 'And you do know a plus one only counts if they're *not* related to you,' she adds before I can mention my cunning plan of roping a sister in.

'My Prince Eric statue! I could drag that along, put a nice jacket and scarf on it and no one would know the difference. It would still be a more talkative date than some of the men I met from those dating apps you set me up on!'

And the less said about those, the better. I'd say I kissed a lot of frogs, but most of those frogs only wanted *one* thing, so it never got as far as kissing, and no actual frog has ever been repulsive enough to deserve the comparison.

Everyone says goodbye and Mickey and I start walking away, but I was wrong to assume I could sneak off that easily.

'Lissa! About my son I mentioned...' Mrs Coombe, who runs the winterwear shop on Christmas Ever After, rushes after us. This is far from the first time she's mentioned her son who's moved back home after working abroad and would, apparently, be my ideal man.

Before I have a chance to respond, Imogen from Sleeping Beauty's Once Upon A Dream marches over. 'No, Mrs Coombe, we discussed this. My neighbour's lad is free this weekend, would you like...?' She turns to me hopefully.

'...people to stop discussing my love life behind my back?' I finish the question for her. 'Yes, I'd love that, thank you.'

'Nope, Ren's art teacher friend has got first dibs,' Mickey interrupts, shutting them both down.

I know she's only trying to save me, but I have as much intention of meeting Ren's art teacher friend as I do of meeting any other potential matches my co-workers can summon out of thin air. It makes me feel like Princess Jasmine when she declares that she isn't a prize to be fought over, and the only thing I've ever wanted to share with Princess Jasmine is her perfect hair. Although a prince riding a magical flying carpet wouldn't go amiss either, if only to appease my well-meaning friends.

'Really?' I turn to Mickey as the other two slink away with suitably guilty looks.

'I was trying to help! You don't want to be set up with Imogen's random neighbour or Mrs Coombe's son any more than you want to meet Ren's colleague, but you're going to need a plus one before the end of the year.'

'That's plenty of time. And if I don't find anyone, what are Sadie and Witt going to do? Bar the doors and lock me outside? It's not like it's actually enforceable. You were all single once. Just because you're rolling in loved-up happiness now, you must still have vague memories of how hard it is to meet someone who's not married, otherwise taken, an axe murderer, or a misogynistic twit.'

We make our way towards our respective businesses, and I wave to her as we reach the fork in the wishbone shape of Ever After Street and she splits off towards her curiosity shop, and I continue towards my museum of fairytale artefacts.

Ever After Street is the best place in the world to work. A cobblestone road full of quaint little shops that are all themed around fairytales, right in the heart of the Wye Valley, at the foot of a real-life fairytale castle in the hills beyond the street. There's a forest, and a river flowing past, and Colours of the Wind museum is on a small hill, overlooking a grassy picnic area which is home to a carousel, craft areas for children, crammed flowerbeds, and plenty of space for families to enjoy the outdoor air and general magical feeling that pervades our quirky little street.

I look up at the grey-brick building as I climb the higgledy-piggledy set of stone steps towards it. The building looks like a large, welcoming house that's been built in three distinct sections. There's green ivy covering one third of the building, but no matter how much I try to encourage it, it never wants to spread to the other sections.

Colours of the Wind has become like a living, breathing thing over the years. Sometimes I feel like the artefacts could talk if they wanted to...

I stop in my tracks. There's a man on my roof.

When I suggested a man might fall into my life, I did *not* mean it literally. 'What are you doing? Get down from there right now!'

The man is wearing a yellow workman's jacket and a hard hat and taking photos. He doesn't even look up at my bellow, but I realise the museum door is open.

What the heck? I locked up before I left for the meeting. I *know* I did.

I *race* up the steps and barrel inside, and I'm greeted by... men. Everywhere. There are men *everywhere*.

Men in yellow work jackets and hard hats. Men up ladders with industrial-sized tape measures. Someone's marking up the wall outside the room where I keep princess dresses and clothing for children to dress up in when they visit, and I'm bewildered by what I'm seeing. I've only been on the other side of the street for half an hour – *where* did all these people come from and *what* are they doing here?

In the middle of the chaos is a man, probably in his early forties, wearing the sharpest suit and smartest tie I've ever seen, with fingers flying across a tablet in his hand. He gives off an air of being the one in charge of all this, whatever *this* is, and I march across to him.

'Excuse me, but what the *hell* is going on here? Who are you and what do you think you're doing in my museum?'

He looks up from his tablet and when his eyes fall on me, he recoils like I've scared him. 'Wow, you are an ex-*plo*-sion of colour, aren't you?'

It does not sound like a compliment, and I shake my hair back and stand taller, trying to embrace the multi-coloured look of my younger sister's hairdressing training.

'Let me guess, Lisa Carisbrooke?'

'It's Lissa.'

'Oh, so that's not a typo?' He uses a stylus pen to correct something on the tablet he's holding. 'I've never heard that one before.'

'I don't think the spelling of my name is too important when I'm moments away from calling the police!' I brandish my phone at him. 'Who are you and what are you doing in my museum?'

'Oh, where are my manners? My apologies. Warren Berrington of Berrington Developments.' He holds his hand out like he actually expects me to shake it. 'Owner of the building, so technically, *you* are the one in *my* museum.'

'No, no, no, that's not right.' I'm struggling to clear my reeling head. 'My landlord is—'

'Mr Mowbray,' he fills in for me. 'Yes, dear old chap, not much of a head for business these days though. Berrington

Developments have recently purchased the building and given him a nice nest-egg for his impending retirement.'

The knots twisting around in my stomach are accompanied by a severe sinking feeling. I was hoping this was all a misunderstanding and he was simply in the wrong place, but that flicker of hope is instantly snuffed out. He wouldn't know that about the landlord if this wasn't legit, would he?

I reluctantly fold my arms, tucking my phone under my armpit because I haven't quite given up on the idea of calling the police yet. I'm still hoping there's some sort of 'breaking and entering, filling my building with random men' law he might have flouted, and surely there's health and safety protocol about the guy on the roof? 'Why has no one informed me?'

His infuriatingly handsome face contorts in confusion. 'What do you think I'm doing if not informing you?'

'I meant in writing. Advance warning, that sort of thing.'

His dark eyebrows furrow. 'Again, what exactly do you think I'm doing right now? I *am* your advance warning, right here in front of you. Arguably cheaper than a first-class stamp these days.'

'Doesn't the landlord have a responsibility to keep tenants informed of changes like this?' I'm clutching at straws, trying to find some loophole that can punch a hole through this ridiculous claim, and we both know it. I know less than zilch about things like property law, and I'm pretty sure it's written all over my face.

'Well, you'll have to take *that* up with Mr Mowbray. You'll probably find him on a plane, halfway to the Caribbean by now. Between you and me, he was looking forward to a break. He'd been struggling to stay on top of his landlordly responsibilities, as I'm sure you know, seeing how you've got away with paying such a pitiful amount of rent for so many years. Any landlord still holding onto all their marbles would've increased that years ago.' He gives me the most condescending of all smiles. 'Fortunately, Berrington Developments are nowhere near as lax when it comes to their duty to their tenants and fair use of their properties.'

Developments. A word to strike fear into the heart of any small business owner who works on a quaint, somewhat old-fashioned street where everyone knows everyone else and every business is run with the heart and soul of its owners, and profit is not the most important thing to any of us. And absolutely no one wears a suit that cost more than my annual takings. I'm trying not to look at him, but it's hard not to appreciate the fit of that very smart suit, even though I'm certain that the price tag would make my eyes water.

A company with the word 'developments' in its name should be nowhere near a street like this. Mr Mowbray has always been a hands-off landlord. He was enchanted by my idea of a museum full of fairytale artefacts, and he stepped back and let me get on with it. I've now got a five-year commercial lease with a guarantee of no rent increases. That doesn't expire for another two years, and there's nothing this guy can do about it.

I hope.

I go to tell him that, but before I've managed to stutter out half a sentence about my long-term lease, he interrupts.

'Oh, yes, your current lease is voided, by the way. New owners – new lease. Rent's tripled and we've added a tiny little redevelopment clause that states you'll need to vacate the property within six months should we decide to forge ahead with redevelopment plans. Here you go, here's the preliminary notice that we *are* intending to redevelop the site, so I'm officially serving you your six months' notice. Advance warning, as requested.' In one swift move, he bends to open a briefcase next to his feet, slides out some papers and pushes them into my hands with a cheerful tap of his stylus pen, like he's just given me the latest weather report rather than delivered news that will upend my life.

'What?' Every word is like a crash-course in gobble-de-gook. *Triple* my rent? Evict me in six months? They *can't*... surely? 'You can't do that.'

'I assure you, I can.' His smile could actually be quite nice if he wasn't in the process of destroying my life. 'We're a multinational property acquisitions and development company. Family run. My mother handles the acquisitions aspect, I handle the development side of the business. Have done since I left university. We've done this *hundreds* of times. I know my rights – and yours.'

'I didn't mean from a legal standpoint, I meant morally.' I'm struggling to keep the emotion out of my voice. There are too many people here, doing things that I didn't approve, and this guy is telling me that I'm about to be evicted and there's nothing I can do about it? It's all too much. 'This museum is part of Ever After Street. It's been here for ten years. The local council have to approve all plans regarding businesses on this street...' I trail off because I am not the biggest fan of our local council and they might describe me as... a thorn in their side, if they were feeling particularly generous in the descriptive department. I've led protests against their unreasonable demands on more than one occasion. If they saw a chance to get rid of me, they'd bite the hand off the person who was offering.

'The local council have no say over private properties. There may be certain conditions for a tenant to meet, but in redevelopment terms, if we can guarantee an increase in revenue and visitors and something that enhances the street, then we're all set. We've already had preliminary plans approved by the council.'

He says it in an upbeat, lofty voice, like it's the best thing that's happened all week, whereas I feel like the whole world is crumbling around me.

How can they swan in and take over everything? How can there not be something I can do, some form of retaliation, some right of being a tenant here for so many years? I mean, maybe there *is*, and this guy clearly isn't going to reveal it to me, but if I can get an appointment with the Citizens Advice Bureau, or throw myself at the mercy of the local council and beg them for help... I can't be kicked out of Colours of the Wind. It's been my whole life for over ten years. My world is centred here. The idea of losing it leaves me feeling like this is a nightmare that I need to wake up from.

I've never been very good at hiding emotions, and something flickers in Warren Berrington's blue eyes. 'I sense you're conflicted.'

'Conflicted?' It comes out much louder than I intended and several of the workmen turn to look at me. '*Conflicted?*' I hiss again, quieter this time as the workmen go back to whatever measurements they were taking and things they were surveying. 'No, actually, I'm not conflicted at all. There is no conflict here. I've poured years of love and work and hopes and dreams and imagination into this museum. You cannot simply waltz in and claim it. There are laws that protect commercial tenants, and I... I...' I intend to find out what they are, but I don't want him to know that I don't already *know* what they are, so I square my shoulders and jut my chin out. 'I intend to use them against you.'

He laughs. I don't think he means to, but he bursts out laughing. And I think about what this must look like. He's obviously used to being in charge, with his frightfully posh suit, shiny shoes, and fancy tablet, whereas my curly hair is wild, mostly blonde with dark roots coming through, and a rainbow of colours in it from my sister experimenting with foils and coloured highlights a few weeks ago. I'm wearing dungarees that have come undone at one shoulder, and a long-sleeve top with a hole in one arm and a paint stain on the other. I'm still clutching my phone like I'm hoping to batter him with it, and I haven't ungritted my teeth since I walked in. He probably feels like he's just been threatened by a poodle.

'Well, don't I feel like I've just been read my rights upon arrest?' He composes himself and stands up straighter. 'Do you know how much trouble a company like ours would be in if we cut corners? Every line of your tenancy agreement has been gone through by multiple experts. Our contract is watertight. I spend my life looking for loopholes and *closing* them. Look, Lissa... May I call you Lissa?'

'I don't know, may I call you a demonic gerbil with no soul?'

He laughs again, not taking me seriously, even though he almost definitely is demonic and quite... gerbilic.

'Petty name-calling aside, you would get a lot more out of this if you work with us, not against us.'

'Work with you to do what?' His words pique my curiosity. So far he's made it sound like I have no options, but this makes it sound like there might be a lifeline after all.

'You and I both want the same thing. You want to save your museum, and I'm here to help save your museum. I know I've made that sound unlikely so far.'

I get the impression of a used-car salesman. A bit of patter, clever marketing phrases, and a charm and affability, with an air of someone who's done this before. Many times before, but I go along with it, because being in this position, even thinking about losing the museum and *having* to save it makes it impossible not to listen. Five minutes ago, everything was normal. How can this happen and how can *this* be the first I'm hearing about it?

'But fear not, all is not lost. Believe it or not, I am actually here to help. I'm quite taken by your concept. I've not heard of anything like it before, and I believe there might be merit in keeping it open.'

I narrow my eyes because I can read between *those* lines. 'Profit, you mean?'

'Yes, profit. A thing that all businesses need to stay afloat. I haven't had a chance to go over your accounting in depth yet, but it's blatantly obvious that this place is struggling.'

'It's not struggling. At least, it wasn't until you showed up,' I snap at him, but if I'm honest, it *is* struggling a bit, and I'm certainly not going to admit *that* out loud. 'It's hard to get people interested and I could do with more advertising, but the budget is limited, and what little there is has to go towards new exhibits and making Colours of the Wind a world of imagination. Things like marketing fall further down the list, but it limps onwards, like a zombie shuffling along with the occasional limb falling off. Okay, every so often, it has to stop and sew an arm back on, but it gets there in the end.'

'Where's it going?' He pushes at his lower lip with his pen, looking bemused by my comparison.

'I don't know. Wherever zombies go. To come back to life.' I've lost track of my own analogy, and he's watching my lips as I speak, clearly trying to keep track of it himself and barely suppressing another laugh. He was probably expecting a suited-up office-dwelling museum curator, and he's got a multi-coloured poodle yammering about zombies. No wonder he looks confused.

'While this certainly feels like walking into a horror film, my goal *is* to help you bring it back to life.'

I scoff in disbelief, because there's no way a guy like this does something to help anyone other than himself. He didn't manage to afford suits like that by helping *others*, did he? This is a head-office man accustomed to sitting behind a desk and giving orders, who's completely out of touch with the real world and what it's like to run a business on a small budget.

He looks at me for a moment, blue eyes blinking slowly as he considers his next move. 'May I show you something?'

Without waiting for an answer, he swivels his tablet around so it's facing me, skims his stylus pen across the screen until an architectural drawing of... a load of geometric shapes on a hill appears in grainy pixels under my nose.

I tilt my head to the side. 'What is that?'

He quirks a dark eyebrow but doesn't answer the question, leaving me tilting my head to the other side, trying to figure out what it's supposed to be. It looks like someone's dropped a Rubik's Cube and the layers have broken apart, and I'm pretty sure that whatever it was he wanted to show me, he's pressed the wrong buttons and brought up the wrong image.

'Nope, you've lost me. It looks like you're trying to invent a building block puzzle to confuse a small child.'

His blue eyes flick between my face and the screen. 'This is what happens in six months' time, if this place doesn't demonstrate that it can do a *lot* better than it's currently doing.'

'*What?*' I grab the tablet with both hands and snatch it from him, and he yelps because his fingers are through a holding strap on the back and he has to yank them free to avoid them being broken. I instantly realise what he means. *What* he's trying to show me. The hill. This isn't a child's puzzle. It's here. It's this place. It's what this place is going to become if I don't do something to stop it. They're going to demolish this gorgeous, eccentric old building and rebuild this hideously modern architectural nightmare in its place. It's all squares and sharp angles and looks like something from a futuristic sci-fi film where there are robots flying around all over the place and people whizz past on hoverboards. There has never been anything that would look *more* out of place on Ever After Street.

The *last* thing I intended to do was cry, but it's a gut reaction and tears have welled up in my eyes before I know it. 'You... *can't*... You're going to knock it down and build this... this... *monstrosity* in its place?'

He's shaking his hand like he's still trying to ease the pain in his fingers. 'We propose to turn it into a cinema and entertainment complex. Multiple screens for maximum film showings, and indoor bowling, indoor mini golf, wall climbing, an American-style diner, a pizzeria, a doughnut chain, an arcade, and a whole host of other entertainment options that haven't been settled on yet.'

'You can't do that,' I repeat, wondering how many times I'm going to plead those words today. What am I expecting him to say? 'Oh, yes, you're quite right, I won't then.' As if. 'Places like that will put the food shops here out of business. Cleo who runs The Wonderland Teapot, and Ali who owns the 1001 Nights restaurant. They won't be able to compete with diners and pizza places and doughnuts.'

'That wouldn't be Berrington Developments' problem.'

'Of course it wouldn't,' I mutter. Did I really expect any different response? 'And why does everything modern have to be indoors? Wall climbing, golf, bowling. Mostly traditional outdoor activities. Shouldn't we be encouraging children to spend more time outside and away from screens? Let me guess, not your problem?'

'I'm a businessman, not a parent. If we give kids – and adults, and families – as many activities as possible that they can do in one place, they spend more time in that one place, and therefore, more money. *That's* the only bottom line that matters.'

'Of course it is.' I echo the same response as earlier. The businesses and shops, and *friends* who are going to suffer because of this are irrelevant to his company.

The magnitude of it starts to sink in as I tap his tablet to turn the screen back on and stare at the drawing again. This is not just about Colours of the Wind. It isn't just me who will lose my business if this plan comes to fruition. This will be the end of Ever After Street as a whole. If everyone who comes here is going to spend hours glued to a cinema screen, or scoffing pizza, or scrambling up a wall or playing indoor golf, they *aren't* going to be visiting the quaint and quirky shops here, like Marnie's *Beauty and the Beast*-themed bookshop, Mickey's curiosity shop, or Imogen's Once Upon A Dream that specialises in all things cosy, like pyjamas, fancy bedding, and candles. Small independent shops will fall by the wayside in favour of this under-one-roof approach where customers can spend their entire day... while the rest of the street stands empty.

The thought makes the emotions rolling through me even stronger, and I turn away and swipe at my eyes, angry at myself for not being able to hide it. I'm trying to pretend I'm not crying, but the unexpected shock of this has undone me.

'I *am* here to help...' He's looking at me warily, like he's not sure if I'm going to start wailing or bare my teeth and try to nip him.

'Why would you help me if *this* is what you intend to do to my building?' I jab angrily at the tablet and he reaches over and extracts it from my hands before I do it any damage.

He lets it slide that this isn't *my* building – it never was, and it never will be. My teeth cut through the inside of my lip until I taste blood as I try to stem the tears again. This museum is the only thing that's ever given me a sense of stability in my life. The security of being a mainstay of Ever After Street is gone in an instant, and I don't know what to do about it.

He taps at the tablet again. '*This* is going to cost a *lot* of money, and I *like* the concept of a fairytale museum, it's interesting and different and could be huge if done right.'

I bristle at the implication that *I* have not been doing it right for all these years.

'The way I see it is that it will cost a lot less to invest in this place as it is, bring in some much-needed upgrades and budget fine-tuning, and see where it takes us. My mother was all for immediate demolition, but it was me who put forward this plan and got us this stay of execution. We have until the end of the year to turn this around and prove that it's better value to keep it as it is – with a few minor adjustments – than it is to build the cinema complex. My company can put up a cinema complex anywhere – I've overseen four already in the past couple of years – but where else are we going to find something as unique as a fairytale museum?'

My hackles have risen at his way of making it sound like I have some sort of choice, when it's blindingly clear that I do not. 'And I will be at your mercy? Constantly waiting for the day you decide you're going to knock it down anyway and evict me at a moment's notice?'

'Six months' notice.' He corrects me by tapping his pen on the papers in my hand. 'And I'll offer you a deal. If you can prove that this place is worth keeping – that it's a worthwhile business venture, and it can make us more money than a cinema complex could, and you can cover the increased rent – then we'll match Mr Mowbray's terms in the lease. Five years, and we'll take out the redevelopment clause.'

'And after that?'

'We'll reassess, as any good landlord should.'

That bit is fair enough, even Mr Mowbray reassessed every once in a while. It's everything else that feels hideously unfair. How can this man swoop in here and act like he's trying to help? 'And what exactly would these "minor adjustments" entail? Is that what all these workmen are doing? Measuring up for your "minor adjustments"?'

'They're surveying, getting a feel for—'

'All good for the fishtank, Mr Berrington!' one of the workmen interrupts by bellowing across the lobby. 'It will fit here nicely, as you thought, sir.'

'Fishtank?' I stand up straighter. 'Why would you want a fishtank? And why would it be so big that you need two men and two stepladders to measure up for it? We've tried a fish-tank before, it had a blue-and-yellow angelfish in it, like Flounder, and the poor thing died and a child found it before I did, and well... let's just say that child was probably trauma-tised for life and I decided not to do living creatures again after that.'

'Ah, but this fishtank won't be housing a fish. It'll be housing a mermaid.'

I flick my head like I've misheard him. 'I hate to be the bearer of bad news but mermaids aren't known for existing.'

'No, but have you seen those shows where swimmers dress as mermaids and can hold their breath underwater for an astound-ingly long time? Everything you do here is so small. You need to think bigger. We need things that are a spectacle. Things that people will *come* to see.'

'I thought we needed "budget fine-tuning" and you want to install a giant fishtank for a fake mermaid?' The clicks of my foot tapping on the black and white chessboard floor echo through the old building.

'I hate to be the bearer of bad news, but I think we'd struggle to find a real one.' He deliberately repeats my own words with a sarcastic smile.

'No. I mean, you can't do that. It's not real. I take pride in every single exhibit being faithful replicas of items from fairytales. The entire point of this museum is so children leave here believing their favourite stories are real. That if the things in them are real-life objects that they can pick up and hold and connect to, then magic must be real too. Mermaids aren't real. That clashes with my entire *raison d'être*. People are going to know it's just a person in a monofin flipper tail.'

'Yes, but the point is, they'll pay an admission fee *before* they do. That's something else we need to address – the absolute pittance you charge for admission. It's laughable. A fiver per person or tenner per family is nothing less than an insult to the exhibits here.'

I'm surprised by how much that sounded like it was partially a compliment. Is it quite nice that he thinks my exhibits are worth more? 'Do you know how difficult it is to find places to take children that are affordable? Some people are struggling to put food on the table. People are behind on bills for essentials like electricity, heating, and hot water – they can't afford big days out, the theme parks and other places children want to go, but they still need to keep their little ones entertained. Everyone on Ever After Street has made it a priority to keep things affordable. The shops keep things reasonably cheap, the attractions charge small. It benefits us all in the long run.'

'I'm not here to fix Ever After Street as a whole, although I've only been here for half an hour and I can already give them an *extensive* list of things that need improvement.'

'Nothing needs improvement!'

'The attitude of someone who doesn't realise that times are changing and businesses need to change with them to stay relevant. If your fellow shopkeepers feel the same, no wonder this street is stuck in the dark ages.'

'No one on Ever After Street needs *your* help. People like you don't get it and you never will. Not everything is about profit. It's about love and dreams and community.'

'As a side note, I would like to clarify that Berrington Developments do *not* accept love, dreams, and community as payment towards the rent, so might I politely suggest that profit inserts itself into the equation somewhere?' He's using that saccharine sweet voice again, and I glare at him for long enough that he rolls his eyes and steps back with a sigh. His voice changes to something softer and more genuine. 'Look, Lissa, you and I are in this together whether we like it or not. I'm here to give your museum a fighting chance. I've been allocated a small budget that I'm willing to plough into certain improvements if I believe them to be worthwhile. You can either work with me towards our shared goal of making your museum better and helping it to thrive, or I can walk away right now, and you can book your moving trucks for the first of March, because that's when my company will be along to start the demolition process.'

The thought makes me shudder, and a feeling of uneasiness floods me. I can't trust him as far as I could throw him. All he's interested in is profit, and that's never been the overarching importance on this little street. How can I ever make someone so businessy appreciate that?

I wait for him to say something else, still trying to get my head around this turn of events, because I feel like my life has been turned upside down six times in the past twenty minutes, and I'm struggling to come to terms with the fact that today was just another lovely autumnal Monday like any other in September, and then this happens. *He* happens.

'Do you know anything about running a museum?' I ask

when, instead of saying anything else and without putting the tablet down, he's also got his phone out of his pocket and is one-handedly typing something on it.

'Nope. That's where you come in. You can show me what you usually do and then I'll suggest ways to do it better,' he says without looking up from his screens.

I stomp down the diatribe I want to bark at him. Who does he think he is – coming in here and taking over, and now he's suggesting that I have to teach him how to do *my* job so he can tell me how many mistakes I'm making, and the urge to literally push him out of the door and down the steps, ideally so he lands in a heap at the bottom with the damn tablet cracked on his head, and his workmen not far behind is overwhelming and so very, very tempting.

But, apart from potential criminal charges for grievous bodily harm, what would it achieve except dooming this place for good? I *have* to believe that he means what he says – that I have a chance of saving Colours of the Wind if I can do things his way for a while.

If I can get that five-year lease again, I can get him out of here and put things back as they were, and at least I'd have time to prepare myself before the next reassessment, and surely anything is better than cinema complexes and moving trucks next spring?

'And you? You're... staying here, are you?' I can barely bring myself to vocalise the words. Is this for real? I'm suddenly going to be sharing my job with someone who looks like he's never stepped out from behind his desk before?

'Hmm?' he mutters like he hasn't heard me, probably because he *still* hasn't looked up from his screens.

'Oh, yes, that's right.' He answers without looking up after I repeat myself. 'I'll be working on my other jobs remotely while

I'm here, so I can give this my all until the end of the year. If you could direct me to your office so I can get set up?'

Ah. Slight problem there. 'Define office?'

He looks up from his tablet and his dark eyebrows furrow. 'If I need to define it, we might have an issue. I would suggest it's a small room where you do important things like paperwork. There's probably a computer, filing cabinets, a printer, strong WiFi coverage...'

'I don't exactly have an office...' I um and ah, trying to think of the best way to frame it. Even though how I manage my space is up to me, I *know* he will find fault with it. He seems like the kind of man who considers nothing more important than an office. 'I turned it into a workshop because I don't have the space at home and the exhibits need to be made somewhere, so now the office *is* the kitchen table.'

His raised eyebrow says it all.

'At least the kettle is easily accessible for tea?' I offer optimistically. 'And there are no other staff, so it's not like you'll be disturbed. An office really wasn't an optimal utilisation of our limited space.' I throw in a couple of words that sound like they might be on his wavelength. He seems like an 'optimal utilisation' type of man, and I can't describe the sense of dread that's settled over me at the thought of letting him run amok in my museum, although I get the impression of someone so uptight that his interpretation of running amok would probably involve nothing more than a slight loosening of his tie...

The end of the year seems a lifetime away, and I have no idea what he's planning, or how on earth Colours of the Wind could ever conceivably earn more than a state-of-the-art cinema complex, and the tendrils of dread twist outwards, making this feel like a fight I can't possibly win. Am I sentencing myself to a few very frustrating months where I will lose the museum anyway at the end of them? If there's one thing I *do* know, it's that you can never trust a company with 'Developments' in its name.

And yet the alternative is unthinkable. I've never in a million years imagined that Colours of the Wind wouldn't continue indefinitely. I've never even entertained the thought of being evicted or of leaving Ever After Street and all my friends here, but if I don't go along with this, what option will there be?

My thought process must play out on my face because he finally closes the case of his tablet and looks at me. 'I *get* that this place means a lot to you, but we've bought this building and we can't keep housing a failing business for the sake of sentimentality. As I said earlier – you've got a chance here. I like unusual concepts and things that are a little bit different. I would also like to avoid as much public backlash as possible. I've been pushing for a while to change the direction my company is going in. If Berrington Developments can do that by working with what's already here rather than facing protests about pulling it down, then that might be the way forward, and this is my chance to prove it. This is important to me too. Let us both show we've got what it takes to change, update, upgrade, and turn things around, and your museum stands a good chance. Otherwise, *this* is built within eighteen months.'

He taps the closed case of the tablet again, and I decide to be forthright too. 'Okay, honestly, *how* can I compete with that? This is a small place. I'm a one-woman band. I can't afford much advertising. My visitors come from word-of-mouth and because people who come to Ever After Street want to see everything it has to offer. I can't imagine the revenue a place like *that* would turn over, but I would guess my annual takings are barely a fraction of it. If I'm wasting my time, I'd rather you be honest about it now. Give me time to... prepare for the inevitable.' My voice wobbles on those words and he looks a bit guilty.

'Okay, honesty, I can work with that.' His dark hair bounces as he nods like he approves of my forthrightness. 'We streamline the budget and give people a reason to come here. We need an increase in visitors and an increase in reasons for them *to* visit. This is a good concept but it has many flaws that need ironing out. Consider me the iron.'

'Have you done this before? Saved businesses that were scheduled to be turned into ultramodern futuristic compounds?'

He presses the rubber end of his stylus pen into his chin, and the hesitation before he answers makes a cold sliver of ice slide down my back. 'Look, this isn't our usual protocol, and I'm not going to get into specific statistics about it, but—'

'That's a no then?' I interrupt his evasive answer.

'If you don't show me to your office space so we can make a start, it's not going to be either, is it? Wasting time like this is the enemy of efficiency.'

I huff and beckon for him to follow me as I start walking towards the stairs.

'I'd also like you to give me a full tour.' He hurries after me. 'Show me the museum through your eyes.'

'And the workmen? Should I give them all a tour too?'

'I've borrowed them from one of our building sites, they're just on loan for the day. They're mapping the place out so we can see what we're working with and where we can make improvements or repairs. Just ignore them.'

'Ignore several men wearing neon yellow, making the noise of a small army, and carrying ladders and power tools? Are my customers supposed to ignore them too?'

He rushes to catch up so he's walking beside me instead of behind me. 'If you ever get any, we'll find out.'

I don't give him the satisfaction of a response, as I sharply turn the corner onto the second floor and pass the closed doors to the now-defunct function rooms and his shiny shoes squeak on the flooring as he rushes to keep up. We reach the stairs to the third floor and he catches up as I'm about to turn onto them.

'You can call me Warren, by the way. Although I'll also answer to a demonic gerbil with no soul, if you prefer.'

He's thoroughly enjoying poking fun at my earlier reaction, and it makes me stomp even faster up the set of stairs to the third and final floor. 'I could think of a few other names for you.'

'And I for you, but I'm too much of a gentleman to say them out loud.'

'Hah. Last I heard, gentlemen don't waltz into buildings that *aren't* theirs and try to take over thriving businesses.'

'I'm trying to help.'

There's something in his voice that makes me want to believe that, but this isn't the sort of thing I can adjust to that easily. 'You've made a problem and now you're trying to sell yourself as the solution to the problem that didn't exist before you arrived. You may wear the suit of a gentleman, but that's as far as it goes.'

'You *really* don't like my suit, do you?'

'There's the office. Make yourself at home.' I stop beside the kitchen and point towards the table to one side of the small room without giving him the satisfaction of an answer. It's not his suit I dislike, the suit itself is really very nice, but how can there be *anything* likeable about a company that wants to tear down gorgeous old buildings and put up Rubik's Cube eyesores in their place, or anyone who works for such a company? The suit is fine and I can't deny that he wears it *well*, but it's everything else that makes him immensely dislikeable.

'This isn't a *thriving* business, Lissa.' He stands in the doorway and surveys his new office space with a wary look. 'As you said yourself, it's more of a limping zombie, and the sooner you realise that we share the same goal in reviving it, the better.'

'It doesn't need your help.'

'Well, *it* hasn't got much of a choice, so I predict that the next couple of months are going to be interesting.'

'At least we can agree on that.' I turn around and stalk away, wondering what on earth I've let myself in for, and somewhat intrigued by why he's so keen to help, if help is genuinely what he's offering.

This museum means the world to me. It's my little corner of the world. It gives me a sense of purpose, and without it, will I lose that too? It's my way of bringing a little bit of magic into the world. My mum made my childhood magical, and after she died, it fell to me to bring that same magic into my younger sisters' lives, and now I try to do it for other children too, because believing in magic and wonder can set people up for life.

And no one is going to get in the way of that.

I can get this show back on the road by myself, can't I? The museum has had tough times before and we've always bounced back. We can do that again, and I certainly don't need the help of some corporate mouthpiece who thinks I'm doing everything wrong. Ever After Street will never have a cinema complex, not on my watch.

2

_____

'That's an intriguing interpretation of office space. I've got a kink in my neck already.' When Warren reappears in the lobby, he's got one hand on the back of his neck and is turning his head from side to side, his tablet is tucked under his other arm, and he's got a water bottle dangling from one finger. 'Shall we start this tour then? Unless you're snowed under with visitors, that is...'

He waves an open hand around the lobby, but even the workmen have gone for a coffee break and I have to accept that the museum is as empty as it usually is. It's not _always_ like this. There _are_ good days, he just happens to have turned up on a quiet Monday. Of course he has. If someone arrives to pick apart your business, it's not like they're going to come on a bright and bustling day when it doesn't look like it needs any help, is it? That would go against the rules of the universe. All right, there are more quiet days than there are bright and bustling ones, but still. It was busier over the summer and it's always quieter on weekdays. Things will pick up.

'Let's start outside and work our way upwards, and don't

worry, I'll let you go if there's a sudden influx of money-wielding guests.' He spins on the heel of his shiny shoes and heads for the entrance doors, and I get out from behind the reception desk and reluctantly traipse after him. I have a feeling that 'tour' may be not quite the right word, and 'fault-finding exercise' might be more apt.

'This sign needs to be much clearer.' He's started speaking before I've even got outside, and he's already jotting something down on the screen of his tablet, and then he steps back and snaps a photo of the large metal signpost that shows what the building is. 'It just says "Colours of the Wind Museum". There's nothing that explains what you have on display here, and the name sounds like it could be a museum for autumn leaves.'

'I would love to see a museum full of autumn leaves.'

'Yes, quite.' His blue eyes flick up to me and blink like he can't quite comprehend someone making a joke about that. 'But the name means nothing. I am *now* aware that it's a song from *Pocahontas*, but only because a member of my staff explained it to me last week. I won't be the only one who doesn't get it, and people are not going to come in if it isn't immediately obvious what it is. We'll need to order a new sign that makes it much clearer. Do you have a logo?'

'I don't need a logo.'

'Everyone needs a logo, for branding purposes if nothing else. You can put it on everything to do with the museum and people will instantly recognise it.'

It's one of those things that I've thought about idly over the years, but a logo has always seemed too businesslike, and the last thing I want is for this place to start feeling like a corporation.

When I shake my head, he sighs and inputs something else into the Tablet of Gloom. He also casts a beady eye over the sandwich board next to the door where the entrance prices are displayed, but he doesn't say anything else about it. 'I believe there's a garden I need to see?'

'Yes. It's only small, but it's special. I've carved gaps in the trees for books, strung up fairylights, and there's a magical wishing well that really grants wishes.'

'I'm sorry?' He puts a hand behind his ear like he needs to hear the sentence again. 'Did you just use the term "magical wishing well that really grants wishes" and keep a straight face?'

'It's real. Come on, I'll show you.' I beckon him to follow me along the paving stone walkway that skirts around the building and leads through a decorative wooden gate that feels like entering a secret garden, and into the museum's outside space.

There are beds of daylilies at the entrance, and he stops to crouch down and read the plaque explaining what they are. 'A real-life version of the Sundrop flower from *Tangled*... I don't know what that is, but these are looking very sorry for themselves. Are they weather-damaged or have people nicked them?'

I look at the once-bursting beds of lilies, but the leaves are a bit on the slug-eaten side, and most of the stems are bare where people have, indeed, helped themselves. 'You can't stop people picking flowers, and it *is* autumn, the summer flowers are starting to have seen better days.'

'If you cultivate these as an exhibition then they should be in cages to protect them from wandering hands. Better to have no exhibit at all than one that looks as faded as this.'

'Do you know how excited children get to see a real-life version of a flower from a Disney film? Most people don't even realise that the Sundrop flower was based on a real lily. It's a bit annoying, but there are worse things people could do than take a flower as a reminder of their time here.'

'If people are going to take anything from here then they need to pay for the privilege.'

'You can't charge someone to pick a flower!'

'No, *you* can't. I, however, have no qualms. If you've put time and effort into growing them, they are not free to take, and that *must* be made clear.' He stands back up and looks around the garden. 'There aren't any "don't pick the flowers" signs up. Not even an arbitrary attempt to stop people taking them.'

'There was, once, but people ignored it, and when it fell down, I didn't replace it because it wasn't doing any good.' I'm reluctant to agree with anything he says, but there's an energy in his voice that makes me feel quite reassured by the value he places on my exhibits. I *do* get annoyed at the thought of people picking them and I've never known what the solution is, but charging people isn't it. What next, oxygen at 50p per microgram if you're inclined to *breathe* while visiting?

'They're one of the exhibits, no different to any other. I've got all the incomings and outgoings paperwork that you have to submit to the council, along with incident reports, so believe me, I *know* you have issues with people stealing the exhibits, but we'll get onto that later because I need to see them to understand what the reports are telling me. I'm not well-versed in this Disney nonsense.'

'And that, sir, is why you have no place in this museum and I don't see how you can help with something you don't understand.'

'Sir? An improvement on what you called me earlier.' He raises a dark eyebrow and one corner of his mouth twitches. 'And I'd venture that precisely the point of you giving me a tour is to *help* me understand what's going on here.'

'What's going on here is that you can't monetise something as simple as picking flowers, and if that's what you're trying to do, you may as well leave now. If you're going to add a fee to *everything*, then the integrity of the museum will be lost. I can't believe I'm saying this, but I'd rather bow out now than watch this place become something unrecognisable.'

My voice wobbles as I say it, but the flowers have given me a biting flash-forward to what the next few months are going to be like. How are we ever going to agree on anything? And even if we do agree on *some* things, we're never going to agree on a solution to them, are we? I have a sudden sense that we're delaying the painful inevitability of me losing this place anyway. Would I be better off spending the next few months preparing for the unavoidable ending rather than trying to fight a battle I can't win?

I have no idea what I'd do without the museum. I can't picture a future without it, and the thought is enough to send me into a panic spiral as I imagine bleak, endless days, and my life feeling as empty as it felt before I found this place. An art gallery at the time, overseen by an old chap who was about to retire, and the idea for Colours of the Wind came into my head and it gave me something to focus on, and brought the friendship of the other Ever After Street shopkeepers into my life, who rallied behind my idea and filled my days with joy and enthusiasm. I don't know what I'd do without the community and companionship of this little street.

'I'm open to anything, Lissa. I'm just trying to get a handle on this place and what's going on here.' I must be terrible at hiding my emotions because he sounds slightly contrite. 'I've heard a little about you while dealing with the local council to get our plans approved. You're not one to step down from a fight.'

'Neither are you, I'm guessing.'

The smile that spreads across his face is the first one that's looked real all morning and it's a thing of beauty. 'And that's what makes it interesting.'

I shake myself and take a few steps to put more distance

between us, and he follows me from the entrance and into the wider part of the garden.

'Wow. It's like someone dropped a library out here.' He goes to poke one of the books. 'A wooden library. Why are all these books made of wood?'

'We're in England. It tends to rain occasionally. Real books and rain don't fare well together?'

'Oh, ha ha, you know what I meant. Why are all the...' He looks above us. 'Wait, are those book pages *growing* on trees?'

'Those are laminated book pages tied onto the tree branches, yes.'

His fingers are rubbing over the wooden book he's picked up, which is one of the many bookish sculptures made by my friend Franca. 'I have so many questions...'

'It was originally going to be a reading nook of a garden. Somewhere people could come and bring a book and a hot flask of tea, with all these little nooks to sit in amongst the tree trunks and roots, maybe an outdoor library to borrow books from – somewhere to escape from the world and spend time enjoying the sunshine and looking at the view of the treetops and the castle.' I wave towards the truly spectacular view, unique from this angle of the street, where I can see out towards the Full Moon Forest and the castle in the hills, surrounded by browning leaves as the trees get into the swing of their autumn colour change.

He glances in the direction I point and, for just a moment, I see his face change to something like awe and he takes a step backwards like he needs more space to take it in. It's the first time he's really looked up from his tablet, and he shakes his head like he isn't taking in what he's seeing. 'I don't believe in fairytales, but *that* is a view from a fairytale.'

It *is* a spectacular view. It's always been my favourite area of the building. Standing down here and looking up, the highest turrets and spires of the castle peeking through the treetops on the hill above us, it's like you've come across the venue for Cinderella's ball or the Beast's enchanted castle hidden in the woods, right here in front of you.

He's clutching the wooden book he's picked up and looking upwards, at the castle, but he also seems taken with the book pages in the branches above his head, and the twisted and gnarled tree trunks that have got wooden book sculptures pushed into every cranny, and the fallen logs that have been structurally stabilised, varnished, and turned into benches. Eventually he comes back to himself and consults his Tablet of Gloom again. 'Why do you have an outside space like this but my reports show that the garden is underutilised?'

'Because my friend Marnie has the Tale As Old As Time bookshop, and she has a beautiful garden there now. She and her other half have combined their gardens into one so it's all books and roses, and people can go to sit and read and while away the hours, and it's not right for me to tempt customers away from her bookish garden. She and Cleo from The Wonderland Teapot run a "books and afternoon tea" experience together in her garden. They've worked really hard to make it perfect and I didn't want to encroach on that or try to muscle in on their customer base, so I just made my garden into somewhere Belle would like to be.'

He looks confused. 'Who's Belle?'

'Belle.' I blink at him in surprise. Is there *really* a person in the universe who doesn't know who Belle is? 'The main character from *Beauty and the Beast*?'

'I've never seen *Beauty and the Beast*, nor read the original fairytale. Why would I?'

'Why would you?' I repeat in indignation. 'Because it's an

endemic part of our society and the lessons learned from it are part of the fabric of our lives? Belle is a role model for every booklover and every person who's ever felt out of place or like they don't fit in. It's the quintessential proof that beauty is only skin deep and people can be nothing like they seem on the surface. It shows us that it's okay to like things that other people don't approve of, and that books are nice and can help us with the answers to most of life's problems, like feeling lonely or ostracised. Give me that,' I almost growl as I take the wooden book sculpture out of his hands. 'You don't deserve to hold that if you haven't even read one of the classics of our time *or* seen at least one version of the film.'

He laughs. He must think I'm joking. Instead of pushing it, he types something into the Tablet of Gloom and walks further into the garden and uses the toe of his mirror-shined shoe to poke at one of the low hedges and his blue eyes trace the other evergreen hedges dotted around the garden. 'This looks like an abandoned maze.'

'It is an abandoned maze. I was going to do a Wonderland thing and create a small maze with the wishing well at the end, but then Cleo opened The Wonderland Teapot, and it didn't seem fair to impinge on her Wonderland theme so I just left it.'

He looks around, his lower lip sticking out as he nods slowly. 'So what you're saying is that the opinions of your fellow shop-keepers are more important than your own livelihood...'

'What? No!' I should have known he'd read something more into it. 'They're not connected. My fellow shopkeepers – *friends* – are important to me and so is my own livelihood. Those two things don't belong in a sentence together.'

When his fingers start skimming across the screen of his tablet, I snap at him again. 'What are you doing? Don't put that in your tablet!'

'I need to understand what I'm dealing with here.'

'*I'm* what you're dealing with here. I'm not some statistic to be analysed by your AI business software. Don't put notes about me in that thing.'

He ignores me and continues typing and I wonder if he's putting a note about *this* conversation in there.

'The others have individual concepts, individual fairytales that their businesses are built around. I have all concepts. I have items from all fairytales. It's not fair of me to take theirs as well.'

'Regardless of what anyone else thinks, you have a right to make the most of *your* business's strengths. It's a cut-throat, dog-eat-dog world out there.'

'I *do* make the most of them, but the garden area is unimportant in the grand scheme of things, and I don't want to use it to take customers from other businesses on this street. We all help each other out and do our best by each other. This is not the place for that many cannibalistic-sounding metaphors.'

'Then perhaps we could work on some sort of cooperation with the others. From looking at the street plans, I don't believe The Wonderland Teapot has any outside space to make their own maze. Maybe we could continue setting one up here that forms some kind of connection – they advertise your maze and you offer a gift voucher for the teashop at the end of the maze, or something along those lines. That way, both businesses can benefit from your outside space. The bookshop too... You say they have gardens, so does the castle, so do you, so perhaps we can join forces with them for a walking tour of Ever After Street's gardens. Surely there are more ways we can tie in to the other businesses on the street as well, rather than worrying about not treading on their toes.' He types *that* into his Tablet of Gloom too, leaving me surprised by the potential in those suggestions.

I've often had ideas that I've abandoned because I don't want to steal customers from my friends' businesses, but leaning into our similarities rather than avoiding them is something I've never thought of before. It's a great idea, and the fact that he's suggested something so thoughtful has disarmed me and made me drop my guard. Maybe he really is trying to help?

I hurry after him when he makes a beeline towards the well at the other end of the garden, surrounded by crumbling brick walls and a wildflower patch of greenery.

'Hmm.' He looks predictably indifferent. 'Looks like an old well strung up with a load of solar lights. I'm impressed that you've managed to convince anyone this is magical. I'd be more inclined to believe it's a hazard.'

'It *is* magical. Children write their wishes on pieces of paper and drop them down it, and then they come true.'

He looks at me for the longest time, like he's expecting me to burst out laughing, but I keep my face stony straight. The wishes in this well will always be a special part of the museum for me, and I have no intention of explaining it any further to someone so dismissive.

He peers over the edge and looks down. 'It's a good thing it's got a safety grid because you would've been shut down on health and safety grounds years ago if it didn't have.'

'Of course it's got a safety grid. Children falling down wells is terrible for business.'

'Another thing we can agree on.'

Next to the well, there's a plastic dispenser box that holds several pens and a few rainbow memo blocks of coloured paper, and I crouch down and get out a green piece of paper and a pen.

'What am I supposed to do with that?' His sceptical eyebrow rises ever higher when I hold them out to him.

'Make a wish, obviously.' I push the paper and pen nearer to him, gesturing for him to take them. 'Write your name, age, and address, and then write your wish, fold it up and pop it through the grid. Once it hits the bottom, your wish will come true.'

'Name, age, and address? That could be termed information harvesting.'

'It's not information harv...' I trail off because the notion is too ludicrous to even repeat. I hoped he wouldn't be *quite* so cynical, especially when I thought he was trying to help just now. 'How else is the wishing well supposed to know who to grant the wishes for and where they need to be granted?'

His eyes flick between me and the well and he looks like he wants to back away slowly.

'Go on, write your wish down.'

'I'm an adult, I don't have wishes.'

I fold my arms and raise an eyebrow. 'Everyone has wishes.'

'Fine.' He rolls his eyes, turns the Tablet of Gloom over so he can use the back as a rest, scribbles something on the paper and then holds it up to show me.

I wish Lissa would shut up about this wishing well nonsense.

'That's not funny.' I crouch down and get out a blue piece of paper this time and hold it out to him again. 'Come on. You have to do it properly or it won't work.'

He goes to protest, but I muster the sternest look in my artillery that's frightening enough to cut his protest off before it's begun, learned from many years of getting boisterous kids to put down fragile exhibits without needing to say a word. 'You want to get to know this museum, and this is a huge part of it. Indulge me. Your heart's greatest desire. Write a *real* wish on this piece of paper, fold it up, and drop it down the well.'

He gives me a doubtful look, but reluctantly takes the blue paper, thinks for a moment before he writes something down, folds the paper, and pokes it through the grid so it floats down into the darkness of the well.

'Happy?' He hands the pen back.

I snatch it from him and put it back in the weatherproof box. 'Rapturous.'

He laughs at my deadpan tone, and gives the wishing well a final mistrustful glance before turning to head back inside.

'Right, let's start down here,' he says once I've caught up with him in the lobby where he's already consulting the Tablet of Gloom again. 'There's a Princess Suite, a Prince Suite, and a Fairytale Homes hall?'

I beckon for him to follow me, and push open the door of the Princess Suite, a large hallway where most of the exhibits relating to our favourite fairytale main characters are gathered.

'Wow.' He lets out a low whistle. '*What* is going on in here?'

'This is the *Tangled* corner.' I point out the area just inside the door where the golden sun crest is on a custom-made shaped rug on the floor, and in the centre stands a mannequin wearing a pink dress and a floor-length wig of blonde plaited hair with flowers woven into it, and the mannequin is reaching up, releasing a paper lantern into an installation of floating lanterns that I've managed to wire together to look like they're suspended in mid-air. I've got the golden glowing lanterns hanging from the beams on wire of differing lengths, so it looks like they're floating all the way across the ceiling and flickering with LED tealights to create a magical atmosphere in the hall.

'One of my sisters is a wonderful artist so the wall of the *Tangled* corner has been painted with a replica of what Rapunzel paints on the walls of her tower – her dream of herself watching the floating lights – and on the mannequin's shoulder sits a clay model version of Pascal, her pet chameleon. And look, there's a little speaker down here and if you press the button, it plays an instrumental version of "I See the Light".' I hold my hand out, encouraging him to press it, and when he does, the music fills the room and he leans closer to the speaker, looking like he's either straining to hear it or he just doesn't want to. 'Cool, right?'

He gives me a blank shrug and I can't help feeling disappointed. After his suggestions in the garden, I had a tiny bit of optimism that he would *get* it, and maybe he'd have other suggestions for how we can pep this place up. *Tangled* is one of my favourite Disney movies and getting my littlest sister involved in creating this corner makes it even more special, and there's a part of me that really wanted him to understand that.

'And this is Moana with her boat.' I go across to another area where there's a traditional Polynesian canoe that had to be disassembled to get in the door and then reassembled once inside. The mannequin is dressed in Moana's orange top and white skirt, there's a soft toy version of her pet pig and chicken, and people can sit in the boat alongside her for a photo opportunity. I lift the necklace from the mannequin to show him and then open it up and take out the metallic green stone. 'And this is her necklace. It's a giant shell that opens and inside is the heart of Te Fiti, which she carries across the ocean to restore to the island.'

'Ah, hang on. This "heart of Te Fiti" thing is mentioned in my reports.' He consults the Tablet of Gloom again. 'According to this, it's been stolen six times so far this year.'

'We don't know that it's been stolen, it's gone missing. There's a difference.'

He reaches over and lifts the green stone out of my hand and holds it up to the light. 'Yes. The perfect size to "go missing" in the pockets of many little thieves and souvenir hunters.'

'I make it out of oven-baked clay and paint it with metallic green paint. I have another two at home ready to replace whenever this one disappears. It's a bit demoralising, but I value it being realistic, and Moana's stone isn't superglued into the necklace in the film.'

'You're enabling children to steal! And wasting your own time and money for the fun of it. There has to be a better solution to this.'

'Well, I'm not putting up signs saying "don't nick the heart of Te Fiti", that's openly telling my customers that I think the worst of them!' I say, even though I'm touched by his protectiveness of the exhibits, and I like his ability to face problems head on. He *is* right, but if there's a better solution then I haven't thought of it yet.

'If they weren't such immoral little thieves, you wouldn't need to think the worst of them.'

'Most of them are under seven years old! You can't call children immoral thieves! What next? Strip searches upon leaving and metal detectors on the doors?'

'Now *there* is a good idea.' His face brightens and I'd *like* to think he's joking, but I don't think he is.

'And parents do bring stuff back sometimes. They've come in looking ashamed and guiltily handed me back something, saying, "I'm so sorry, my son walked out with this. I had no idea."'

'And those parents would be the exception, not the rule. Most people are not that decent. Most people would keep it as a trophy or it's the parents themselves who steal it.'

'Do you have such an exceptionally low opinion of *everyone* or is it just people associated with this museum?'

'No one's ever asked me that before.' He looks up at the lanterns hanging above our heads and chews his lip, giving it some thought. 'Yes, I suppose I do really. I've never thought of it like that.'

I should probably be annoyed at his cynicism, but he looks

unexpectedly downbeat, and it strikes me as a bit sad. It seems like his front has dropped for a moment, and I'm intrigued by the shift in his demeanour.

He shakes himself and consults the Tablet of Gloom yet again. 'And there's something about a Lego model of Agrabah palace being broken by children fighting with Rapunzel's frying pan?'

'It wasn't *broken*, it was... temporarily deconstructed, and I put it back together again. The owner was fine about it. No harm done.' I don't tell him about the sleepless nights, endless phone calls to the Lego collector who'd lent Colours of the Wind his Disney palaces collection, printed downloads of instructions, and help from at least three other Ever After Street shopkeepers to get the palace looking as good as new again after the unfortunate frying pan incident. It's another one of those demoralising things where I wish parents would keep an eye on their children and not let them run wild, but I feel helpless to do anything about it, and a stern look can only go so far.

He turns back to the *Tangled* area and lifts a frying pan down from a display hook on the wall and waves it towards me. 'Why *are* there frying pans here?'

'It's a thing from the film. If you'd seen *Tangled*, you'd understand.'

'I'm an adult man,' he says again, sounding like he thinks I've failed to notice.

'Only men who are threatened in the masculinity department are afraid to watch Disney movies.'

'Or men who just don't like them.'

'No one dislikes Disney movies. They are timeless and ageless.'

'Okay, people who simply aren't interested in them then. If I sit in front of my TV to relax and switch off for a while, some cutesy cartoon for children is not my first choice of viewing material. Each to their own and all that. You can like them and I can not be interested in watching them and we can still co-exist peacefully. Who knew, eh?'

All right, that's a fair point, and 'each to their own' is one of my main mottos in life, but no one *really* dislikes Disney movies. 'I didn't mean it like that, but you're being judgemental when you haven't even seen one. People of all ages and all genders enjoy Disney movies, and it's narrow-minded to suggest you won't enjoy one because you're—'

'A demonic gerbil with no soul?' He interrupts me to offer it as such a polite suggestion that it makes me laugh.

I meet his eyes across the room, and there's a glimmer of something much warmer about him, and I'm intrigued by another peek behind the front I saw earlier. He seems much more down-to-earth than his standoffish façade has led me to believe so far today. Maybe working with him won't really be so bad, even though I'm filled with misgivings and reservations too. 'We don't all have to like the same thing, but you reckon you can overhaul a museum that you have zero understanding of. You're not best placed to be involved here.'

'I don't know what you want me to say. I don't have children. I don't have siblings so there are no nieces and nephews. I don't have an extensive family with gazillions of little cousins. I've drifted apart from friends who have children because our lives are on different paths. If I've ever watched a Disney movie in my life, it's before I was old enough to remember. That doesn't mean I can't see the potential here from a business perspective, and it seems like *your* passion is enough to drag us both through kicking and screaming, so can we get on with it? You explain what I need to know and I'll ask if anything doesn't make sense – deal?'

'Deal,' I say after he gives me another tight, sarcastic smile. I saw a hint of a real smile earlier, and if he let that out more often, he'd be a *very* good-looking man, with his dark brown hair and blue eyes – if he wasn't threatening to demolish my museum, that is.

'Is there *anything* in this room that you recognise?'

Warren looks around, and I almost feel sorry for him over how bewildered he seems as he takes in the model versions of Princess Jasmine, Pocahontas, and Elsa from *Frozen* with a large snow-covered polystyrene mountain behind her and a billowing blue dress and snowflake-covered cape, and Princess Aurora, wearing the pink-and-blue splodged dress that Sadie has painstakingly recreated from the final scene of *Sleeping Beauty*, and Belle in her yellow ballgown, carrying a single red rose.

'Well, that's Cinderella and the pumpkin carriage.' He points to the mannequin wearing a silver-blue ballgown and standing in front of a pumpkin-shaped carriage, and then to the shoes on a pedestal plinth beside it. 'Glass slippers!'

He looks momentarily excited to have recognised something, and then his face turns serious again. 'These are in my report.'

I groan involuntarily and drag myself after him as he hurries across the room while reading from the Tablet of Gloom and then tucks it under his arm and picks up the shoes from the display.

'These are actual glass?'

'No, that would be dangerous. These are multi-faceted crystallised acrylic that are much safer and less breakable than glass.'

'You let children actually wear these? Actually put them on and walk around in them?'

I nod.

'And they cost £200 a pair?' The look of horror on his face

suggests he does *not* see that as a bargain. 'And you've had to replace them more than once?'

I reluctantly nod again. I know it's not the most cost-efficient way to run things, but the price of an occasional replacement is worthwhile to see the look on a child's face when they slip their feet into what could be the *real* Cinderella's magical glass slippers. They have to be realistic, realism costs money, and children occasionally break expensive things. It's another law of the universe, even if it feels like I'm throwing money away sometimes, and when he says it like that, it does sound a bit daft.

Warren gives me a 'hold that thought' gesture, puts the shoes back on the plinth, and hurries towards the lobby, and then returns holding a carrier bag. 'A member of my staff was able to source these this morning.'

He pulls something from the bag and deposits it proudly into my hands. 'These were £2.50 from a nearby market. Budget friendly *and* much less susceptible to breakages. Win-win. Your ones can go in a display case, never to need replacing again, and *these* can be worn by children who want to feel like Cinderella.'

I look down at what I'm holding and let out a gasp of dismay. He *cannot* be serious! I tear the plastic cover off the cardboard backing and extract the shoes, which look like a larger version of a Barbie doll shoe. 'They're pink! And plastic! And so poorly made that they have sharp bits inside.' I knock them together and they make a hollow clunking noise. 'They're cheap trash. Even £2.50 is a rip-off considering how bad the quality is. No one would believe Cinderella wore these!'

'I don't give a monkey's what Cinderella wore. Her budget was in magical pumpkins and bibby-bobby-something...'

'Bibbidi-Bobbidi-Boo,' I say, wishing I could wave a wand and magic *him* away.

'Yes, that.' He sounds like his patience is wearing thin.

'Whereas *our* budget is limited by the pesky confines of reality and cold, hard cash. You cannot let children run around in something so expensive. So I'll take these and put them somewhere safe, and you put those on display for all to play with.'

Warren lifts the glass slippers from the plinth again, and gestures for me to put the pink plastic ones back in their place, but I have a much better idea.

I take my glass slippers from his hands and push his plastic pair back into them. 'You like them so much, *you* wear them. A colour-blind orang-utan with really low standards wouldn't be seen dead in them, never mind a child. Cinderella's glass slippers will *never* be pink plastic rubbish. Take them away and never even *think* such a thought again. The recycling bins are out the back.'

He laughs. Again, I get the impression that he thinks I'm joking, and I think we'd best move on before I give in to the temptation to pick up Rapunzel's frying pan and threaten him with it. I'm a bit annoyed because I know he's got a point about the shoes. They *are* too expensive to let little ones run wild in them, and maybe they *would* be better in a display case, but doing that goes against everything I've always wanted for this museum.

'And then, to get to the next room, we have to walk through Ariel's grotto of treasures.' I push open the door at the end of the Princess Suite and hold my hand towards it, encouraging him to step through. 'The previous owner used it as a storage closet, but it connects the two main halls on this side of the building, and I saw an opportunity to turn it into something much more special.'

He turns around a couple of times, looking at everything, but of course, he decides to comment on something practical. 'Have you taken the *ceiling* out?'

'Not me personally, but a builder has, yes. It's just a small corner of the room, away from any joists or structural necessities, and it now looks right up to the third floor – to give the impression of being underwater and looking up to the surface like Ariel does.'

There are models of Flounder and Sebastian, and Ariel's orange bag is hanging on a hook, and the walls are lined with shelves right up to the ceiling and they're filled with all sorts of oddities that Ariel may have discovered on her undersea adventures, from dinglehoppers to smoking pipes to seashells, paintings, costume jewellery, and treasure chests, and the *pièce de résistance* is a life-size replica of the statue of Prince Eric that Ariel recovers after the shipwreck in the film.

'I've never seen anywhere like it.' His tone doesn't give away whether that's a bad thing or a good thing.

'I believe in making the most of every space. And listen to the sound of lapping waves.'

He puts a hand behind his ear, tilting his head, but his face remains blank, obviously not impressed with what I thought was a nice immersive touch. 'And then, we open this door and we come to the Prince Suite.' I invite him to go in first and he has to duck through the small-ish door.

'There's Aladdin, with the Magic Carpet, and the Genie's lamp.'

He goes over, takes the golden lamp from the podium and rubs it, and actually looks disappointed when no genie pops out. 'Aren't kids going to be disillusioned when a genie doesn't appear?'

'Genie's got his hands full with the wishing well.'

Warren laughs loudly and puts it back. 'Something tells me you've been asked that many times before.'

'Yep, usually by people a lot younger than you though.'

He wanders around the dressed-up mannequins, from Prince Charming in his cream and red suit, to Prince Philip from *Sleeping Beauty*, Prince Florian from *Snow White*, Flynn Rider from *Tangled*, a model frog which doubles as Naveen from *The Princess and the Frog*, and the Beast in a costume given to me by Darcy who runs The Enchanted Rose Garden flower shop. I haven't found much inspiration for the Disney princes lately. It feels like this part of the museum needs a rethink, and judging by the apathetic look on his face, Warren agrees. I just have no idea *how* to inject some more life into it. He obviously recognises almost nothing in this room either, so I hurry us back out into the wood-panelled lobby because no one's manning the front desk, although there are so few visitors today that no one's needed to.

'Through there is the dressing-up room, and the Fairytale Homes hall.' I gesture to both doors opposite us, and then turn towards the far end of the lobby. 'And you've seen the enchanted rose and the painting of Prince Adam.'

The panelled walls throughout the elongated lobby gives the room an elegant, old-fashioned feel, almost like walking into the finest castle, and the walls are full of nooks and crannies that are the perfect size to display smaller things, like my statues of Lumière and Cogsworth, but Warren heads towards the fairy-light-filled table at the end where the enchanted rose stands, and above it, the Beast's painting from when he was still human, just like the one Belle finds in the forbidden West Wing, complete with torn claw marks.

Warren reaches out and lifts one of the tears, unwittingly copying Belle in the film. 'Someone's ripped this.'

'Oh, for heaven's sake. Watch *Beauty and the Beast*. It's supposed to be torn. The Beast has swiped at it in anger because he doesn't look like this any more.'

He ignores me. 'And you just have this openly on display? Anyone can touch it? Pull it? Yank it? Tear it?'

'That's exactly the point. It's a significant scene from the movie. People love being able to recreate it.'

'It's going to get damaged with so many hands playing with it.'

'What do you think someone's going to do? Come in and throw a can of soup over it? I would rather it get damaged than my customers have to look at it through an acrylic box. This is not some stuffy, hands-off museum where you're terrified of touching anything. I pride myself on being the opposite of that.'

'You're not protecting your investment.'

When he puts it like that, it sounds like a reasonable point, but the last thing I want to do is let him know that. At least people are mostly gentle with the painting and the photo opportunity it provides. 'My investment is in people being able to pick up and hold things. If a child wants to try on Pocahontas's necklace or walk around with Princess Jasmine's headband in their hair then I *want* them to be able to do that – and adults too, for that matter. You never truly grow out of your Disney phase. This museum started out really small and I've added things to it whenever I've been able to afford to or been able to make things or find things. This is ten years' worth of work and love and help from my friends that's built up gradually. It's here for people to enjoy it, and that's how it's going stay.'

'No, it isn't. Your museum *can't* stay as it is. Your finances must be barely ticking over at best, and although I can't fault your passion, it seems to eschew your business-sense. Rent cannot be paid with wishes and magic, and no building in the Berrington Developments group can continue in this way.'

'We'll see about that.' I fold my arms and glare at him, and he looks like he's about to fire something else at me, but instead, he backs down.

'You know what, I feel like I've been whacked round the head by a humungous book of fairytales, so let's agree to disagree. I'll be upstairs, in *my* office, going through your accounts to see where we can make some much-needed adjustments. If you continue to be opposed to change, that's up to you. Your beloved museum can stay as it is for exactly six more months, so enjoy it while it lasts, *or* we can work together to ensure many people get to enjoy it for much, much longer. The choice is yours.'

'I'm not opposed to change!' I shout after him as he disappears up the stairs. 'I'm opposed to men who waltz in and think they can enforce change upon me!'

He doesn't respond, which is probably a good thing, because I have a stone gargoyle from *The Hunchback of Notre Dame* and thwacking him round the head with it is unlikely to end well for either of us.

I'm trying to hold onto my rightful anger about the injustice of all this and not to think about the sense behind his words. I *know* he's not wrong, and I really, really didn't want him to be right about anything, but money *is* tight. The budget is *always* overstretched, and it's extra upsetting when I have to spend more of it on replacing something that's been damaged, lost, or stolen. I'm unsettled by the fact he's been here for half a day and he's already addressed some problems I'd been hiding from, and it feels like a bit of a reality check. Maybe it's been a long time coming. The museum *is* failing, and this might be the push I need to do something about it... while I still can.

3

'*Who* is that insanely attractive man in your office?'

I groan, because there's only one person Mickey can be referring to, and I was trying not to think about *quite* how attractive he is.

'Do not tell me *that* is the evil squirrel with no soul?'

'Gerbil,' I correct her. We're in the Fairytale Homes hall and she's helping me rebuild the Hansel and Gretel-style gingerbread house after a child has started dismantling it and, judging by the teethmarks, tested it for edibility too.

'If we're going down the animal comparisons route, there's something much more vulpine that I'd use, because he is a *fox*. A seriously hot Robin Hood-type fox. I thought you said he was horrible?'

'Just because he's nice looking doesn't mean he's not horrible.'

'He's quite Mark Darcy-ish, isn't he?' Mickey carries on like I haven't spoken. 'With the suity uptightness, and the tall, blue-eyed, dark-haired handsomeness.'

'I doubt he even knows who Mark Darcy is. He doesn't read

fairytales, I can't imagine he'd spare the time of day for a rom-com either.'

'Even so, from what you've said, I was expecting a cross between Jim Carrey in *How the Grinch Stole Christmas* and a Gremlin who's eaten after midnight. Is he single?'

'I have absolutely no idea, and even less interest in finding out.' I nudge Mickey to hold a clay-gingerbread wall in place while I slot a brick back in. 'And yes, presumably he is, because he's not wearing a ring, and no one would be stupid enough to put up with him. He's surgically attached to the Tablet of Gloom, and he's a "no" guy, you know? All he says is "no". No, no, no, no, no. Without thinking anything through or weighing up the merits, he just says no instantly. He can't see the magic in anything.'

I try to ignore the prickle that I'm being a bit unfair when all Warren really did was spot problems I've been trying to ignore and be annoyingly sensible and blunter than I was ready for.

'That's a lot of information to have garnered when you only met him yesterday.'

'And I would rather not have met him *at all*.' I roll up a piece of air-drying clay and poke it into a hole between the ginger-bread walls. It's not the first time we've had to fix this house, and it undoubtedly won't be the last. Usually I tell myself that I don't mind, but everything Warren said yesterday has got to me, and I'm suddenly wondering why parents can't keep a closer eye on their little darlings when they're walking along the Yellow Brick Road that winds throughout this room between a selection of fairytale houses. Some are Lego models, some are garden sheds with added bits to make them into something special, and some are built entirely out of foam bricks and clay, like this one. 'You haven't seen the other ruby slipper, have you? It's gone missing from the witch's legs under the Oz house. Again.'

Mickey shakes her head as she glues the gingerbread chimney back on. 'Have you told him about the wedding?'

I stop what I'm doing long enough to give her a disbelieving look. 'Why, on this green and verdant earth, would I tell him about the wedding?'

'Because you need a date for it and he's *gorgeous*?'

'He's also trying to destroy my business, enforce his opinions on me, and will undoubtedly end up evicting me anyway, after months of misery for both of us. He's cynical and uptight and his entire existence revolves around business. He doesn't understand what I'm trying to do here.'

'Oooh, this could be just like *Pocahontas*! He could be your very own John Smith! You know, two different people from two different worlds, learning the ways of each other's lives and to respect each other's beliefs...'

'Well, John Smith does get shot at the end, I could get behind that aspect...'

'I knew this place was called Colours of the Wind for a reason!'

'It's called Colours of the Wind because I thought it was a good way of representing all the different colours and flavours of the fairytale world. It's supposed to suggest there's something for everyone.'

She squeaks and pulls her phone out. 'I'm going to google him.'

'Please don't.' I glue a line of clay gumdrops back on the roof, but she continues ignoring me. Even though she's loved-up with Ren herself, the appearance of an attractive man in *my* vicinity seems to have eroded either her common sense or her eardrums, because it feels like she hasn't heard a word I've said.

I hold the gumdrops in place for the glue to dry while scouting around the room for the missing sparkly red shoe.

We've got the pastel-coloured house from *Up* with a multitude of colourful balloons coming out of the chimney. Behind a curtain of green vines, there's Rapunzel's hidden tower, and a small version of Dorothy's house from *The Wizard of Oz*, complete with the Wicked Witch of the East's legs – the famous black-and-white-striped stockings and the ruby slippers on the feet – ready for anyone who wants to try them on and click their heels together three times. It would be nice if they put them back on the witch's feet afterwards though.

'Uh-oh,' Mickey says, staring at her phone.

'Good uh-oh or bad uh-oh?'

'I don't think there's any such thing as a good uh-oh, Liss.' She glances up at me and then looks back at the screen. 'You know that library just outside Cheltenham?'

'That gorgeous old building that had a campaign to save it all over social media? The one they knocked down and replaced with a "leisure complex" that looks like something from a futuristic sci-fi movie where AI has taken over the world?'

'The Berrington Developments logo is all over that leisure complex website.' She scrolls a bit further and then reads aloud. 'Redevelopment project led by Warren Berrington.'

'Oh.' I feel my stomach sink and echo her earlier sentiment. 'Uh-oh.'

'How can any company be proud of doing that?' She ponders her phone screen. 'It's everything that's wrong with the world these days. Beautiful old buildings are being destroyed in exchange for eyesores like this.'

I can't bring myself to tell her about the sketch I've seen of their broken Rubik's Cube vision for *this* building. 'And with *him* involved, I bet you have to pay a pretty penny to get into that leisure complex, whereas a library would've been free for everyone. A hub for the community. Books for people who can't afford to buy them. A place for children who had nowhere else to go and for lonely pensioners to meet and natter.' I try to remember some of the other things that were written online in the campaign to save that library a couple of years ago, but the realisation has made an even larger pit of dread settle in my stomach. That library had *everything* on its side. A massive amount of support on social media. Articles about the injustice of its proposed demolition in newspapers. Even a spot on local TV about a sit-in protest they staged.

And it was all for nothing. None of it made any difference against the power of Berrington Developments. The library was still torn down. So what hope do I have? What can I possibly do to save my museum that would be bigger than their extensive community campaign that, ultimately, did nothing at all?

'The library was structurally unsafe.'

I yelp in surprise as Warren appears in the doorway and my cheeks instantly burn red. How long has he been standing there? How much of that did he hear?

'It was a matter of time before those "beautiful old bricks" you're lamenting fell down and crushed one of the library patrons to death. The library needed investment but couldn't get it. The council gave up on it and sold it to us. It was too old and too weather-damaged to patch up well enough to pass inspections. The electrics had started to fry where rain was leaking in. No matter how much people loved it, *they* didn't see the state the roofspace was in. For someone who loves books so much, you should know that there are two sides to every story. And I believe you're looking for this.'

He's got a sardonic smile on his face and the missing ruby slipper dangling from his finger. Great. Not only does he overhear me berating him, but he finds the shoe I am unable to keep track of too.

'I didn't mean...'

'I know exactly what you meant, but not everything plays out in your stereotyped "corporate greed versus beloved community non-profit" narrative. Some old buildings are exactly that – old. Some businesses fail because they have no patrons. That library couldn't get investment because it had been unused for years. Not everything you read on social media is the whole truth.'

'I didn't know about that,' I admit, feeling a bit guilty that I may have misjudged this. There was nothing in those online campaigns about the structural integrity of the library or the reason behind their lack of investment. It seemed like a good-versus-evil fight where evil ended up winning. Was I wrong not to consider that there might have been something more going on behind the scenes? 'Did you try to cut their costs and save them too?'

'Nope. You're the first, that makes you special. You *could* be grateful.'

He walks along the Yellow Brick Road with the red shoe held out in front of him, and I meet him beside the scarecrow and take it. 'And you could be grateful that no one's rammed this shoe up your—'

He cuts me off by laughing hard, and I turn around and stomp over to Dorothy's house and put the shoe back on the plastic legs that are sticking out from underneath it.

'Those are damaged.'

I check the witch's legs and feet, and realise he means the shoes where a few patches of glitter are coming off at the heels, but not enough that I've got them on my 'things to be replaced' list. Yet. 'People put them on and try clicking their heels together, like in the film.'

'It's fun,' Mickey suggests. 'You should try it.'

He keeps his eyes on me and doesn't reply and I can't work

out if he hasn't heard her or, more likely, he thinks her suggestion is so ludicrous that it doesn't deserve a response.

'This is my friend Mickey.' I go to introduce them, but he stops me before I get any further.

'I know. We met in the kitchen. Apparently your friends have free run of the place, and every cup of tea comes with an impassioned plea about how wonderful this museum is and how much Ever After Street would suffer without it, regardless of the fact that *some* of us are trying to concentrate on work. There's a reason people have offices and it's so they can shut the *door*.'

I send her a scolding look. I didn't ask her to do that, but my heart is warmed by the fact she did, even if *he* isn't best pleased about it.

'Well, sorry for interrupting, but as you'll come to understand, Colours of the Wind means a lot to people around here.' Mickey stands up for me again, and when he stays determinedly unimpressed, she claps her hands together and tries a change of subject, and I shoot her another look, wishing I was near enough to stamp on her foot and stop her. 'So, apart from the heartless developer aspect, are you single? Because Liss here is Pocahontas and she really needs a John Smith.'

He looks taken aback for a moment, probably not used to Mickey's particular brand of directness, and then he laughs. 'You see, I actually know who they are because they were real people. *That* is the kind of info that belongs in a museum, and not the romanticised, unrealistic Disney version.'

He glances between us and that sarcastic smile creeps across his face again. 'And yes, I am. No one would be stupid enough to put up with me, and I'm surgically attached to my Tablet of Gloom. Oh, and I'm a "no" guy. All I say is no, no, no, no, no.'

'Apparently you're also an eavesdropper guy.' I try to cover the embarrassment burning through me from my toes to the tips of my hair. *Why* did I have to go and say all that without even considering that he might be lurking outside the door? If the ground could swallow me up right now, it would be very much appreciated.

'Not voluntarily.' His mouth is set in a hard line as he gives me a serious look. 'One might think it prudent to ensure their new boss isn't in the vicinity before talking about them behind their back.'

'You're not my boss.'

He raises an eyebrow. 'My company owns this building and I'm the lead on the redevelopment project. I'd like to hear your thoughts on what that makes me if not your boss...'

'Oh, trust me, you would *not* like to hear my thoughts on anything about you.' I smile such a falsely sweet smile that it makes him laugh, and I feel something ease a little that he doesn't seem truly angry about what he's just overheard.

He glances between me and Mickey. 'And for the record, I'm not a "no" guy. I'm a "maybe, if it's a sensible allocation of budget, usage of time, and expenditure of effort" guy.'

'He's also a laugh-a-minute guy,' I say to Mickey, but my deadpan tone makes it sound more sarcastic than it was intended to.

'Clearly,' he says good-naturedly, poking fun at himself as his laugh gets stronger and it sounds genuine, and I find myself giggling too, a mixture of nerves and embarrassment. Until now, I hadn't realised that he *could* be funny or not take himself too seriously, and I catch his gaze across the expanse of Yellow Brick Road, and for just one moment, nothing exists apart from his blue eyes, brighter with the twinkle of merriment shining in them, and something fluttery stirs inside me. He dips his head towards me and a weight momentarily lifts.

Maybe we're not that different after all. We don't have to like the same things to find common ground and compromise, and knowing he has the ability to laugh at himself and not take *everything* too seriously is a good place to start.

The unspoken truce lasts for a matter of seconds before he sobers up and straightens out his suit. 'Oh, I can laugh *many* times a minute, I just don't find failing museums very funny. You'd do well to remember that.'

'Failing museum, you've got a nerve!' Mickey shouts after him as he stalks out, and I let out a long groan.

'That wasn't embarrassing at all.'

My best friend giggles. 'Oh, come on. There's plenty worse he could have overheard. He took it pretty well.'

'Yeah, until he realised he was lightening up for a moment and got quickly back on form.'

'I don't know, I saw a little something there.' She waggles her eyebrows at me. 'He didn't seem evil. He seemed... disconnected, like he was *trying* to be antagonistic rather than actually being antagonistic. When I spoke to him in the kitchen, he didn't seem to know what to say. He seems a bit lost. Maybe it's more of a... misalignment than being a soulless evil chinchilla.'

'Whatever he is, he's my only chance of saving this place.'

'He's not your only chance, Liss, he's *told* you he is. He wants you to believe he is. But he doesn't know Ever After Street. He doesn't know the community around here and how much we love and support each other. If he messes with one of us, he messes with *all* of us.' She's holding another gumdrop in place on the gingerbread roof while I'm still over by Dorothy's house, trying to get the dead witch's legs to look right.

'I am 100 per cent confident that there is *nothing* the Ever After Street shopkeepers can't do if we put our heads together, including turning Mr Suity Uptightness into a magic-believing Mr Darcy who wants to snog Bridget Jones.'

I deliberately ignore any insinuation she's placing on snogging and concentrate on the *important* part of this conversation. 'He seems to be immune to Ever After Street magic. It was all I could do to get him to make a wis—'

She cuts me off with an excited squeak, and then stops herself, runs to the door to double-check we're not being overheard, and then comes back and whispers to me. 'You got him to make a wish? Liss, that's fantastic! You've got to go down there and get it and we'll grant it like we grant other wishes. Make him believe in magic. If he finds out for himself that wishes from that well come true, he can't demolish this place.'

I give her my most sceptical look. 'What could a guy like that possibly wish for? Especially that I can afford to grant for him. A new sports car? New high-priced suits to add to his extensive suit wardrobe? We grant wishes for kids, not multinational company execs who undoubtedly already have everything their tiny little hearts desire. And whatever it was, it'll probably be a joke. He wasn't taking it seriously.'

She grins. 'Not then, maybe, but he will do when he realises that magic really does exist on this street – and it might not be from magical wishing wells, but it *is* from how much we all love and care for each other. No one is shutting down Colours of the Wind on my watch.'

I swallow hard because it's such a lovely sentiment, but it hammers home how devastated I'll be if I end up having to vacate this building. There's nowhere else on Ever After Street, or even nearby, where my exhibits could possibly fit, with rent I can dream of affording, and the thought of having to leave my friends here is soul-destroying. The wishing well will be wiped out too. Who else will grant wishes that children drop into a well and make them believe in magic?

After my mum died, our family struggled. I watched my

younger sisters complain about hand-me-downs and not being able to afford the toys their friends had. I tried to make life a little bit nicer for them, and now I try to make it nicer for the children who visit here, who wish for something that the Ever After Street shopkeepers can grant between us, and it makes my life better in return.

But if everything Warren's said is true, it's not just about proving the museum's worth. I've also got to find enough customers to cover the cost of triple-increased rent, and whatever other surprises they're likely to throw my way, and I suspect Berrington Developments is the kind of company that *always* has a few surprises tucked neatly up its sleeve.

'I don't know what to do, Mick. This is bigger than me. He's got all these facts and figures and reports. So many reports that I thought were private. I'm not business-minded. I don't care about cold, hard numbers. I care about how people *feel* when they visit here. I want children to believe in the magic that my mum brought into my childhood, that was sorely missing from my sisters' lives after she died, and he's never going to understand that. Our visions are never going to align.'

'This is exactly what I've just said. You don't need children to believe in magic – children believe in magic anyway, but *he* doesn't. If he did, this would be different. He just needs to see this place the way you do. And I've got an idea...'

'What?' I ask at her cryptic connotation.

She grins and strokes her chin in a scheming way that would be mildly concerning if she wasn't my best friend. 'You'll see, my friend, you'll see.'

4

_____

The following day, when Warren comes down the stairs, there's a mum at the front desk trying to wrangle a ten-pound note out of her purse while simultaneously attempting to keep her excitable young boy out of trouble. He's around four years old, and she's got a grip on his wrist but he's bouncing and wriggling and jumping up and down so hard that it shakes coins out of her purse and they clatter onto the smooth wood of the reception desk.

It doesn't take long before he squirms out of her grasp and makes a beeline for the _Beauty and the Beast_ area in the lobby with a cry of, 'Beasty! Rosey!'

'It's his favourite film,' the mum explains, but he's bounded up to the enchanted rose and lifted the cloche off it before she's finished paying, and there's a scattering of foam petals as they all fall off simultaneously under his eager little hands. 'Oh, no, I'm so sorr—'

Surprisingly, Warren cuts off the mum's apology. 'It's okay, allow me.'

He puts his water bottle down on the front desk and strides

after the little lad and I'm wondering how to shout after him that he can't discipline someone else's child without worrying the mum, but I'm even more surprised when he crouches down beside the little boy and asks him what he likes most about *Beauty and the Beast* while surreptitiously scooping up the fallen red petals before the lad treads on them.

The mum apologises again as she pays their entrance fee while her son babbles excitedly at Warren, who's listening intently while looking like he hasn't understood a word.

'Don't worry about it, the petals are meant to come off,' I reassure her as she thanks us both and goes over to take a firmer grip of her son's hand and they start walking around the Prince Suite.

I go over to the enchanted rose where Warren has laid the petals out on the table and is looking confused as he tries to work out how they fit back into place.

'That was very mellow of you. I half-expected you to get a cane out and punish him.' The stem of the rose is made of wire that twists around and I start sliding the inner petals back on.

'Am I really that much of a Neanderthal?'

'Not so much Neanderthal, but... there's a bit of a "strict Victorian" vibe about you. The Child Catcher from *Chitty Chitty Bang Bang* springs to mind.'

He lets out a loud laugh but doesn't seem offended. Instead, he holds his hands up and puts the petal he was holding back down. 'I give up. I don't have the coordination and the delicate touch you obviously have.'

I put this rose back together multiple times a day, so I carry on with something I've done so many times, I could do it blindfolded, and try not to think about the way he's stayed crouching and how those blue eyes are intently watching my hands work.

I suspend the final petals on fishing line so it looks like

they're floating downwards, turn the glowing fairylights back on, and then stand back and replace the glass cloche.

'Is it worth it?' His voice sounds distant and when I glance over, there's a faraway look in his eyes.

'Every moment. Especially when you see a reaction like that little boy's. A lot of kids grow up with no wonder in their lives, and being part of bringing that, even for a moment... that's what makes it worth it. Even if I *do* have to put fallen petals back several times a day.'

He nods and it takes a moment for the distant look to disappear as he shakes his head. 'And you really made that yourself?'

'I bought the cloche. The rose is just wire, fairylights, and repurposed petals from other artificial roses. More assembled than made.'

'I admire your dedication, I can't deny that.' He stands up with a groan and both his hands go to his lower back.

'Ugh, that office,' he complains as we both go back to the main desk, listening to the sounds of delight as the mum and little boy enjoy themselves in the halls. 'But you knew that, of course. It's not an office at all – it's a bloody uncomfortable chair at a bloody uncomfortable table.'

'Well, if I'd known you were coming, I'd have ensured it was a lot *less* comfortable for your arrival. A sort of "bed of nails over hot coals" type of desk.'

His laugh has taken on a sarcastic tone again. 'I could always come and sit down here with you and appreciate the *silence*.'

'There's instrumental Disney music playing all the time.' I point towards a music player in one of my nooks, not far from the main doors, and next to Thumbelina's tiny bed in a walnut shell.

He glances at it and tilts his head, but the look on his face remains blank. 'Oh, right, *that* music. Yeah, of course.' He does a vague handwave when I look at him expectantly. Maybe he just doesn't recognise *any* Disney songs whatsoever. 'I didn't mean that – I meant where I'll be uninterrupted by anyone because there aren't any customers.'

'There are customers.'

'I've seen two since I got here, and one of them broke something.'

'He was adorable, and he didn't *break* it. The petals detach on purpose. And just because you don't see them doesn't mean customers aren't here.'

'Oh, so invisible customers are a thing now, are they? Jolly good, all your business woes are solved.' He hooks his shiny shoe around the leg of the stool I was about to sit down on and pulls it out from under me and over to himself.

'I meant you've been upstairs. You haven't seen every coming and going.' I give him a *look* as he sits down on my stool, and I don't add that, admittedly, it *has* been a slow day today, like so many other days recently.

'To be fair, even down here, I'd be interrupted less by random people inviting themselves to get a cup of tea and *six* biscuits.'

'Mickey is not a random person. Half the stuff in this museum wouldn't exist without her. She runs The Mermaid's Treasure Trove over the road and she always picks up anything she knows will fit in here or that I can make something of. Pretty much everything in Ariel's cave came from unwanted stock in her shop. She can have as many cups of tea and biscuits as she likes.'

Talking of Mickey brings our encounter yesterday back into sharp focus when I'd been trying to forget all about it, and I force myself to face it head on. 'I'm sorry about yesterday. That was unprofessional of me. I'm not used to—' I stop myself and rethink. 'No, actually, there's no excuse. I shouldn't have been having a private discussion in a public place, and I'm sorry. I didn't mean for you to overhear that.'

He nods slowly, bending forwards on the front desk, almost leaning around me so he can see my face from where he's sitting and I'm still standing. 'Thank you for that. I appreciate the directness. I guess we can agree that I could have made a better first impression than barging in unannounced like that. I felt the need to appear in control of the situation, and I deserved your assessment of me.'

I'm surprised by how much I appreciate *his* directness too, and his open admission that maybe he isn't as unflappable as he seemed at first.

'And look...' He splays his hands out and places them both on the desk. 'No Tablet of Gloom. And no surgery necessary to remove it. Just thought you might like to see proof.'

I don't know why, but it makes me laugh, and I appreciate that he can make a joke out of what he heard yesterday rather than making me feel bad about it. It really wasn't my most professional moment.

Another customer comes in and pays the single person's entrance fee, and I can feel Warren's eyes on me as I put her money in the till and give her quick directions around the building.

'I'm not your enemy,' Warren says gently when we're alone again. 'You want to keep your museum – I'm here because I believe there could be merit in keeping your museum, but for any business to stay *in* business, they need to earn more than they pay out. Looking at your accounting, I understand that's a foreign concept to you, but...' He trails off when I frown at him. 'Look, I'm not completely heartless. I can see what this place means to you and that you weren't expecting this takeover to happen, but I firmly believe that we can find a middle-ground solution that works for both of us. You get to stay here, and I get to prove to my mother that my ideas aren't always terrible ones, and she can retire safe in the knowledge that I won't run our family company straight into the ground.'

I knew there was something more personal behind his initial explanation for his interest here, and I appreciate his honesty and the hint at something much deeper going on behind the scenes, and the fact that nothing I've said so far has deterred him. I haven't exactly been the most welcoming host or receptive in any way to his plans, but there is still the unspoken truth that makes it difficult to trust him – what plans does he have for this place for it to feasibly compete with a multi-million cinema and entertainment complex? He doesn't understand a love of fairytales and the magic of seeing an item in real life that you thought only existed in a storybook. He thinks installing a human mermaid to swim around in the lobby is the way forwards, and doesn't realise that the strength of this place is in small things that people can pick up and hold and touch, even if there's a trade-off that things might get damaged. It's not about spectacles, it's about making things that don't exist in real life seem like they do.

'There's a gap between ticking over and thriving. I want to bridge that gap.'

'Why?'

He picks up a pen from the desk and twiddles it between his fingers as he thinks about it. 'Because this place is different to anywhere I've ever seen. When I first heard of this, I read the reports, and I could see somewhere that had so much potential but was missing the mark, and—' He must see me bristling because he changes tack, and his voice switches from accusatory to persuasive. 'You must be able to see that – even though there's nothing *wrong* per se and what you do here is charming and good-intentioned, things could definitely be better? I'm not wrong in saying that, am I?'

Annoyingly, he isn't, but it irks me to admit it. I *know* he has a point, but the last thing I want is for him to think I need his input. If my museum needs to be saved, it should be up to me. All right, maybe it could do with an upgrade or two, and I should have done something about it earlier, but when things *are* ticking over, it's easier to bury your head in the sand and convince yourself that everything's fine and always will be.

When I don't answer, he chuckles like he can hear the unspoken war between my head and my heart, but he doesn't push me on it. 'All right, what do you think the problem is? You know this place better than anyone. It's blindingly clear that no one could love it more than you. Why do *you* think it's not doing better?'

'I think we're invisible.' I answer his question instinctively, and only stop to think about what I've said after the words have come out, but now I've said it, I realise it *is* true. 'We have a wonderful vantage point on Ever After Street – right at the end of the road and at the top of a hill. Grey stone steps leading symmetrically to the doors of this three-storey grey-brick, partially ivy-covered building. Shoppers literally can't miss us, and yet, I feel that we stand here like a ghost, in plain sight but somehow unseen. I don't have the budget for adding new exhibits very often, and most of the existing ones have been here for a long time, so there's nothing new to advertise, nothing to encourage people to come back, so we sort of blend into the background and disappear from public perception.'

He fiddles with the pen he's still faffing with, turning it over and over, pressing each end against the wooden desk. 'So what we need to do is turn the museum into the architectural equivalent of you then, because you could stop traffic.' He leans over and uses the pen to lift a pink section of my curly hair and then quickly drops it when I frown at him because it doesn't sound like a good thing.

He sounds like he means it in a 'could cause a multi-car pile-up resulting in multiple deaths and horrific injuries' sort of way, either that or he's comparing my colourful hair to a set of traffic lights.

And he's got it so wrong. I couldn't stop traffic. I couldn't stop anything. I can't stop some uppity development company swooping in and taking this building. I can't drag enough visitors in. I fight causes for other people who need help on Ever After Street, but I find it impossible to admit it when I need help myself. I learned early on in life that people you rely on can be taken away in an instant, so it's better not to rely on anyone. I'm used to people assuming I'm coping fine, and it's hard to admit that sometimes, I'm not, and now I spend my days skulking around here like an apparition in my unseen museum, waiting for someone to look for me. 'I feel like I'm invisible too.'

I don't realise I've said the words out loud until the pen drops onto the desk and he slides the stool back far enough to look at me.

Why did I say that? I've never even said that to Mickey, never mind a man I only met this week. My cheeks blaze so hot that surely lava is about to explode out of them like a bubbling volcano, but something about him equating the colourful streaks of my sister's hairdressing practice to some sort of strong, confident personality has rubbed me up the wrong way. I know how people see me around here, like a warrior, always on hand to fight for a good cause, and no one realises that I'm frantically treading water and trying to stay afloat in a sea of falling visitors and declining profit. Colours of the Wind does need help – for me or *because* of me?

'Intriguing...' he murmurs, and gladly we're saved from any further awkwardness when the mum and little boy cross the lobby and ask if there's anything upstairs, and telling them it's staff-only gives me a chance to hope Warren develops sudden-onset amnesia and instantly forgets everything I just said.

'You need a map,' he says when they disappear into the Fairy-tale Homes hall.

'Maps cost money.'

'Not all extra expenses are unnecessary. Nice quality post-card-sized maps with some marketing info on the back, a link to the website, social media accounts and hashtags to post about their visit. Something people would keep as a memento... You do have a website, right?'

'Of course.' I cringe internally. News and announcements of new exhibits are posted on the Ever After Street website, but the museum's own website is... shamefully neglected.

He gets his phone out of his suit pocket and I have a *horrible* feeling that he's about to look up my website.

I see him wince as the drab background and bright, blocky text assaults his eyeballs. 'Oh. Wow.'

It is *not* the good kind of wow.

'I'd say it looks like a five-year-old put this together, but a five-year-old would do a vastly better job. This is not a website, this is a school project from before the internet was widely used. It wouldn't have been up to date in 1998.'

'Look, you didn't ask me if I had a *good* website. The Ever After Street social media is—'

'Nothing whatsoever to do with your own online presence. This... needs help.'

I can't disagree with him there, and that's the nice way of

putting it. 'I'm not a techy person. I don't know the first thing about websites. I bought the domain name and used a template thingy to put some stuff about the museum in. I couldn't afford to hire a professional.'

'I see that.' He types something into his phone and I catch a flash of a notes app as he presses send.

'The Phone of Gloom is just as bad, you know. Did you just type something about me into that and send it to your own tablet?'

'Just trying to keep all my notes together. You may not realise it, but there's a *lot* to do around here. Every aspect of this place needs attention. You excel at the exhibits, but... um...' It's like he runs out of sentence before he can get to the really insulting part, but I can see his point. I *love* the exhibits side of Colours of the Wind. I do *not* love the paperworky, admin-type tasks that come with it, and I have a tendency to put them off for an impressively long time.

'...do not excel at other aspects?' I offer, because he's got a way of shining a spotlight on the things that I *should* have dealt with by now, and I can't help thinking that I already *knew* everything he's saying but I ignored it, and maybe I'd be in a better position by now if I hadn't.

He doesn't confirm or deny my words, because it's probably so obvious that it doesn't need any concurrence. Instead, he stands up with another groan and walks out from behind the counter until he's standing opposite me, and I take my stool back and plonk myself down on it with a huff.

He paces, twirling his phone between his hands. 'Tell me about the empty rooms upstairs.'

Oh, *joy*, he's found them. I was hoping the three locked doors on the second floor might escape his notice. 'They used to be function rooms. I used to offer things like children's birthday parties, a space for art and craft classes, the occasional wedding reception...'

'But...?'

'Well, Witt came back and he and Sadie turned the castle into a functioning destination venue. They hire rooms of the castle out to birthday parties, weddings, receptions, they offer a space for classes in the grounds, and who would want to have a function held here when they could go to the Ever After Street castle itself? It was worthwhile when the castle was a closed-down shell, but now it's up and running again, I can't compete with them, and I don't have enough exhibits to fill three more rooms so...' I trail off, unsure of how to end the sentence.

He's stopped pacing long enough to raise an eyebrow, but he doesn't say anything.

'I *am* trying. They'll be full of exhibits one day. I was thinking of moving things around. Splitting the exhibits into movie franchises rather than the princesses together, the princes together. I could divide those large rooms and have each section dedicated to a single fairytale...'

'Or you could hold functions again. Was it profitable?'

'It had its moments. Children's birthday parties were a big thing, but no one wants their birthday party here nowadays when they can have it in an actual castle or in The Wonderland Teapot across the road.'

'So you have these huge rooms of empty space just sitting there?'

'They're not hu—'

'I have the master key, Lissa. I let myself in. They're *huge*.'

I huff again. The truth is that I haven't known what to do with the function rooms since people stopped booking them for functions. Fill them with more exhibits, certainly, but new exhibits take time and money, and filling three huge upstairs rooms is a daunting impossibility when there's still empty space on the main floor and my focus has always been on making the downstairs halls the best they can be.

He's quiet for a while, still pacing back and forth in front of the desk. 'It's easy to build a picture of what's happened here, you know.'

'Oh, please, do enlighten me. I can't wait to hear the insight of someone who got here two days ago. You must know *everything* when little ol' me who's been doing this for ten years is completely clueless.'

He chuckles at my sarcasm, but it doesn't deter him. Instead, he comes over and leans his elbows on the desk and looks up at me through his dark eyelashes, and my breath catches for just a second. His eyes are so intensely blue and I feel like he can see right through every wall I put up. 'You're not invisible, but you make yourself small to accommodate others. The museum is ticking over rather than thriving *because* you're more concerned about not upsetting anyone. You have a right to make the most of your space even if it means treading on a few toes.'

I roll my shoulders, trying to ease the uncomfortable feeling because he is, once again, not *totally* wrong. I *do* consider the other businesses and their owners whenever I do anything here, but it's a mutual respect that goes both ways. My Ever After Street friends have all helped me out with the museum many times, and the last thing I want to do is undermine their shops by offering something similar. 'We don't do that around here. We help each other. We love each other. It might not be the most businessy way to do things, but it works for us on Ever After Street.'

'Does it though? *Is* it working for you?'

'Yes.' I glare at him and a challenge flashes in his eyes, and I'm determined to out-stare him, but I find my cheeks turning red under his gaze and not more than a few seconds passes before I turn away, leaving him wallowing in his self-satisfied grin of winning our unofficial stare-off. 'We're colleagues with the same purpose, not competitors. And I'm still here, aren't I? Still "ticking over" well enough to be in business after ten years, so I don't get *everything* wrong.'

'Your visitors are people who come to Ever After Street anyway and pop in for a look, whereas people should be coming to visit *here* and having a look at Ever After Street afterwards. This should be a destination. This place could be worth a hundred cinema complexes with a nudge in the right direction. You are by far the most interesting attraction on Ever After Street, and the others should be gaining customers from you, not the other way around.'

I'm touched by what seems like an authentic belief in my museum, and bristling at yet another hint that what I already do isn't good enough, and also at his ability to say things that need to be said, in a way that makes them impossible to ignore. Yes, things could be better, and maybe I could have done more to make them so, and that's not an easy thing to admit.

Before I can respond, he pushes up off his elbows so he's grinning down at me where he's standing and I'm sitting. 'Do you know what I'm good at?'

'Oh, the endless possibilities of that answer...' I can't help laughing to myself as I run through options in my head, and only share the least offensive one with him. 'Suit shopping?'

He laughs. 'Improving visibility. And that's what we're going to do, together. Between us, I think we can give this place exactly what it needs.'

His words give me a shard of hope and an equal sinking feeling. I want to believe him. Everything he's said so far hasn't been entirely unfair, and he does make some good points, but I still don't know what he gets out of this. He's mentioned that he's trying to prove a point to his mother-slash-boss and take the company in a different direction, but is that really all there is to it? He's come in like he's the only thing standing between my business and certain doom, but is he? How can I trust him when I think that, whatever his reason for getting involved in this, I haven't yet heard the *real* one?

5

'This isn't funny, Warren!' I stand looking at the empty display plinth where Cinderella's glass slippers usually are, but this morning, they're nowhere to be seen. My instant assumption is that Warren has taken them in another attempt to replace them with the pink plastic monstrosities he's already been firmly rebuffed for.

He's arrived early this morning. At least, there's a fancy black supercar in the Ever After Street car park and no one else around here owns a car like that.

I shout his name again because he is *not* replacing those glass slippers on my watch, and when I still don't get a response, I stomp up the stairs towards the office. 'Warren!'

I'm halfway up the second flight of stairs before he appears on the landing above me, his mouth full of something he's munching on. 'Did you say something?'

'No, I've only been shouting at you for the last ten minutes. Where are my shoes?'

He glances downwards. 'On your feet, I wouldn't wonder.'

'Not *those* shoes, the glass slippers.'

'What glass slippers?' He's good at pretending not to know what I'm on about.

'Cinderella's gla—' My eyes fall on what he's eating and I gasp in shock. 'Why are you eating that?'

He holds up the toffee apple he's already taken several bites of. 'It's very nice. Thank you.'

'It's Snow White's poison apple!'

His face turns *whiter* than Snow White's porcelain skin. 'It's not really poisoned, is it? Because I know you don't like me but that would be a cruel trick if it is. Was I supposed to recognise it and find it funny?'

'What?'

'You left it on my desk! I thought it was a breakfast-shaped peace offering!'

'I did nothing of the sort! And no, of course it's not bloody poisoned, it's just a red apple with green candy mixture poured on through a stencil so it's got the Evil Queen's skull motif on it. You're eating one of my exhibits!'

'Oh.' He glances down at the apple, and then shrugs and takes another bite. 'And very nice it is too.'

'Warren! This is not funny! Where have you hidden the glass slippers?'

'I haven't touched the glass slippers. Why, what's happened to them?'

'They're not where I left them last night and you're the only other person here. And you certainly have no qualms about tampering with my exhibits!' I jerk a hand towards the apple he's taking another bite out of.

He brandishes it at me. 'You left this on the kitchen table beside my stuff. I assumed it was for me.'

'No, I didn't! It was displayed in a box in the Princess Suite when I last saw it yesterday!'

'Well, it was on my desk when I arrived this morning.' He motions for me to go back down the stairs as he follows me.

I march into the Princess Suite and point out the empty display box where Snow White's apple usually stands, with a plaque explaining how the Evil Queen disguises herself as a haggard old woman and tricks Snow White into taking a bite, and then I turn around and point to the empty plinth where the glass slippers have disappeared from.

'Maybe a Fairy Godmother turned them into lizards overnight.'

'She turned the lizards into footmen, not shoes, and— Oh, for God's sake, this has nothing to do with the Fairy Godmother!' I snap as my frustration gets the better of me. He's obviously been messing around with things and is trying to get out of it now he's been caught. 'Did you think I wouldn't notice?'

He goes to reply, but a noise makes its way to my ears and I hold up a finger to shush him. 'What *is* that noise?'

'What noise?'

We both listen to the usual silence of the museum at this time of morning, but today it's interrupted by a... sort of whirring noise. '*That* noise? Like a droning... burring... noise. You don't hear it?'

He shrugs and gives me a blank look.

'It's coming from...' I turn around and head for the Fairytale Homes hall. The whirring is definitely coming from in here. I follow the noise over to the far corner, a little nook filled with straw and a sole spinning wheel... which is spinning by itself. It's always threaded with gold thread, and the clockwork mechanism that powers it has clearly been wound up, which it definitely wasn't last night, and now the straw that fills the corners of this little nook is covered by masses upon masses of golden thread.

I turn to Warren. 'Hilarious. I thought you didn't know any fairytales.'

'I don't. What are you talking about? What fairytale is this?' He puts his head round the room divider and peers in, looking between the piles of gold thread and the spinning wheel. 'Sleeping Beauty?'

'Rumpelstiltskin!' I crouch down to turn off the wheel and look around at the masses of thread in despair. What the heck am I going to do with all this?

'Spinning wheels feature in more than one fairytale?' Warren sounds confused.

'Sleeping Beauty pricked her finger on the *spindle* of a spinning wheel. It's— Oh, it doesn't matter. Rumpelstiltskin spins straw into gold in exchange for a woman's firstborn child, and she only gets out of the deal if she can guess his name correctly, and when she does, he tears himself in half.'

'He sounds like a nice chap.'

In the middle of what's been a crazy morning so far, where I can feel my stress levels climbing higher by the second, the laugh that bursts out makes everything stop for a moment. My stress levels plateau and I can suddenly see us standing here, watching a spinning wheel spin by itself while he eats Snow White's apple and I wonder where a pair of glass shoes have got to. I sigh and roll my shoulders, trying to loosen up and take a few deep breaths. 'Look, this is very funny and all, but—'

I'm interrupted by a knock on the front door, and I dodge around Warren and run to see who it is. I open it when I recognise the familiar figure through the glass in the door.

'You haven't lost Cinderella's shoes, have you?' Witt is standing outside, holding the glass slippers in his hands.

'Yes! Where did you find these?' I take them carefully from him as Warren appears behind me and I introduce them, even though I *know* that news of Warren's presence had spread around Ever After Street within minutes of his arrival last week.

'In the castle ballroom. All on their own, in the middle of the dancefloor… waiting for their princess, presumably?'

I can't see Warren's face, but I can *hear* his sceptical raised eyebrow. 'How the heck did they get up there? Is this a joke?'

Witt shrugs. 'No idea. Sadie and I were shocked to find them there. We left a window open last night, that's probably how they got in.'

'By themselves?' I say in confusion. *What* is going on this morning?

'Well, you know what these magical exhibits are like,' Witt says with a nonchalant shrug. 'Maybe the Fairy Godmother put a spell on them.'

For a non-existent fictional character, the Fairy Godmother is getting blamed for a lot of things today. I call a thank you after Witt as he hurries back down the steps, and while I'm watching him go, Warren takes the shoes from my hands and knocks them gently together.

'So you're telling me that these inanimate objects somehow got all the way up to that castle *on their own*?'

I take them back from him because I'm still convinced this is his doing, even though breaking into the Ever After Street castle seems far-fetched, even for him. 'I don't know.'

'And you *really* didn't put the apple on the kitchen table? I assumed it was something you sold to customers and you'd left one for me to try.'

'I do sometimes have them to give away to customers, but only if I've had time to make a batch the night before, and I haven't for a few days now.'

'By "give away", I hope you mean "sell for a reasonable price".'

I don't reply because, honestly, I've thought about it, but I feel guilty charging customers for something extra when they've paid the entrance fee. If I force myself to get over that, maybe it would be a small way of bringing in some much-needed cash?

He takes my silence for the answer it is. 'You have a very, very strange approach to running a business.'

'And you have a strange approach to practical jokes.' I brandish a faceted crystal shoe at him, more than a bit annoyed that he's made yet another good point about the toffee apples. 'If you're trying to mess with me, it's *not* funny and it *won't* work.'

'Lissa, I haven't touched any of this stuff. It was probably a customer at the end of the day yesterday and we didn't notice it before we left.'

'No, I do a quick walkaround every evening before I lock up. Cinderella's slippers were on their plinth and Rumpelstiltskin's wheel definitely wasn't spinning, and I don't even have *that* much gold thread in the museum. I have one roll upstairs in case anyone wants a demonstration. That's way more than one reel of thread. Someone's brought it in.'

'Yeah, and you were still here when I left last night, so my guess is that this is a ploy of *your* doing to mess with *me*.'

'Why would I do that?'

'I don't know, your mind works in mysterious and mildly concerning ways. Why would I do it either?'

'I don't know, your brainwaves are probably affected by the tightness of that super-stiff collar. That's tight enough to cut off oxygen to the brain and cause moments of madness.'

It's his turn to stop and laugh, a slightly unhinged laugh. 'What would any rational person think if they overheard us now? This is by far the most bizarre conversation I've *ever* had.'

Even so, I can't help feeling a bit guilty when he undoes the top button of his white shirt and loosens his stiff collar, and his forehead furrows as he looks at the shoes I'm still holding. 'Are you saying that *you* haven't done this? That someone else has come in and moved things and started up a really strange spinning wheel, thrown a load of gold thread all over the place, and stolen a pair of shoes? Like... vandalism and theft?'

'It's not vandalism, is it? No harm has been done, apart from a shedload of thread to clear up... and the shoes have found their way back to us,' I say, even though I can't get my head around it. It's quite possibly the strangest thing that's ever happened in the museum, and *that's* saying something after being here every day for over ten years, but I'm flummoxed. Warren *must* be involved – there's no other possibility.

'But they didn't go walkabouts on their own in the first place, did they?' He raises that sceptical eyebrow again, and I *know* how it sounds, but it doesn't seem malicious.

'Oh, maybe it's like that film? You know the one with Ben Stiller where the exhibits come to life at night?' Warren's still holding the apple core in one hand, but he flaps the other one like he's trying to remember.

'*Night at the Museum*?' I suggest and he nods in agreement, looking the most animated I've seen him until now. 'Oh, yes, that's *much* more likely. Glass slippers that walk by themselves, a spinning wheel that's spun itself into a frenzy of gold thread, and a poison apple that's magicked its way up three floors to the kitchen all on its own. That's unquestionably the most reasonable explanation. Good job, Warren, you've solved the mystery.'

'You've spent the past week going on about magical wishing wells, but you think *Night at the Museum* is absurd?'

'Everything about this morning so far has been absurd,' I mutter, wondering why he's so blasé about this. The obvious answer is that he's messed with things to wind me up or make me think there's something sinister going on.

'Does anyone else have a key?'

'No. Only me, and now you.' I gulp a bit too loudly as the lie slips off my tongue. Mickey has my spare key, but it's not like she's going to have come in and done something like this during the night, and seeing as he's already complained about her using the kitchen, it's better not to mention it.

'Maybe I should call the police...' I suggest, not really intending to, but certain that it will force him into admitting culpability.

'Oh, yeah, that'll be great for business. Blue lights and officers swarming the place because a spinning wheel started up by itself.' He rolls his sharp blue eyes and looks around the lobby. 'Let's sit tight for now. Nothing's really happened, has it? Nothing's been damaged that we know of, and the only missing thing has been returned. Let's see if anything else happens before we jump to conclusions.'

Ah-ha! Almost as good as proof of guilt. If he didn't already *know* what was going on, he'd want to find out, wouldn't he?

'And if it *is* the exhibits coming to life by themselves, then we don't want to scare them because *that* has so much potential to go viral and get everyone talking about Colours of the Wind.' He cups his hands around his mouth and calls out to the whole museum. 'You hear that, exhibits? If you want to move by yourselves, feel free! You have our full support!'

'No, they don't!' I squeak in horror. 'No sentient exhibits, thank you! Don't encourage them!'

'Are you kidding? This is the most exciting thing that's happened in years. Sentient exhibits would really put this place on the map. I'll even clear up the gold thread so they don't feel bad about it.'

I'm sure it's a way of directing suspicion away from himself, but I appreciate it anyway. I can't remember the last time there was a mess made around here and *I* wasn't the one clearing it up, and it feels nice to not be as alone as I usually am. No one is ever really alone on Ever After Street, but this is the first time I've ever had someone *here* to share the day-to-day running of the museum with, and it feels much better than I expected.

'Oh, maybe it's a ghost!' He sounds genuinely excited, and the grin on his face is one of pure childlike joy, even though I'm almost certain he's pulling my leg. The best course of action is to go along with it, bide my time and try to figure out exactly what his angle is with this.

'Did I forget to tell you about the museum ghost?' I call after him. 'It's been haunting these halls for years. Tries to murder anyone who wants to change things. It's especially fond of all those property developers who come a-knocking.'

'Good job I'm not your average property developer then.' He turns back and gives me a wink and a cheeky grin. 'And I thought my competition had lessened in recent years.'

I laugh despite myself. He has a way of being funny at unexpected moments, and I'm starting to suspect that the first half of that sentence is very true indeed.

6

'This room should be a gift shop.' Warren is not spending enough time upstairs. Warren *hasn't* been spending enough time upstairs since the other morning when he cleared up the mystery gold thread and then spent the day untethered from his Tablet of Gloom, telling me all the ways he'd change things if he was in charge, and he hasn't stopped since. 'Every museum needs a gift shop.'

'The worst part of every museum is the gift shop! People feel obligated to spend money they don't have on things they don't want, especially if they've got kids pressuring them. Besides, what would I sell in it?'

'With that logo we talked about the other day, the possibilities are endless. Any memento that people can take home to remember this place. Something they might catch sight of a year from now and think about coming back for another visit. You have nothing to leave a lasting impression, nothing to remind people of their visit here. Nothing for them to stick on their fridge doors and tell friends when they enquire about it.'

'I didn't know friends gathered around fridge doors,' I say to cover my irritation because he's right again, which he's annoyingly good at being.

He gives me a scathing look and I roll my eyes. 'So I'd have to invest in loads of items, probably hundreds of them per batch, only for them to sit on shelves gathering dust? It's a waste of money, and that room is the dressing-up room. Kids love being able to wear these elaborate gowns for the duration of their visit, it makes them feel like part of the fairytale.'

· 'Yes. It's going really well, isn't it? That last child made *me* feel like I was part of a horror film.'

He's just witnessed a tantrum from a little girl who had put on a yellow Belle dress to walk around and really objected to having to take it off again when it was time to leave, and had to be wrangled out of it by harassed parents who looked like they'd rather get antibiotics down the throats of a fleet of angry cats than try to get the dress off her. She hissed at them at one point. Warren looked quite shellshocked afterwards and started googling for local exorcists.

'It's a bit of fun. It makes kids feel special and immersed, like a princess or prince.'

'Apart from the ones who don't fit in the clothes. For them, it just makes them feel like outcasts.'

'I have various sizes of dresses and jackets. It's impossible to have every option to fit absolutely every child, but there are enough options that most kids can find something.' I try not to show that I'm quite touched by his sensitivity and thoughtfulness. This is something I've worried about too, and there are often tantrums from a child who wants to wear an item of clothing that is simply the wrong size for them, but these are Disney-inspired clothes that Sadie has made for me or that I've found in charity shops and got her to alter. 'Most of the dresses tie on so they'll tie on to anyone of any size, and at least the headdresses and crowns fit anyone.'

'And then you have issues where kids don't want to give them back.' He was, of course, also present when a parent ran in the other day and returned a tiara after their precious munchkin had snuck out with it hidden under a hooded coat. I've become quite good at surreptitiously running my eyes over kids as they leave to make sure they're not still wearing anything that belongs here, but it does happen occasionally.

'Look, I was an oversized kid. Bigger than my classmates and taller than most of my teachers. It wasn't something I wanted to celebrate. A room like that would have made me feel like even more of an outsider. Dressing-up clothes aren't inclusive enough because they can't possibly include everybody. Only the kids that "fit" the clothes can enjoy them. By trying to include everybody, you end up excluding some anyway. For kids who don't fit in, that room is the stuff of nightmares. It still makes me feel uneasy in a PTSD-type flashbacks sort of way.'

'You were bullied?' I ask, surprised by his openness.

'No,' he says swiftly in a way that clearly means 'yes' and expertly sidesteps the question. 'Do you offer school trips?'

I chew on my lip as I look at the defensive stance he's developed and the way he's squared his jaw. I desperately want to know more but I don't push the topic. I don't know him well enough and he's trying to take over my business so I have shouldn't have any interest in poking around in his private life. I try to pretend I'm not intrigued, but it does make me think about the dressing-up clothes. It wouldn't be the first time it's caused ructions. I thought it was a unique part of the Colours of the Wind experience, but Warren's view has given me pause for thought.

'Lissa?' He waves a hand in front of me like it's not the first time he's tried to get my attention. 'School trips?'

'Oh, yes, sometimes. School trips can be complicated because the ideal age range is pretty small. If the classes are young enough to believe in fairytales then they aren't familiar with all of them, and a lot of it goes over their heads. Old enough and there's too much peer pressure to appear grown-up and think stuff like this is childish. I do take them, but it's usually chaotic and more hassle than it's worth. I have to close to other customers to accommodate them and the schools don't pay as well as the potential customers lost, but generally if a school class wants to come here then I like to have them.'

'Hmm.' He's standing in front of the reception desk, pushing a clicky pen against his stubbled chin. 'I wonder if there's anything we can do there to make it more worthwhile. Of course, if there was a gift shop, loads of schoolkids with pocket money to spend would buy things...'

I reach over and thwack his arm with the papers I was looking through. 'A day is just not complete for you without extorting money from a child, is it?'

He sidesteps me easily and his laugh sounds warm and genuine. 'With a school trip, we could extort money from several children at once. A win all round, I'm sure you'll agree?'

I'm still laughing when a customer comes in, a grandfather with a little boy in tow. I greet them with my usual cheery greeting, and Warren steps out of the way so they can come up to the counter, and I see the way the grandfather side-eyes him and the little boy clings onto his grandfather's trousers as he gets his wallet out to pay. He's trying to hide behind the elderly man's leg, all the while peeking at Warren uneasily.

'Apparently I also terrorise small children,' he mutters as they walk off, confirming that he *did* notice it too.

'You *are* a little overdressed,' I venture, trying to be tactful, especially after his mention of clothing-related childhood trauma just now, but really, his suit looks like it's stepped right out of a fancy business meeting with millionaire banking cronies, and in an easy-going place like this, it makes him stand out like a sore thumb.

'Overdressed? Do you have any idea how much these suits cost?'

'More than my monthly household bills, I would imagine, but regardless of what they cost, your look is giving, "I'm senior management, I sit behind a desk all day and have no idea how to connect with real people".'

I can see him prickling after the ease of earlier, and I wonder if I've been too harsh and misjudged the jokey way of getting non-funny points across we've developed in recent days, an acquiescence that we don't have much choice about working together and trying to make the best of it.

'Yeah, well, I am senior management and I do sit behind a desk all day, and I don't think you can really criticise my clothing choices, do you, Little Miss leggings and sweater-vest?'

'It's a jumper-dress!' I pull my brown and orange extra-long jumper down to my knees self-consciously, even though my thick black leggings keep any modesty well and truly covered. 'It's seasonal and it looks welcoming and approachable. Unlike your suit collection, which screams... undertaker. Don't stand too close, I might embalm you.'

He choke-laughs at that, but I'm on a roll. 'And your shoes are so unsuitable that they screech on the floors. It's off-putting.'

It takes him a moment to recover his composure, and then he clears his throat and pulls himself up to full height. He's over six foot but spends most of his time hunched, or bending over, or leaning on something so he rarely looks as tall as he is. 'It's a good job I don't live my life with an onus on *on*-putting you then, isn't it?'

'It's not about me. It would help *you* to remember that you're not in some stuck-up business meeting now. We're easy-going and warm and friendly around these parts. If you're staying here, you're customer facing, or more specifically, *my* customers have got to face *you*. The suits are imposing and unapproachable.'

'Good. I *am* imposing and unapproachable.'

With those words, I see someone desperately trying to put on a front. No one who is imposing and unapproachable has to *tell* you so, and I realise there's something much deeper going on behind the smart suits and guarded attitude, but I don't know him well enough to dig further into it, even though I want to. 'It's autumn. Put on a nice jumper or something.'

'A nice jumper?' Both his eyebrows rise like he needs to look up the definition in a dictionary.

'Something friendly and cosy. Cuddly.'

'*Cuddly*?' he repeats in horror. 'I am the least cuddly person on the planet. Why on earth would I...' He trails off, shaking his head like the thought is too much to bear. 'There's such a thing as looking professional, you know.'

'And there's also dressing appropriately for your job. Most of my customer base are under-tens. The fancy suits are superior and out of place here. End of story.'

My attempt at being tactful failed miserably, but he's been here for nearly two weeks now, and I was expecting him to realise for himself that casual clothes are encouraged and much more fitting for a fairytale museum, but he hasn't, so it was time to say something.

'Do you have any other complaints about my conduct, dress sense, or otherwise?'

'Yes, I do, actually.' I see an opportunity to bring up something else that's bothered me this week. 'Can you please not ignore customers if they speak to you? I know engaging isn't your strong point, but ignoring people is really rude. I felt so sorry for that little girl yesterday afternoon. Kids don't understand that not all adults are open to talking to them.'

His face screws up in confusion. 'What?'

'Yesterday in the Princess Suite. You were standing there, analysing something or other on your Tablet of Gloom, and that little girl started babbling at you. You glanced down and then point-blank ignored her, until her mum gave you a death glare and moved her away. For as long as you're here, you're a member of *my* staff and I will not have anyone treating customers like that. Even if you didn't know what to say, you could have at least acknowledged her.'

I didn't have an opportunity to bring it up last night, but now I'm glad to get it off my chest. It bothered me, and it was quite surprising after how unexpectedly nice he was to the boy with the enchanted rose. I assumed he was out of his depth and didn't know what to say to an excitable little girl, but I can't have him skulking around, looking like he works here, and then point-blank ignoring any customer who asks him a question.

'I don't know what you're talking about. I didn't ignore anyone.' He snaps the words out and folds his arms defensively, but his face has gone volcanically red, and I can *see* his cheeks prickling with heat.

'I literally watched you. You need to be more mindful in future, okay?'

He pushes out a long breath and closes his eyes like he's trying to remember yesterday afternoon and then he shakes his head. 'It was busy... Noisy... I didn't... I couldn't...'

He trails off and looks momentarily flustered, but then, in an instant, his body language becomes closed off and it's like he shuts down. 'No one talked to me. If you're making that up as a way of saying I'm spending too much time down here, just say that. I'd go back to the office if you had one I could use undisturbed. That's always my choice – undisturbed.'

He grabs his water bottle and stomps back up the stairs, leaving me listening to his irate footsteps across the upper floor, and wondering what button I just unintentionally pushed to get a reaction like that, especially as he seems to have been enjoying getting to know the museum lately, and I haven't been entirely opposed to having someone to share each working day with. That was a strange reaction. I got a sense of panic rather than anger or taking offence, and although I know he appreciates directness, I wonder if that was a bit *too* direct and I shouldn't have brought it up. It's yet another insight into something much deeper going on with him. There's more to that man than meets the eye, I'm sure of it.

7

'You should know that this is the most ridiculous thing I've ever done in my life!'

'Oh, really, I would never have guessed.' I huff under the weight of the pumpkin carriage, which Warren and I are in the process of rescuing from the riverbank, after it's gone off on a jolly all by itself.

I got in early this morning, hoping to make it before Warren, but annoyingly he was ahead of me and I caught up to him walking down the road from the car park. When we arrived, there was no sign of forced entry and nothing was out of the ordinary, until I did my usual pre-opening checks and discovered that Cinderella's life-size pumpkin carriage was missing.

Before we could call the police to report it stolen, Sadie phoned to say that she and Witt could see a pumpkin carriage down by the river.

'No wonder the Fairy Godmother turned lizards into horses to pull this thing!' Warren pants through gritted teeth.

'Mice. She turned lizards into footmen and mice into horses.'

I'd been wondering if Warren's early arrival this morning was a cover and I'd accidentally caught him on the way back from dumping it by the river, but I'd forgotten how heavy it is.

This is, at best, a two-person job, and even with the two of us, we're struggling. If I'd caught him in the act, even if he is hiding super-size muscles under those sharp suits, he'd have been sweaty and dishevelled and out of breath.

As sweaty and dishevelled and out of breath as he is now, actually.

'All right, let's take a break,' I say because he looks *hot*. In both the sweaty sense and the not totally unattractive sense. It's hard to deny how good-looking he is, even if I *want* to, because I'm fairly sure I shouldn't be seeing a property developer who's considering demolishing my museum in that way. Piercingly light-blue eyes, dark stubble tinged with the tiniest hint of grey, wide-set features, and dark bouncy-looking hair that would defy gravity if it wasn't swept backwards and tamed with product.

We've taken a shortcut around the side of the castle and now we've reached the edge of Ever After Street and the birch trees give us some shade from the blazing mid-autumn sun before we have to tackle getting the pumpkin carriage up the steps to the museum.

Warren leans against a tree, bending over with his hands on his knees, panting for breath. 'I always enjoy an opportunity to showcase how unfit I am.'

'Oh, I wouldn't say that...' I clear my throat and tear my eyes away from the way his chest is heaving. 'I mean, yes, me too, obviously. I don't have time for... fitness things.'

'Same. I sit at a desk all day and...' As he looks up, the wind blows and a snowstorm of yellowing birch leaves float down around us, making him laugh and bat them away from his face. '...hadn't realised how long it's been since I've been outside in nature or done *anything* that didn't involve staring at a screen.'

It doesn't sound like the way he intended to end that sentence, and it's something I can't imagine ever finding any joy in. The creative side of the museum is what I love. The fact that it's varied, that you never know who's going to turn up next or what you're going to be faced with on any given day.

He hasn't mentioned our discussion of his clothing choices again since the other day, but he's ditched the tie and the suit jacket, and now he's wearing perfectly pressed suit trousers and a long-sleeve office-type shirt with a button open at the collar, and when we got to the riverbank, he rolled the sleeves up to his elbows, putting his forearms on *full* display.

And he *is* knackered. He's leaning against the tree and we're both still breathing hard and sweat is glistening on his neck. I thought he was responsible for taking the glass shoes and starting up the spinning wheel the other day, but this is something different.

'Did you really not do this?' I didn't intend to let him in on my train of thought, but I blurt it out anyway.

He looks up and meets my eyes. 'No.'

I'm never sure whether I can trust him or not, but in that one simple answer, I believe him. It brings to mind all sorts of questions about who *did* do this, and how they got in to the museum in the first place, or why. I know Mickey's got the spare key, but there's no way she could have got this out either, and there's certainly no reason for her to go into the museum at night without telling me. There has to be something else at play here, I just don't know what it is yet.

'You didn't either, I'm guessing.'

I swipe the back of my hand across my forehead to wipe away sweat and shake my head.

He nods like he believes me too. 'Now we can't say that nothing's been taken. We're calling the police as soon as we get back.'

Something doesn't fit quite right about this. The pumpkin carriage was taken from the museum, yes. It was left on the edge of the riverbank, yes, but it isn't damaged. It didn't look like it had been dumped there, it looked artfully arranged, its own image reflecting on the water, and I feel like I'm missing something. 'What happened to sitting tight?'

'We're in the middle of hauling an extraordinarily heavy pumpkin carriage up from a riverbank. That's where sitting tight ends for me. I can entertain the joyous thought of sentient exhibits to a degree, but this... This did not get down there on its own.'

'But it doesn't feel malicious...'

'It *feels* like someone is breaking in at night and having a laugh at our expense. It's probably teenagers who have either managed to pick the lock or stolen a key and are going there to hide out, drink, take drugs, and whatever other illegal things teenagers do when they get together to do things they shouldn't do. Of course, if you had CCTV...'

It's not the first time he's lambasted my lack of CCTV, but it's yet another expense that I can't afford, and now I'm wishing I'd made it a priority because it would soon sort out what's going on at Colours of the Wind while our backs are turned.

'Do any of the other shops have CCTV that might cover a part of the street?'

'I doubt it. Most people around here are traditional and CCTV feels like too much of an intrusion. The council have cameras covering the main street and the car par—'

'The council! Lissa, you're a genius!' He pushes himself upright and darts out onto Ever After Street and I watch him stalking up and down the cobblestones, taking stock of where the CCTV cameras are. One of them covers the area around the carousel at the base of my steps, so there's a small chance that it might have picked something up and probably an even smaller chance that the council would willingly share it with us.

He points out all four cameras when he comes back, looking excitable. 'That's got to have captured something. One of us can stop by the council building later and see what they've got.'

I don't mention my not-so-wonderful relationship with the local council, but if anyone's going to try, it will need to be him. 'I think there's about as much chance as us getting this back up to the museum without one of us dying, but I'm surprised you're such an optimist.'

'I am.' His grin changes his whole face from its usual default semi-frown look and makes his eyes gleam like a kid again. 'I don't think we'll die. Maybe rupture something and be hospitalised for weeks though? And you think I don't know how to look on the bright side.'

It makes me laugh as we set off again, alternately pushing and pulling the pumpkin carriage across the bumpy cobblestones of Ever After Street, ignoring the *very* strange looks we're getting from families visiting the street.

'How did you even get this thing anyway?' Warren wheezes.

'Mickey found the frame at an antiques fair and knew I'd be able to do something with it. So I bought it, scrubbed it and sanded it down, added some rounded wooden panels to make it pumpkin shaped, painted it, and voila.'

'That's... pretty impressive.'

'Thanks.' If my face wasn't already red enough to rival the spot on Jupiter, I'd be blushing at how sincere he sounds. 'Visitors love that they can actually sit in Cinderella's carriage. It's a great photo opportunity.'

He goes to speak but I interrupt him before he has a chance. 'And no, we can't start charging for photos.'

'Actually, I was going to say that we need more photo opportunities. I've noticed that your visitors like them.'

I appreciate his perspective and it *is* true. People love a photo op. 'And more opportunities for photos people can share on social media would be a good thing.'

'Good thinking. We'll make a businesswoman out of you yet!'

We're both as embarrassingly out of breath as each other while we push the pumpkin carriage up the grassy verge beside the steps leading to the museum's door.

'I am impressed, you know,' he says as we reach the top of the hill, gasping, and stop outside the doors and look back at the climb we've done. 'That you make pretty much everything yourself. That's a lot of time and dedication. I can't imagine giving that much of myself to anything.'

'Your job?' I ask, and it makes me realise that I know next to nothing about him, despite him getting under my feet for many days now. He hasn't revealed anything about himself, his life, his likes and dislikes, any hobbies. There's keeping a professional distance and there's just *being* distant, and I still get the feeling that he's not being honest about something, and maybe it's part of that. If he's trying to keep something hidden, maybe it's easier to keep *everything* hidden? Or maybe it's my fault. I haven't been as welcoming as I could have been. I haven't asked him any questions or been particularly friendly. I haven't embraced the 'working with him' aspect that he suggested, despite his insights being right on the mark. Maybe he'd have been more open if *I* had been more open too?

He shrugs and makes a noise of indifference. 'A job is a job. I could live without it. Unfortunately, I couldn't pay my bills without it, so it's a necessary evil.'

I'm surprised by his apathy. Since he's been here, his job is the *only* thing I thought he was dedicated to. The only thing that's broken through his wholly professional façade is the possibility of exhibits coming to life, and I'm determined to find out more about him. If I knew more about him, maybe I'd have a clue about what he might be hiding.

'Well, that was a fun morning I'd like to *not* repeat in a hurry.' He looks back down the steps behind us and then jerks his head to one side to make me look too, because we've got a small audience of people, watching us haul, lug, and heave the pumpkin carriage, and now waiting to come in and see it in its rightful home.

'Two minutes, folks!' I call down. 'Just wrangling the exhibits that have escaped again!'

The small audience laughs and I flash my eyebrows at Warren. 'Tell you what, I bet Cinderella never had this much trouble.'

He laughs, but it gives me another pause for thought. We've attracted a bit of attention in dragging this along the street. I don't know how the pumpkin carriage got down to the river, but getting it back up hasn't been an entirely bad thing. It might even have helped business.

Warren's forearms flex in my view. Yeah, it hasn't been an entirely bad thing at all.

8

'No, absolutely not, that would go against every privacy law in England. Bugger off!'

Mr Hastings, the local council leader, gives a much more polite response than I expected to our request to see the CCTV from the Ever After Street cameras.

Somehow Warren persuaded me to come along and present a united front, and we've accosted Mr Hastings in his office just before closing time, but our request has had a predictably unenthusiastic response.

'Oh, come on, please?' I try again in my most persuasive voice. 'Someone has broken into the museum at least twice, and last time, they brought an extremely heavy pumpkin carriage out with them. Your cameras must have captured some part of that. We just want to know who and why.'

'No one gets a look at our CCTV footage without a warrant, it would be a breach of privacy.'

Mr Hastings is standing firm on this one, and I get an idea. I point at Warren. 'He's the owner of the building! He has rights! He can subpoena you to show us that footage!'

'No, I can't!' Warren holds both hands up, trying to stay out of this.

'Miss Carisbrooke.' Mr Hastings leans forward across his desk with his fingers steepled together. 'Why would I do *anything* to help you? You're a stone in my shoe, and that's the *nice* way of describing you. Every time I make any suggestion, any tiny little thing whatsoever, for the benefit of Ever After Street, *you* are at the helm of every protest. You are *always* the one riling up the other shopkeepers and making them think I'm serving some great injustice upon them rather than simply suggesting something that might be an advantage to us all. Over the years, I have realised that it doesn't actually matter what the council's suggestions are, they will *always* be met with opposition from *you*. You are an idealistic obstructionist and always will be.'

'I don't like change,' I mutter as embarrassment sends heat racing to my face. I'm not really that bad, but if Mr Hastings and his fellow council cronies are suggesting something that would have a detrimental effect on someone's business then I stand up for them, and I'm good at organising protests for things to stay exactly as they are. If it ain't broke, don't make needless and convoluted suggestions to fix it.

Every time anything has changed in my life, it's rarely been for the better. After Mum died, our lives became unstable, and I put a huge amount of effort into keeping things stable and steady for my sisters. Life is easier when it's smooth and unchanging, even if it does leave you feeling a bit stuck sometimes.

'I find this quite a turn of events that you now seek my help, and then I remember how you assisted Cleo Jordan in trying to outsmart me, and helped Raff and Franca over Christmas last year, and I don't think it would be in my best interests to do *anything* you ask me to, do you?'

I huff because I will never regret standing up for my friends who were being unfairly targeted by the council, but right now, I feel belittled and I wish I had someone to stand up for me in return.

Warren steps forward. 'Maybe you could have a look yourself and tell us if you've captured anything then?'

'Oh, yes, I'll be sure to pop it right at the top of my priority list, just behind clipping my toenails and taking the bins out.' He leans back in his chair and crosses his feet at the ankles, and I fight the urge to poke my tongue out at him. He's made so many of us jump through unnecessary hoops since he became council leader and it's been perfectly reasonable to push back against his power sometimes. 'Quite frankly, Miss Carisbrooke, I think Berrington Developments' proposal for the museum site is impeccable. It would be a huge asset to Ever After Street and bring in a vast number of jobs and new visitors, and there would be endless re-visit value too. Your museum never changes. Once people have seen it, they've seen it. An extra mannequin in a new costume occasionally doesn't give them enough reason to come back. But a cinema complex with a multitude of films showing every day, a pizzeria, diner, climbing, golf, bowling... Now we're talking! A reason for people to return every week and bring their families and friends. In fact, I was quite opposed to Mr Berrington's rescue plan, as Berrington Developments have the full support of the council. Their proposal would do wonders for Ever After Street, and I have no doubt that this olive branch has only been offered in an attempt to allay the number of shopkeepers who would fight for you, given how often you appear here, hammering my door down to speak up on *their* behalves.'

'It's not just an olive branch,' Warren says. 'Lissa's got the first right of refusal to stay in place. The museum brings a lot to the street and surrounding area. She deserves a fair chance to defend her position there.'

I can almost hear the unspoken, 'Even if it is pointless' that *should* follow his words. I appreciate his attempt at showing Mr Hastings a united front, but this does nothing but confirm the local council would be glad to get rid of me. Usually I feel invisible, but this makes me feel seen in the worst way possible. It makes me feel like the only person on my side is the *one* person who's responsible for starting all this in the first place, and leaves me feeling alone and unimportant, and scared for what the future may bring. I don't know if I can trust Warren, but without him, there is *no one* who would be on board with saving me.

'Either way, neither of you have a right to go poking your noses into our CCTV footage, and I'd like to get home before my dinner goes cold, so if you please...' He motions towards the door, and Warren and I meet each other's eyes and simultaneously decide that we aren't going to be able to wheedle anything further out of him tonight.

'Thanks for your time.' Warren remains the epitome of politeness as he holds the door open for me to go through first, which is nice because I can't get out fast enough. I knew Mr Hastings didn't like me – I didn't expect him to be quite so gleeful to see the museum shut down.

Without either of us explicitly stating where we're going, we head back towards the Ever After Street car park together, and I like the sense of not being alone, especially after our encounter with Mr Hastings has left me feeling small and browbeaten.

'You're very quiet,' Warren observes.

'Questioning every life choice I've ever made,' I mutter, assuming he will find Mr Hastings' clear dislike of me *very* helpful for the prospects of his cinema complex.

'Oh, don't worry about that stuffed-up cucumber with a

puffed-up sense of his own importance. I'm sure you've had many vast and varied reasons for obstructing his wishes time and time again.'

'We've all been forced to jump through hoops to fulfil some stupid requirement or another. He holds threats of eviction over anyone who doesn't comply. He doesn't care about the shopkeepers. He's all about money and not what makes the street better.'

The noise of passing traffic is loud, and he's leaning so close to hear me that he nearly walks into a lamppost. 'Yeah, imagine a businessman who wanted to make money. What a bizarre concept.'

'Hah hah,' I grumble so he knows how utterly amusing he is, but in a strange way, I appreciate his support and roundabout way of trying to make me feel better.

Instead of saying anything else, he turns around so he's facing me and walks backwards before continuing the conversation.

'What are you doing? You're going to fall over and crack your head open.'

'I don't mind staring death in the face,' he says with a cheerful shrug.

'It's not death you're looking at, it's me. Walk normally, for goodness' sake.'

'Don't worry about it.' His blue eyes are focusing so intently on my face that it makes my cheeks heat up and a tingle run down my spine, and I almost forget to worry about how likely he is to trip over his own feet.

He really is the strangest man. Businesslike to a worrying degree for 99 per cent of the time, and then he randomly turns into a naughty toddler who walks backwards in the street and gets abnormally excited about the prospect of sentient exhibits.

I'm lost in my analytical thoughts, so he says, 'On the plus side, at least we've learned that Mr Hastings knows you really well. I've yet to hear better descriptive words for you than idealistic obstructionist.'

It sounds like he's poking fun and I can't help the snigger that escapes. 'And I've yet to hear a better descriptive word for him than stuffed-up cucumber. You were spot on there.'

He laughs too, lines crinkling up around his eyes, and they distract me so much that I blurt out, 'Is it really a rescue plan?'

'Hmm?'

'You. What you're doing? He called it a rescue plan. I still don't understand why you'd try to rescue my museum. There's no conceivable way it will ever be more profitable than a cinema complex.'

'Not everything's about profit.'

I do an exaggerated double-take. 'From the moment I met you, you've repeated endlessly that *everything* is about profit. Half the time, I think you understand the language "money" better than you understand English.'

His face heats up in an odd way, and he ducks his head and nearly overbalances when he steps on a grate covering a drain, but he still continues walking backwards. 'I'm scratching an itch to do something different. When I heard about your concept of a museum, it... grabbed hold of me. Like I said, this would be the fifth cinema complex I've been involved with lately. However, there's only one of *you*. And having met you, seen your passion, seen Ever After Street as a whole, I think there's a lot to be said for helping and upgrading what already exists. I'd like to take the company in a more organic direction. We have a reputation for being modern and innovative, and I've always liked that, but in recent years, I think I've become more mindful that the past isn't always best knocked down and built over and there's room for preservation as well as forward thinking.'

Again, I find myself believing him even though I have no reason to. 'I like that.'

'It feels like the right thing for the company. In some situations, how we do things is not always the best approach, and there's room for compromises and looking at things from different angles... but I'm not the boss, and the boss still needs some convincing.'

'The boss is your mother?'

'Indeed.'

Again, it's an answer he could expand on, but he doesn't, and we're almost at the car park entrance so I don't push it. You can't *force* someone to reveal something they don't want to share.

'Where are you going back to? Where's home?' I ask instead.

'I don't know.' We've reached his car and he stares at it blankly for a moment before shaking himself and giving the black roof a pat. 'Where's home to anybody?'

'Somewhere they feel safe and free to be themselves?' I suggest and he shrugs another blank shrug, and it strikes me as incredibly sad. If home doesn't feel like home, then what have you got?

'But I live in Bromsgrove, if that's what you want to know,' he says quickly, like he's trying to circumvent how unexpectedly melancholy that answer became. 'It's about fifty miles away from here. My mother runs the office in London, but I'm usually based out of our Midlands office.'

'Fifty miles?' My eyes widen. 'So you do a hundred-mile round trip every day just to make my life a misery?'

'Yep.' He looks up at me with that naughty toddler twinkle in his eyes again. 'And it's worth every penny in petrol costs.'

I laugh out loud and retreat towards my own car. 'Thanks for the united front today.'

'Thank you for...' He trails off like he doesn't have a clue what he was intending to thank me for and then shakes his head. '...the carriage-related workout this morning, I guess. See you tomorrow.'

I echo his words with a wave, and surprisingly, I feel a bit lighter as I get into my car and wait, watching in the wing mirror while he starts his engine and pulls out. For once, seeing him tomorrow doesn't feel like an entirely bad thing.

9

'Lissa, I know you've got your hands full, but there's something quite odd going on...'

It's a few days later and Warren's gone out for his lunchbreak. There haven't been any suspicious exhibit incidents since the pumpkin carriage, but the hair stands up on the back of my neck as I answer the phone, and it's Imogen on the other end, sounding apologetic, but also quite worried.

'It's this spinning wheel, you see. It's, well, it's everywhere, and it's starting to make me a bit uneasy...' Imogen runs a shop called Sleeping Beauty's Once Upon A Dream that specialises in all things cosy for a perfect bedtime. Pyjamas, luxury bedding, snuggle hoodies, bath bombs and pampering kits, among other things, but this is the first I've heard of any spinning wheel problems.

'It was a bit strange when I arrived this morning and it was outside the front door, but I thought it was just kids playing a prank, but a little while later, it was outside the back door, then there was a tap-tap-tap on the shop window and it was out there, lurking in the bushes round the side, but now it's turned up in my office and every time I look at it, it's creeping closer.'

'Wait, it's *in* the office? It's actually moving?'

'Well, I've not seen it, but I shut the door and locked it in, and now every time I look through the glass in the door, it's moved a bit nearer, like it's coming for me. You don't know anything about it, do you?'

I *do* know this is the most ridiculous thing I've ever heard in my life. 'We know something's been going on with the exhibits, but we're still trying to get to the bottom of it. I'll come and get it as soon as Warren gets back. Just try not to... provoke it?' I say before she hangs up, and I wonder if I should take a defensive weapon or something to fight it off with. How the flipping *heck* is a spinning wheel taunting someone *inside* their office? And in broad daylight? How is it circling her shop with no one seeing it?

I quickly go to check on the spinning wheel that usually stands beside the mannequin of Princess Aurora, and it's definitely missing, and I go back to the lobby, perplexed by how it escaped my notice earlier, never mind how it *escaped* at all.

'Everything al—' Warren comes back in from his lunchbreak carrying shopping bags and clocks the look on my face instantly. 'What's wrong?'

'I've just had a phone call from Imogen in the Once Upon A Dream shop. She's being taunted by Sleeping Beauty's spinning wheel, and—' I don't get to finish the sentence before the phone goes again, and this time, it's Ali, the head chef and owner of the 1001 Nights restaurant.

'Look, I know this is just a big joke,' he says down the line. 'But putting a big, furry Remy from *Ratatouille* in my kitchen is not in the slightest bit funny. It might only be a fake rat, but *any* kind of rat in a restaurant kitchen is a terrible omen.'

'I didn't put it there!' I say indignantly.

'Oh, I know that, but if you could come and collect it as soon as possible, I'd be much obliged.' Ali puts the phone down without waiting for an answer.

'Remy, the rat who loves cooking, has appeared in the kitchen of 1001 Nights,' I explain to Warren. 'Ali starts work around this time of day, he must've just got in and found him. And he and Imogen are a couple, they started dating last Christmas, is that weird? Someone's targeted them both at the same time. It must be someone who knows they're together.'

Warren shakes his head, looking like he doesn't know where to start dismantling everything he's just heard. 'There's a *rat* who loves cooking?'

'Oh, you *really* need to watch some Disney films...' I realise that he's changed since I last saw him. 'What are you wearing?'

He transfers his shopping bags into one hand and curtsies to me. 'A nice jumper or something.'

He's still got on the suit trousers, but like I told him to the other day, he's now wearing a cosy-looking brown rib-knit jumper with orange leaves around the bottom hem, and it looks *good*. 'Have you just been out and bought that?'

'Maybe. I'm not a big "autumn jumper" kind of person, or at least, I *wasn't*...' He shifts the bags he's carrying between his hands again.

'You're not a big comfort person then.'

'No, I'm not.'

It's another thing that strikes me as being incredibly sad. There's something comforting about big, cosy, baggy jumpers at this time of year, something that brings in the season and makes you feel snug, and I feel quite sorry for anyone who misses out on this particular joy of autumn. 'It was a good choice. It's a very *nice* jumper.'

He blushes and the thought that a little compliment from me could make him blush makes *me* feel flushed too.

'Let me put these down and we'll go and rescue the rogue exhibits.' He lifts the bags again and heads for the stairs. 'Ali didn't sound particularly happy, so I'll take 1001 Nights in case he's angry and you take the spinning wheel.'

'You're a real gentleman, volunteering to battle a fake rat that's about thirty centimetres tall,' I say when he comes back down.

'Nope, just marginally more terrified of a stalker spinning wheel. If you prick your finger and fall asleep for a hundred years, don't blame me. You're single so finding true love's kiss might be difficult.'

'Ahh, Prince Philip, the man who ruined me for all others. Quite frankly, if a man isn't going to fight through roses and thorns and battle a dragon for you, then is it really love at all?'

He goes to reply but I cut him off. 'And don't tell me that's an impossible standard like my friends do.'

He laughs and holds his hands up. 'Wasn't going to say a word. I fully support anyone with high standards, no matter how unrealistic they are.'

I laugh too, and secretly I'm quite glad that he's swotted up on at least *one* fairytale.

* * *

'What do you think it wants?' Imogen whispers.

I'm standing beside her and we've both got our faces squashed against the small glass window in her office door, peering through nervously. 'I don't think it wants anything. It's a spinning wheel,' I say, wondering how my life got to a point where I'm having a conversation about what an escaped non-sentient object might want when the wooden thing really has *no* desires of its own whatsoever.

'Do you think it's after blood?'

I try to contain my laughter because she sounds legitimately concerned, but it gets the better of me and bursts out. Imogen is a perfectly sane middle-aged woman who has worked here for almost as long as I have. She isn't prone to flights of fancy or anything out of the ordinary, but she sounds honestly worried that the spinning wheel in her office is here on some sort of revenge mission that can only end bloodily.

The office is at the back of the shop, down a narrow corridor between her till area and her storage room, and there is *no* feasible way that anything could have snuck down here without her seeing it, and yet, somehow, one of my exhibits is in her office, and she has no idea how it got there.

There is something really strange going on here.

In fact, at this point, the *most* reasonable explanation is that my exhibits have turned into ghosts and developed the ability to phase through walls, which is really, really unlikely.

I go to open the door, but she stops me and hands me a long-handled umbrella with a sharp tip. 'Here. Just in case.'

I have to bite back the laugh again as I take my new protective weapon and go into her office, but the spinning wheel is just a spinning wheel, sitting there... menacingly.

There aren't any clues for how it got there. It's a small, windowless room with only the one door, tucked away at the back of the shop, and there's no hint of how it could possibly have moved each time she looked at it, and I'm half-wondering if Imogen's secretly had a bottomless brunch. Eventually I give up on trying to understand it, give the spinning wheel a gentle nudge with my foot while holding the spike of the umbrella out threateningly, just to make double-sure that it's not about to attack, and then I pick it up and carry it back out.

Imogen jumps aside and gives me and the spinning wheel a wide berth as I hand her umbrella back and apologise again, wondering if I should reassure her that I'll put it in a cage or something in future, lest it escape and seek her out again.

When I get back to the museum, Warren's water bottle and the model of Remy the rat are now sitting on the front desk, and Warren looks up when I come in. 'Should you be carrying that thing? What if it tries to bite? Do you need a tetanus jab after a spindle bite?'

'Very funny,' I say, despite the fact I'm trying not to laugh.

'This is the best thing I've seen in years. I have no idea what's going to happen next. I need to know what's going on, and at the same time, I actually don't want to know because it's marvellously fun, and it's sent my imagination into overdrive.'

Mine too, but mainly because there *has* to be a logical explanation, I just don't know what it is. 'Either way, budge over, because there's a bicycle lock in one of those drawers and I'm going to tie this thing up and lock it in place. Just in case.'

He laughs as he gets off the stool behind the counter and gives me space to crouch down and rummage, and when I stand back up, Remy has moved along the counter and is looking over, and I let out a yelp of surprise at his rodenty face staring at me, and Warren is nearly doubled over with laughter.

I laugh too, and take Remy and the spinning wheel away to put them somewhere safe, consistently surprised by his sense of fun when he doesn't overthink it. Half the time, it's like he forgets to be all businesslike and serious, until he remembers and quickly censors himself, and I wonder again if there's more than I thought hiding behind the fancy suits and excellent taste in jumpers.

10

Warren is a conundrum, and despite working together for a few weeks now, I feel like I know hardly anything more about him than I did on the day he arrived, and I keep thinking of what Mickey said – about finding his wish and granting it. He seems to love the idea of the exhibits coming to life, and I wonder if he'd be more open to the possibility of wishes coming true than I thought at first. It *has* been a couple of weeks since I collected wishes from the well, so it's as good an excuse as any to go down there and just have a little look...

Last time I saw him, he was hunched over his computer at the kitchen table, not looking like he'd be going anywhere for some time, and it's past 5 p.m. so the museum is closed for the night. I'm tidying the Fairytale Homes hall after a busy afternoon, but I realise this is the perfect opportunity to sneak down to the basement and find out if his wish was something we could realistically make come true.

And I'm 99 per cent positive that the basement is haunted and I prefer the idea of going down there while someone else is in the building. Usually I make Mickey come with me as a safety in numbers thing, but at least Warren would hear me scream.

The basement has an access door through Ariel's grotto, and I listen at the bottom of the stairs but it doesn't sound like Warren's going to move anytime soon, so I grab a torch, and click open the lock that allows one side of the cave to be pushed inwards, and venture down the long, hollow, freezing corridor that runs underneath the garden.

This is an old building that's had many uses over the centuries it's stood here, and this part of it must've been some sort of dungeon once, because I'm fairly sure that I can still hear the distant sound of ghostly, rattling chains every time I come down here.

The basement door creaks as I unlock it and push it open with my shoulder, and flick on the light that Darcy got working for me a couple of years ago, which is the only thing that allows me to come here without having a fear-induced heart attack.

The other end of the room is directly underneath the wishing well in the garden, and although it was probably used for water once, many moons ago, by now, the old stone has crumbled and fallen away, and the well opens out directly into this room, and all the colourful pieces of paper that children have pushed through the grate above now litter the floor in here, waiting to be granted.

Warren's wish was written on blue paper, and I bend over and rifle through the scattered wishes, picking up every blue one I can find and discarding it when it's not the right one.

There aren't as many as there once were – testament to my declining visitor numbers and, I think, a declining number of children who believe in magic, but there's still a good few all over the uneven stone floor, and I keep looking for that one piece of blue paper, until I find it...

...and wish I hadn't.

Warren, 41, Bromsgrove.
  I wish to find some meaning in this miserable life.

It feels so raw and vulnerable and I can feel my throat constricting. After the first joke of a wish he wrote down, I wasn't expecting something so personal and honest. I was expecting him to have written something superficial, the kind of thing any guy would wish for – a new car or the latest games console or something, but this... This is much, much deeper. His life is miserable? He doesn't find any meaning in it? I think about what I thought the other day when we talked about autumnal jumpers and cuddly, cosy clothing – he doesn't seem to enjoy much at all.

'So that's how you're doing it.'

The sound of my own scream takes me by surprise at a voice in the silence, and I don't think I would have jumped so much if an actual ghost had materialised in front of me.

I spin around and turn to face Warren where he's standing in the doorway, and then quickly hide my hand behind my back and let his wish flutter to the floor like I'd never picked it up. The last thing I want him to know is that I've seen that.

'What are you doing down here?' I demand, a hand on my chest which is still heaving from the shock. 'You can't sneak up on someone in a haunted basement!'

'Haunted, really?' He raises a sceptical eyebrow as he pushes the door fully open and ducks in.

'Oh, you can believe in exhibits that move of their own accord but you don't believe in ghosts?'

'Didn't say I don't believe in 'em. Just thought that most ghosts would choose somewhere more inspiring than this to haunt.'

'All right, it's not the best basement in the world, but it's mine and I love it. You don't get to come down here and insult my basement.'

'You're terrified of it. I can almost guarantee that you get your friend to come down here with you every time.'

'I do not!' I lie. How the heck did he get to know me *this* well when I know so little about him?

'So...?' I ask again, trying to redirect him back to my earlier question.

'I have the floor plans, Lissa. I could see there was a room beneath the wishing well and I've heard too much talk about wishes being granted in this place for it to be coincidental. Plus the information harvesting was very, very weird, even by your exceptionally strange standards. I knew something was going on and figured you'd enlighten me sooner or later. I was just leaving and you were suspiciously missing. I wondered if you'd been kidnapped by one of the exhibits and thought you might need a Prince Charming-type to rescue you.'

It's my turn to raise an eyebrow, and he laughs. 'God knows where I'd have found one at this time of night so I came looking for you myself instead.'

'Surprisingly chivalrous of you.' I laugh, but I'm still breathing hard from the shock and I feel shaky and unbalanced at being caught looking for *his* wish, which I'm sure he's realised.

I step away from the scattered wish papers and try to look innocent as he comes closer, the footsteps of his shiny shoes echoing around the hollow room. He crouches down and does exactly what I did – picks up a few pieces of blue paper and discards them until he finds the right one, then he folds it again and puts it in his trouser pocket without a word.

'So what *did* you wish for?' I say breezily, trying to pretend I didn't find it.

'The usual. New socks, nice cologne, the latest PlayStation. Like putting in an order with Santa and not having to wait for the hassle of Christmas.' His voice is just as breezy as mine as he pats his pocket and stands upright again, looking down at the rainbow of coloured papers littering the floor around him. 'So, what is this? Is it pure nosiness or are you throwing the budget away on every entitled little blighter who puts a piece of paper down that well wishing for games and laptops and smart phones and I-something-or-others, and anything else their greedy little minds can come up with?'

'No! Of course not!' I say indignantly. 'This is nothing to do with children who want *things*. There are families who are struggling to get by, and Ever After Street comes together to help them. Anyone with such a cynical attitude has no business being surrounded by the magic of children's wishes. Go on, out!' I've turned around mid-sentence and started marching towards the door to order him away, but his fingers clamp around my shoulder and force me to turn back to him.

'Sorry.' He drops his hand and steps away instantly. 'But don't turn your back on me when you're talking. I can't...' He sighs and pushes a hand through his hair. 'If I'm being talked to, I want to be talked *to*.'

'As opposed to the more time-efficient multitasking of walking and talking?'

'Exactly,' he mutters, which is surprising for someone who seems to value nothing more than efficiency.

'So you have spoilt only-child syndrome then? Used to having undivided attention?'

'Something like that.'

There's something in his tone that suggests it's *nothing* like that, and I'm once again certain that there's something I'm missing here, and I don't know where to begin in finding out.

'Tell me, please,' he says in a gentle, curious tone. 'You're not just some year-round Santa who delivers endless expensive presents to demanding children?'

'Children wish for the most heartbreaking things. Things you can't imagine any child ever needing, never mind needing so badly that they have to wish for it, but they do...' I stop myself saying anything further, because it's the kind of thing he's never going to understand. He'll tell me it's not my responsibility and I shouldn't be wasting the budget on something so frivolous and unrelated to the business.

'Like what?' he prompts.

'Things that someone who can afford your suits and your car could never comprehend. Just forget—'

'They're work suits. It's a company-issued car to make sure all employees look the part and impress potential clients. I'm just a normal guy with normal struggles... who never usually lets the professional front slip this much.'

A professional front. In those few words, he answers so much about himself. I'm not used to people who are all-business. On Ever After Street, everyone's businesses are run from the depths of their hearts, and everyone is emotionally invested in everything we do, but Warren has always seemed aloof and determined to keep a professional distance at all times. Is that front *exactly* why I don't know much about him? In fact, the only moment it's cracked even slightly is when he's been intrigued by something the exhibits have done, and unable to hide the little boy buried deep down inside.

I relent and answer his question. 'Like food. Enough food to have breakfast as well as dinner. Enough food that Mummy can eat too. Clothes without holes in them. Clothes warm enough to keep out the winter chill. Blankets warm enough that their parents don't have to worry about putting the heating on.'

'Wow.' He's chewing his lower lip as he looks at me, making me self-conscious of how intently he's focusing on my mouth again. 'That's... unthinkable.'

'That's the reality of what life is like for a lot of people these days. People have to choose between buying food and paying their heating and water bills. Children go to bed hungry. Children go to school hungry. Mickey's partner is a teacher and he confirms this is true for many families. It was true for me when I was younger. After my mum died, my family *struggled*. Dad's grief was overwhelming. He lost the will to work, and when he did work, he struggled with childcare, and one inconsistent wage wasn't enough to bring up five girls and pay all the bills. I was the lucky one. I grew up with two parents. I was the oldest, so I had no hand-me-downs, but after life changed, I watched my sisters fight against every second of not having the things their friends had. Wanting new clothes and toys and having to put up with clothes that didn't fit the rest of us any more, and toys the rest of us didn't want any more, and there was nothing I could do about it. I watched Dad go without so the rest of us had full dinner plates. And now, I see the same happening to other families, and I feel that if I'm in a fortunate enough position to be able to help, then I want to. I didn't know that's what the wishing well was going to become, but when you read some of those wishes, it's heart-breaking, and when the other shopkeepers found out what I was doing, they got involved too. Now I get the kids to write down their info so we can find them again, and every few weeks, I gather the wishes and we all get together and see what we can do between us.'

I didn't expect to reveal something so personal, but he's listening intently with a slow and understanding nod. 'I lost my dad at an early age too, so I get it. I realise that I'm lucky never to have gone without anything, but childhood wasn't easy. I relate to that, very much so.'

I can't help responding to the soft smile he gives me. That's the first time he's mentioned his father and I had no idea that we shared a childhood experience like that, and it gives me an urge to hug him that must be avoided at all costs.

He must sense it too because he looks down at the colourful pieces of paper on the floor. 'May I?'

It's nice that he asks permission and I nod, and watch as he crouches again and picks up a folded green paper, and then laughs loudly and holds the paper up to me. 'Way to prove a point. This kid wants *a new Xbox so I don't have to share with my brother, and more games than he's got.*'

I take the paper from his fingers and roll my eyes. Trust him to pick one that goes against everything I've just said. 'Not everyone takes it in the spirit it's meant, and we just ignore those ones. It's the really personal ones that we do something about if we can.'

He picks up a yellow piece of paper and reads it. 'Nappies for her baby sister because Mummy keeps worrying about the price and Daddy goes to work all the time to pay for them.'

'A very young interpretation of how expensive babies are. Parents don't realise that children pick up on the things they're worried about. As long as she's put the full address, we can send them a small gift voucher for a babycare shop. I suspect "nappies" is a generalised term and they probably need a few things.'

'And you just... knock on their doors, hand them a gift, and tell them their kid wished for it at your magical wishing well?'

'No! That would spoil the magic. We send everything by post.'

'You don't leave things outside the door, knock, and hide to see people's reactions?' He sounds surprised.

'I have done occasionally, if they live nearby, but I don't want anyone to know who's doing it and most people have got doorbell cams these days.'

'That's... nice. Surprisingly nice. People do realise it's you though. Like I said, I've seen enough talk online about your magical wishing well. Some kids have put two and two together and told their parents.'

I shrug. 'I deny all knowledge. No one can prove where it came from. I *want* people to think there's a little magic in this old well. That's the point – to send a bit of wonder into the world.'

'I really am impressed by your dedication, you know. You put a lot of effort in to make people believe in that little bit of magic. It's...' His eyes find mine and he swallows hard and seems to lose the ending of the sentence.

'Whimsical? Fanciful? Idealistic?' I offer, knowing all too well the sorts of words he'd use to describe me.

'Inspiring. And really, really lovely. I can't remember the last time I met a person who *cared* as much as you do.' He says it quietly and looks away as he speaks, but his eyes quickly flick back up to my mouth when I answer.

'Many people would say that's not a good thing.'

'Yeah, they would...' He goes back to looking through the wishes without clarifying whether he'd agree or not.

He reads aloud from a pink bit of paper and then holds it up questioningly. '*Amy, eight, 55 Fleethall Road, I wish for a new Barbie, my Barbie is lonely...* Doesn't sound quite as demanding as the Xbox lad?'

'Ones like that need approaching with balance. She could be some spoilt millionaire's daughter who gets a new Barbie every week and gets bored of them within a day, or she could be a normal eight-year-old who's struggling and has only got Barbie to turn to. It could be a metaphor for her own loneliness. On balance, you can get Barbie dolls for under a tenner online and it could make a huge difference to her life. If nothing else, it could bring her a moment of joy, so it's worth it.' I furrow my eyebrows at the sceptical look on his face. 'And if we look them up on Google Maps and the house is a mansion, then we'll keep Barbie for the next kid.'

He laughs and picks up an orange piece of paper and his eyes go distant as he reads it. '*I wish I had a dragon to fight off the bullies at school...* That's so sad, and yet so inventive. That's exactly what I would've wished for when I was a kid.'

It's not the first time he's mentioned being bullied, and it intrigues me again. It's not something I'd expect someone to be open about, and yet he is. As an adult, he seems like the *last* person who would ever be intimidated, and it makes me wonder if that's *because* of what happened in his childhood, and if that's a big part of the front he's obviously hiding behind. You never know what a person has been through in their lives, regardless of outward appearances. I want to ask him more about it, but he swallows hard and goes back to looking through the wishes. 'Aww, this one's sweet. *I wish to come back here again.* That's...' He swallows again and sounds a little bit emotional. 'Can I keep this one? I think we should stick it up in the office as a reminder of why we're doing this.'

I nod wordlessly as he tucks that one into his pocket too, alongside his own. 'I've never had that with one of my properties before. Never imagined a child would like a place so much that they'd make a wish to return to it.'

'What, in your multi-million-pound cinema complexes with new films showing every day and endless popcorn and dough-nuts and diners, and scurrying up indoor walls and lobbing balls around, literally designed for comeback value? Kids must beg their parents to take them there every weekend.'

'Yeah, but not like this.' He pats the wish in his pocket. 'That's just entertainment. This is... heart. Of all the things a child could dream of wishing for, this little girl wished to come back here. That's so charmingly simple that it's special.'

Whenever I'm in this basement alone, I often feel my heart in my throat, but this time, it's not because I think a ghost might be about to pop out at me, but because of how earnest he sounds. I thought the wish-granting aspect would meet his immediate disapproval, but he seems surprisingly accepting of it.

He shakes his head and gathers up the remaining wishes in one swoop and holds them out to me. 'How do we do this?'

'There's a shopkeeper meeting on Friday, I'll take them with me and we usually divide them up between us so everyone takes a few and gathers what we need, and then we get together to package everything up and get it ready for sending off.'

'Can I help?'

'You want to?' I reach out to pull him up, and even though he doesn't need my assistance, he slips his fingers around mine and lets me tug him to his feet, and that simple act of accepting the tiniest bit of help feels like a metaphor.

'Yes, I do.'

For as often as I think he's hiding something, in that simple answer, he isn't. 'I'd like that.'

'I'd *love* that.' He realises he hasn't let go of my hand yet and yanks his fingers away quickly. 'Now, can we get out of here before we get attacked? I might not believe in ghosts, but I'm pretty sure I can hear spiders salivating in those darkened corners.'

I laugh as I herd him towards the door. 'No, no. We don't mention the spiders. If we don't acknowledge their presence, they can't see us. I don't need any more reasons to beg Mickey to come down here with me.'

'I knew it!' His laugh fills the corridor with warmth as we walk back towards the Princess Suite, and it's yet another day that ends with me feeling like his presence isn't altogether a bad thing. He's the first person in a long while who makes me feel *seen*, and he's the also the last person I ever imagined could do that.

11

Mysterious happenings are afoot on Ever After Street! Just days after Cinderella's glass slippers went to a ball all by themselves, Imogen from Sleeping Beauty's Once Upon A Dream is being taunted by a vengeful spinning wheel, 1001 Nights has got a new chef, and the pumpkin carriage has escaped the museum and gone to admire its reflection in the river... Just what is going on here? Leave your answers in the comments section!

I stare at the Ever After Street social media in surprise. Usually, I only check it once a day, but the marked increase in notifications this morning made me wonder if something was happening, and sure enough, the shared account that every shopkeeper has access to has posted a selection of photographs of my escaped exhibits.

There's a picture of the glass slippers, all alone in the castle ballroom, a photo of Ali posing with the model of Remy wearing a matching chef's hat, several photos of the spinning wheel – outside Imogen's front door, outside her back door, hiding in the bushes at the side of her shop, and one of it in her office – and a few arty photos of the pumpkin carriage beside the river too.

These pictures were taken before they called us, they had to have been. Something is going on here. And I have a sudden deep suspicion that my fellow shopkeepers are up to their necks in it.

'This is very interesting...' Warren comes downstairs from the office, Tablet of Gloom in hand and the usual water bottle hanging from a finger. 'Ali's doing a thumbs up with Remy. He's hardly got the angry "get your rat out of my kitchen right this second" attitude that he had when I saw him, has he?'

'And someone's taken these photos all around Imogen's shop and *in* her office. Not exactly the petrified "take an umbrella to fight it off" attitude that she had when I got there either...'

'Intriguing...' He goes to stroke his stubbled chin but stops short when he looks around. 'There are people.'

'There are,' I confirm. It's not a huge increase, but this morning has been slightly busier than other mornings lately, which is always a nice boost.

'Have you read the comments?' His fingers flick across his tablet screen.

I shake my head and quickly navigate there on my phone as well, and can't hide the gasp at the ever-increasing number.

Aww, pumpkin carriages need love too!

The glass slippers in the ballroom by themselves are a metaphor for modern life!

BRB, going to 1001 Nights for a dish cooked by Remy now!

That spinning wheel is the funniest thing I've ever seen! How have they managed to make an inanimate object look so menacing?

Never bothered with going in the museum before, but we will next time we come! It looks excellent!

'I didn't even know we had *that* many followers who engage with our posts. Social media feels like shouting into the abyss most days, we only usually get "likes" from bots or advertisers.'

'This is brilliant. It's captured *my* imagination, I can see why other people are interested too. I didn't even think about putting it on social media...' He trails off and his blue eyes find mine again. 'However, *someone* did, and this provides quite a clue. My money is on your friend who seemingly has free run of this place... and *you* really didn't know about this? This hasn't been your plan all along?'

'I *wish* I was clever enough to come up with this, but I'm not that good at marketing. Can you cover at lunchtime? I'll go and find out if Mickey knows anything.'

He takes a drink from his water bottle. 'I can guarantee that she will.'

I think she might too, but I can't believe she'd do anything like this without telling me.

* * *

Mickey's shop is suspiciously empty. The front door is locked so no customers can get in, so I go round the back and find the back door unlocked, but my best friend is nowhere to be found.

Her shop backs onto a narrow path on the edge of the forest that surrounds this end of the street. All the shops on this side share the same back access route, and as I stand there for a moment, wondering where she could be, I hear voices coming from further along the path and I creep closer.

'What next?' a familiar voice says.

'The spinning wheel was genius, but next time, we need to double-check how heavy something is before we volunteer to move it, I think I'm still sweating from dragging that pumpkin carriage out.' That's Darcy, the florist and castle gardener who's also Marnie's other half.

'So the Notre Dame gargoyles are a no-go then, they're solid stone.' Mickey's voice filters over the hedge surrounding Marnie's bookshop garden.

'Lumière and Cogsworth could get up to some mischief,' Sadie suggests. 'If we borrow some of your stock, Marnie, we could set up a scene of them reading Belle's books.'

'Or they could go for tea in The Wonderland Teapot.' Cleo's voice is quieter than the others, like she's the only one aware that they could be overheard.

'What about Aladdin's lamp? That could get up to mischief... We could hang it from the Christmas Ever After arch so it looks like the genie is trying to fly off somewhere?' That's Franca speaking, who runs The Nutcracker Shop on the year-round festive offshoot of the street.

I clear my throat as I peek around the hedge. 'Is this a private coordinated scheming or can anyone join in?'

A few screams of surprise fill the air, and I can't help enjoying the little bit of vindication I feel at making them all jump so much. 'So it's all of you? You're *all* using Mickey's key and going into the museum at night to move things and take things?'

'I can explain.' Mickey holds up both hands. 'It's not as bad as it sounds – we're trying to help.'

'We thought that if we could make it seem like the exhibits are coming to life – like those *Night at the Museum* films – then the museum would gain some interest and get the public talking, and then you'd be in a stronger position to fight back against those evil developers. Today's post was just the start. We're going to—' Marnie looks at me before amending. 'We *want* to carry on, every night, if you'll let us.'

'I've had quite a few visitors comment on the spinning wheel already this morning,' Imogen ventures.

'Ah, yes, the spinning wheel.' I turn to her. 'You deserve to be nominated for an Oscar over that. I thought you were terrified!'

'Oh, thank you so much!' She clearly misses my point. 'Ali and I practised together all morning!'

I shake my head, unsure whether to laugh, cry, or be really, really annoyed. 'Why didn't you tell me?'

'We wanted you to believe in the magic that you help others believe in,' Mickey says. 'And I thought it would be best if you really were in the dark as well. If the evil gerbil is anywhere near as sharp as his suits, he'd figure out that you knew what was going on straight away. It was better if you didn't have anything to hide.'

'Yeah, but he's invested in this now. He's determined to figure it out. Even without knowing that Mickey has a key, he's already guessed it was you lot. He knows I was on my way over to ask Mickey about it.'

'Just tell him it wasn't us.'

'Tell him we took photos of the exhibits that had already escaped, but we had nothing to do with them escaping. This whole thing is to try and protect the museum *from* him and his rotten company, you can't let him in on this.' That's Bram, Cleo's other half and the Mad Hatter from The Wonderland Teapot. 'It would defeat the entire object.'

They're right, of course they are, and they're all bloody geniuses too. I could never in a gazillion years come up with something like this, but at the same time, excluding Warren and lying *to* him feels uncomfortably prickly.

Mickey knows me well enough to know I'm the world's worst liar, and I kind of wish I'd heard that first voice over the fence and walked away, so I wouldn't know, and I wouldn't be part of the deception. Just like they said.

'This has so much potential. People are already intrigued. We've had more "likes" on social media since that post went up than we have in months. The more exhibits we can move, the more interest this will generate, and if there's a lot of interest around the museum, then his company can't waltz in and close it down, there would be a public outcry.' Sadie nods encouragingly.

'I'm not sure outcry makes much difference to them. Look at that poor library near Cheltenham,' Mickey mutters. 'As long as he doesn't know I have the spare key, he'll never know.'

I shake my head because although he still doesn't know that part, it's unlikely to be long before he figures it out. 'What happened to the Pocahontas and John Smith comparison? I thought he was a "Mark Darcy-esque fox who needed to be taught my culture"?' I paraphrase what she said when she first saw him.

'I don't know, Liss. He's staying here until the end of the year for what reason? He's given you nothing tangible. No set goal. He says you need to prove the museum is worth saving, but he hasn't told you *how*. No "you need to earn such-and-such amount of money" or "gain X number of visitors". None of us understand what he's getting out of this. Without set goalposts, he can change them at any moment. You were right to be suspicious in the first place and we all need to keep our guards up. A company like that cannot be trusted, no matter how handsome the man they've sent as their liaison is.'

It feels pointed, like she knows I've been softening towards Warren lately, especially since reading his wish last week.

'Exactly that,' Darcy agrees. 'What is he really doing here? What's his purpose? Because a man like that *always* has a motive, even if it's well hidden.'

Are they right? It bolsters my doubts about Warren and how honest he's been about the *real* reason for his presence here. I know he's trying to prove something to his mother-slash-boss, but he hasn't elaborated much. However, it makes me want to stick up for him too. It might be well buried, but there's something deep about him, and I don't think he's anywhere near as bad as I thought he was at first. He was openly touched by those wishes the other day, and I'm getting the sense that he's enjoying the museum more than he expected to, but I have to remind myself that I've been friends with everyone in this garden for years. I *know* they're being protective because they want what's best for me, whereas I've known Warren for a matter of weeks and I *do* feel like he's hiding something.

'Did you find his wish?' I'm so lost in thought that it's definitely not the first time Mickey's asked.

I hesitate and then lie. 'No. I tried, but he came in and caught me and then took it.'

I hate not being honest with my best friend, we share *everything*, but it doesn't feel like something I should share with anyone. Would Warren have written something so personal if he'd known I was going to read it? Of course he wouldn't, as shown by how quickly he took the piece of paper when he realised that I might.

No matter which side we're on, I can't tell my fellow shopkeepers that he finds life meaningless, only for it to be passed around Ever After Street like the juiciest gossip. It would be different if it was something tangible, something we could actually get him, a way of proving the magic of the wishing well, but it isn't, and his feelings aren't mine to share.

Mickey makes a noise of frustration. 'What a shame, it would have been so handy to have that. Oh, well. Mr Hastings told us he put on a good show?'

'Mr Hastings *knows*?' I say in disbelief.

'We knew he'd see us on the CCTV, and we knew you'd go looking for it. We had to get him in on the plan,' Cleo says. She knows Mr Hastings better than the rest of us and insists that he *does* have a nicer side, somewhere.

'But he *hates* me. He'd be glad to get rid of me. And he's already approved the Berrington Developments plans – he sounded like he couldn't wait to visit their cinema complex!'

'Ahh, but he's learning to listen to what the shopkeepers in his area want and we all want *you*,' Cleo assures me. 'He had to get on our side or face the wrath of all of us. I think he's more neutral than you think. He'd like to see the museum doing better, because you've been a fixture here for so long. Ever After Street wouldn't *be* Ever After Street without you, Liss. Even Mr Hastings can admit that. Who else would he have to call him out on his nonsense if you weren't here?'

'Well, he did an absolutely sterling job of making me think I was the biggest thorn he's ever had in his side and he couldn't wait to see the back of me. And you lot. You're all wasting your lives running shops here when you should clearly all be auditioning for roles in *Coronation Street*. I can't believe you guys did this, and at the same time, of *course* you did. Who *else* would have come up with something so astoundingly brilliant?'

Mickey is the first to come over and give me a hug. 'And now you're involved so we have your imagination too. The possibilities are endless.'

I don't feel as excited as I should. The possibilities *are* endless, and I can see where they're coming from and that their intentions are nothing but good, but the prospect of going back to the museum and telling Warren it was nothing to do with them weighs heavy. He's going to know I'm lying, and the ease that's been building between us is going to be eroded.

But they are right. I trust my friends with my whole heart, but I have zero idea of whether I can trust him.

There is no concrete goal. What would he consider to be 'proof' that the museum is worth saving? What if we get to the end of the year and he says I haven't done enough without ever defining what 'enough' is? Since he arrived, I've made peace with him being here. I know he's looking at the budget, at things that can be improved here and cut there and streamlined everywhere, and I've tried to embrace that – believing him to be my best chance to save Colours of the Wind, but what if it's the biggest mistake I've made? What if joining the others and really embracing this escaped exhibits idea could give me a leg to stand on and might be *my* way of saving my museum – with or without him?

12

'Is he climbing in or climbing out?' a boy of around eight or nine comes up to the front desk and asks me shyly.

'I don't know, what do you think?' I say with a grin. He's talking about my model of Lumière, who is currently trying to scale the tower of the Ever After Street castle.

'Maybe he's trying to rescue Plumette?'

'Oh, yes, of course, why didn't I think of that?' I realise it should be reasonably easy to get a feather duster and do it up in the style of Lumière's love-interest in *Beauty and the Beast*, and I wonder why I've never thought of it before.

'Either way, it's awesome,' the boy says and goes back to the mum and little sister who are waiting for him.

'Was that about the candlestick?' Within moments of the boy walking away, Warren comes down the stairs, his eyes on the Tablet of Gloom in his hand.

'Do you do nothing but sit up there monitoring social media?'

'Hmm?' His eyes were on the screen and I have to repeat myself before he answers. 'No, I sit up there working. You're not the only job I'm overseeing at the moment, you know. I'm choosing to do my usual work from here because it's easier than commuting. I got a tip-off from my boss to check the Ever After Street account again.'

'Your mother?'

'One and the same.'

'That must be strange.'

'It has its moments.'

It's typical of Warren's terse responses in recent days.

Things have been awkward between us. When I got back from catching the others, I told him that no one knew how the exhibits got out, but the other shopkeepers had spotted them and decided to have a bit of fun for social media. For added flair, I claimed they thought it was me doing it and laughed in my most unhinged manner.

As predicted, he knew I wasn't telling him everything, what-ever respect had built up between us was eroded instantly, and he's spent almost all his time hunched over his laptop at the kitchen table since then, although he's stuck to wearing the comfy jumpers rather than going back to the intimidating suits.

'So, *is* he climbing in or climbing out?'

'I don't know. It's up for interpretation. Although have you seen that castle? Why would anyone want to get *out* of it? Lumière and Cogsworth lived in the Beast's castle in the film, maybe he's trying to sneak in so they can get back to the comfort they're accustomed to.'

'That's the story you're sticking to, is it?' He twists the water bottle around on his finger.

'I don't know, Warren. I don't know how he got there. Last I saw him, he was on that shelf by the door.' I hate how easily the lie rolls off my tongue when the reality is that Sadie tied him to a rope made of knotted fabric scraps and lowered him from the tower window at 1 a.m. last night, while Mickey and I stood in the street and helped her position him perfectly to catch the most eyes, and then took photos as soon as daylight came, and now there's a post on the Ever After Street socials asking people to comment if they spot anything untoward at the castle today, and to leave their guesses on what the cheeky candelabra is up to.

'Right. Of course he was.'

I don't know who's right – my fellow shopkeepers telling me to keep this from him, or my gut feeling that tells me I should be honest with him, but what I do know is that everything seemed better when it felt like Warren and I were on the same side.

* * *

All I can hear are clattering and scraping noises. It's after 5 p.m. and now the museum is closed to the public, Warren is up to something upstairs. 'What are you doing up there?'

No answer.

I go up a few steps and call his name again, and this time, he pops his head around the wall of the landing and looks down at me. 'Did you say something?'

I repeat myself and he beckons me upwards, and when I reach the second-floor landing, I find he's cleared a spot beside a statue of Tinkerbell who's been put up here due to a pair of broken wings, and has dug out my collection of dustsheets and covered the floor with them, and he's looking exceptionally proud of himself.

I give him a clueless shrug because it requires further explanation.

'Oh, you have to get down there to see the point.'

I get the sense of that mischievous little boy coming to the surface again because he's taken his shoes off and is bouncing on the balls of his feet and he's got that 'I'm up to something' glint in his blue eyes, and I indulge him by unzipping my boots and stepping out of them to kneel down in the spot he points out.

It's behind the baluster posts of the landing banister, looking down the stairs and directly into the lobby from above, towards the main doors, and when I still can't figure out what he's getting at, I look up at him questioningly.

'I've found the perfect spot for a stakeout!' He looks so pleased with himself that it would be adorable if it wasn't the *worst* suggestion ever. 'I'm going to stay here tonight and keep watch. This is the ideal hideout – I can see the doors and the lobby, a perfect view of anyone coming in or going out, but no one will ever know I'm here. Tonight, I will catch whoever it is red-handed.'

Panic fills my mind and I scramble back to my feet. 'You can't do that!'

'Why not?'

'You just... er... you can't...' I'm on thin ice here. If I protest too much, he's going to know I'm hiding something, because if I didn't *know*, I'd want to find out too, wouldn't I? What possible objection could I have that wouldn't be even slightly suspicious?

I can surreptitiously text Mickey and make sure she tells everyone not to do anything tonight and meanwhile, I can reinforce the belief that I don't know anything either, can't I?

'You can't – on your *own*!' I amend my previous sentence as a moment of inspiration strikes. 'I'll stay too. I want to know what's going on just as much as you.'

'Of course you do.'

I often feel like I'm invisible, but at the moment, I feel like he can see straight through me. 'Two pairs of eyes are better than one, right? One of us might spot something the other one misses.

Besides, I couldn't possibly leave you alone with the museum ghost, could I? Yes, this is a good idea.' I nod sagely. 'I can't believe we didn't think of it sooner.'

And I can't believe that *we* didn't foresee this as a possibility.

I walk slowly down the stairs until I'm out of his sight and then *race* down the remaining steps until I can grab my phone from the front desk and quickly text the shopkeepers' WhatsApp group to warn them to stay far, far away.

I'm still texting when Warren comes down the stairs with his briefcase and his car keys jangling in his hand and I put my phone down quickly. 'Where are you going?'

'To change and get something to eat before I settle in for the night, and also to make it look like I've gone home in case anyone's watching the building. When I get back, can you let me in round the back way?'

I nod, surprised by how seriously he's taking this. He's really going to the trouble of returning by going through the forest and scrambling up the hill and over the garden wall at the back? I feel that guilt again. No one's watching the building because their 'inside woman' is literally spilling the beans right at this second.

'Can I get you anything?'

'Oh, I'm okay...' I trail off, surprised that he's offered something so thoughtful. I didn't expect him to consider that although *he* might've been semi-prepared to spend the night here, I'm not. 'Food, I guess. I'm not fussed, whatever you're having.'

He nods and loudly says goodnight like he really is expecting that someone's eavesdropping.

As he leaves, I quickly text the group.

> He's just gone out. I could fetch something out now and stash it somewhere until later...

Mickey's reply comes through instantly.

> Too much of a risk. This could be a trap and he's watching the building from somewhere to test us.

I laugh out loud to myself about him saying the exact same thing about them not five minutes ago, until another message comes through.

> You'll have to smuggle something out to us later. It'll be a dead giveaway if you don't! Either he catches us in the act or he proves that nothing happens if he's watching. The only way to get past this is if something happens right under his nose – while he's watching! None of us can get in or out unseen if he's there. You're our only hope of calling his bluff.

They have a point, of course. He'll either catch who's really responsible or he'll know that I'm involved and I've forewarned them not to come, but if something was still to escape without him seeing or suspecting anything and then, in the morning, he can't prove how an exhibit could still have got out then it would be a good thing...

More messages come into the group chat, and I should feel as excited as the others are about this opportunity to beat him at his own game, but I feel like this is going from bad to worse. Now I'm not only pretending to be on a stakeout with him, but I've got to somehow smuggle something outside without him catching me. How am I *ever* going to pull that one off when I'm certain that he's also staking out *me* tonight, and making sure that I *don't* smuggle something out?

It isn't long before there's a quiet knock on the back door, and when I open it, Warren ducks in. He's wearing a grey T-shirt and black jogging bottoms, carrying a paper bag from a health food shop a couple of streets over, and has what looks like a sleeping bag rolled up and held by a strap over his shoulder.

'How long have you been planning this?' I say, at a loss for anything else to say as I lock the door behind him.

'Only since yesterday. It's long past time we got to the bottom of this.'

I go to ask him if anyone saw him coming back, but realise how ridiculous it is before the words come out, so I change the question. 'You do wear something other than suits sometimes then?'

'Of course. For sleeping or lying around the house. I'm intending to spend tonight on the landing with only dustsheets for padding. A suit wouldn't cut it in this situation.' He fiddles with the drawstring of his jogging bottoms. 'Although you do have a *lot* of views on my wardrobe choices.'

'Well, you dropped the mermaid in a tank idea, so you've left me with nothing else to complain about.'

He's laughing as he dumps the bags he's carrying at the bottom of the stairs and pulls the Tablet of Gloom out. 'Just going to do a walkaround and make sure nothing's missing at this point, and hope it stays that way.'

I debate following him, but I decide I've already aroused enough suspicion tonight with my overzealous protest about his stakeout idea, so I go back to the till and finish cashing up for the night, pleased to see the marked increase in takings since the social media posts went live, and that distracts me from thinking about how the ever-loving heck I'm going to manage to smuggle something out without him catching me.

It's definitely going to be a long night.

* * *

'Today's Lumière post has got a fantastic response.' Warren's sitting cross-legged on the spread-out dustsheets when I get to the upstairs landing, his water bottle in front of him, and his fingers are flying across the Tablet of Gloom's screen while the other hand holds a sandwich he's munching on. 'There are 233 comments and they're almost all positive. People saying they've forgotten about this place and want to come here again. People saying they loved their visit here and this is great fun. People saying they're long overdue a visit to Ever After Street or that they wish they lived close enough to visit. Someone's started a "fairytales in the wild" hashtag. This is really capturing imaginations. There's so much marketing potential in this, I hadn't realised how big it could get.'

'Big?'

'The fairytale museum with exhibits that come to life at night. The secret lives of the museum exhibits. *Night at the Museum* in real life. This has turned itself into a huge selling point.'

'The others have turned it into a huge selling point. They saw the social media potential and acted on it, even though they had nothing to do with the rearranging of the exhibits themselves.'

He raises an eyebrow without looking up from his tablet. 'We have to tap into this while we can. Tomorrow, we'll film a little promo video, I'll record and you can move things offscreen so it'll look like they're moving on their own. We'll overlay it with some music and post it online, and on your website, which I've got a designer working on as we speak, and—'

'Have you?'

'Yeah. I told you I've got a small budget and that website needed some serious investment. I've seen some early preview pages and it's great. He's got a little animated wishing well in one corner with butterflies fluttering around it, and he's going to do seasonal themes that can be changed easily. It'll really help with your presence online.' His voice speeds up when he's excited about something, and it's easy to see he's wholly invested in this.

'Thank you. That's really nice of you. Surprisingly nice.'

He looks up and the smile he gives me is nothing but sad, and I wish I hadn't added the bit about it being surprising, because it feels like I've just kicked a puppy for no reason. I immediately want to apologise but I'll only end up digging myself in deeper, so I pretend I haven't said anything while feeling silently guilty for being so cynical. His first impression all those weeks ago might not have been great, but there's nothing surprising about him being nice now I've got to know him a bit.

I've turned all the lights off downstairs so it looks like the museum is closed for the night, but up here, Warren's put a super-beam torch on a stand, ready to turn on when darkness falls later.

'Come. Sit.' He pats the space opposite him and when I take my boots off and sit down, he pushes the health food shop bag towards me. 'Help yourself to anything. There's sandwiches, crisps, chocolate, I didn't know what you'd like.'

I have a better idea and go to make us a cup of tea each, and he looks surprised when I come back a few minutes later and put a mug down on the floor in front of him.

'Thanks,' he murmurs, sounding perplexed by such a small gesture, but I haven't exactly been the most welcoming host, and nattering over cups of tea isn't something we've done before, and maybe it should have been. There's a twinge of guilt inside me that I've held back so much and given him a hard time rather than being open to his suggestions. I'm starting to feel like his presence here is exactly the push I needed, but I haven't been able to admit that to him yet.

I sit down again on the side of the landing nearest the stairs and he immediately shifts around so he's facing me, but doesn't put the Tablet of Gloom down, so I pull the shop bag over and rummage through it. 'You brought *crisps* to a stakeout? They're, like, the noisiest food ever!'

'They're not crisps, they're unsalted baked lentil curls. And I'm sorry, but I'm not an experienced stakeouter. I've never had to base my snack choices on their perceived noise levels before.'

'What do you normally base them on – nutritional content and value for money?'

'Doesn't everyone?'

'No! Most people choose snacks based on how good they taste and how much they enjoy them.'

He makes a noise of indifference. 'Enjoyment is overrated.'

'I'm trying to remember if I've ever heard a sadder sentence spoken that that. Don't you enjoy anything?'

'I might enjoy those. Open them and we'll find out.'

I do and hold the bag out to him, and he takes one and pops it in his mouth and makes a face. 'If I enjoyed eating concrete.'

I take one too, hoping it won't be as bad as it looks, but if anything, it's *worse*. 'Concrete might be more appealing. Why on earth would you choose these?'

He laughs. 'I apologise. I'll know for next time I'm on a stakeout.'

It makes me laugh too. 'Do you expect to spend a lot of your career from now on staking out non-sentient objects that start coming to life?'

He's still laughing as he takes another crisp, holds it between his teeth and speaks around it. 'You never know.'

I can't help smiling at his cheeky grin. 'I've spent many hours in this place after closing time, and I can honestly say I've never done anything quite as strange as this.'

'That's been a regular occurrence since I got here. Every day brings another iteration of "I've never done anything as strange as this before".'

'Well, this *is* a museum of "things that go bump in the night".'

'Oh, if going bump was the only thing they did, I'd have no problem with it. Unfortunately what your lot do is a lot more complicated than "bumping" and makes them a lot harder to track down afterwards.'

The sheer surrealness of this conversation washes over me again, and I'm unsure if he's pulling my leg or if he's serious, and I get the sense that *he* isn't sure if it's *me* who's pulling *his* leg either, and how bizarre this is makes me chuckle nervously. I want to confess that I know exactly who's doing the bumping in the night and it's not the exhibits themselves.

He's looking at me with one side of his lips tilted into a smile. I meet his eyes and the urge to tell him the truth clamours at my throat, so I look away and shift around, moving so I'm lying down on my front and looking out through the baluster posts.

He lets out the most minute of sighs, but it feels like it's aimed more at himself than at me, and I furtively glance over my shoulder and watch as he looks upwards at the ceiling like he's silently trying to vent frustration, and then reluctantly gets to his feet, stalks across the landing to pick up the sleeping bag, and unrolls it as he pads back, wearing only white socks under his black jogging bottoms, and stops on my other side.

'It's cold tonight.' His words are interspersed by the snick of the zipper opening, but instead of getting into the sleeping bag himself, he opens it fully, so it becomes a big puffy sheet, like a duvet, and then he holds it out to me, offering to share some of its warmth.

I'm again touched by his thoughtfulness, and I reach up for it, but he stops me. 'Budge up, I prefer this side.'

This time he motions for me to shift across the landing to the space he was just occupying because he clearly wants my spot, and it's such a strange, random thing that it catches me off-guard and I edge across the landing, and only afterwards do I stop to think how odd a request it is.

He joins me in lying down on his front next to me, seemingly satisfied that he's on my left side now, and then he spreads the sleeping bag out and lets me pull half of it across myself, which I do on autopilot because my mind is stuck on how strange that was. Why could it possibly matter which one of us takes which side of the landing?

'What was all that about?' I ask when he's finished wriggling around to get comfortable.

The bag of lentil curls is open between us, and instead of answering, he stuffs two of them into his mouth and then mutters something entirely unintelligible around them.

I'm not sure what's more bizarre – the inexplicable swapping of sides or the deliberate action to avoid giving me an answer, but I decide not to push it. Anyone willing to eat two of those dreadful crisps in one go has suffered enough. 'Ah, well, at least if the museum ghost comes up the stairs, it'll get you first and give me time to get away.'

The unexpected laugh makes him choke on his crisps, and I reach across to his original spot and pass over the mug of tea he left behind in his eagerness to swap places, and he gulps it gratefully.

'You're very weird,' I say when he's got his breath back. 'Has anyone ever told you that?'

'Nope.' He looks over at me. 'I've never let anyone get close enough to find out.'

It's another sentence that sounds unbearably sad and I nudge his arm with mine. 'I didn't say it was a bad thing.'

I *see* the blush sweep up his body from the uncomfortable shiver to the red blotches that colour his neck. His cheeks go crimson, even the tips of his ears turn pink, and I'm unable to take my eyes off him. The bashful look on his face is more endearing than it has any right to be, and he doesn't seem to know what to say, so I force myself to look away and take another *dreadful* crisp.

'You've criticised my museum a lot, but you've never told me what *your* favourite childhood story was... Maybe we could create an exhibit from it.'

He looks over at me again and closes his eyes, thinking about it for an abnormally long time. 'I don't think I had one. My mother never read me fairytales, she read me newspapers. She wanted me to grow up knowing what the real world was like, not with my head in the clouds of make-believe stories.'

'That's terrible! It's unthinkable for a child not to have a favourite story. You must have been young once.'

'No, I don't think so. I think I attended nursery school in a suit and tie. My dad was always at work and my mum didn't have time for childish frivolities.'

'There is no such thing as childish frivolities *to a child*.' I look over at him again, and then poke his leg with my toe. 'Don't worry, it's not too late to rediscover your lost childhood. Maybe you came to the right place after all.'

'I'm a little old for children's stories.' He looks at me again and seems to be carefully considering his next words. 'I did buy a subscription to the Disney online thing though so I can watch the movies. I thought it might help me to understand you... this *place* better.'

'I'm surprised you want to. Me *or* this place.' I deliberately draw attention to his quickly amended choice of words, enjoying the way it makes him blush again.

He seems quiet tonight, like the unexplained swapping of sides has exposed something I don't understand, and I feel that familiar sense that I'm missing something.

'So you're just going to lie here all night and hope you see something?'

'I'll probably get uncomfortable in a while and sit up, but that is the general point of a stakeout, yes.'

'And you're not going to get tired or fall asleep?'

'I'm on the clock. Getting to the bottom of the mysterious exhibits is literally my job. Trust me, I'm not going to fall asleep.'

He thinks I'm asking to make conversation, but really I'm trying to gauge how much chance I'll have of smuggling something outside, and we lie in silence for a while, the quietness only interspersed by the occasional crunch of an unsalted baked lentil curl, and the buzzes of my phone with notifications from the shopkeepers' WhatsApp group.

At first, I check the messages covertly, but I realise that trying to hide it will do nothing but tip him off, so I answer them as I would any other messages, like I've got nothing to hide. He's got his Tablet of Gloom in his hand, but when I catch a glimpse of the screen over his shoulder, it looks like something spreadsheety, so I assume he's trying to get some work done, and I continue sharing updates from the stakeout with the others.

They're trying to come up with excuses I could use to go

outside for a minute and take something with me, although it would have to be something pocket-sized because he's watching the main door, and *nothing* is going to get out unseen.

Mickey texts.

> I could create a distraction? Make a clatter outside and then you could rush out to investigate it? Or while he goes out to investigate it, you shove something out the back door?

I glance at him and catch him watching me and he quickly averts his eyes.

> Too suspicious. He is literally waiting for exactly that to happen.

'You don't have to stay if there's somewhere else you need to be,' Warren says after I send off another text and put my phone down, racking my brain for a non-suspicious way to sneak an exhibit outside.

'Nowhere else I'd rather be.'

He looks over at me solely so he can raise a disbelieving eyebrow. 'On a freezing cold, probably haunted landing, eating the most dire crisps in the history of the world, in the company of a demonic gerbil with no soul?'

I laugh out loud, mainly to cover the awkwardness at the reminder of my initial judgement of him.

'Who are you texting then? The others to warn them I'm still here?'

'No. My little sister. Boyfriend trouble. Do you want to see?' The lie rolls off my tongue because, more often than not, whenever I get a slew of text messages, it will be one of my younger sisters asking for love-related advice. I hold my phone out towards him, hoping against hope that he'll refuse, because if he really did take my phone, he certainly wouldn't see anything about boyfriend trouble on there, and I feel that frisson of guilt again. He hasn't done anything to deserve being lied to. What difference would it make if he knew who was responsible for the escaped exhibits?

'No, of course not. That would be an unthinkable invasion of privacy.' He sighs and shakes his head at himself. 'I didn't mean for that to come across as entitled and control-freak-ish as it did. Obviously you can text anyone you want and it has nothing to do with me. I shouldn't have asked in the first place. Sorry, this is messing with my head.'

The Tablet of Gloom drops out of his hand and onto the padding of the dustsheets as he clonks his head down onto his arms and lets out another long sigh. 'I know you know something.' He doesn't lift his head and his voice is muffled behind his arms. 'I know it's your friend doing all this, and obviously you're going to be on her side and keep her secret, which is fine, of course you are, but I thought...' He shakes his head again, like he's trying to shake loose the right words. 'I don't know what I thought. But I'm not your enemy and I've been enjoying my time here, getting into the swing of things, and I... I thought you knew that.'

'I do,' I say quietly. When it seems like he hasn't heard me, I reach over and press the backs of my fingers against his forearm to give him a nudge and then repeat it, and it's enough to get a smile out of him.

'I know my job has a bad reputation, I know property developers are seen as unscrupulous and untrustworthy, but we're not all like that. Some of us are trying to make the world better, one place at a time, and are just trying to please everyone and keep all the plates spinning at once.'

His voice is quiet and he looks away as he says it, and it feels like another big chip in his professional armour. And it leaves me with a decision to make – share the secret with him, or stick by my friends who I've worked with for years, who have always bent over backwards to help me in every conceivable way, and tell him another outright lie, when he sounds vulnerable enough to really *need* a bit of honesty.

'It's not Mickey.' I swallow hard. I *have* to choose my friends. I have to stick by the people who have always stuck by me. 'It's not anyone here. They don't know what's going on either, they just saw the exhibits outside and thought it would give people a laugh on social media. That's it, that's all I found out.'

'Okay.' He looks over at me. 'Okay. If that's what you're sticking with, then that's that. We aren't going to get anywhere if we don't have any trust between us, so I'm going to choose to believe you. I do understand loyalty, and distrust of strangers, and I understand Ever After Street coming together against me, but I don't want to see this place closed down any more than you do. You can choose to believe that or not, it's up to you.'

I don't intend to let out a scoff, but one escapes anyway because no one could possibly be as invested in this place as I am. 'Maybe it would be easier to trust you if you were honest about what you're doing here. How does helping my museum benefit you? What do you *really* get out of this? You're trying to prove a point to your mother?'

He looks at me for a long time, so long that I can almost see the war playing out behind his eyes and I hold his gaze, because I can't tear myself away from the depths I can see hidden behind his sarcastic quips and uptight seriousness.

'Yeah, in a way,' he says eventually, sounding exhausted from thinking about how to word it. 'No matter what I do, no matter how much I achieve, she always knows better. That parent-child dynamic never goes away. She never says "well done", but only ever points out what I could have done better or handled differently, and I always feel inferior and like a child still finding my feet, even though I've been in this industry since I left university. She dismisses every suggestion I make without giving it consideration, and I spend every moment of my working life desperately wanting her approval, and never getting it, and being stuck in an endless cycle of trying to prove myself only for it to never be *enough* because I have this thing that makes *me* not good enough, and—'

'What thing?' I didn't mean to interrupt him, but that's piqued my curiosity in a way that can't be ignored.

I see the moment he realises what he's just said and sheer horror crosses his face and he gets a rabbit-in-headlights look, like he doesn't know which way to run. His whole body has stiffened, like he's about to leap up and bolt at any second.

'It's okay, I get it,' I say quickly, because I don't know what he's talking about, but I *do* know that he isn't ready to explain it right now either, and I'm enjoying getting to know more about him. The last thing I want him to do is scarper. 'It can't be easy working with a parent.' I try to smooth things over and let him breathe, because it looks like he's breathless from spilling all that out. 'Every child will *always* be their parents' child, no matter how old they are. I can see that making for an interesting working dynamic...'

I leave the sentence deliberately open-ended, hoping he'll fill in more if I give him time.

'The museum is not so much about proving a point but proving that I can do something right,' he says after an abnormally long pause. 'I was fascinated when I heard about it and I know other people will be too. It's important to the community and has local support. I thought if I could take this concept and turn it around, make it bigger and find investors, show that we can take what's already here and improve it... but I never realised how personal it is, and how much *you* are a force to be reckoned with. I didn't expect to come up against someone like you.'

It's my turn to blush. Generally I feel ineffectual and invisible, and the last thing I am is a force to be reckoned with, but he makes it sound like a good thing, and I like how I feel in knowing he sees me that way.

'I admit that I didn't factor escaping exhibits into my original plan, but the attention they're bringing will help. If we can prove this place is worth saving – that it can do just as much for the area and for the company profits as another cinema complex could – then my mother will be forced to approve of something I believe in, and realise the company can move forward in a different way.'

I feel like he's both said more than he intended to and still not really answered what I was asking him, because there still aren't any set goals, any parameters, and maybe that uncertainty is something I have to accept.

'I should be taking over the company. My mother is seventy-two, she should be thinking about retirement, slowing down, taking time to enjoy her life, but she won't because she doesn't think I know what I'm doing.'

'I doubt it's just that,' I say carefully.

'No, of course not. Berrington Developments was my dad's thing – his life's dream. He worked for so many years to be in a position where he could start his own company, and he did, and later that same year, he died. I was only fourteen so I was too young, and it wasn't what Mum wanted to do, but she knew how hard my dad had worked and how badly he'd wanted it, and she couldn't stand by and let his new company fail, so she took over it. She grieved *through* it. She poured every ounce of grief and heartache into his company, she worked every hour imaginable, and she did it. She made Berrington Developments into a huge success. She made it into exactly what he dreamed of it being. No one could fault her for that, but...' He trails off with a shake of his head, another sentence he doesn't know how to finish.

'What about what *you* dream of it being?'

He fiddles with his water bottle for a long time before he answers. 'I don't know, but different to what it is now. I'd like to save buildings, invest with a purpose of preservation rather than just... destruction.'

I can't help thinking about his wish. If he's unfulfilled at work, is that why he feels that life is meaningless? I can't shake the need to prod further. 'And your mum doesn't agree with that line of thinking?'

He shakes his head.

'Maybe it's not you at all.'

'No, it's me, trust me.'

'But if the company was tied up in your mum's grief then maybe it's more connected to that. Maybe she feels like she keeps your father alive by working. For as long as she does the job he should have been doing, in a way, he's still there. That's a long time to work so hard, and if she stops, does she have to finally face the fact that your dad is gone?'

'He's been gone for twenty-seven years. I think she's noticed by now.'

'I meant metaphorically, obviously. She sounds like someone who worked rather than grieved.'

'And you sound like a psychologist, not a museum curator,' he snaps.

'You already know my mum died when I was twelve and my dad didn't cope. It's not the same, but I understand all too well what it's like to lose a parent at a young age, and how unbearable it can be on the parent left behind.'

His neck is twisted around so he can watch me as I speak, and it looks like the most uncomfortable position, but he makes no attempt to move. 'I know you mentioned it the other day, but I never expect to meet people and have that sort of thing in common. I'm sorry.'

'So am I – for you. I didn't know your company had a story like that behind it. I thought you were...' I trail off because it's not the right moment to add 'heartless, money-grabbing, evil gerbils', and instead I shuffle forwards on my elbows so he can untwist his neck because he's intent on watching my face every time I speak.

'Oh, I know exactly how that sentence ends and I appreciate you not finishing it.' He lets out a self-deprecating laugh that turns into a drawn-out groan, and he moves his head around, one hand going to the back of his neck, trying to unkink it.

His brown hair falls forward as he makes a physical effort to relax his tense shoulders, and I have to fight the urge to touch my fingers against his arm again, because it's such a surprising insight and I didn't expect him to be that open.

'I don't know where that came from,' he says after a while and moves to sit upright. 'I should, er, stretch my legs. Bathroom break. Want another cuppa?'

Bathroom! The inspiration comes in a flash. The customer bathroom downstairs has a window that opens to one side of the museum – the opposite side to where we are. It's perfect, and another cup of tea is the perfect excuse to use it.

'That'd be great, thank you.' I give him a genuine smile because it *is* nice of him to offer, but the second he's gone up the stairs, I grab my phone and text the shopkeepers' group to tell them my plan and ask someone to be ready under the window.

When Warren comes back with two mugs, I down mine as quickly as the temperature will allow, and then tell him I need the bathroom and rather than using the staff bathroom upstairs, I make an excuse about double-checking the exhibits while using the customer toilets downstairs, and I run away before waiting to see if he believes me or not.

I've spent the past few minutes trying to think of something small enough to fit through a narrow-opening top window, and I've come up with Aladdin's Magic Carpet, which can be rolled up and pushed through, and on my way to extract it from its usual display, I spot Pascal sitting on Rapunzel's shoulder and shove him in my pocket.

By going through the supply closet door into the Fairytale Homes hall, I can avoid the front half of the lobby altogether and remain out of sight, and I'm holding my breath so hard that I'm panting by the time I make it to the bathroom.

I clamber onto the toilet seat and put one leg up on the cistern behind it, and push the window open. Sure enough, Mickey and Cleo are standing below and I shove a hand through to wave to them silently, and then push the Magic Carpet through a centimetre at a time, being careful that it doesn't snag on anything, but also that I don't make a sound.

There's a whoosh as it finally falls from the window and drops into Mickey's waiting arms, and we all freeze for a moment to make sure Warren hasn't overheard and doesn't come to investigate, and after a few seconds have passed with no movement from upstairs, I hold Pascal out and drop him down to Cleo.

I do a silent thumbs up and give them a grateful smile that's obscured by the window before I close it, clamber back down, and flush the chain so Warren doesn't get suspicious.

Who knew that bringing exhibits to life could be so stressful?

13

When I get back upstairs, Warren's lying down, leaning on his elbows and using the Tablet of Gloom, but he puts it down when I settle beside him.

'Anything unusual going on down there?'

'Not a thing. All present and correct,' I trill so chirpily that he's bound to know I've been up to something, if the overly long bathroom visit didn't clue him in, or my heart pounding so hard that he can surely see it hammering in and out of my chest.

He's got the sleeping bag over him and has left one half free for me, so I step across him and lie down on my front again, sticking on his right side where he clearly wanted me to stay, and wriggle around to get comfortable, glad of his thinking to pad the hard floor with dustsheets.

'So...' He stretches both arms out in front of him, lays his head down on them and turns towards me.

'So...' I furtively pat my forehead in case he can see the nervous sweat beading there. I have no idea what the girls are going to do with the Magic Carpet and Pascal, but I'm looking forward to finding out while also dreading how I'm going to fake it when *he* finds out.

He makes no move to pick up his tablet again, and I get a little thrill that he wants to talk and maybe he enjoyed the little connection we shared just now.

'So you're in the "lost a parent at an early age" club too?'

I don't mean to laugh, but his way of phrasing it makes a snort escape. 'The one club that no child should ever have to join.'

'Exactly. The club membership that separates you from your peers and makes you stand out in all the wrong ways.' He looks away and casts his eyes over the lobby below before looking back at me. 'Go on, I've told you my tale of woe, it's only right that I get to hear yours…'

I don't talk about it very often because it was so long ago, and with Dad gone now too, it's not easy to re-open old wounds and dwell on the past, but there's something about knowing Warren will understand – really, truly understand in a way that no one possibly can unless they've been through something similar – that makes me *want* to talk about it. 'I was twelve when Mum died. It was sudden, unexpected, and for us, it was like the ground fell out of the world and we were all falling down a long, black hole of loss. Dad didn't cope with his own grief, never mind with helping me and my sisters navigate ours. Childhood ended in an instant. I became the one trying to look after my sisters *and* my dad. I had no one to turn to because the others all turned to me and Dad relied on me. Life was difficult, and these days, it's easier to block that out and not think about it because of *how* tough it was, but somehow all five of us made it to adulthood almost unscathed.'

'Apart from a bit of boyfriend trouble.' He nods towards my

phone, which has suspiciously stopped buzzing now the exhibits have been smuggled out.

'Ah, ha ha, yes, right.' My unhinged laugh is back. There is *no* way he hasn't worked this out by now. I knew I was the world's worst liar, but I hadn't realised I was quite *this* bad at it.

'You have four younger sisters?' he asks, but before I can answer, he adds, 'I'm sorry I haven't asked about this before, but I try not to get personal when it comes to work.'

I tilt my head to the side, unintentionally mirroring the way he does because he's impossible to work out sometimes, and I feel like I'm constantly one step behind when it comes to getting a handle on who he *is* as a person. This seems like yet another chink out of his professional front, a crevice showing a glimpse of the man underneath. 'What's different tonight?'

'We're sharing a sleeping bag, eating the worst crisps in existence, and hoping to catch either a ghost or anthropomorphic museum exhibits in the act of leaving under their own power. We passed getting personal long ago.'

It makes me laugh and I take another vile crisp to disguise how much I appreciate his directness.

'I'm the oldest of five girls,' I say eventually. 'So when I accidentally stepped into the role our mum left behind... no one noticed. I was old enough to cook and feed myself and the others. I was old enough to go to the shops and buy food when Dad couldn't get out of bed. I didn't need help getting dressed and tying shoelaces, I didn't need to be herded into the car for school runs, and I ended up being... overlooked. No one ever realised that I had taken on the role of parent. My youngest sister doesn't remember Mum at all, she just remembers me doing all the parental things that Dad struggled to do. Everyone worried for the younger ones, but I was old enough to cope, and no one ever seemed to worry about whether I *was* coping or not. No one ever saw how much I was doing.' I stop myself abruptly when I realise how much has just spilled out. All of us Carisbrooke girls tend to brush our younger years under the carpet and only reminisce when we all get together and have too much wine at Christmas, and I had no intention of sharing something so personal with Warren, but there *is* something about talking to someone else who's a member of the club that no one wants to be part of, a feeling that he'd understand even though he doesn't have siblings himself.

He sucks in a breath and nods slowly, understanding written on his face. 'So you grew up feeling invisible and you still do?'

I intend to snap something at him for calling me a psychologist earlier, but it cuts right through my bristling and leaves me speechless for a moment. No one has *ever* put it into such simple terms before, and yet I feel those words inside my heart. I *did* grow up feeling like I was working hard in the background, and no one ever acknowledged that, and that's followed me into adult life. I stay in the background, making sure I don't tread on anyone's toes, because I'm so used to feeling invisible that now I don't know what I'd do if anyone *did* notice me.

'I get it.' He's turned onto his side and is propped up on one elbow facing me, leaning his head in his hand. 'I really related when you said that. Sometimes, I feel like I'm invisible too. I think most people have that existential crisis at some point. Why do we keep going, keep trying so hard, working so hard, if it never makes any impression on anyone else's life? Sometimes I feel like no one would notice if I didn't show up for work tomorrow.'

I blink in surprise. It feels like not just a chink in his professional armour, but like a huge chunk has just fallen out of it.

'How could you ever be invisible?' I'm shaking my head in disbelief and not concentrating on what I'm saying. 'You're tall, gorgeous, well-dressed, funny, clever, obviously good at your job...'

'Gorgeous?' Both of his eyebrows shoot up so fast that they almost merge with his hairline.

Oh, heck, did I say that out loud? I cringe at myself. 'I didn't mean gorgeous. I meant... um... I must've got my G words muddled up. I meant gruesome, that's it!'

He laughs so hard that the elbow he's leaning on gives way and he rolls over onto his back and meets my eyes upside down. 'None of that's me. Well, the height, I guess, I can't do much to change that, but I'm just...' He looks away, his eyes swivelling towards the ceiling as he rolls his head back and forth, like he doesn't know what to say. 'Half the time, I feel like I'm still just a kid who made a promise to his dying father to be strong and look after his mum, and I spend my life living in fear that someone will realise I'm not a forty-one-year-old businessman at all, but still a child trying to find his way in the world and keep everyone happy.'

Now, *that* I understand. 'When you lose a part of your childhood, there's a part of you that's always searching for a way to get it back.'

'What do you do if you reach forty-one and you still haven't found it?'

'It's never too late.' I chew on my lip as I say it because I'm still expecting him to ridicule me or make fun in some way.

'Is that *why* you're so dedicated to childhood magic?'

'I guess so. I think every child deserves to feel wonder and to believe in magic. I was lucky because I was old enough to spend my younger years with my mum. I have those memories that my sisters missed out on. I remember the fairytales she read to me, the dandelion clocks she made wishes on, the toadstools she claimed were fairies' houses, the way she dragged me outside to look for Santa's sleigh *every* Christmas Eve, even when I was far, far past the age of believing in Santa. I didn't realise how special those moments were at the time. And if I can do something that helps adults feel like that again too, then that's my goal. I wanted this place to be great for kids, yes, but I also wanted adults to come in and be able to momentarily forget that they *are* adults. I lost that, and I've been trying to find it again, and granting wishes, trying to make children's lives better than mine was, is as close as I've come so far.'

'That is...' He pushes himself back up onto his elbow so he's facing me. '...probably the nicest concept I've ever heard. You have no idea how many times in my adult life that I've wished I wasn't an adult and wanted a better adult to come along and tell me what to do.'

'Same.' I smile at him and the grin he gives me in return causes lines to crinkle around his eyes and makes him look completely unguarded for once.

After a moment, he schools his smile and looks me in the eyes again. 'And you're the brightest person I've ever met. No one could ever *not* see you.'

'That's just—'

'And I don't mean the hair.' He somehow knew exactly what I was going to say, and he picks up his stylus pen and uses it to reach over and lift a half-pink and half-purple curly lock of my hair and hold it up, and I appreciate him understanding that too. Colourful hair gives an impression of confidence, but sometimes it's masking the exact opposite.

'Everything about you makes you the most memorable person I've ever met. A real force of nature, and I wish I had something I cared about as much as you care about this place. It's inspiring.'

Something in my chest catches and I push out a stuttery

breath because it sounds like one of the most unfiltered things he's ever said.

His eyes are locked on mine, and I forget where we are, I forget *who* we are, and everything around us evaporates apart from the desire to get closer to him, and in my head, I can *see* how easy it would be to lean forwards, inhale the subtle leather scent of his aftershave that I keep getting hints of, to hold his face in my hand, run my fingers over his dark stubble, and…

He clears his throat and drops the curl of my hair with a shaky huff of breath, and then flops down onto his back again, almost throwing the stylus pen back towards the Tablet of Gloom like *it* was solely responsible for whatever just happened, and I feel like someone's yanked the dustsheet out from under me and left me sitting here wondering what *did* happen.

Unexplained creaks of the museum's quirky floorboards fill the awkward silence, and eventually I swallow hard. 'I'd notice. If you didn't show up for work, I would notice.'

'Yeah, *now*, because I'm here every day and I've taken over your office space, and if I didn't show up, you'd probably do a dance of joy and be like, "Oh, thank God he's not here today!" but before?'

'We'd never met before. You can't notice someone you don't know.'

'Yeah, I know, I just meant…' He meets my eyes again and he looks deeply tired in a way that has nothing to do with the time of night. 'I don't know what I meant. The late night is making me punch-drunk. Just ignore me.'

'You meant that you want to be important to someone. You want your life to matter.'

'Yeah, but in a good way. The impact I have on the world now is…' His eyes look up at the ceiling as he struggles to find the right words. 'You bring magic to life. You make children believe in something. This museum is something they'll remember for the rest of their lives, whereas I... I don't think I've ever left anything better than I found it. Nothing has *ever* been improved by my input. That's something I keep thinking about lately. That's why I'm really here. This seems like a place to discover what life *should* be like rather than what it *is* like, and I saw a chance to help it rather than destroy it.'

For once, I believe him. He's so laid bare and open that it's impossible not to. 'We can implement the gift shop. Not *all* your suggestions are bad ones.'

He laughs so hard that he curls in on himself and it's the first time I've seen him laugh so unreservedly. It eases the tension and I flop down beside him and realise I've forgotten that we're anything other than two friends having a very strange sleepover.

Darkness has long since fallen, and somehow it's nearly midnight, the hours have passed in a flash, and the room is only lit by the otherworldly glow of the streetlamps outside coming in the window behind us. I get up to turn the torch on when I realise he's struggling to see my face in the dark. He's shifted closer and he's squinting every time he looks at me, looking like he's struggling to make out what I'm saying.

'Has your Tablet of Gloom got enough battery to make use of your Disney movie subscription?'

He laughs. 'I knew I was going to regret telling you that.'

'Oh, come on, what better way to stay awake than by watching a Disney movie? Call it doing important research for the gift shop you're going to implement,' I suggest, knowing that a 'sensible use of working time' is something he can't deny the appeal of. 'You choose it while I go and make another cup of tea.'

He pushes himself up with a groan. 'I think this is only going to work if *you* choose it. Whatever you think is most important for me to see. *I'll* go and make the tea.'

Once he's standing upright, he stretches and it shouldn't be as sexy as it is, but my eyes are glued to the sliver of stomach that appears as his grey top lifts, and the flex of a forearm as his sleeve catches and rises up.

'And Liss?' He's looking at me like he knows exactly where my focus was, and I try not to think about how much I like him shortening my name. It feels friendly and easy-going, something we've struggled with until now. 'Thank you.'

'For what?'

'I'm not sure.' His head tilts as he thinks about it, making his dark hair flop to the side. 'Watching my professional front splinter and helping me hold it together?'

He disappears up the stairs to the kitchen before I can formulate a response. Even though I'm not much of a 'professional front' kind of person, I think he's done exactly the same for me too, and I force myself to stop pondering it, otherwise I'll still be staring at the blank tablet screen when he comes back.

I straighten out the dustsheets and plump up the sleeping bag, and then prop the Tablet of Gloom against the baluster posts in front of us, open his browser and find *Beauty and the Beast*, and it's almost as difficult to get his words out of my head as it is to stop thinking about the colour of his eyes, the fall of his hair, and the scent of his aftershave, and how I expected this to be the longest night of my life, and now I'm wishing morning would never come.

14

I wake up in the most uncomfortable position known to mankind. My head is pillowed on a pile of dustsheets and I'm still covered by Warren's sleeping bag, and there's an ache in my hip that suggests I'm too old to be spending nights on the floor. And yet, as I turn onto my back and stretch luxuriously in the daylight streaming in from the windows above, it doesn't feel like a bad thing.

I don't know how long I stayed awake last night, but it wasn't long enough to see the end of *Beauty and the Beast*, but talking to Warren, getting to know a *real* part of him was worth any stiffness and aches this morning. I might have failed on the stakeout part, but it feels like a win on some level.

The smell of coffee is wafting down from the kitchen upstairs, and I haul myself to my feet and run to the bathroom to clean my teeth and try to make my hair stop resembling the nest of a not-very-houseproud bird, and I groan as I drag myself up every step towards the kitchen on the third floor.

'You sound like you slept on the floor last night.' Warren's sitting at the kitchen table with his water bottle, a mug, and the

Tablet of Gloom in front of him, and he looks up when I arrive in the doorway, sounding like I've just run a marathon, not climbed a couple of flights of stairs.

'I think I did, for a bit. You didn't really stay awake all night, did you?'

'Sleepless nights are a regular thing in my job. It makes no difference whether I'm having them here or at home.' He lifts the mug like he's making a toast and takes a sip of his coffee. 'And no, I gave up too. Put my head down for a few minutes at 5 a.m., woke up two hours later. I'm clearly too old for stakeouts.'

'Aren't we all?' I go over to the kitchen unit to re-boil the kettle and try not to be touched that he's put a mug and the jar of instant coffee ready for me.

'It was nice to talk to you last night,' he says as I busy myself with making the much-needed coffee. 'Something I don't do very often.'

'Lie on a hard, cold landing and eat dreadful crisp-type things?' I turn around to look at him while stirring my drink, even though I don't like instant coffee, there is nowhere near enough caffeine in tea for mornings like this.

'Talk.'

I'm surprised by his openness again and I meet his tired eyes across the kitchen. 'You should do it more often. *We* should do it more often.'

'I can't disagree with that.'

I splosh milk into my mug, give it a final stir, and take the seat opposite him at the kitchen table.

'At least you didn't see me cry at the end of *Beauty and the Beast*.'

I don't mean to snort, but I can't help it. 'You did not. If you did, you wouldn't openly admit it.'

'I've never been so captivated in my life. How had I not seen that before? When I next see my mother, I'm going to have a go at her for withholding Disney movies from my childhood.' He leans forward in his seat and whispers the next bit like he's worried someone might overhear. 'And when I'd recovered my manly dignity after that, I watched *Pocahontas* because I wanted to understand the connection to the museum. And now I want a racoon and a hummingbird as friends.'

It's a good job I hadn't just taken a sip of coffee because I would've spat it halfway across the kitchen with the unexpected laugh. 'You are normal after all then, because trust me, no one has *ever* watched *Pocahontas* and *not* wanted a greedy racoon friend and to go paddling in some nearby river and talk to a few trees afterwards.'

He laughs. 'I know there are cultural appropriation issues and historical inaccuracies with it, but I liked the message. Two people who are very different can learn to live alongside each other, learn something from aspects of each other's lives, and truly come to respect each other.'

It's a metaphor that I'm too tired to fully untangle, but I like what he's hinting at, and we sit opposite each other, smiling, until his phone buzzes and he gives it a cursory glance, and then looks between me and the Tablet of Gloom on the table in front of him.

'Okay, riddle me this.' He sits forward again, turns the tablet screen on, and spins it around to face me. 'How?'

On the screen is a post from Ever After Street's social media, showing a photo of the Magic Carpet dangling from a tree, and the caption reads, 'Crash landing!'

I laugh out loud. The girls are *brilliant* to think of that. I couldn't imagine what they were going to do with that rug when I posted it through the bathroom window last night, but this is hilariously ingenious.

'Oh, that is amaz—' I quickly swallow back my gleefulness when I glance up at his definitely-*not*-laughing face and force a frown to appear. 'Well, if it broke out by itself, it didn't get very far, that tree is only on the edge of woods, just beyond the carousel.'

He reaches over to tap the screen. 'That carpet was there last night, I remember seeing it when I checked. And I didn't spot anything. Not a movement. No one – and nothing – came or went last night, I'm sure of that. So... *how?*'

He sounds completely and utterly defeated, but rather than annoyed or curious, he sounds like he's just fed up now, and it makes that guilt race through my veins again. He *must* know, and he's *waiting* for me to be honest, and I want to, but the others are right. Without him and his company, there would be no need for moving exhibits and sneaky Magic Carpet jiggery-pokery in the first place, and I can't let him in on the one thing that's making a difference to my chances. Mickey and Cleo went hugely out of their way for me last night. I can't return the favour by betraying what they've asked me to do – *not* tell him.

'We were distracted for a while,' I stutter, trying to find the right words. 'Maybe it waited until we were both asleep and then snuck out.'

'Yeah, I think it's *really* likely that a Magic Carpet was waiting in the wings all night, floating around, watching us, eager for a chance to make its escape.'

'Thank you for making the Magic Carpet sound like something from a horror movie. That's a really disturbing thought.' I force out a laugh, going for redirection instead of anything close to the truth.

His eyes bore into me from across the table, and I *know* he knows, but I can't bring myself to spit it out. I might have enjoyed getting to know him better, but my museum is never going to bring in more revenue than a cinema complex, and I can't shake the feeling that, sooner or later, someone's going to pull the rug right out from under me and, somehow, *he's* going to be responsible. To even stand a chance, I have to come up with the rent that *he's* increased, and I can't let him in on something that might help me to raise it. I keep my lips sealed and force a nonchalant sip of coffee down under the scrutiny of those intense blue eyes.

'You know what, I give up.' Eventually he sits back and shoves a hand through his hair with a sigh. '*Whoever* is doing *whatever* they're doing, they're actually helping us. The comments on this are hysterical. People are really responding to the "escaped exhibits" angle, there are independent social media posts asking for theories about what's going on, and we've seen an increase in visitors. This is exactly what we need, and we can tap into this ourselves with that promo video I mentioned last night. So that's it. No more stakeouts, no more trying to catch someone out. No more questioning. Let them get on with it.' He meets my eyes again. 'If you could pass that message on to the "sentient exhibits" that would be great.'

He does the air quotes, leaving me in no doubt that he knows full well the Magic Carpet didn't escape by itself, and I must admit to feeling a sting of disappointment at the thought of no more stakeouts. I could do without the whole balancing one leg on the toilet cistern and poking valuable items through a very small window aspect, but everything else about last night was pretty good. I wouldn't be entirely opposed to doing it again, even with the offensive crisps, the bad night's sleep, and the aches this morning.

He sits back in the chair, rubbing his fingers over his dark, unkempt stubble thoughtfully, but whatever he's thinking about, he doesn't share it with me. Eventually he downs the last of his coffee, shudders because it was almost definitely cold by now, and stands up. 'I'm going back to the car to change so I look vaguely presentable for work today.'

'If you were up most of the night, don't you need to sleep?'

'Nah, I'll catch up tonight. However, coffee.'

I laugh at how he uses the word like it's the all-encompassing answer to every problem.

'I need something stronger than this instant stuff. I'll bring you one back too.'

'Thanks. Although after those crisps, I'm not sure I trust you to be sent out for supplies ever again.'

It looks like the laugh takes him by surprise and he hesitates for a moment, leaning one hand on the table, looking like he wants to say something, but again, he doesn't, and I can see him chewing the inside of his cheek as he looks at me.

The moment passes and he shakes his head and pushes himself off the table and picks up the Tablet of Gloom and his water bottle as he walks out. 'Luckily I'm much better at coffee than I am at snack choices.'

I get my phone out and open the Ever After Street social media account and scroll to the comments.

Don't drink and fly!

One-too-many Arabian Nights!

A whole new world… of pain!

Without even realising it, I've been chuckling at my phone for ten minutes, and new comments are being posted every few seconds. I see what Warren meant about the people responding to this idea, and I get the sense that our daily update was being waited for today. And visitor numbers *are* up, and so are mentions on social media and website hits. Could we really be onto something here? Something that could truly make a difference to not only my chances of keeping the museum, but to what I can do here? Even with the higher rent, with more visitors, I'd have more money to invest in the exhibits and we'd be able to grant more wishes... Especially if I stop resisting Warren's suggestions for small changes here and streamlining tweaks there. It was unfair of me to say that not all of his ideas are bad ones last night because, to be fair, apart from the whole mermaid tank debacle, most of them have been very, very good.

I refresh the page again and one of the girls has posted another update.

> Pascal's gone missing! If you can find Rapunzel's camou-flaged chameleon friend in his hiding place on Ever After Street, take a photo and tag us, and you'll be entered into a prize draw to win an 'Unbirthday party' at The Wonderland Teapot!

I'm so touched that I have to bite my lip to stop myself tearing up. I had no idea they were going to do something like that, or that Cleo was going to offer a prize at her Alice-themed tearoom, and I send a text to the shopkeepers' group saying that they didn't have to do that.

> Just seen HIM leave.

Mickey texts back immediately.

> He must be so annoyed that we outfoxed him on his stakeout idea. The tweets are getting so much attention on social media. This is brilliant!

I type an agreement, but it niggles at me and I don't end up pressing send. I sit back and look at my phone again instead. While the social media engagement is truly fantastic, and I'm having a 'pinch me' moment on that front, it's everything else that doesn't feel brilliant. It feels like Warren knows exactly what's going on. He knows I'm lying to him, and he's given up on caring. I can't help feeling that I've approached this all wrong. Fooling the public for a bit of social media fun is one thing, but trying to fool someone who *knows* I'm trying to fool him is quite another.

15

Far from sitting back and letting them get on with it, Warren has seen the potential in the living exhibits and is fully embracing whatever they get up to next. After he goes home at night, me and a couple of the other shopkeepers hang around until after dark, when Ever After Street is closed to the public, and then we do *something* with the exhibits. So far we've had Flynn Rider's wanted posters put up all over Ever After Street and a few *Tangled* lanterns that have broken free, the balloons from the *Up* house escaping from the chimney of the museum, and the Wicked Witch of the East's legs sticking out from underneath Marnie's bookshop walls. The statue of Prince Eric has been found peering into Mickey's shop window, and multiple orange feathers from Peter Pan's hat keep turning up, along with thimbles and acorns to represent Peter and Wendy's interpretation of a first kiss, and rather than pushing for an explanation, Warren has quietly worked in the background, figuring out the times when our audience are most active, keywords, hashtags, and something to do with algorithms that I would've needed a degree in rocket science to understand.

The new website has gone up, and between the two of us, we've filmed several short promotional videos to appeal to different explanations for the mysterious goings-on.

There was one where I filmed as Warren walked Lumière down the street and then used video editing software to edit his arm out, so it looks like the candelabra is walking down the street alone. Another one with a focus on a spooky haunting, where we turned the lights down and filmed at night, and tied fishing wire to some of the exhibits and I stood out of shot and used it to turn them around without being seen, and Warren overlaid it with creepy music, and then another one with a *Night at the Museum* focus, where we filmed a few of the Disney prince and princess mannequins in one position at night, and then moved them all around and filmed again in daylight, trying to make it seem like they'd moved of their own accord overnight. Each video is only thirty seconds long, but they were fun, and an aspect of marketing that I'd never thought of before, and there's been something really nice about experiencing Warren's creativity. It's not something he gets to showcase often and he's obviously been having a blast doing it, and I've been all too happy to stand back and let his imagination run wild. Marketing has never been my strong suit, but Warren instinctively knows what will get views and what will get people talking.

The video of Lumière walking down the street has got a couple of hundred *thousand* views now, with hundreds of comments guessing what he might be up to and where he's going, and the other videos aren't far behind it, with the haunted museum angle gaining traction as well, and so far we've had requests from two ghost hunters to film overnight and exorcise our museum ghosts, and visitor numbers are up, up, up.

Children come in and excitedly tell us that they've seen Cogsworth having tea in The Wonderland Teapot, or Genie's lamp getting up to mischief, and some of the other shopkeepers have offered prizes for more scavenger hunt-type quests now Pascal has been rescued from the flower bed, and we've had Mary Poppins's parrot umbrella on the roof of Mickey's shop, and Chip the teacup hiding away in Marnie's window.

The increase in visitors has been hard to stay on top of, so Warren's been spending more time at the front desk and I've cleared out the dressing-up room and he's arranged for shopfitters to come in this week to give it a makeover, fill it with shelves, and turn it into a gift shop.

I've found a site that sells wholesale Disney-inspired bits, and with the extra takings, I've been able to order a couple of hundred mugs that are identical to Chip from *Beauty and the Beast*, vases in the shape of the Wicked Witch's striped stockings and sparkly ruby slippers, and tiny little replicas of the Beast's enchanted rose.

For the first time in years, it feels like something is going right. I've been unmotivated when it comes to the museum, happy to sit back and take the visitors that come my way without putting enough effort into *getting* more, feeling like an outsider up on the hill, but having someone to bounce ideas off, someone who works in the business industry and whose expertise has proved nothing but helpful so far has been a revelation, and so have the lengths that my fellow shopkeepers will go to in order to help me.

It's made me feel valued and more important to the street than I thought I was. I've always wondered if anyone would miss me if I wasn't here, a feeling that has followed me through life since childhood, but everything the others are doing has made me feel loved, important, and like it would really *matter* to them if something was to happen to the museum. At the same time, it's starting to feel like the museum will be safe. I can easily afford the increased rent this month, and I try not to think about the likelihood of sustaining this level of interest in the escaped exhibit escapades, and what might happen after it fades.

It's a Thursday morning, the beginning of November, and the weeks are flying by. I've just finished tidying the Moana mannequin after having to replace the green heart of Te Fiti stone in her shell necklace after it's been stolen yet again, a fact that I don't intend to share with Warren because he's even more concerned that the increase in visitors means an increase in exhibits being potentially damaged. I would *hate* to make the necklace off-limits or make it unrealistic by gluing the stone inside it. I *have* put up signs asking people not to take anything from the exhibits, and I'm prepared to put up Warren's suggested 'Smile, you're on CCTV!' signs if the more moderate approach doesn't make a difference.

When I go back out into the lobby, he's sitting in an old computer chair that he's dragged out of a storage room, leaning backwards with his feet up on the wooden desk, and it's a good thing there aren't any customers at the moment, because he's loosened up lately, and I can't help smiling at the sight of him looking so comfortable. It's something I never thought I'd see last month.

He looks up and grins at me as I go and lean over the desk so I can get a look at what he's doing with the pencil in his hand and sketchbook on his lap. 'Are you using actual paper and a real pencil? Not the Tablet of Gloom?'

'Some problems call for non-technological solutions.'

'Which particular problem is this?' I reach over and rifle through some of the discarded pages scattered across the desk in front of him, spinning them towards me so I can see what they're meant to be.

'The problem is that we'll have a gift shop ready this week and you still don't have a logo.'

'Oh. Wow.' I grab a handful of the pages and spread them across the countertop in awe. 'These are amazing. Did you *draw* these?'

He makes a noise that sounds like an agreement, clearly embarrassed by the attention, but he deserves every compliment because these are incredible.

With coloured pencils, he's designed a circular logo with an outline of the museum building on it, almost crown-shaped with its three distinct sections, tiny door and windows, and it's coloured in shades of blue and green. He's even got the ivy climbing one side with tiny tendrils twirling outwards, and it sits inside the outline of a pumpkin with the words 'museum of fairytales' written in neat printing around the lower edge. With one glance, anyone would know exactly where it is. If someone had asked me to imagine an ideal logo for this place, something that captures it perfectly and condenses it into one instantly recognisable, memorable image, *this* is a million times better than anything I could have ever dreamt of.

'These are *so* good, Warren. *You* are so good at this.' I shake my head in surprise at this until-now hidden talent. 'I didn't know you could draw.'

The discarded pages are all different variations in some way, with one small thing or other changed. It's so much effort for one little thing, and yet he looks the most relaxed I've ever seen him, and I think he's completely unaware of the smile tipping up his lips as he adds something to the version he's still working on.

'It's kind of a relic to times gone by, back in the days when I thought I might do something creative with my life, rather than... destructive.'

I look across at him and his cheeks are flushing brighter by the second, but neither of us look away, and I want to press him on those words, to ask about what he thought he'd be doing with his life versus what he *is* doing with it, but it feels like the wrong moment, and the opportunity passes when he clears his throat and breaks eye contact to look back at the book on his lap, and then he leans over and holds it out to me.

On the page is the most recent version of his logo vision. He's added sparkles and tiny stars around the top part and it's such a perfect, beautiful addition that I have to bite my lip to stop myself welling up. I wasn't sure he'd ever really understand this place, but this is absolute proof that he *gets* it, and I'm surprised by the sense of relief I feel.

Like he can tell I'm fighting to contain my emotions, he leans forward and taps the sketchbook I'm still holding. 'It's circular so it'll fit on supermarket trolley tokens. Keyrings. Coasters. I like a nice coaster.'

I laugh so hard and so unexpectedly that it takes me a few moments to recover. 'You have a knack for saying sentences I've never heard before and never thought I would.'

He looks confused. 'Who doesn't love a good coaster?'

'I don't know. Some of us just prefer mug stains on the tables.'

'No one prefers mug stains on their tables.' He leans over and takes the sketchbook from my hands and sits back again to add another few sparkles, and I instinctively push myself up on the desk and reach over to stop him.

'This is perfect. I know I baulked when you suggested a logo all those weeks ago, but I imagined something corporate and meaningless, not something that captures the essence of the museum like this, and makes it look so inviting. If I saw this, *I'd* want to come here. You make it look like such a... home.'

'It is. *You* make it into a warm and inviting home.' He holds my gaze again for a long moment and then looks away and quickly adds, 'For all the sentient exhibits, obviously.'

'Obviously.' I chew on my lip and echo his words, but I'm certain there's a deeper meaning there.

'Bookmarks.' He redirects the subject back to the gift shop. 'If we come up with some clever slogans or something, we could put them on bookmarks with the logo and a link to the website on the back... Magnets. Mugs. Pens. The possibilities are endless, but at least with this, you can build a real brand for the museum and tie everything together with one logo. Ooh, tote bags! Everyone loves a tote bag. And badges! You and I could wear badges so people can identify us as staff.'

I laugh at how enthusiastic he is about the gift shop. It was something I never thought would be worthwhile, but now it's something I wish I'd done years ago. The dressing-up aspect has always had its problems, and he cut through all my waffling about it and saw exactly what needed to be changed, and I hadn't realised how much I needed that.

Now I've stopped him tweaking the already perfect design, he leans back in the reclining chair and looks up at me. 'What were you up to?'

'Fixing Moana. Someone had tried on her flower crown.'

'Ah, yeah, I've got a bone to pick with you about that. Is there *any* Disney movie that *won't* make me cry? Because I watched that last night and when her grandma died in the beginning, I am hideously ashamed to admit that I bawled like a baby. These movies are turning me into an emotional wreck.'

I'm not sure which I like more – the fact he cries at Disney movies or the fact he openly admits it. 'What that tells me is that we should watch more Disney films together because I feel like I need to witness that.'

'I would be remarkably okay with that, even though I'm a grown man who should not be getting emotional at animated children's films.'

'The most attractive thing about any man is his feelings and a lack of fear when it comes to showing them.'

'Then I must be George Clooney.' He waggles both eyebrows.

He thinks he's joking, and while George is certainly okay, I don't think he's a patch on Warren Berrington. 'George *wishes* he had your hair.'

He laughs in a disbelieving way, but his face has gone redder than red, and we grin at each other across the desk, and then he considers something for a moment and beckons me to come round to his side. 'There's something else I wanted to show you, but it's just an idea, something you mentioned a while back and I played around with...'

He pulls another piece of paper out from his sketchbook and holds it up to show me, and I stand next to him and look over his shoulder.

On the paper is a pencil-sketched drawing of... a floorplan? It takes me a minute to understand what I'm seeing, and I can't help the intake of breath when I do.

The mini-map I mentioned weeks ago that I'd wanted to get made but was too expensive to even consider commissioning... he's *drawn* it. And not just drawn it, but drawn an absolutely beautiful, eye-catching map of the building that could not be any *more* perfect.

He's got the black and white checkerboard floor look of the lobby, with a 'you are here' arrow at the front desk, and then small depictions of the Prince and Princess Suites on one side, the Fairytale Homes hall on the other, and the soon-to-be gift shop, customer bathrooms, the stairs with a barrier crossing it off because I spend half my days answering questions about whether there's anything up there, and he's paid attention to that without me saying a word.

The whole thing is inside a cloud, and to fill the empty space around the edges, he's doodled the shapes of glass shoes, the genie's lamp, Rapunzel's sun symbol, Ariel's seashells, and enchanted rose petals.

It's the sweetest, most thoughtful gesture, something I hadn't even thought of again, and a real display of understanding this place, but also of how much research he's been doing for someone who'd never even heard of most fairytales a month ago, and it's the first time that I have *zero* doubt that his intentions are honourable and he really, truly cares about Colours of the Wind. No one could put so much effort into something they weren't fully committed to.

'It's just doodling.' He sounds endearingly nervous, like he honestly expected me not to like it. 'Maybe I shouldn't hav—'

Before I know what I'm doing, I've thrown my arms around his chair from behind and dragged it back against me, causing him to slide backwards and his feet to fall off the desk and hit the floor with a thunk.

He makes a choked-off noise that sounds like he's swallowed his own tongue as my arms tighten around his chest and hug him, despite the chair's high back between us.

His breathing has sped up because he clearly wasn't expecting it any more than I was expecting to do it, and it takes a few moments for him to relax and sink into it.

He turns so his head is leaning against mine, his breath coming in sharp pants, making me shiver as it skims across my neck, and I lose track of the minutes ticking by as we stay in that position.

'What's this in aid of?' he whispers against my hair, sounding relaxed and dreamily distant.

I consider it before I answer, because I want to be honest, and at the same time, I don't want to make it any weirder or more awkward than it already is. I swallow and force my tongue to wet my suddenly dry lips before answering. 'Being you.'

He makes that choked-off noise of surprise again and I hear the gulp as he swallows hard. He turns further into me, so his mouth is against the skin of my neck. 'If you said what I think you just said, it's really unfair to try to make me cry in the middle of a working day.'

I laugh and hold him tighter, and he shifts closer, his stubble catching in the lengths of my hair with every movement.

'No one's ever said anything like that to me. I'm not someone who makes people feel like that.'

It sounds like something he didn't intend to say, and he seems curiously starved for affection, because he holds onto my arms tightly, his fingers curling deeply into my skin like he's clinging on and silently asking me not to let go yet, and he holds them around his chest long after my back is protesting the bent-over awkward angle and the chair is digging into my collarbone.

It makes me long for a proper hug without the physical barrier between us, but nothing is more important than this connection that I'm not ready to break yet.

He doesn't say a word even though his hands gradually slide down my arms as his grip starts to loosen, until eventually his fingers wrap around my fingers and tangle our hands together, and then his chest arches as he stretches with a groan and starts to lift my arms from around him. I'd happily stay here for longer, but—

'Excuse me, dears?'

We're interrupted by an elderly lady with a granddaughter in tow. I let out a squeak at their sudden appearance, and I feel Warren physically jolt in surprise at the unexpected ending to... whatever that was.

We dive apart so quickly that he barely misses running over my toes with the wheels of his computer chair. I'd forgotten we were at the front desk and could be interrupted at any moment. For a minute there, I'd totally forgotten about *everything*.

Warren's leapt up and is leaning on the desk, breathless from the shock of the interruption, or possibly wondering what spell I cast to get him to allow physical contact like that, and I'm trying not to think about when it was that I started feeling this much affection for him.

I smooth my hair down and try to compose myself, feeling as embarrassed as I might do if a visitor had found us in an intimately compromising position, and not just two friends hugging because one did something nice for the other one. That's all it was, right? I glance at him. A thank you hug, nothing more.

'I just wanted to say that you've got such a lovely place here.' The woman is leaning on a walking stick with one hand and clutching the little girl's hand in the other. 'I'd never heard of it before but I saw something about the escaped exhibits online and my husband and I decided to bring our granddaughter, and it's been one of the best days out any of us can remember, hasn't it?'

She jiggles her granddaughter's hand until the little girl confidently declares, 'It has!'

'It's made me feel like a child again.' Her watery eyes flit between me and Warren. 'Walking around here has been like watching the years slip away. My own mum has been gone for decades now, but there's something about being here that makes me feel like *I'm* a little girl again, standing at her side and holding her hand, and looking at something magical. I can't describe how special it is to feel like that at my age.'

And I can't help but smile because *this* is exactly what I've always hoped my visitors would feel, no matter their age. 'No one is ever too old to reconnect with their inner child. In fact, I happen to think it gets *more* important as we get older. It's all too easy to forget what it's like to be young and to find wonder in anything.' I glance at Warren again. 'The world is good at snuffing that out, and if I can do anything to help people get that back, then that's the best thing I could ever hear. Thank you.'

She smiles too and I love the sense of connecting with someone who truly gets what I wanted to do here.

'Those naughty exhibits escaping just adds another layer to the magic too. I don't know how you're doing it, but very well done, both of you.'

Until now, Warren has been frozen to the spot, utterly transfixed by her words, but at this, he stands upright, looking surprised that she's included him as well.

'I want to knoooow!' The granddaughter looks up at us, sucking a thumb shyly.

'No, no, we mustn't spoil the magic,' her grandmother says.

'You really want to know?' Warren steps out from behind the counter and crouches down to talk to the little girl, and when she nods enthusiastically, he carries on. 'The exhibits are *magic*! They're real and they only come to life at night when no one's watching them. Lissa and I stayed here one night and we hid from them and do you know what we saw?'

She looks so excited that she might burst before he reaches the end of his tale.

'We saw Aladdin's Magic Carpet flying around all by itself!' He waves his hands through the air, depicting the movement a flying carpet might make.

'No, you never!'

'We did, scout's honour.' He does the scout salute and the little girl giggles in delight.

He holds his hand up for a high five and she smacks it much harder than he was expecting, and he falls onto his bum, pretending that the force of her hand knocked him over, making her laugh even harder, but it makes something inside me melt.

There's something infinitely trustworthy about someone who isn't afraid to make a fool of themselves to make a child laugh. He's wonderful with kids, and it makes me think of the things he's said over the last few weeks, about being bullied, losing his father at a young age, not having much of a childhood, and still feeling like a kid in adult's clothing. There really is an inner child in there, *screaming* to get out.

'Anyway, we just wanted to pass on our compliments and say thank you and keep doing what you're doing, there's not many places like this in the world, and it's been a joy to find one. We'll be back again very soon!'

The little girl choruses, 'Byeeeeeeee!' as they walk away, waving over her shoulder to Warren as he picks himself up off the floor.

'You're really getting into the swing of things here...' I comment, leaving an open-ended space for a response.

'I love it. I wish I could stay forever.' He's got a distant look on his face where he's leaning on the counter with his chin resting in his hands, watching the woman meet her husband at the door and the little girl takes his hand too and swings between them.

'Really?'

'Ye—' He realises what he's saying and quickly corrects himself. 'I mean, no, obviously. Just, er, winding you up. This is a job, just like any other.'

If there's one thing I've learnt since opening this museum, it's that this is a job *unlike* any I have done before, and if it is to end, it will be unlike any I might find in the future either.

The thought makes a sense of melancholy settle over me, and clearly unwilling to expand on *any* of the things that have just happened, Warren busies himself tidying up the sketch papers still strewn across the counter. 'So if you approve this design, I'll get the logo scanned in and send you a useable image file, so you'll always be able to use it after I've gone, and I'll send you a link to the wholesaler's website our company uses so you can pick the best products for the gift shop. On the map front, if I colourise this, scan it in, and scale it to the right size, it's only an investment of forty quid to get a thousand of them printed as postcards, I'm happy to expense that, and if they're popular then we'll know it's worthwhile. The map will be on the front, and I'll design a back with the logo, encouragement to leave a review on travel websites and to come back again sometime.'

In the middle of his shuffling of the papers that he's already reshuffled beyond any shuffling need, I reach over to grab his hand and give it a squeeze. 'Thank you.'

'You're welcome.' He hasn't taken his eyes off the spot where my fingers are curled around his, and they twitch like he wants to squeeze them back, but he doesn't, and enough time passes that it becomes awkward.

'That was a reference to the *Moana* song, right?' I joke to ease the tension.

'Hah. Good spot.' He pulls his hand away from mine and shakes it like my fingers have squeezed too tightly, and then nods towards the stairs. 'I should get back to the Tablet of Gloom. Er, I mean, vitally important piece of work equipment that I couldn't do my job without. How have you even got me calling it that now?'

I can't help laughing at how bewildered he looks. 'The magic's getting to you, Mr Berrington.'

'Something is all right.' He looks like he wants to say more, but his phone rings in his pocket and he pulls it out, looks at the screen, and puts it back in again. It's not the first time I've seen him ignore his phone or the constant notification noises coming from his tablet lately, and I'm intrigued by what's changed between now and the almost surgical attachment of a few weeks ago. 'Do you need to get that?'

'Yes, I do.' He looks down at the pocket of his trousers like he's contemplating it and then looks back up at me. 'But I'm not going to.'

'And you're okay with that?'

He thinks for a moment and then grins at me and starts heading for the stairs. 'I'm getting there.'

* * *

It's not the last time I hear Warren's phone ring. When the museum is quiet, the loud ringtone filters down through the floors, and I also hear how abruptly he shuts it off when he rejects call after call.

It's a few days later and the museum is closed for the night. I don't intend to eavesdrop on a private conversation, but he's been upstairs all afternoon, and now I've shut the door to visitors, I'm on my way up to check in on him when I hear his phone ring again, and for whatever reason, this time he decides to answer it with a snarled, 'What?'

I freeze on the spot halfway up the stairs. I hadn't realised until this very moment that I've never heard him answer the phone before. He doesn't talk on the phone, ever. He does absolutely everything by email, and hearing him answer is so unusual that it doesn't occur to me that I shouldn't be eavesdropping until it's too late and I already *am*.

I should turn and go back down the stairs, I know I should, but I'm intrigued by the fact he's answered this time and by the razor-sharp *way* he answered, because Warren is a lot of things but rude isn't one of them, and the temptation to stay put is impossible to resist.

'Why are you phoning me?' he barks, presumably into the receiver. 'You know I'm useless on the phone, put it in an email.'

A pause. Of course, the problem with eavesdropping on phone calls is that you can only hear one side of them.

'Yes, so I gathered,' he says from upstairs. 'Yes, I know it's taking off, that was the point.'

A longer pause, peppered with noises of frustration on his part. 'What?'

Another pause. Another, 'What? Say that again?'

A, 'Slow down!'

A muttered, 'Well, that's their bloody problem.'

'Will you *please* talk slower?'

An endless litany of different noises of aggravation. He sounds beyond frustrated, and like he keeps starting to say something but being interrupted.

Eventually he says, 'Whatever the problems are, email them to me. I literally cannot do this, as you well know. Goodbye.'

There's the sound of a phone being slammed down onto the table, and another growl of annoyance at, presumably, the person on the other end who he's hung up on.

And I realise I'm stuck. If I go back downstairs *now*, he's going to hear the floorboards creaking and know I was up here listening in. And if I make myself known, he's going to know I was up here listening in.

Honestly, the intricacies of eavesdropping should be taught

in schools so nosy people know what to do when they find themselves in these situations.

I decide that head on is the best way to tackle it, and take a deep breath and force myself to run up the rest of the stairs. Maybe he'll think I'm so fast at climbing them that I was downstairs this whole time and made it up here in three seconds flat. That's possible, right?

Except... when I go into the kitchen, he's sitting at the table with the Tablet of Gloom and his laptop open, his elbows on the table and his head in his hands, massaging his temples like he's trying to stave off a headache, and I'm surprised by how harangued he looks. 'Are you okay?'

He jumps at my unexpected arrival and lifts his head, revealing a face that looks even more exhausted than the rest of his demeanour does. 'Yeah, fine.'

I can see the cogs in his brain turning as he mentally calculates how much I might've overheard, and I'm about to say something about keeping fit by running up the stairs, but he desperately looks like he needs someone to talk to, and I drop any form of act. 'Are you in trouble?'

'In every conceivable way.' He answers instantly without thinking it through as he goes back to rubbing fingers across his forehead, looking like his attempts to avoid the headache are failing fast.

I could prod for more info, but I'm a firm believer that there's nothing a cup of tea won't make better, so I go over to put the kettle on and throw a teabag into a mug each.

His head is still in his hands and his fingers have moved on to rubbing his scalp when I put the mug of tea down in front of him and give his shoulder a squeeze to make him lift his head and slowly blink tired-looking eyes open.

Those eyes follow me as I walk round the table and take the

seat opposite him, and then he looks down at the mug like he's still trying to work out what it is.

I sit down and take a sip of my own tea and then raise the mug like I'm doing a toast, and it's like he's been in a world of his own because he blinks back to awareness and connects everything that's happened in the past few minutes all at once. He wraps both hands around the mug like he's cold and takes a long sip.

'Ahh, that's good. Thank you.' He looks over at me and shakes his head. 'So much. You have no idea how much I needed that.'

'I like to think one of my hidden talents is a sixth sense when it comes to tea.'

He lets out a laugh and sits upright, putting one hand on the back of his neck and rolling his head around to ease the stiffness, and when he takes another sip, he slumps down in the chair and leans backwards, letting his eyes drift shut again.

I stretch my leg out under the table until I can push at his foot with mine. 'You can talk to me, you know.'

'That's what I'm afraid of.' It's a quiet mutter that sounds like he didn't intend to say it out loud, and then, yet again, his brain catches up and he blinks weary eyes open and looks at me across the table and backpedals. 'Yeah, thanks. It's nothing. Just... my mother. The company. Phones. I've got this thing where I... I can't...' He stops mid-sentence and his eyes flit away from mine and focus on a cobweb in a high corner of the kitchen ceiling, and he shakes his head. 'Nothing. That parent-child dynamic. My mother has a unique ability to make me feel like a child with one lash of her tongue. There's nothing like having a parent as your boss to make you feel inadequate and undermined.'

'I'm sorry.' I nudge his foot again with the toe of my shoe, wishing that he'd complete a sentence without abandoning it halfway through. 'Is this because of me? Because of what we're doing here?'

He gives me that look again, like he's trying to see *inside* me and determine whether I can be trusted before he decides how much to share, and I get that all-too-familiar sense that everything he does share is strictly curtailed into the most palatable version, and not necessarily the most *true* version.

'Yeah, it is.' He eventually settles on an answer, and it sounds like an honest one. 'This whole living exhibits thing is gaining a lot of attention. People are talking about it and my company's on the warpath. But you know what, if I'm going against them then maybe for the first time in my life, I'm doing something right.'

He takes a fortifying sip of tea and his words sound fierce, but the look on his face is nowhere near as assured. 'The attention the escaped exhibits are getting is reflecting badly on our company because we *were* intending to knock it down. My mother has got investors questioning our morals. One has threatened to pull out because of the potential backlash surrounding this project. Another has got a son who's following us online and he's threatened to cut ties with us if we were to forge ahead, and no one's happy about the conflict of interests.'

'What's the conflict of interests?'

'I am.'

'Oh. Right. I thought your job was to save the museum,' I venture carefully, feeling like he's going to realise I'm wheedling for information at any moment, because I *still* feel like I'm missing something about this whole situation.

'It is. But my job and my mother's vision don't always align. Basically, investors aren't happy and she's not happy, and no one's happy either way.'

'But that's a good thing, right? In terms of trying to save it, backlash from the public and especially from investors is likely to turn this around, right?'

'Yeah.' He runs a hand through his hair and shakes his head. 'Yeah.'

It sounds like he's trying to convince himself, and it makes me reconsider my certainty that he's truly on my side. Anyone objecting to my museum being demolished has to be a good thing – at least for someone who *wants* it saved, and I'm once again left wondering which side of the line Warren stands on.

16

Chaos. Chaos is how I'd describe the nights when the other Ever After Street shopkeepers descend on the museum en masse to put together all the wishes we're able to grant, package them up in pretty parcels and get them ready for sending.

'I still don't see why we can't deliver them in person.' Warren's comparing an address to a map on his phone. 'Surely the point of doing this is to *see* the joy it brings to a child who's wished for something?'

'We'd be caught,' Franca says.

'Everyone has doorbell cams and CCTV these days,' Marnie cuts in. 'You can't walk up to someone's door without them identifying you.'

'So let them know,' he replies. 'Put the Ever After Street branding all over the boxes and let everyone know how above and beyond you all go to help kids who wish for something.'

'That would defeat the object and spoil the magic, and none of us want it to become a way of getting freebies,' Cleo says. 'You've got to retain some level of cynicism. The wishing well has to be organic. We know there's chatter online, we know people post about wishes coming true, but firstly, we can't grant every wish because some are heartbreakingly impossible, like "I wish my mum didn't have cancer" or "I wish my nan was still alive", or things that can only exist in imaginations, like "I wish I was a fairy", and we don't want those kids to feel left out or like the wishing well's magic isn't strong enough to grant *their* wishes, and secondly, we don't want this to become somewhere that children post a wishlist of expensive items down the well and expect to get everything on it. The wishes we try to grant are sentimental, ones that mean something. It's Lissa's magic, this was all her idea, her doing, and we're only along for the ride.'

'She's done so much for everyone on this street that we'll all do *anything* for her.' Mickey's tone is vaguely threatening as she gives Warren a warning look. 'No one messes with our fairytale museum and gets away with it.'

While it warms my heart and gives me goosebumps to hear that, he laughs and holds his hands up in a surrendering gesture, but it's easy to see we've veered into uncomfortable territory too, and my best friend is one step away from baring her teeth at him like an angry guard dog.

As much as I appreciate her protectiveness, I also want her to like him. *I* like him, and part of the idea of getting him involved tonight was so everyone would give him a chance instead of writing him off as an evil property tycoon, like I did before I got to see behind his professional front.

'Plus, people might be watching for us,' Cleo says, inadvertently defusing the tension. 'There's a lot of interest in the exhibit escapades and who's doing it, and it's not beyond the realm of possibility that someone could be trying to catch us out.' Cleo stops abruptly and glances at Warren, suddenly remembering that he's here and he doesn't know. She quickly corrects herself. 'Them. I mean, *them*, the exhibits, obviously.

Someone might be trying to catch *them* out, and it would be suspicious for *us* to be caught... doing anything... in the vicinity.'

I have zero doubt that Warren knows exactly what's going on with the exhibits without being explicitly told, and the small, silent smile that creeps across his face only serves to confirm my suspicions.

'Messing about here overnight, it could put ideas in people's heads, and we wouldn't want them thinking that we have anything to do with it or that the exhibits *aren't* moving of their own free will. All by themselves, no siree.' Cleo hasn't yet realised that she needs to stop digging.

'I'm fielding a lot of questions. People keep asking about the spinning wheel that, er...' Imogen glances at Warren. '... tormented me.'

'I am too. Raff and I both had a journalist in the other day, asking about it all. I think he went to every shop,' Franca says, and the others chorus an agreement.

'No one told him anything.' Marnie is packing books into a box for a child who wished for new books so she could be like Belle. 'But this has taken on a life of its own. People are keen to uncover the real truth behind the moving exhibits.'

The *us* truth. And that would be a Very Bad Thing. If it comes out that *we* are the ones doing this, that it was me all along, it will spoil the magic entirely. I mean, parents have probably figured it out, but the excited little faces that have pointed out Lumière on the castle wall or jumped up and down when they've spotted Pascal hiding amongst the flowers, they'll never believe in magic again if they discover it's all been a con. A clever marketing ploy in an attempt to keep my museum relevant. Children wouldn't understand things like rent increases and contract clauses, but they'd understand that I'd been fooling them all along. The others are right – we *do* need to be careful that no one realises what we're up to.

'These are the sweetest wishes. Listen to these.' Warren is sitting at the counter with a rainbow of pieces of paper scattered in front of him and he reads some of them out loud.

I wish for a new husband for Mummy so she won't be so sad since Daddy moved out.

I wish I could talk to animals.

I wish a wizard would turn my brother into a toad!

'*I* wish we could actually grant these ones, they're so... innocent.' He looks around, blinking like he's trying to stave off emotions. 'Exactly what childhood *should* be like.'

I see the curious looks pass between the other shopkeepers. Marnie raises an eyebrow at Cleo, and Franca gives Mickey a questioning look, but this is exactly why I wanted us all to get together. Warren isn't as heartless as we thought he was, there's a soft side there that's really touched by the wishes, and I feel like *this* is the real value behind Colours of the Wind, and I want both sides to come together and see that.

I'm packing up a cape for a little boy who wished to be a superhero, and Mickey's sitting at a temporary table opposite me, putting a few mermaidy bits together from her shop for a little girl who wished she could be a mermaid.

It's never much, usually things we either already have or can order from suppliers at a discount, or cobble together from our combined stock, but I'd like to think it can bring a moment of magic to a child's day to find something they wished for delivered to their door, and it's never been about the recognition but about the opportunity I saw with the wishing well to make a small difference in strangers' lives.

Although tonight, I'm struggling to concentrate on the wishes because of how many times I keep looking at Warren. He was uneasy about the others all being here, but since we got started, there's a wide grin that hasn't left his face and a sparkle in his eyes every time they catch my gaze across the room, although most of the chatter seems to be going over his head, and he watches as an observer rather than getting involved in the conversations all around him.

Ali is folding a giant teddy bear into a box that is really too small for it, and Warren leans over and reads the wish that's being fulfilled. '*I wish for my teddy to get better. My brother set him on fire and Mum tried to fix him but he's all black and smells of smoke.* Wow. I'm suddenly extremely grateful to be an only child. Who knew children had so many problems with brothers?'

'Can't fix his teddy, but my grandson didn't want this one, so maybe he'll like it instead, and hopefully it will escape the wrath of any pyromaniac siblings this time. Either way, it's a little thing that costs us nothing but the price of postage, and might make this little lad feel special and like he's important to someone, somewhere. It's not easy to feel like you *matter* when you're young and your parents are busy – working, taking care of the house, their own parents, running around after multiple kids, pets, and everything else families have to keep on top of. This has quickly become my favourite part of working on Ever After Street.'

A loud chorus of agreements sweeps through the lobby and between that and their earlier comments, my heart continues warming until my chest feels like it might explode. I knew they enjoyed doing this, but I'd never *really* realised that it matters to everyone else as much as it matters to me.

The warm feeling is quickly replaced when Ali jabs the pen he's holding towards Warren and wields it threateningly. 'And if you even *think* of doing anything to this museum and destroying the magic of that wishing well, we will hunt you down and torture you until *your* only wish is that you were dead so the pain would end.'

'Oh. That's... um... quite violent. A bit scary.' He reaches over and gently pushes Ali's pen away from his jugular and gulps loudly. 'I'm doing the best I can.'

'Make it better!' Mickey turns around to snap at him. 'If you evict my best friend from this place, or are in *any* way responsible for her having to leave it, we will fight your cinema complex every step of the way and sabotage it at every chance we get. You'll regret the day you ever set foot on Ever After Street!'

I'm feeling warm all over and touched by their impassioned protectiveness of me, and also a little uneasy because I thought tonight would be a good time for them to get to know Warren, not for threats of quite so much violence and channelling Liam Neeson's famous *Taken* speech.

'I think Warren likes this place more than he expected to,' I say, because I feel bad that no one's even giving him half a chance. 'Ever After Street has a way of getting under your skin. We all know that.'

'Joking aside,' Warren says with his hand on his throat, sounding hopeful that it really *is* a joke, 'this is amazingly fun. Thank you for letting me be part of it. Since I came here, it's been eye-opening to have an insight into how kids see the world, how they're always so hopeful and believe in things like wishing wells, and fairytales, and magic. Makes me wish I had a childhood like that.'

'It's never too late,' Ali says to him.

'Where have I heard that before?' Warren's tone is soft and

fond as he looks over his shoulder to catch my eyes again, and only looks away when he spots that Marnie, Cleo, and Franca are all watching us.

Mickey kicks my foot under the table we're sharing and waggles her eyebrows.

'*Soooo*, what are we getting Sadie and Witt for a wedding gift?' Marnie says, sounding like she's deliberately steering the topic towards the wedding and I have an instant premonition of exactly where this is going. 'Should we all go in on something together?'

There's a chorus of agreements, but no one makes any suggestions. It's like they all get that the point of this conversation has nothing to do with a wedding gift and everything to do with the look they've just clocked between me and Warren.

Taking up the baton from his other half, Darcy says, 'Are you *still* desperately searching for that plus one, Lissa?'

He puts such an emphasis on it that the word sounds like it's in capital letters, like I've been spending my every waking moment since the wedding invitation frantically hunting for a mythical plus one, and not had anything else like museum takeovers and escaping exhibits to worry about.

I've always liked Darcy, he's the castle gardener and owner of the florist shop next door to Marnie's bookshop, and her partner of over two years now, but that sentence makes it sound like they collaborated to get onto this topic.

'I don't need a plus one. It's not compulsory.' I can't help glancing at Warren. Any discussion of my love life should be banned in front of people I fancy, or actually, banned completely, regardless of who's listening in. I can't help thinking he looks uneasy. He's following the conversation back and forth, like a tennis match, but he's looking at the wrong person when someone else is speaking, and he looks like he's *fighting* to keep up.

Although maybe that's a good thing with this particular discussion.

We've all worked together for years and get used to when to let each other talk and when to make our own voices heard, but I can imagine it would be a *lot* for someone who isn't used to it, especially as it's after-hours now and the professional masks that we hold up in front of customers slip and we can be ourselves amongst friends. There's constant chatter about how our days have gone, and everyone moans about difficult customers or things that happened this week or Mr Hastings's latest antics, or the most favoured topic of conversation lately, my eternal spinster status.

'I've got a mate who's just broken up with someone,' Bram offers. 'He'll probably be out of rebound territory before the wedding comes around.'

'A delightful thought, but no, thank you. Can we focus on the wishes and not my love life?' I'm blushing hard and I can *feel* Warren's eyes on me. I'm embarrassed by the fact that everyone I know is more invested in this than I am, and that they think I need *this* much help in the love department.

'Surely we could find someone who'd pretend or join you as a platonic date,' Cleo suggests. 'No one specified it had to be a romantic plus one. Any mate will do.'

'Someone who'd pretend out of pity?' I raise an eyebrow. 'I don't want to go to a wedding with someone who feels sorry for me.'

'Raff's brother-in-law has got a single colleague. He's a tad younger than you, but no one would ever know,' Franca offers.

'Oh, good. I'm not sure what's worse – someone who makes

me look like I've taken my *grandson* to a wedding or the fact that you've all been putting feelers out on my behalf. Plus ones are not mandatory. Sadie and Witt are not *really* going to bar me at the door if I turn up alone.'

'Listen to this one,' Warren says loudly, and when I look over at him, he tips his head in my direction, and my heart melts a little bit at his clear attempt to rescue me from this awkward conversation. What he's doing is so obvious, and the others will undoubtedly notice and read something into it, and I think he realises that and doesn't mind taking the flak on my behalf. '*I wish I was an astronaut so I could live on the moon and make friends with an alien.* How sweet is that? Does anyone have a little alien we could send her?'

When no one does, he turns to me. 'Can I keep this and do it tomorrow? I'll go and buy an alien soft toy or something and send it?'

I nod, pleasantly surprised by his eagerness because that was a wish from the 'ignore' pile, and even though I know he loves being privy to children's wishes, I didn't expect him to offer to do something so sweet off his own back, and I can't help the smile as he slips it into his pocket.

As soon as he's turned away, Mickey kicks my foot under the table again and cups her hands around her mouth and whispers to me, 'Who is that and what have you done with the evil gerbil with no soul?'

I try to give her my best 'shut up, everyone's listening!' look, but I can feel my face pulsing with redness, and she barely contains a squeal. 'Pocahontas and John Smith! I told you, you're showing him how to paint with the colours of the wind! Literally!'

'Having fun, Warren?' Franca is boxing up one of her handmade nutcrackers for a child who wished it could be Christmas every day.

He ignores the question. Which, again, is strange because he's never usually so impolite.

'Warren!'

'Sorry, what?' He turns around to her and I notice how red his face has gone.

'Are you having fun?' she repeats.

'Oh, yes, thank you, yes.' It's a strangely curtailed answer, and he looks wildly embarrassed, and it makes me think again about how much he's struggling to keep up tonight.

'Sorry, I didn't realise you were talking to me.' He adds it as an afterthought and the whole exchange makes him hunch over the counter, like he's trying to make himself smaller, especially when everyone else has turned to look at him too, and something sparks in my mind, a realisation that remains frustratingly just out of reach.

'Who's got the nicest handwriting to write the little boy's name on this teddy bear's collar tag?' Ali asks. 'My handwriting's terrible and I don't want to mess it up.'

'Warren's really artistic,' I say, glad of the opportunity to let the others see there's more to him.

He's blushing as he glances at me and then turns back to Ali to take the pen and the plastic tag and Ali murmurs the little boy's name to put on it.

I go back to holding my finger on the ribbon around Mickey's box so she can tie it in a neat bow, and don't think anything more of it until Ali snaps, 'For goodness' sake, Warren, didn't you hear me? I said Jaden, not Aiden! We've only got one of those and now it's ruined!'

For one moment, the world freezes, and I instantly know what Warren's been trying to hide all these weeks.

With one comment, Ali has blown open what I've been trying to put my finger on and never quite getting there.

Everything that didn't add up suddenly makes perfect sense.

It's why he's struggling so much tonight. There are too many people, all talking at once, interrupting and talking over each other, saying things to him when he can't see their faces. He didn't ignore Franca just now – he didn't *hear* the question.

He doesn't watch my lips when I'm talking because he's got a weird lip fetish, but because he's *lip-reading*.

The little girl I accused him of ignoring, and how oddly upset he seemed by it at the time. I thought it was because I'd called him out for being rude, but it wasn't, was it? He didn't ignore her – he didn't *hear* her. He probably didn't even know that a little girl *had* tried to talk to him.

The inexplicable changing of sides on the night of the stake-out. And the way he moves so he's facing people. He's always got to be opposite someone talking to him. Front-on, never sideways. The way he leans in when someone's speaking, turns slightly to his right. I'd noticed it but I'd never realised it was anything more than a quirky little habit.

Even the phone call the other day. *I literally cannot do this, as you well know.* I wondered what it was he couldn't do and what the other person was supposed to know, and this is the answer. He never takes phone calls because he *has* to see someone's mouth moving to catch what they're saying.

The number of times I've mentioned the instrumental music playing in the lobby and he's given a brush-off or an empty agreement and I've half-wondered if he even knew what I was talking about.

'Liss?' Mickey clicks her fingers in front of my face and her tone sounds like it's the tenth time she's said it. She's tied my finger into the ribbon when I didn't move it from the box in time, and I hadn't even noticed.

I pull it free and look around. 'Where did Warren go?'

'Did you not see him stomp upstairs in a sulk?' Bram asks. 'He's a weird one, isn't he?'

'I think it might be more complicated than any of us imagine...' I murmur, unable to get my mind off what I suddenly understand. I don't know why someone would go to such great lengths to disguise having an issue with hearing, but there's something going on there, and it must be a touchy subject, otherwise he would've been open about it. He obviously doesn't want anyone to know, and Ali's just unintentionally put it in a very public space, even though it doesn't seem like anyone else has made the same connection that I have.

'I don't trust him, Liss,' Mickey says gently. 'He's hiding something.'

'I think it might not be what you think it is. I'm going to...' I point upwards. I was going to say 'make sure he's okay' but whatever his reasons for hiding this are, I don't want to openly suggest that he *isn't* okay, so I finish lamely with, '...bathroom.'

When I get up to the kitchen on the third floor, Warren is standing at the table with cardboard laid out in front of him and a pair of scissors in hand. 'What are you doing?'

He jumps at the unintentional volume of my voice, but now I know he's struggling to hear, it came out louder than intended.

'Oh, good, it's just you.' He lets out a sigh of relief and holds up a star-shaped piece of cardboard that he's cut out. 'Trying to make a new tag for the bear. Cardboard isn't ideal but I messed up.'

There are so many things I could say, but like an out-of-body experience, I walk across the room, take the scissors out of his hand and drop them on the table, and pull him into a tight, tight hug.

'What the—' He chokes off the protest when I squeeze him tighter, and after a few moments, his arms slide around me and pull me against him and, breath by breath, some of the tension starts to seep from his body as he breathes into it.

It's not the first time we've hugged, but it *is* the first time we've hugged without a computer chair between us, and I let myself get lost in his arms and in the luxury of his leather-scented cologne.

One arm stays around his back and the other slides further up, until my fingers are playing with the ends of his hair on the nape of his neck and he tries to disguise the shiver that goes through him, but it's impossible to ignore the way he curls just a little bit tighter around me.

'What's this in aid of?' he says into my shoulder, sounding happily faraway.

'Nothing,' I murmur, but I'm on what I've realised is the wrong side.

'Hmm?'

I've never thought anything of it, but now I realise how often he says that. How often he gets people to repeat themselves. There is so much behind that 'hmm?' now, and I shake my head, knowing he'll feel it and take it as being unimportant. I want to tell him I know, but here, right now, with half of Ever After Street downstairs thinking he's hiding something, *now* isn't the moment.

Instead, without a word, I revel in the cuddle for a couple more minutes and he does the same, doing nothing but holding me and letting himself be held, and I especially enjoy the noise of disappointment he makes in his throat and the way his arms tighten when I start loosening my grip and he holds on for a few moments more.

When we pull back, I force myself to take a step away in case I leap on him again, and he looks so knocked off-balance that he has to rest a hand on the table to stay steady.

'That was nice.' He pinches the bridge of his nose and flicks his head like he needs to clear it. 'Unexpected, but nice.'

'It was.' I hold his gaze and silently *will* him to let me in, but he doesn't.

Instead, he picks up a pen and leans over the table. 'What's the name for the tag again?'

He gets me to spell it out, and I make an effort to form each letter clearly and loudly, and he adds a few floral flourishes to the cardboard and then takes the new tag back downstairs, hoping to catch Ali before he's sealed the box.

I could follow him, but tonight has rapidly taken on a different tone, and I stay put, waiting for him to come back because I have a feeling there are too many people downstairs and he's going to segregate himself up here for the rest of the evening if I let him.

I listen from the landing, I hear him give Ali the new makeshift tag for the bear, and then he comes straight back up. Before I can think it through, I blurt out, 'Fancy a walk?'

'A walk?'

'Yeah, what you said earlier about hand-delivering wishes. That bear and the superhero cape aren't far from here and are only about fifteen minutes apart. We could do that easily. Why don't we?'

'Just you and me?' he asks, and when I nod, a grin breaks across his face. 'I'd like that. My car's in the car park and I can charge petrol to my work expenses.'

'No. On foot. It's a beautiful autumn evening and you seem like you could use a break.'

He gives me a curious, questioning look, like he's trying to figure out what my hidden agenda is, and I raise an eyebrow until his mouth twitches into a smile. 'Okay, okay, you had me at getting out of here. And autumn. You had me at autumn.'

He tries to correct himself, but the first answer was the most honest and exactly how I imagined he'd be feeling after what just happened.

He tidies the cardboard offcuts away and puts the scissors back while I go and grab my coat and autumn scarf. 'Do you have a coat or a hoody or something? We can't just walk up to people's doors, you need something to cover your face so no one will recognise you.' I wave the end of my scarf in his direction.

He shrugs. 'Nope. Only the jumper I'm wearing. All my coats are at home and I don't think I've ever owned a scarf.'

'Then you'll have to borrow something from one of the mannequins.' I give it some thought and then hit on the perfect idea for a quick disguise. 'Prince Florian's cape! You can wrap it round your shoulders like a shawl and pull it up when we get near any doorbell cameras.'

'I don't even know who Prince Florian is.'

'Snow White's prince. His kiss wakes her up after the bite of poisoned apple.'

'I suppose that's another one I'll have to add to my watchlist.' He jokingly rolls his eyes as he holds his hand out towards the stairs, inviting me to go first, and we trundle back down together.

Usually, I love being around the others, but tonight, with everyone trying to set me up, coupled with my sudden realisation about Warren, it's started to feel a bit suffocating and I need some space too. While he disappears into the Prince Suite to find the mannequin of Prince Florian and borrow his cape, I ask

Mickey to get the others and smuggle out a couple of exhibits while we're gone, and she thinks my idea of hand-delivering a couple of wishes is a clever ploy to get them the privacy to do it, and I don't tell her that it's nothing to do with smuggling exhibits out and everything to do with a sudden and overpowering desire for some air, and to get Warren alone, where there's no one questioning his motives, and find out exactly what he's hiding and why.

17

'You think you've lent me this as a disguise, but I'm actually going to put it on.' Warren settles the red cape around his shoulders and ties it at the front as we walk down the steps from the museum. 'Reading all those wishes has made me realise that it's never too late to indulge your inner child. And now *you* get to walk down the road with a full-grown man wearing a cape and you've only got yourself to blame.'

I can't help giggling at his childlike grin. I never in a gazillion years would have imagined that the sharp-suited, uptight man who I found in my lobby six weeks ago would voluntarily wear a Disney prince's cape. 'Luckily it's dark and I'm firmly of the belief that no one is *ever* too old to wear a cape. It suits you.'

'Being here suits me. *This*. You actually grant wishes for children, Liss. That's such a privilege.'

'It is.' It's impossible to hide my delight that he *gets* it, and I hadn't realised how much I wanted him to.

I'm carrying the boxed teddy bear and the package containing the cape, and as we turn the corner at the end of Ever After Street and go through the car park, Warren's got his phone out and is checking the route on his GPS app, and he quickly realises that I wasn't *exactly* honest about how far away the houses are.

'I thought these houses were only fifteen minutes away! It's going to take us nearly an hour to walk there!'

'I meant fifteen minutes away from each other, I didn't specify how far from here. Besides, it's a beautiful evening. Look at the stars! Look at the trees! Feel the wind blowing your cape!' I look over and meet his eyes. 'And it was getting a bit... over-crowded inside tonight, don't you think?'

He gives me that curious look again, like he knows I'm getting at something, and his response comes out as more of a mutter than he probably intended. 'You can say that again.'

It sounds pained, and I can only imagine what it's like to be in a room full of people, all talking at once, and to be struggling to hear while also desperately trying to hide it, and more than anything, I *wish* I'd known. I wish he'd told me, because I would never have put him in that position tonight.

It's 8 p.m. and darkness has long since fallen, and as we get further away from Ever After Street and onto quiet country lanes, Warren double-checks his phone to make sure we're on the right path and then turns around and walks backwards again so he's facing me, and now I know it's because he's making sure he can see my lips moving, it hurts like a physical blow that he feels like he needs to do it rather than being open.

'Don't do that.' I transfer the box and package so they're both under my left arm and then reach out with my right hand until he takes hold of it, and then I use my grip on his fingers to pull him nearer again. 'I don't have to speak. We can just walk without a word being said.'

He blinks in surprise for a few moments, and then silently falls back into line beside me and drops my hand, and I wonder if I should have given such an open hint, because this is obviously something he doesn't want anyone to know about, but at the same time, now I know, I *have* to know all of it, no matter whether he's ready to share or not.

Time passes as we walk side by side in silence, punctuated only by the occasional falling leaf or call of a fox from the fields on the other side of the road, and I hear his intake of breath a couple of times, like he's building himself up to saying something but never managing to get the words out, and I keep looking over at him, trying to smile encouragingly, and fighting the urge to reach over and take his hand again, but with him walking normally, I can't think of an excuse to do so.

'You know, don't you?'

It's almost a relief when he finally faces it head on and I look over at him and nod.

'Because of Ali's comment just now?'

'No. I already knew, but Ali's comment made me realise what it was that I knew, does that make sense?'

'No! Not even slightly!' He looks over and meets my eyes. 'Which I'm starting to see is part of your charm.'

It makes me blush, and I decide to be honest with him too. 'And you know about the exhibits, don't you?'

'Of course I do,' he says with a good-natured laugh, sounding glad of the lighter subject. 'Long before they just admitted it in front of me and forgot I didn't know.'

I start to apologise for not being open with him about it, but he stops me. 'It doesn't matter, Liss. I'm an outsider, I know that, and you're all very protective of each other. Scarily protective.'

His hand goes defensively around his throat again and he makes a face of abject terror, and I can't help giggling, but I'm also not leaving the hearing thing there. 'You know you have to tell me, right?'

'No, I don't think I do. I think we could just pretend this conversation never happened and carry on working alongside each other in blissful ignorance.' He's smiling and his tone sounds jokey, but I suspect that if I agreed, this would be his preferred plan.

'That doesn't work for me.'

'As I knew it wouldn't.' His smile turns into a sigh and he looks off into the distance. 'When I was twenty-two, I was diagnosed with Ménière's disease.'

'I've never heard of that,' I admit, wishing I had more hands because my fingers twitch towards my phone to google it, but I'm going to drop these gifts if I try to juggle that as well.

'It's a chronic inner-ear disorder. Causes bouts of vertigo, tinnitus, and hearing loss in my left ear. It progresses with age so it's getting worse as I've got older.'

'If I'd known, I'd have never invited so many people over tonight.'

'Yes, you would, because I will *not* have people changing their plans to accommodate my failings.' There's a sharp look in his eyes and a determined set to his jaw, and when I go to protest that it's not a failing, he doesn't let me. 'But yes, I was struggling tonight. One on one is fine as long as I can see someone's lips moving, but with so many voices all at once, everyone talking to each other as well as to everyone else at the same time, I got really lost, and then I misheard the name Ali said for the tag and made it so obvious, right there on display for everyone to see, and I just needed to get out of there.' He steps closer and nudges his elbow gently into my arm. 'Thank you for recognising that and coming to rescue me.'

'Says the man in a superhero cape.'

He laughs and does a twirl, his Disney prince cape spinning

out around his shoulders and then catching up with itself all at once to thwack him round the face.

'For what it's worth, no one else put two and two together. They don't know you like I do,' I say, as he straightens it out again. Would it really be such a big deal if anyone *had* realised the truth behind his quietness tonight? If any of my friends had known that he was struggling to hear, they would have made a huge effort to ensure he could, we *all* would.

I know it isn't as simple as sounds, he's obviously got some issues around this and I feel like I shouldn't push too intensely and let him talk in his own time, so I venture gently, 'Is there anything that helps?'

'Staying hydrated. That's why I've always got a bottle of water with me. And the reason those crisps were so bad was because it supposedly helps to avoid salt, but—'

So many little things. It's like a crushing realisation and it makes me grab his arm to pull him to a halt, put the boxes down the on the pavement and throw my arms around him again.

This affects *every* aspect of his life and he's fighting *so* hard to keep it hidden. There are so many things about him that didn't make sense, but now do, and I don't know what to do other than hug him to bits. I knew he was hiding something, and all along I've thought it was something underhanded, and I had absolutely no idea it would be something like this.

He laughs at the unexpected hug. His arms slide around my back and he bends until he can lift me off the floor. 'What's got into you tonight? It's just a... thing... I have to deal with. You don't have to hug me to within an inch of my life.'

I squeeze him tighter and nod hard, knowing he'll feel it, because if there's one thing I desperately *do* need to do tonight, it's hug him.

I feel his face shift through my giant scarf like his smile is widening, and we cling onto each other for a little while, until something changes and I can sense his body language tightening up.

'And you certainly don't have to feel sorry for me.' He abruptly plonks me down and stalks away, and I have to grab my box and package and catch up to him.

'I'm not hugging you because I feel sorry for you,' I explain when I realise why his body language changed so abruptly. 'I feel bad for all the things I didn't know. I accused you of being a spoilt only child when you asked me to talk *to* you. I've said – and thought – so many things about you because I didn't understand.'

'I don't mind that. I'd rather people think things like that about me than know the truth.'

He's clammed up now we've gone back to walking side by side, and I'm making an effort to turn towards him every time I speak, determined to ensure he doesn't stop opening up yet, even if *he* is more than ready to. 'Do you get the other things as well? The vertigo and tinnitus?'

'They come and go. Bouts of vertigo usually pass quickly. Tinnitus drives me mad for weeks on end and then stops until the next time.'

'Why didn't you tell me?' I ask the question that's screaming the loudest to be answered, because everything would have been so much easier if he'd told me straight away, but what he said about accommodating his failings is replaying in my head too, and I feel like he's got a distorted vision of how people might react.

'Are you kidding? I don't tell anyone.' He lets out a scoff and then looks worried. 'And you can't either. I don't want *anyone* to know about this, ever. You have to promise me, Liss. No one can know.'

'I promise.' I rush to reassure him because he sounds so *urgent*, and every doubt he's ever had about trusting me is flashing across his face all at once.

'Thank you.' His sigh of relief is the loudest I've ever heard. 'Apart from my mother, you're the *only* person I've ever told. I haven't got my head around talking about it yet.'

I try not to think about how special that makes me feel. I know we've worked together for a while now, but he could've pushed on with denying it tonight. He *chose* to let me in. 'How can that be?'

He glances at me with a raised eyebrow, like it's a question I should already know the answer to. 'Because I don't want anyone knowing my weaknesses, obviously.'

'It's not a weakness, is it? It's a... difference.'

'People take advantage of differences. People use them against you. I was a bullied kid – I refuse to be a bullied adult as well.'

'But people must know. People you work with. Friends. I figured it out in the few weeks we've known each other.'

'Yeah, but *this* situation is unusual. I don't usually work so closely with someone for so many weeks. I'm usually alone in my office. I can cover it in face-to-face meetings and there's almost nothing that can't be achieved through emails at best, or video calls at worst. I can get away with delegating other staff to take phone calls for me. Trust me, *no one* knows. I wouldn't still be working there if they did.'

'Yeah, but—'

He checks his phone again before interrupting me. 'Look, I appreciate that you care, but we're not far from the house for the teddy bear, and it's strange to talk about it. I'm not sure I've adjusted to sharing this yet, so can we just...'

He doesn't finish the sentence but I understand what he

means. 'Leave it for now?' I suggest, putting a strong emphasis on the 'for now' part.

He looks over and gives me that wide, unguarded smile again. 'You're consistently tenacious, I'll give you that.'

I take that as a compliment and give him an expectant look until he laughs. 'Fine. For *now*.'

18

Once we reach the street where the teddy-wanting little boy and his pyromaniac brother live, I unfurl my scarf and settle it in a complicated tangle that goes over my head and covers my face from the nose down, and Warren watches me with an impressed look, and then bends down to let me do the same with his cape, giving us both a bit of protection from doorbell cameras and nosy neighbours.

We stop to identify the right house, and sneak along in the middle of the road like a pair of burglars, hoping to avoid detection.

'Can I?' Warren takes the teddy bear box from me when we reach the right place, and I look for somewhere to hide, but it's an exposed house with a short path and no fencing or hedging.

My only option is a set of two wheelie bins on the pavement outside, surrounded by black bags of rubbish, but I'll take it over being spotted and having to explain who we are and why posting a wish down a well has led to this.

'Put it down, knock, and *run*,' I whisper-shout at him. 'We *cannot* get caught.'

It's not my first rodeo at this, I hand-delivered a few wishes in the early days, but once the others got involved and someone suggested posting out wishes was a much more sensible solution, I haven't done it since, and this is bringing back memories of good old days and reminding me of how special this is, and what a privilege it is to have such an insight into children's hopes and dreams.

He nods and readjusts the red cape hiding most of his face, and I sneak over to the hiding place behind the bins and crouch down to stay out of sight, and watch as he creeps up the path on tiptoes, taking such comically wide strides that he may as well be wearing a black-and-white-striped top and an eye mask. He silently puts the box on the doorstep, knocks loudly, and rushes back out of the garden and skids to a halt behind the bins.

I yank him down until he's crouching next to me as a light comes on in the front hallway, and a woman wearing a dressing gown opens the door and looks down at the box on the step curiously, reads the label and then yells, 'Jaden!'

Moments later, a little boy wearing Paddington pyjamas appears and the mum points to the box, and he kneels down and tears into it excitedly, and then lets out a squeal of delight as he pulls the teddy out and hugs it to his chest.

'Where did that come from? Did you take my credit card and order that?' his mum asks.

'Noooo! It's what I wanted! I wished for him!' It's a big teddy, not much smaller than Jaden himself, and he pulls back and looks at the teddy and touches the cardboard tag around its neck like he can't believe it's real, and the porch light above catches the sight of happy tears glistening in his eyes.

'Oh, you silly thing.' The mum ruffles his hair and he buries his face in the bear's brown fur.

He babbles something about the museum on a school trip to

Ever After Street to his mum, but it's muffled from how tightly he's clinging to the bear, and I should be watching the little boy, but I can't tear my eyes away from Warren, who's got his lip held between his teeth and is absolutely mesmerised by the scene playing out on the doorstep in front of us.

'Thank you, wishing well!' Jaden calls out.

'Wishing well, my foot. I'm going to check my bank statement,' his mum mutters as she picks up the empty box and herds him back inside with his new bear.

When I glance at Warren again, his eyes are still on the doorway and they're damp too.

I reach over and touch his hand. 'You okay?'

He blinks fast and shakes his head, but it seems more like he doesn't know what to say, even though he's grinning from ear to ear too. 'Greatest thing I've ever done in my life.'

He leans over to press a big 'mwah' to my cheek and it takes me by such surprise that I squeak and overbalance. I grab at him to keep myself upright, and end up with both hands behind his neck, holding him in place against me, and once his arms have steadied me, and we're both rebalanced and safely crouching, he touches his lips to my cheek again, and it's nothing like the big 'mwah' it was just now.

This time it's a soft, gentle kiss, with purpose behind it. His nose rubs against my skin and he rests his forehead against my hair and pushes out a breath, so close I can feel his every blink, and it might feel vaguely romantic if we weren't crouched behind overflowing wheelie bins and a pile of binbags.

He doesn't move away until we've kept an eye on the windows for a few minutes to make sure no one's looking out, and only when I've deemed it safe to move do we run past the house and dash up the street.

'We actually brought someone to tears of joy.' He still sounds awestruck as we stop to take our scarf and cape off and put them back to how they should be.

'Jaden isn't the only one it brought to happy tears.'

'Oh, I'm an emotional wreck, you know that.' He laughs a thick-sounding unstable laugh. 'That was the best thing I've ever felt. I *love* that wishing well. I love that you do this. I love that you gave *me* a chance to do this. Thank you.'

'Thank you for helping. It's been a long time since I hand-delivered wishes. It makes a difference. Makes it feel more special. Reminds me of *why* I value the wishing well so much.'

He checks his phone again to make sure we're on the right route to the next house, and then turns around and walks backwards.

'Warren, don't. You don't need to—'

'It's easier, I promise. I don't want you to feel like you have to keep stopping and looking over at me, and I don't want to not-talk to you. It's fine, you don't have to worry.'

At a loss for what else to do, and feeling a need to hang on to what feels like an unspoken connection between us tonight, I reach out and take his hand. 'At least I can *try* to keep you upright.'

He laughs loudly. 'Yeah, this is not weird at all. Not least because if I did fall over, you'd never be able to hold me up, all it would achieve is pulling you down on top of me.'

'Worse things have happened.' I give him a smile, but I can still feel the imprint of his lips against my cheek, and I'm certain he realises that this is nothing more than an excuse to touch him, because being with him tonight is making me feel alive.

'What's your favourite ever wish?' His fingers squeeze mine, even though my eyes are glued to the pavement, convinced he's going to fall down an open manhole at any moment.

I give it some thought. 'There was a kid who used seven

pieces of paper to give a long and complicated breakdown of why school term times and school holiday times should be reversed so kids only have to go to school for six weeks in the summer, which to be fair, was such a brilliant and well-thought-out essay that he could've presented it in parliament and tried to get the government on board with his plan. And there was one girl who said she wished she could live in the museum, and one who must've had a wish granted because the piece of paper just read, *Thank you, wishing well! You're the best! I love you!'*

'That's really sweet.'

'What would you have wished for as a kid?' I give his fingers a squeeze because I haven't let go of his hand yet, but I'm hyper-aware that I'm edging around the wish he made on his first day here – the one he doesn't know I read. I can't openly ask him why he doesn't find any meaning in life, but the more I get to know him, the more obvious the answer is becoming.

'Honestly?'

I nod.

'I don't know. I never believed in things like magic and wishes and fairytales. If I wanted something, my parents tried to "instil a good work ethic" by making me earn it in one way or another – household chores or good marks at school or some-thing. Christmas and birthday gifts were always of the practical variety – never toys. Everything was very sensible. I can't imagine what the young me would have made of a supposedly magical wishing well or what I would possibly have asked of it. I guess if I could go back now, I'd ask for a childhood where wishes and fairytales were commonplace and to grow up knowing what it felt like to believe in magic. To feel like I feel right now, but thirty years ago. How's that?'

I can barely speak around the lump in my throat. 'The

perfect answer. *You* are exactly why it's so important that we get to do this.'

'So kids don't turn out like me?'

I know he's winding me up, but I give him a scathing look anyway. 'Exactly. Not that how you turned out is a bad thing, obviously.'

'Ah, so you want *more* kids to grow up to be evil gerbils without souls?'

I blush at how harshly I judged him at first and his grin gets even wider because that's exactly what he was aiming for. 'Every child should get to experience hunting for fairies and looking for magical lands at the top of big trees, and believing in whimsy and daydreams and letting their imaginations run wild.'

He uses his grip on my hand to tug me closer and then turns and falls into step beside me, finally facing the right way again. He drops an arm around my shoulders and leans his head towards mine. 'Agree. Very much agree.'

The closeness shuts out the chill in the breeze of the November night, and I'm quite disappointed when it's only a few more minutes before we reach the street of the boy who wished for the cape, identify the right house, and re-do the knotted tangle of our face coverings again.

At least the second house has got a wall, and a creaky gate that announces our arrival like a Tannoy system, and a dog inside that starts barking instantly. Warren insists on taking the package to the door again, so I crouch behind the wall and watch as he runs up the path, presses the doorbell, and I can't help giggling at how much the barking dog makes his pace quicken as he flails out of the gate and scrambles into a hiding spot beside me just as the door opens and a little boy comes out, picks up the package with an 'Oooooooooh!' and takes it back inside.

'Not gonna lie, I hoped he was going to open it and try it on right there and then.'

'Why, so you could compare capes?' I tug his playfully where it's starting to unravel from the knot hiding his face.

'Mine is better, obviously.' He leans down to whisper to me. 'I've always thought capes were more becoming on people who are thirty-something years too old to wear them.'

I'm fighting off an increasingly familiar urge to hug him again. How could an evil gerbil with no soul turn out to be *this* adorable?

We're on the right side of the house for a quick getaway, but the curtains are open and the lights are on in the living room, and within minutes, we're able to see the boy inside, zooming around with the cape flapping behind him and an excitable Labrador jumping up at him, barking loudly, and probably wondering what the heck is going on.

'Best night ever.' Warren pushes himself up and holds a hand out to pull me up too, and even though I'm quite capable of getting up from a crouching position on my own, I give in to the temptation to touch him again.

He doesn't let go until we get safely out of sight and drop hands to pull our face coverings down. As soon as his cape is back to being over his shoulders, he holds his hand out again and I take it instantly.

He walks beside me this time, swinging our hands between us, but we're both meandering, wandering slowly, putting off heading back towards the museum because that will mean saying goodnight and not holding his hand any longer.

'I don't want to go back to work,' he says eventually. 'Can we just stay out here giving presents to kids all night?'

'I'd like that, but we're all out of nearby wishes.' As I say it, my eyes fall on a streetside hot drinks van at the edge of a park, and I nudge him to look in the right direction. 'However, we *could* reward ourselves with a hot drink and take the scenic route through the park... If you weren't in any rush to get back.'

'You had me at hot drink on a cold autumn night... It's freezing out here. Someone needs to teach Disney princes to wear scarves and warm coats.'

We left in such a hurry that he hasn't got his wallet with him, which gives me free rein to choose the most autumnal drink possible, and I order us a Black Forest hot chocolate each, and we head through the iron gates of the park and meander along a leaf-strewn path in comfortable silence.

'It's going to get worse as you get older?' I say eventually, and he groans.

'When we agreed to leave it "for now", what I really meant was "for forever".' He automatically knows I'm talking about his hearing and I'm pretty sure he knew I was never going to leave it very long before questioning him again, and he probably would have refused the drink if he *really* minded.

He sips his hot chocolate and looks over at me contemplatively. 'If you hadn't just bought me the most autumnal drink of all time, I'd tell you to shut up.'

'No, you wouldn't.'

'No, I wouldn't.' His laugh turns into a long sigh. 'It *has* got worse as I've got older, I know that. When I was in my twenties, apart from a few rounds of vertigo, it barely made an impact on my life, but now I'm in my forties, the hearing in my left ear has slowly declined, and there's no cure, nothing that can improve things.'

'What about hearing aids?'

'I'd have to retire first because my mother would sack me for coming to work with a hearing aid in my ear.'

I don't realise my mouth has fallen open until a moth nearly flies straight in. I bat it away, but I feel like I've missed a part of that sentence and it doesn't make sense without the missing part. 'You can't be serious.'

He does a noncommittal shrug, and we pass a bench surrounded by piles of crispy leaves, and I reach out to grab his hand again and pull him over to it. 'Sit. Unpack that for me.'

He raises an eyebrow.

'Please?'

He's trying not to smile as he lets me drag him the few steps across the grass and push him down onto the wooden bench.

'It's a weakness, Liss.' His foot kicks at one of the leaf piles collected around the base of it.

Goosebumps break out across my body and I reach over and take his hand. 'No, it's not. Surely you *make* it into a weakness by pretending you can hear when you can't.'

'I *can* hear, I've just got reduced hearing in my left ear. It's usually fine, but it becomes noticeable if there are a lot of people, or background noise, or loud music playing or something. It's not a big deal.'

If there's one thing I know about someone who tries *so* hard to keep it hidden, it's that it's a *much* bigger deal than he's letting on.

'I have a disability,' he says eventually, focusing intently on a brown leaf blowing along the path in front of us rather than looking at me. 'Do you know how hard it is to admit that? And to wear a hearing aid would be to *show* that. Everyone I encounter, every day, would *know*, instantly. You can't begin to imagine what that would be like.'

'No, admittedly, I can't, but many people can. Many people overcome disabilities of every sort, every day, and are stronger for it.'

'I'm not many people. In my family, a disability is a failing, a failing equals failure, and failure is weakness. Any form of weakness is unacceptable. In my world, weakness makes you the most likely to be picked off and ripped to shreds, like those wildlife programmes you see where a gang of cheetahs surround a herd of wildebeest and attack only the weakest calf. You don't put your failings on show for all to see – you hide them.'

Despite the tangent into David Attenborough territory, it *hurts* to hear the disdainful way he talks about himself. It's the kind of attitude that makes me wonder about his mother, and how anyone can grow up feeling like a disability should be hidden and masked, rather than doing something that might improve it. 'Weakness is human. Everyone is different. Everyone has many forms of abilities and disabilities. None of us know what people we encounter in our everyday lives are going through, but everyone is overcoming *something*. Wearing a hearing aid wouldn't make you any less of a person.'

'It would make me less of an opponent. It would give my opposition something to pick up on and take advantage of. A way to undermine me. A weakness they can chip away at. If anyone knew I had a problem with my hearing, they could hold it over me. They could use it to gain their own advantage. People could create issues or lie about things that have been said and blame it on me for mishearing. I have a lot of board meetings. I wine and dine a lot of investors. I have property disputes that I have to win. I *must* appear sharp and on the ball, and I can't let people think there's something inferior about me.'

I sigh. 'Does your life have to be about nothing but opponents and opposition? Fighting, winning, losing, failing. Can't you just... live?'

He meets my eyes again and holds my gaze. 'You... this place... it makes me wish I could.'

He sounds surprised by the words, like he didn't intend them to come out quite so vehemently, and he takes another sip of his drink and looks away, his eyes distant and his mind clearly anywhere but here.

The wind and the cape have knocked his dark hair loose and it's blown wild by the wind and looking gorgeously dishevelled for a change, rather than held down by styling product, and it's incredibly hard *not* to reach over and stroke my fingers through it.

He looks over his shoulder at me. 'Would you have treated me differently if you'd noticed a hearing aid in my ear? On that first day, when I had to come in and take over your museum and present myself as confident and in charge and make sure you knew there was no choice? Would it have made you see me in a different light? Would you have felt the slightest bit of pity? Shown me extra kindness because of it?'

'No. But I would have been more mindful that you couldn't hear everything exactly the same way I could.'

'Of my limitations, you mean.'

I go to deny it but the words stop halfway, because I can see his point, and yet... 'But part of your limitations is not being able to hear clearly, and if a hearing aid would improve that, then you'd be in a stronger position anyway.'

'But everyone would know I had an impairment.'

'But it would *be* less of an impairment.'

He huffs like he can see my point too. 'My mother would not allow me to continue running our Midlands branch if I put my impairment on show for all to see. Hearing aids are for elderly people. It's something I'll look into when I retire.'

'You're forty-one! You're not retiring for another twenty-something years.' It makes my thoughts return to his mother again. Him at twenty-two, diagnosed with something that he must've known would have a big impact on his life. If she was the only person he opened up to, I can't imagine how any parent could encourage him to hide it, to be embarrassed, and treat it as something shameful. Those are the kind of shackles that are hard to shrug off, even so many years later.

I try a different angle. 'You must have meetings with serious, scary businessmen who wear glasses all the time. Glasses are an aid to an impairment, no different to a hearing aid. Do their glasses make you think any less of them?'

'Glasses are more socially acceptable. Hearing aids in a man my age are an anomaly, something people would notice. Not the norm.'

'Be the change you want to see in the world. Change the norm.'

'You're the type of person who can do that. I'm not. I'm just a shy bullied kid who goes through every week desperately trying to come out unscathed at the end of it, without having to explain intensely personal things about myself to strangers who would undoubtedly feel entitled to ask.' He sits back and looks over at me. 'I appreciate you trying to help, but we're from different worlds, and mine isn't like yours.'

No wonder he's struggling to find any meaning in life. He sounds so defeated, completely and utterly fed up of every little thing, and the urge to hug him is unreal.

'I'm sure they make incredibly discreet ones these days. Technology has advanced so much that they're no longer the squealing brown things that everyone's granddad was always fiddling with.' I know I'm probably pushing too hard, but this feels like something that would make his life so much better if he was open to it. 'If you wanted to try it while you're here, while you don't have to go into the office and face your horrible "opponents"...' I do the air quotes because, admittedly, I don't know much about his job, but it sounds *awful*. 'If you could get fitted for a hearing aid, being here could be an opportunity to try it out and see how much it would help... No one on Ever After Street would think less of you. If they knew you like I know you, they'd like you for exactly who you are, and there is nothing in your ear that would make the slightest difference to that.'

'I believe that.' He pushes a hand through his hair, looking like even the thought has made him nervous. 'I already have one but I've never been brave enough to wear it. Maybe I'll give it some thought.'

'And if anyone was to say anything, they'll have me to deal with. I have Rapunzel's frying pan and I'm not afraid to use it.'

He laughs so hard that he throws his head back against the bench, the lines around his eyes crinkling up as he rolls his head to look at me. 'I think you might be the most wonderful person I've ever met.'

I expect him to turn serious and sit up, but he stays as he is, holding my gaze, and instead holds the hot chocolate cup up and examines the writing on the side. 'Are we sure this hot chocolate isn't spiked with alcohol? I didn't mean to say that. I meant, um... I'm going to have to watch *Tangled* now, aren't I?'

'One of my favourites. We could watch it together...'

There's something about his smile when it's so completely unfiltered, spontaneous, and like a burst of sunshine on a dark autumn night, and I wring my empty cup between my fingers to keep them occupied, which might be the only thing preventing me from reaching over and dragging his lips to mine.

Eventually, the chill of the night air gets to both of us and when we get up, he leans over and brushes my hair aside, and then ducks down until he can touch his lips to my forehead. 'Thank you for not making me feel like there's something wrong with me.'

'I'm so sorry there's anyone in your life who ever has. Every part of you is *you*, Warren. No one should be picking and choosing which bits to love. Everything about you makes you *you*, and *you* are... not a bad person to know.'

I hear his breath catch and he pushes it out shakily, and the atmosphere feels charged, like he wants to say something but can't find the right words.

We throw our cups in a nearby bin and when he holds his arm out to me, I can't resist slipping my hand through the crook of his elbow and tugging him close to me, and not another word needs to be said, because I think he might be the most wonderful person I've ever met too, and there is no ability, disability, or otherwise that could change that.

19

'Liss, I hate to state the obvious, but are you aware that you're drilling a hole into the ceiling?'

From halfway up the stepladder, I lift my safety goggles and turn around to face Warren where he's standing in the doorway of the Fairytale Homes hall. 'Oh my God, am I really? How did I get up here?'

He laughs as he comes over and reaches up to put a steadying hand on my lower back as I push myself upwards to inspect the hole. It's gone all the way through and into the floor cavity of the landing above, so I start to climb down and he holds a hand out to help me. I slide my wood-dusty hand into his, even though I've managed to get down off many, many ladders without assistance before now.

'I'm trying to work and all I can hear is this burring vibration coming from below.'

'Oh, sorry. I didn't think it would disturb you on the third floor.' It's after closing time and I assumed he'd be going home soon anyway, but I've got a project planned for tonight so I'm not going anywhere yet.

'No worries. Your burring vibration is more interesting than my work.'

It's not the first time I've heard little throwaway comments like that, but it's the first time that quite so much contempt has laced his voice when talking about it.

'Dare I ask what you're doing?' He lets go of my hand and brushes wood dust from his, and I take my goggles off and shake my hair out.

'I'm building a beanstalk.'

He laughs like he thinks I'm joking, but I get an idea. 'Actually, seeing as you're not busy now, *we're* building a beanstalk. I could do with the help.'

'Do people not traditionally grow beanstalks?'

'Not this kind.' I can't help grinning as I nod towards my boxes of craft materials. 'This is a floor-to-ceiling beanstalk with a giant living at the top of it. The hole is so we've got something to attach it to, I've just got to go and take a landing floorboard up so I can put a hook in place.'

He glances between me, the hole in the ceiling, and the craft boxes with a look of both wonder *and* trepidation. 'I've never heard anything like the things you come out with. You never stop. You'll never give up on this place, will you?'

'No, of course I won't.'

'Neither will I, I promise you that.' He takes a step closer and reaches over to brush a bit of wood dust out of my hair and then tucks it back with a wistful look in his eyes. 'We're in a good position now. You can pay the extra rent. The gift shop looks fantastic and every time I come downstairs, you're running between that and the front desk. The interest in the escaped exhibits is increasing every day. My company can't... I mean, they *won't*... want to change things now. We're bringing in revenue and gaining fans left, right, and centre on the internet. That alone would create more backlash than they'd want to deal with. We've done what we set out to achieve.'

There's something in his voice that still doesn't sound as confident as it should, and it intensifies the niggling doubt in the back of my mind. Things might have improved for Colours of the Wind, but we are *not* bringing in more money than a cinema complex would, and we never will be. I try to let his words reassure me. *He* is the property expert, after all. He's going to know what his company wants, and if he says we've done what we needed to then I should take his words at face value. I trust him so much more now I know what he's been hiding was nothing to do with his job or the museum.

He never actually said he wasn't busy, but he seems happy to get involved, and I can't help watching as he pulls his brown-and-cream-striped jumper off, revealing a black long-sleeved top underneath, and he pulls the sleeves up to his elbows, oblivious to the fact I'm ogling him, but those forearms really do deserve to be showcased *far* more often.

My mouth has gone dry and I only realise I'm staring when he claps his hands together and asks what I want him to do.

'Right, I've just got a wholesale order of jumbo pipe cleaners, so we're going to wind them together for vines to build the framework for a beanstalk from the floor to the ceiling. Then we're going to add giant paper leaves, paper tendrils, crepe paper flowers, glittery oversized beans painted in bright colours, and I've got some cotton wool for clouds at the top, and a big planter for the bottom so it looks like it's actually growing out of a pot.'

'If anyone had asked me, two months ago, if I'd ever build a beanstalk, I would have cackled at the thought, but you make beanstalk-building seem normal.'

I laugh out loud, giggling until he meets my eyes again and it suddenly feels like the room has shrunk until I'm forced to take a step closer to him, and it would be so easy to reach out, tangle my fingers in the thermal material of that black top and haul him down until I could kiss him... We blink at each other for a few moments, his eyes are on my lips and this time, it's *not* because he's reading them, and my fingers twitch with the urge to reach out, but I force myself to take a breath and look away.

Rather than confronting what that was, I grab an armful of green pipe cleaners and shove them at him, and he grunts at the unexpected weight of the humungous things. 'Start twisting the dark green and light green ones together for structural integrity and colour variegation,' I tell him, and then pick up my electric screwdriver and metal hook and run upstairs.

On the second-floor landing, I unscrew the floorboard and lift it so I can fit the hook into the cavity that will give us something to attach the top of the beanstalk to, and then because everything is better with tea, I go up to the third floor and make us a cuppa each in the kitchen.

'I've never seen pipe cleaners like these,' Warren says when I get back to the hall carrying two mugs and holding a packet of biscuits between my teeth. 'I didn't think anyone used them outside of nursery school crafts.'

They're hefty, sturdy, and furry, and the second I saw them, I knew they'd make perfect vines for a giant beanstalk with some creative twisting, which he's got down to a fine art in the five minutes I've been gone.

His double-thickness vines will form the base of the beanstalk, which will get narrower as it goes up, so I put the mug and biscuits down, and start using singular pipe cleaners, twisted lengthwise, and start creating the top section so we can, somehow, meet in the middle.

'So I know I missed a lot of the discussion the other night, but one thing I heard loud and clear was the wedding stuff...' he says after we've both got into the swing of twisting beanstalk vines around themselves.

'Conveniently, that was the one part I hoped you'd missed.' I groan, having also hoped that if he *had* heard it, he'd have the courtesy to never mention it again.

He laughs. 'You have my utmost sympathy. There's nothing worse than a wedding as a single person. They should rename them "pity-fests" and be done with it.'

It's a welcome giggle and I appreciate the solidarity, even if I'd have appreciated him pretending he hadn't heard it *more*.

'This is the quiet guy from the castle who brought the glass slippers back and the girl who makes dresses in The Cinderella Shop?'

'Witt and Sadie, yes.' I appreciate him making an effort to get to know my friends, especially when it's obvious that most of the Ever After Street shopkeepers are still hostile towards him, and I wouldn't blame him for not even trying.

'They're not really doing mandatory plus ones, are they?'

'I think it's mostly for my benefit.' I put down one section of beanstalk when it's reached two foot long and start twisting pipe cleaners together for the next part. 'Everyone else around here has found their perfect match, been set up, or paired off in some other way in the past few years, apart from me. I'm the last single one left on Ever After Street, and I suspect they conspired to think this would be the perfect excuse to search their phone books, friends, siblings, colleagues, and long-lost acquaintances far and wide to find me a pity date.'

'Trust me, anyone lucky enough to be on a date with you, it would *not* be out of pity.'

My hands freeze on my beanstalk section and I look over at him, trying to work out if he's pulling my leg or not, but he doesn't sound jokey. 'Thank you. That's a lovely thing to say.'

'I could come. If you want a way to get them off your back, I mean. Not out of pity. Just because it would make me feel like the luckiest man in the world, and—' He hesitates like he didn't intend to say that, and then tries to backpedal. 'I meant, like I said, I sympathise with anyone forced to attend a wedding alone, I've been there too many times, and we could do it together, poke fun at all the daft traditions... er, if the others would let me in, I know I'm persona non grata around here, but... Sorry, I've become really bad at thinking before I speak. I didn't mean you should go with me, you're probably sick of the sight of me, I just meant...' He trails off like even he doesn't know what he really meant.

'I'd like that.' I meet his eyes and then amend my choice of words. 'I'd *love* that.'

He smiles that wide, unguarded smile again, the one that blazes across his face like the sun peeking out from behind a cloud on a dull day, and I can already imagine the pitch of Mickey's squeal when I tell her I've got a wedding date, and the others can stop desperately searching the passing acquaintances of their partner's brother's colleague's neighbour's ice-sculpting classmate's barber, and even though it's not a *date* date, it should still work for getting everyone to leave me content in my singleton status.

'It's not until December. You won't still be here, will you?'

'I can come back. It's *only* a hundred-mile round trip. Worth every penny of the petrol costs.'

I grin at the curious throwback. Last time he said that, it was sarcastic, but this time it's genuine.

'Besides, I think I might miss you when I'm not here any more.'

'I might miss you too.'

His smile gets impossibly wider, and we hold each other's gaze across the room and that urge to march over there and haul him into a kiss tingles in my toes like they're trying to propel me across the room, and my fingertips twitch like they're encouraging me to grab him and snog the living daylights out of him, but at the same time, my feet are – thankfully – glued to the floor and stop me doing anything I would almost definitely regret.

Eventually he shakes his head and picks up another pair of pipe cleaners. 'I'd definitely miss making beanstalks.'

'A regular occurrence round here. Not beanstalks specifically, but you know, crafty fairytale things. Your artistic touch will be missed.'

He looks at the beanstalk vine in his hand, but seems like he's looking straight through it. 'Yeah, it will.'

We get on with twisting our vines until we're surrounded by sections of beanstalk that will hopefully equal about ten foot when joined together. The mugs are empty and half the packet of digestives has gone before Warren asks his next awkward question. 'Why is it that the others are trying so hard? Are they just overbearing or do you really have such bad luck in relationships?'

'Me?' I say, like he could possibly mean anyone else when there's only the two of us here.

I'm still twisting pipe cleaners to join the upper two sections of beanstalk together, and he's moved on to sitting on the floor and putting his artistic talents to good use by cutting giant leaf shapes out of green paper, and he nods without looking up.

It's not that I'm uncomfortable about being single, but how desperate my friends are for me *not* to be single is getting increasingly frustrating. *Every* interaction lately seems to circle back to it in some way, and it's making me feel even more invisible. I know they mean well, but they aren't listening to my repeated requests to leave my love life up to me, and I think Warren will understand that.

'Mickey would tell you that my standards are too high and I'm searching for a Disney prince in a world where a Phil Mitchell lookalike is about the best you can hope for, but I just... I don't want to settle. It's a big deal to share your life with someone. I know what happens when someone you love is ripped away and it's always made me hesitant to be open to relationships. If you love someone, you can also lose them, and it takes a lot of bravery to put yourself in that position. I don't want to open myself up to that kind of heartbreak if it's not life-changing, world-shaking *love*. I've always wanted to meet someone who gives me the feeling I got when I was young and I watched Princess Aurora dancing in the forest with Prince Philip to "Once Upon a Dream", or when I watched Cinderella spinning around the ballroom with Prince Charming, or when Prince Eric dives into the ocean to save Ariel even though *he* can't breathe underwater, but I've never met anyone who sparked butterflies *and* didn't turn out to be a creep after another couple of dates, and I'm fine with that. If the right guy falls from the sky and lands in front of me, great. If he doesn't, that's also fine. Wherever we are is where we're supposed to be, and however things work out, that's right for *us*, even if our friends don't agree.'

He looks up at me from his sitting position and a smile spreads slowly outwards. 'I like that. That's a really nice attitude.'

'How about you?' I watch his nimble fingers slicing the knife around the leaf stencil he's made from cardboard like it's an art form. 'Why hasn't someone snapped you up? Tall, dark-haired, blue-eyed, and handsome... in the right slant of light,' I add quickly. God forbid he gets the impression that I fancy him. Whenever I'm around him, I go back to feeling like a teenage girl with a crush on the hottest boy in school who'd be laughed at if anyone found out.

'...partially deaf, hell of a chip on my shoulder, mother issues, have occasionally been compared to a demonic gerbil... Yeah, it's a mystery for the ages.'

'Sarcastic. Artistic.' I nod to the paper leaves. 'Fancy car. Good taste in suits and even better taste in autumn jumpers.' Nice forearms. Beautiful smile. Lovely eyes. Better not say those last three out loud.

He's laughing so hard that he's almost doubled over. 'Oh, Liss, don't flatter me so much, I might start thinking...' He looks up and meets my eyes, and even though my cheeks are blazing, I don't shy away from his gaze, because he *is* funny and sarcastic, but there's a little bit too much depth behind his self-deprecation, and I *want* him to know that he's lovely, and although I thought the worst of him at first, getting to know him changed that.

He shakes his head and goes back to concentrating on the leaves. 'I've never been open to it. My mother always told me not to fall in love. Drummed it into me all the time – the worst thing you can ever do is open your heart. It's not worth the heartache. When my dad died, it *broke* her. She wasn't the same person afterwards. It was like she didn't know who she was without him, and she still doesn't. She still hasn't reached the "happy memories" stage of grief. Instead, she resents him for dying, and for the impact it had on her. She says that meeting him was the worst thing she ever did because losing him was the worst thing she's ever had to go through. None of this "grief is the price we pay for love" thing. She says love is a myth, a fairytale that only the gullible believe in, and if you're going to fall in love at all, it should be a mutually beneficial business transaction, and feelings should never come into it.'

'And you took that to heart?' I bite my lip. I might never have fallen really and truly in love myself, but it's demoralising to hear anyone talk about it like that, and I hope I never have to meet his mother because I'm fairly sure I would dislike her immensely.

'I did. I grew up being told that the worst thing my mum had ever done was fall in love. That it was a mistake I must never repeat. I've dated, but nothing that's ever gone anywhere. Like you said, it would take a *lot* for me to let someone in, and anyone who could get past the chip on my shoulder and the mother issues would have to be someone *spectacular* with the patience of a *very* tolerant saint, and I wouldn't even mind if they did look like Phil Mitchell.'

I giggle, but he continues. 'Did your dad ever get over losing your mum?'

'No. He struggled with the grief for the rest of his life, but he was firmly in the "your mum was the best thing that ever happened to me, being married to her was my wildest and most wonderful adventure, and I wouldn't change it for the world" camp. He never even considered another relationship, but he always encouraged us girls to look for someone who made our hearts soar.'

'A nice thought. My mother lost her heart when my father died and it made her heartless in every sense of the word. It's nice to think that grief didn't affect everyone in that way.'

'You didn't lose yours.'

'It feels like I did, sometimes. Until I came here and *you* reminded me of the things that matter in life, and that some people are proud of having a big, beautiful heart and sharing it openly with the world.'

I'm chewing the inside of my cheek so hard that I can taste blood, and my need to hug him must be tangible because he looks at me like he can sense it, and changes the subject quickly.

I'm balanced on the top rung of the stepladder, having attached the top section of the beanstalk to the hook in the ceiling, I'm now tying the next section onto it, and Warren has moved on to following instructions to make red and white bean flowers out of crepe paper, and we're both quietly concentrating until I reach the bottom, and he comes over to help me bury the base of the beanstalk into the planter and fill it with gravel.

Mickey found some oversized bean-shaped objects that were probably once part of a children's playset, and the two of us have already painted them in sparkly pastel colours, and I'm intending to scatter some in the pot and hang others from the beanstalk itself, but Warren picks up a handful and tosses them in his palm.

'We could hang these all around Ever After Street to advertise the new beanstalk exhibit. It could be part of the social media campaign. "Have you spotted a magic bean? What could it mean?"'

I love how much he's getting involved in all this, and mainly, I love feeling like we're on the same side and both have the museum's best interests at heart.

'Are beans in season? As in, what time of year would you plant them?'

'I don't know. Autumn-sowing ones, I guess...?' I say questioningly, wondering where he's going with the thought.

'We could give away little bags of beans for planting! Get some small paper bags with the museum logo on, fill them with beans and put them in this planter with a "one per customer, help yourself" sign. That would be a fun little extra, right?'

'Now you're getting it,' I say with a grin, thrilled by the

change in his attitude since the early days. 'If property development falls through, you've got a future in magical museum management.'

'Despite the impressive alliteration,' he says with a laugh that turns serious, 'I've been in my job for twenty years, I'm too old for change now.'

'You already have changed. You wanted to charge visitors for picking a flower when you first arrived, now you're voluntarily suggesting that we give away seeds and happily spending your evening building a beanstalk. You're not the man you were two months ago, Warren Berrington.'

'Ahh, this is by far the most fun I've had in ages.' His jovial laugh sounds like he's deliberately avoiding the implications of what I said. 'The only thing I'm disappointed by is that I can't actually climb it. And *please* tell me that you're going to put up a sign telling people not to do exactly that, because if there's one thing I've learnt about your visitors, it's that they *will*.'

'Of course. I'd love you to draw it actually. "Fee-fi-fo-fum, don't wake the giant by climbing on the beanstalk!"'

He's blushing again as he agrees, and I want to make the most of his artistic abilities while he's here, because any signs will never look as good as he can make them once he's gone.

The thought brings all sorts of other unpleasant thoughts to mind, about how much I've enjoyed his company recently and what the end of his tenure here will mean for the museum in a wider sense, as well as how much I'll miss him. I try not to think about it while he goes back to poking holes through the magic beans to hang them up, and I wrap strips of paper around a pencil to make curly tendrils to pin onto the beanstalk.

Eventually I gather an armful of paper leaves with wire ties to tie them onto the vines, and he drops the beans and rushes over to help me, and I'm quite touched when he insists, even though I tell him that there isn't much in this museum that *hasn't* been constructed by me on a ladder with an armful of things.

'Is there a Disney movie where the prince helps the princess up a ladder and then catches her heroically when she falls off?' He takes the stack of leaves out of my hand and steadies the ladder while I climb to the top of it using *both* hands.

'No, but it happens in every rom-com I've ever seen, so it counts.' I get to a step where I can reach the ceiling and hold my hand out for him to give me the leaves back, but he shakes his head.

'Let me help.' He insists on standing beside me, holding the ladder so it doesn't wobble every time I lean over to twist a wire tie around a vine, and passing everything up one by one so my hands are free to hold on, and it feels so nice to have that companionship and to be not-alone here. I know I could have roped Mickey or one of the others into helping me, but something special happens when it's just me and Warren, alone here after dark.

'Tell me something about you,' I say as he hands me up a crepe paper bean flower.

'I've already told you the biggest thing about me that I've never told anyone before. What else could you possibly want to know?'

'I don't know. Something weird and random that most people wouldn't be privileged enough to know. Favourite food?'

'Pizza. Ice cream. That is one after the other, *not* together.'

'You really are just a kid in an adult-sized body, aren't you?'

'There is no age limit on enjoying pizza or ice cream, I'll have you know.' He hands me up a curled paper tendril and a pin to attach it with and seems to be thinking about something more revealing to share. 'I collect Tamagotchis.'

The laugh is so surprising that I stab my own thumb with the pin. I don't mean to laugh so hard, but I don't know where he gets this knack for saying the most unexpected sentences at the most inopportune moments. 'You can't say things like that to a woman standing at the top of a ladder. You *collect* Tamagotchis? The virtual pets? Those little blob things that were popular in the nineties? The things teachers confiscated in school so we had to leave in the care of our parents and beg them to feed our virtual pets while we were out? Do they even still make them?'

'Yep. A Tamagotchi shop opened in London a couple of years ago. I go in and get another one every time I'm in the city for work.' He gets his phone out of his pocket and I step down a couple of steps to see as he swipes his fingers across the screen a few times and hands it to me.

On the screen is a photo of a glass-fronted display cabinet, full of shelves filled with the colourful packaging of the flattened egg-shaped plastic toys that I honestly had no idea still existed. I zoom in on the photo and admire the vast selection he's amassed and impressive colour coordination of the display, and the sheer unexpectedness of something so completely random that I can't imagine what other surprises might be hiding under his serious façade.

I'm taller than him from my vantage point on the ladder, and his fingers brush against mine and linger as I hand the phone back, and I bite my lip as I look down at him. He's clearly trying to fight embarrassment and probably wishing he hadn't said anything.

'How does a Tamagotchi collection start?' I ask gently, because there's *got* to be a story there.

'When I was young, I always wanted a dog. I begged my parents for one, but they would never agree.' He puts the phone back in his pocket. 'And then my dad bought me one of these instead, thinking it would shut me up about wanting a real pet. It didn't work, of course, but he started bringing me one back every time he went away for work, which was often, like he thought that if I had *enough* virtual pets, I'd eventually stop wanting a real dog. From my dad's point of view, they served a practical purpose, but to me, it was the only toy I had that actually felt like a toy. After he died, I have an uncle in America who sent me one, a rare one you couldn't get in this country that apparently my dad had asked him to get for me, and then I saw one the following year and something compelled me to buy it, and it just spiralled from there. It felt like a little nod from my dad every time I saw one. I guess I thought I'd share them with my own kids one day, but that hasn't happened yet, so now I'm just an adult who collects a children's toy and doesn't share that with many people due to fear of ridicule.'

'Do you play with them?'

'Noooo. I mean, there are a couple that I've opened and started up, but then adult life calls and they die before I have time to look at them again, as is the common problem with being an adult – far too little time to play with toys.'

'I agree. I think that's one of the reasons I like working here so much – often it's part of my job to put together Lego sets or build beanstalks.' I wave a leaf around, and he reaches up to take it from my hand and leans across to tie it onto a vine at his height. 'Did you ever get the dog?'

'No. Another casualty of adult life. Since I've been old enough to have one without parental permission, I'm at work all the time and could never leave a dog alone for so many hours a day, so it's another childhood dream left unfulfilled. Maybe when I retire.'

For someone who's only forty-one, he spends a *hell* of a lot of time thinking about retirement. I can honestly say I've never even considered putting something off until such a distant time in the future. 'That is probably the sweetest, most unexpected thing I've ever heard. Thank you for sharing that.' I know I shouldn't, but I'm at a height where my arms are level with his head and it's too easy to reach out and run my fingers through his hair, brushing it flat where it got ruffled earlier and he hasn't bothered to straighten it out, and his head tilts into my touch.

'Thank you for not laughing *too* hard.' He smiles up at me like he doesn't mind the hand in his hair *at all* and his eyes drift shut so I keep letting my fingers glide through the dark strands.

'I was laughing at the unexpectedness of it, not at your collection. It's nice to have a sentimental hobby like that. Marnie collects original Ladybird books, and Mickey collects... well, absolutely everything, but she runs a curiosity shop so that's allowed, and—' I gasp as an idea hits me out of nowhere. 'Would you display them? Here?'

His eyes pop open and he remembers that my hands are in his hair and takes such a sharp step backwards that he nearly falls over the beanstalk planter. 'What?'

'What if we displayed people's collections? What if we did an exhibit of the things people collect?' I say excitedly as the idea snowballs through my mind. 'So many people must have these hidden collections at home, things that hardly anyone gets to see, so what if they'd let us share them with museum visitors? It would put the empty rooms upstairs to good use. We could put out a call for anyone who collects something and might be interested in having their collection on display here... It would be a great way to diversify and offer something other than stuff I can dream up, and it ties in to what Mr Hastings said about re-visit value. Once someone's been here, they've been here. There aren't enough new additions to make it worthwhile coming back very often, but this, this would be something ever-changing if we rotate the collections on display regularly... I know it doesn't really fit the fairytale theme, but it could be quirky and unusual and would add a real point of interest, and give people something to talk about.'

'What about that one weird guy who's going to offer to bring in his collection of old toenail clippings and teeth of unknown origin? It could be like a museum of two halves – first floor, the hopes and dreams of all things fairytale and a magical wishing well. Second floor – nightmares for life, an urgent need for therapy, and a desperate need to unsee the cold, dead eyes of someone's taxidermy roadkill collection.'

I smack at his arm even though he's joking, and *no one* is going to be displaying their toenail clippings or any form of dead thing on my watch, thank you very much.

'It's a great idea. It'll take a long time to implement though. Assuming we get any responders, there will be logistics to sort out. Presumably, people would send us photos and we'd decide if it would be a good collection to display, and then we'd have to figure out if we're going to help them transport it here, if we're going to pay them for loaning it to us, how long is each one going to stay, how we're going to make sure they're protected, if the people themselves want to come and present their collections to visitors or just write the story behind them to display on a noticeboard or something, if it means we can increase the admission price...'

'No.' I hold out a warning finger, although maybe he's got a point, especially with the increased rent to keep on top of, and the fact we're going to run out of exhibits that can 'go walkabouts' pretty soon and either have to dream up new scenarios and re-use some of them, or try a new approach. 'I didn't think we could get it up and running *tonight*, but it's something to think about. We could start small – your Tamagotchis, and I bet Marnie wouldn't mind showcasing her Ladybird books, and I could ask the other shopkeepers if anyone collects anything or knows someone who does. We could do a test run with people we know, to see how it goes and what niggles need to be worked out, like how to make sure things are safe and unable to come to any harm, and if the general public would actually be interested in seeing things that other people collect.'

When I look back down at him, he's got a huge grin on his face and he's shaking his head fondly, but he hasn't taken his eyes off me. 'What?'

'Just trying to work out how anyone can get so overexcited while standing on a ladder and *not* fall off.'

'It's a gift.' I swing both arms out and do a bow, and then have to grab on fast as I nearly overbalance, making him cackle.

'Seriously. There has never been a more perfect match between human and job. You were *made* to do this, Liss. I'm not going to let anyone take that away. I want you to know that. There won't be any issues going forwards, I'm sure of that, but if there are, then they're going to have to go through me, and I can be a *vicious* opponent when I need to be.'

'When you're not busy doodling, cutting out paper leaves, and collecting Tamagotchis?' I make a joke out of it because of how uneasy his words make me feel, both because of imagining him in that role when in recent weeks, he's been so happy to be away from work, and because every time he assures me there won't be any issues, he sounds anything but sure.

He laughs that same uneasy laugh, clearly feeling the same discomfort, which is made even more obvious when he hands me up another leaf, silently urging me to get *on* with the beanstalk and *off* the subject of him, his job, and the future of Colours of the Wind.

He stays next to me, steadying the ladder and passing up leaves, tendrils, and flowers, and threading wire hooks through our magic beans and handing them up to hang from the vines, and one hand splays on my lower back to steady me whenever I come down a step, and every time, I like the feeling of it there.

By the time we've finished, it's been dark outside for hours and I can't help wondering how it's possible to lose an entire evening with someone and not even notice it passing.

Warren stretches with a tired groan as he pins the final paper tendril onto the bottom vines and stands back up to help me down from the lowest step of the ladder.

When he lets go of my hand, he gets his phone out to check the time. 'It cannot be 10 p.m.'

'Did you have a lot to do tonight?' I ask as I fold the stepladder and cross the room to return it to the storage cupboard.

'Yeah, but none of it would have been as enjoyable as this, so I regret nothing.' He stretches again and his stomach lets out a loud growl of hunger. 'Apart from the fact I'm *starving*. Do you want to...' He hesitates, seeming to reconsider his next words before they come out. 'Do you want to go out for a pizza or something? Just you and me, away from work? Like a practice run for the wedding date next month?'

I don't know if he means a *real* date or not, and how adorably red his cheeks have gone while asking makes me not want to push it, because I would do *anything* just so I don't have to say goodnight to him yet. 'I'd like that.'

'I'd love that.' He deliberately echoes what I said earlier, his smile so wide that his jaw *must* be aching, especially when we've already laughed so much tonight.

'And we can hang up some magic beans on the way,' he adds. 'Because I'm not ready for tonight to end yet.'

'Me neither,' I murmur.

'Good.' His tongue wets his lips and his eyes fall to my mouth again in a way that makes a warm flush run through my entire body. '*Good.*'

Somehow I never imagined that building a beanstalk would be quite so magical, but I do know one thing. Tonight, the butterflies are *soaring*.

20

It's the following week and Warren's late for work. Recently, he's always here before opening time and I'm ashamed of how much I look forward to sharing the first cup of tea of the day with him, and as the weeks tick past, I keep getting little twinges of thoughts about how, sooner or later, he's going to have to go back to his normal job and he's not going to be here every day. In two and a half months, I've gone from loudly objecting to his presence to wondering how I'm going to manage without it.

It's a relief to finally catch sight of his dark hair coming up the steps towards the front door, and I can't hide the wide grin as he comes in, wearing a zip-up jumper with panels of light blue and navy, and stops in the doorway, a huge smile on his face that matches mine. 'I really hope that grin is because you've won the lottery and not just because you're happy to see me.'

'Can it be both?' I joke to cover how much I *can't* stop smiling, and the sole reason is because simply seeing him tends to have that effect lately.

'Is there anyone here yet?' He looks around, trying to gauge how many visitors there might be, and when I shake my head, he continues. 'Can you do me a favour and humour me for a minute?'

He goes over to the music player near the door and turns the volume of the instrumental Disney music up until it's unpleasantly loud, and then comes over to the front desk and points to the far end of the lobby. 'Can you go over there, face the wall, and say something quietly?'

I almost laugh at the absurdity of the request, but he asked me to humour him so I walk to the furthest end of the room while giving him a questioning look, and face the wall. 'You're a very strange man, Warren Berrington.'

'I know I am.'

There's no way he heard that over the volume of the music, and when I turn back to face him, he's still smiling, and he turns his head, revealing the hearing aid in his left ear.

I'm unprepared for the wave of emotion it sets off in me, but before I know it, my eyes have welled up and I *run* back across the lobby and throw my arms around him with such force that the pair of us nearly crash to the floor.

He bends to catch me just in time and lifts me up to spin us around, and I bury my face in his neck, inhaling the hint of dark citrus in his leather-scented aftershave, as my fingers curl into his jumper and pull him closer.

'I have no right to be as proud of you as I am, but I'm *so* proud of you. You actually did it.'

'With difficulty. I'm late because I couldn't pluck up the courage to get out of the car. I thought everyone was looking at me as I walked down the road.' His voice sounds hoarse, like my arms are holding him so tightly that I'm cutting off his oxygen.

'They weren't. You know that, right?' I pull back until I can look him directly in the eyes. 'It's your own self-consciousness you're projecting, not what anyone else is actually seeing.'

'Yeah, I guess.' He lets out a shaky breath. 'I don't even know if I can keep it in, if it's going to get the better of me, but I want to try, while I'm here, while I can be myself and know you're not going to judge me or ridicule me, while I have a chance to see how much of a difference it makes where I know I'll be accepted as I am, and...'

I'm holding his face in my hands, my thumb brushing his cheek, the fingers of my other hand underneath his earlobe, twiddling with the ends of his dark hair, and everything becomes too much, and so much affection for him bubbles up and bursts out of me and there's nowhere for it to go except to press my lips to his.

It's just a peck, but I do it again and again and again. He makes a surprised noise, and his lips press against mine, his hands tighten on my back where he's still holding me up, and I can feel his breath speeding up, sounding unstable as his emotion builds, and...

...suddenly, my feet hit the floor when he puts me down abruptly and takes a step backwards so fast that his body jolts when his hip knocks so hard into the front desk that it will definitely leave a bruise.

I cover my face with my hands. I can't believe I just did that.

Our pizza date last week ended with a lingering hug and a kiss on the cheek, and I got the impression he was holding back from taking it any further, and I definitely wouldn't have been opposed, but I had *no* right to kiss him like that.

'I'm so sorry, I shouldn't have done that.' My face is *throbbing* in time with my speeding pulse, and I'm so hot that I swear steam will start pouring out from between my fingers at any moment, and I want the ground to swallow me whole. Why did I do that? Why did I think that was even in the *realm* of appropriate? Why did I think he wanted it? And maybe that's exactly the problem – thinking. It's clearly not my strong suit.

His hands close gently around my wrists and try to lift my hands away from my face. 'No, you *should*, I'm the one who...' He makes a noise of frustration and steps away, and I blow out a breath between my hands and force myself to part my fingers and look out.

He's turned away and is pushing a hand through his hair. 'Liss, I'm sorry. Everything about my life is so *wrong*, and you are so *right*, and you deserve a Disney prince and I can never be that, and...'

It *hurts* to hear that because, to me, the opposite is true. I *don't* want a Disney prince. That's always been a metaphor. What I've always wanted is someone who makes me *feel* like I'm living in a real-life fairytale, and Warren more than qualifies on that front, and I wish I knew how to put it into words that he could hear – not with his ears, but in his soul.

He makes an even more frustrated-sounding noise. 'Can we pretend the last five minutes didn't happen? Just rewind time, so you're standing there and I'm here, and...' He comes back over and this time, when his fingers touch my wrists, I let him move my hands, and he's standing in front of me, like we were a few minutes ago but without the whole jumping on him and kissing him thing. I take a few deep breaths and try to go along with it, because forgetting all about the last five minutes is *fine* by me.

My hair is scrunched by his hands so I shake it out and square my shoulders, and try to sound casual and like my voice isn't shaking *at all*. 'So, you're wearing a hearing aid?'

'Yeah. It's the one I got about ten years ago and never wore. It's not a perfect fit now because your ears never stop growing, but if I'm going to continue wearing it, I could go back to the hospital and get fitted for a newer, more discreet one.' He sounds normal, apart from the fact his hands are shaking, and he notices when I do and hides them behind his back.

'How does it feel?'

'Weird. I'm so self-conscious, you wouldn't believe. It feels like I'm wearing a brick on my head and just as conspicuous.'

'It's barely noticeable. Your hair mostly covers it anyway.' I go to reach up and then hesitate. 'Can I?'

He nods, and I run my fingers through his hair, loosening it around his ear and covering most of the brown plastic device that's now sitting there, and I let my fingers trail down, and my thumb rubs over his earlobe…

Suddenly, his lips are on mine again. It's my turn to be surprised as he leans down to kiss me, nothing more than a peck that's probably only intended to be one, but like I couldn't either, it's impossible to just kiss him once and pull away, but after his reaction just now, the surprise has taken my breath away. I'm not even sure which part of him I'm holding, but my fingers dig in as he kisses me again and again.

'Warren…' I say warningly.

'I know, I know,' he murmurs against my mouth, forcing himself to pull back just far enough to rest his forehead against mine, breathing hard, more from the emotional impact than from any ferocity in the gentle kisses, and I feel as head-swimmingly oxygen-deprived as if we'd been kissing for hours without coming up for air.

I open my eyes and brush my fingers through his hair, and he blinks his eyes open too and pulls back far enough to focus. I hold his gaze and there's so much emotion reflected back at me, and I see the moment he drops his front and gives in to the desire blazing in his blue eyes, and this time when he kisses me, it's *properly*.

He pushes until my back is against the desk, and it's so much more than just a peck. Our tongues tangle and my arms wrap around his neck and claw into his hair, and one leg hooks around his to pull him closer, holding him against me, clutching at him in case he gets it into his head to pull away again, although he's kissing me so desperately that it doesn't seem like he's going anywhere now.

'This is not rewinding time,' I gasp against his mouth.

'This is making the same mistake twice and really bloody enjoying it.' Every word is punctuated by kisses and his voice is so breathy that I laugh into the kiss, my fingers wound in his hair tightly enough to pull it out, his hands splayed on my hip, one underneath my loose jumper, his fingertips burning into the skin of my lower back, and I let out such an indecent-sounding moan that it makes him laugh, but his laugh quickly turns into a groan when it gives me a chance to press closer against him, his leg between mine, and his hands move, running down my body like he's about to lift me up onto the desk...

'At least someone's having a good morning.' A woman clears her throat in the doorway, and we both screech in shock at the unexpected interruption and dive apart. I'd got so caught up that I'd forgotten where we are, never mind the fact that we're open to customers.

'Sorry, dears, I'd have left you to it but walking up those steps isn't for the faint of heart at my age and I couldn't face coming back again later.' The elderly lady is leaning on a walking stick, looking red in the face, although whether it's tiredness or embarrassment because of walking in on *that* is anyone's guess.

Warren rushes over to turn the music back down to a non-offensive level and smooths his mussed-up hair out, his chest heaving, and I race back behind the desk as she hobbles over and pays her entrance fee.

My hands are shaking as I hand her a map postcard, and try not to die of mortification. At least she's alone and doesn't have any impressionable young children with her.

I decide to face it head on. 'Sorry about that. We're not usually so unprofessional first thing in the morning. Mitigating, er, circumstances.'

'Yes, very mitigating.' She gives Warren an appreciative look as he comes back over. 'I was the same when I was your age and I met my husband. Thirty years later and he still steals an unexpected kiss now and then. You two enjoy yourselves while you're young enough not to have to worry about certain positions flaring up sciatica and being able to enjoy yourselves like that without pulling a muscle!'

Warren and I both laugh marginally deranged laughs, and the lady is still leaning on her walking stick and looking out of breath, and he hits on an excuse to get himself out of this cringeworthy situation. 'Water! I'll get you a glass of water! Be right back!'

The lady reaches over to pat my hand. 'You make the most of it, my love. It's not every day you find one like that.'

'No, it's not.' I glance up the stairs after him.

It's *really* not.

* * *

If it's not every day you find a man like Warren Berrington, it's certainly easy enough to lose him.

After quite a few visitors this morning, Warren has made himself scarce. He disappeared into the garden ages ago, and now it's lunchtime and he still hasn't come back. I stand at the top of the steps and survey Ever After Street, but it's quiet enough that I can justify closing the door and putting the 'gone for lunch' sign out, and I venture round the side of the building and into the garden, unsure if he's avoiding me after what happened this morning.

He's sitting on one of the log benches with his legs stretched out in front of him, his head leaning back against the tree trunk, his eyes closed and the low autumn sun streaming onto his face.

I step between him and the sunlight, casting a shadow that makes him open his eyes and look at me. 'What are you doing out here?'

'Listening to birdsong. I can *hear* birdsong, Liss. I didn't realise...' His voice catches and he has to stop and take a breath. 'I didn't realise how long it had been since I heard a bird singing. I forgot how much I was missing. There's so much I've let pass me by and I hadn't realised until you pushed me to.'

He closes his eyes and shifts until the sun hits his face again, basking in it, and it makes me wonder how much time he spends outside in his day-to-day job, because I get the impression it mainly involves staring at the four walls of an office.

'I'm in love. With this place. With how I feel when I'm here. With...' His eyes open and fall on me, but he doesn't complete the sentence, but the look he gives me makes those butterflies take flight again, except this time, they're joined by a million more and they're all outrageously fluttery.

'I thought you might be avoiding me.'

'No. Why on earth would I be avoiding you? I guess you could say I'm avoiding the temptation to do something inappropriate in front of visitors... That was a close call this morning. I forgot where we were, lost my mind, took leave of my senses. I've never done anything so unprofessional in my life before then... and I loved every bloody minute of it,' he says with a naughty grin and waggling eyebrows.

The throwback to his words in the middle of the kiss makes

my stomach flutter and I go hot all over, and the temptation to simply dive on him and snog him senseless again has to be stamped down *hard*.

I try to keep my sensible hat firmly on. 'I'm sorry about earlier. The whole thing. I shouldn't have been so bold when I didn't know for certain it was reciprocated.'

'Don't apologise for being brave. I've wanted to do that for weeks now and it's been impossible to hide. I'm *glad* you were braver than me. You kissed me out of sheer joy at seeing me trying to accept my issues – that makes me the luckiest man alive.'

The words and the infinite smile on his face makes the butterflies swoop inside me again, and he opens his arms, inviting me to straddle his lap and do it again and I can't get down there fast enough.

I take his face in my hands and let my fingers brush gently over his ears and into his hair, and he makes a wanton noise in the back of his throat and pushes up until his mouth crashes into mine, and it's such a relief to know that we both *want* this and I haven't been second-guessing his signals or misinterpreting whatever it is I'm feeling towards him, and it all floods out into an impassioned kiss that leaves us both panting for breath and really, really uncomfortable. Who knew that fallen log benches weren't designed for fevered kissing?

When the pain spearing through my knees wins, I sit down beside him instead and he drops an arm around me, his fingers tangling in my hair as he pulls me tight against his side, and we drift into slow and lazy sunshine kisses, my hands stroking his thigh, running over his chest, a gentle feeling of relief because it's been building up for *months* and now it's out there, in the open, and everything feels right with the world for a moment.

Contented quietness has fallen over the garden. My head is

against his shoulder, his chin resting on it, moving only to drop occasional kisses on my forehead, and his hand is inside my mass of colourful curls, his fingers running up and down my back, and I could quite happily fall asleep right here.

'Is the well significantly older than the rest of the building?' He sounds like he could too, and when I lift my head far enough to see his face, he's smiling softly and looking at the wishing well.

'I have no idea. Why?'

'Just wondering. The crumbling stonework below and the difference in style between that and the rest of the basement makes me think it was here long before the museum was.'

'I don't know. Never thought about it. Witt might know. He's a history buff and his father owned the castle...'

'Liss?' After a few minutes of silence, he shifts so his mouth is against my forehead and makes sure I'm listening to him. 'If anything goes wrong... If anything doesn't go to plan with what we're trying to do here... Look into that well.'

'What, and make a wish?'

'Something like that,' he mumbles in response.

'Not quite the "unsafe hazard that someone's strung lights on" it once was then?' I paraphrase what he said on the first day.

'Are you sure I said exactly that? It wasn't more along the lines of, "Ooh, a wishing well, how delightfully charming and magical!"' When I giggle, he leans down to kiss me again. 'No wonder you called me an evil soulless gerbil. That feels like a lifetime ago, like that man was a stranger. Thinking about that is like an out-of-body experience, like I'm watching someone else, but that man wasn't *me* at all. I don't think I've been myself for years now.'

I think I already understood that, on some level, but there's something about hearing him admit it to himself that feels significant.

'While I've been out here, a mum with two kids came to look around, and I could *see* the wonder this garden inspired. The little girl was holding a Belle doll and had found a place where she *belonged*. They said hello to me, the mum asked if I worked here, and when I said yes, both the kids gasped and told me how lucky I am.' His head is resting against mine, but his eyes are on the wishing well. 'And a little boy went to write a wish, and then he came over and asked me if I knew why the things in the museum kept getting out, and I said it was magic, and he just accepted it, and I envied him. How lovely it would have been at that age to believe in the impossible.'

'You don't need to be a child to believe in magic. There's magic everywhere, in all the little moments of every day. In patches of wildflowers where fairies dance, in dandelion clocks and falling sycamore seeds, in sunrises and sunsets and chance meetings with people you run into along the way.' I let my hand run over his jaw until I can pull him down for another kiss. 'In unexpected connections with the most unlikely people.'

'It made me so proud to be a part of this.' He sounds raw and emotional and I hold him closer and he lets out a long breath against my hair. 'And no one mentioned the hearing aid.'

'No one would. I'm not trying to downplay your feelings, but it's so much more noticeable to *you* than it is to anyone else. It's a part of you, no different to your nose or your collarbones or your shoulders. It doesn't define you.' I let my hand drift up until it gently covers his left ear, and then push myself up so I can murmur into his right ear. 'This does *not* make you any less of a person.'

We're pressed so closely together that I can feel his breathing stutter, and he takes a few deep breaths before he speaks again. 'A person with a problem.'

'Every person has problems. Most of them, we'll never see or know about, but everyone is dealing with something. Every person we walk past on the street, every stranger who offers a smile or a nod, every single one of them will have something going on in their lives, some adversity to overcome, and that doesn't change the importance they bring to the world.' I kiss his cheek. 'Having an issue with your hearing and doing something about it should be celebrated.'

My lips are still pressed against his cheek and his hands tighten on my body, like he's trying to hold me in place and a long few minutes pass of us simply holding each other.

'You've made me realise how much I've isolated myself. I never accept invitations to go out with friends, or to work dos, or anywhere, because I know I'll struggle and I live in fear of someone realising the truth. It's always been a shameful secret that no one must ever find out about, something that I'd be ridiculed for and treated like an outsider, so I've made myself into an outsider so I could get in first and prevent anyone else doing it. Your acceptance makes so much difference. I wish there were more people in my life like the ones on Ever After Street. Everything you do here is so full of heart. I don't want this to end.'

I kiss his cheek again and then settle my head back against his shoulder. 'I don't want you to go.'

'In three weeks' time, my office closes for the Christmas holidays. That's the end of my time here.'

He sounds so sad and so... *final*... that it makes a boulder of anxiety settle inside me. 'But you could come back, right?'

'I've got an acquisition to oversee in Southampton. I've got to be there on the third of January. I've already cancelled once so I could stay here, I can't pull out again.'

I try not to show how surprised I am, but it hits me like a punch to the gut. I didn't know he had any other commitments like that, or that they were so... *imminent*. I thought he'd be here for longer in a professional capacity, and in a personal capacity... Well, I didn't think he'd be going very far at all. Southampton in January is so... conclusive. I swallow hard. 'How long will you be gone?'

'About a month, maybe. I don't know, it's never mattered before.'

'Okay, so you'll be gone for a few weeks, but after that... you could come back, right? You've been working remotely since September, how difficult would it be to continue doing that?'

'Prohibitively so.'

I don't lift my head but I feel him move to look at me. 'I need to get back to the office because if I stay here, my focus will be on the museum, and while that's been the intention for the past couple of months, it can't continue, no matter how much I want it to.'

His words sting, and I know I'm responsible for roping him into helping with museum jobs, but I've got lost in how much I've enjoyed his company and valued his input and somewhere along the way, I've forgotten that *this* isn't his job, and I appreciate his honesty, even though it isn't what I was hoping to hear. I feel a bit discouraged at how cut-and-dried he makes it sound. It sounds like I'm never going to see him again, and that makes my heart beat faster for all the wrong reasons.

'Okay, but there'll still be... *us*, right? We can still see each other? Fifty miles apart isn't that far, we can still...' I waggle my finger between him and me, not quite sure what label to put on it right now.

'If you still want to by then.'

'Why wouldn't I?' There's a guarded tone in his voice that makes me pull back until I can look him in the eyes.

It was a rhetorical question but he shakes his head like he doesn't have an answer, and the hairs on the back of my neck stand up. I tell myself I'm imagining the feeling of unease that settles over me.

To chase it away, I lean up until I can kiss him again, and his hands are in my hair, and on my back, holding me closer, and the kiss feels increasingly desperate, like he's clinging on, kissing me as though it's the last chance he'll ever have. The mention of him leaving has given us both the realisation that this is coming to an end, sooner than I'd hoped, and I'm surprised by how much I wish it wasn't.

'Before we have to think about that,' I say when we pull back, but instead of snuggling up against him again, I decide it's time to share an idea I've been toying with. 'There's an idea I've been wanting to run past you and I could do with your expert opinion, but it clashes with your cinema complex and maybe takes inspiration from it a little bit...' I blurt out before I second-guess myself. It's something that felt impossible when I was by myself, but with Warren here, it feels doable, but I don't know how he's going to react to an idea of screening films after my rejection of his cinema complex. 'Have you seen the performances where they put on a musical in bars and pubs?'

'Taking children to bars? Great idea, can't go wrong.' He gives me a sarcastic thumbs up, and I grab his thumb and pull it down and then don't let go of his hand.

'No, I mean, the singers perform a musical, but they mingle with the crowd. They act out the scenes and sing live in the space they've got. They use the whole area as a stage and make the crowd part of it. So I was thinking... what if we used one of the empty rooms upstairs to install a cinema screen, and we could screen Disney movies while actors act out some of the parts in front of the audience. *Beauty and the Beast*, while Belle in her yellow ballgown and the Beast in his blue suit dance between the kids who are watching. We could watch *Cinderella* on screen scrubbing the floor and blowing bubbles while someone playing Cinderella actually scrubs the floor and uses a bubble wand to blow bubbles across the audience. *Tangled* while Rapunzel and Flynn hand out floating lanterns to release at the "I See the Light" moment in the film. A real experience. Something immersive. It pays homage to your cinema idea, but retains the integrity of the museum. Anyone can watch Disney movies at home, but we could give them something different, a reason to come here that's more than just staring mindlessly at a screen. And we could do popcorn, and maybe have quizzes and prizes afterwards, and...' I trail off because he's watching me with an unreadable look on his face. 'You think it's awful, don't you?'

'Lissa, you're like living magic.'

'What?'

'You love this place *so* much, you never stop thinking about it, trying to improve it, make it better and even more magical. I understand what the others said now about this being *your* magic. You're the most inspirational person I've ever met. I wish I had as much love and conviction in my entire body as you have in one toe. This museum is not magical, but *you* are.'

'That's the nicest thing anyone's ever said to me.' I'm fighting back tears at how genuine he sounds. I squeeze the hand I'm still holding and his fingers tighten over mine. 'You can't say things like that and be leaving in three weeks.'

'No, I can't.' He breaks eye contact and clears his throat, trying to cover emotions that sound like they're clamouring to get out. 'I love this idea. The quirky collections don't need to take up more than two of those rooms, and it's a great use for the third one. I'll support it as much as I can, but I can't be part of it.'

He seems sad and downtrodden, and that undercurrent of how soon he's leaving is flowing through this entire conversation and clouding everything. It's unreal to consider that two and a half months ago, I thought his arrival was the worst thing that had ever happened to me, and now I feel like his departure is going to change everything again, but this time, in the worst way possible.

21

'One thousand crochet flowers.' Warren sifts through the box that Mrs Coombe who runs All You Need is Gloves has just delivered. She makes a selection of warm winter clothing for humans and pets in her shop on Christmas Ever After, and in her spare time, she crochets flowers, which no one knew until she answered the request I put out for collections we could put on show. 'How on earth are we going to display these?'

'These ones on wire stems can go in a vase on a table as a centrepiece, and Mick's got a stack of foam boards we could borrow, so we could line the wall with them and then pin each flower on, like 3D wallpaper...'

Mickey is downstairs, watching the front desk and gift shop, while we're in one of the rooms upstairs, figuring out the best way to display our collections. We've got Warren's display cabinet full of Tamagotchis, and a couple of room dividers to separate each collection and create a cohesive walkway around the room. We've put up shelves to hold Marnie's Ladybird book display... and now, for the opposite wall, crochet flowers.

I'm loving every minute of this. The room feels alive with the love and attention our friends have put into these collections for years. It's an honour to be trusted with them, and I'm excited to see where it could go if we invite people from further afield to show off their collections here. The room is alive with the sizzle of something else too because Warren steals a kiss every time we cross each other's paths, finds any reason he can think of to touch me, and it's an internal fight to *not* wrestle him to the floor and make good use of the time he has left before he leaves.

While I'm trying not to think about that, I hear the noise of the stairs creaking like someone's coming up, even though the upstairs is off-limits to the public at the moment.

'Liss! Visitor!' Mickey yells up from below, presumably because she's concerned that Warren and I being alone in a room together is likely to end in only one way and she's trying to prevent us being interrupted again.

We both spin around at the exact moment that a woman appears in the doorway. She's tiny in stature, probably older than she looks in her black pencil suit with once-grey hair dyed the darkest of black and cut in an angled bob. The only splash of colour is her postbox-red lipstick and her leather handbag that's somehow an exact colour match.

'Mother!' The easy smile on Warren's face *plummets*.

Mother? Oh, blimey. I was *not* expecting to come face to face with her, ever, let alone *today*. Has she come all the way here from London? Why would she do that? I glance at Warren to see if he's as surprised as I am, and the look on his face leaves me worried. He does not seem okay, and I wish I was standing close enough to give his hand a supportive squeeze.

'What are you doing here?' His voice sounds unsteady, like her sudden appearance has knocked him sideways.

Instead of answering, she makes no secret of the way she's looking him up and down, and I *see* her taking in the Converse he's wearing with jeans and a casual jumper. His hair isn't stuck down, and he's holding a handful of crochet flowers. 'I think a more pressing question, dear boy, is *what* are you doing here?'

He recovers his composure and goes over and gives her an air kiss on either cheek, and I see her eyes stop on his ear, the hearing aid, and her red lips press themselves into an even thinner line of disapproval.

He holds an arm out towards me. 'This is Lissa, who I've been telling you about.'

'Hello.' I feared I might be about to commit an etiquette crime by going over to give her a hug, but her standoffish nod suggests that physical contact would be as welcome as a thunderstorm when you've just put your washing out. Although her red manicured fingernails make her look like the type of person who would not concern herself with menial tasks like housework.

'It's nice to meet you, Mrs Berrington. I've heard so much about you.' I give her my most charming nod back.

'So have I, dear. So have I.' It does *not* sound like a good thing.

'This is the display of people's collections I mentioned,' Warren explains, shifting uneasily. 'We're getting them set up, ready to open to visitors at the weekend.'

She peers around the room and her eyes fall on the Tamagotchi collection. 'Oh, your father's silly little game things. I never could abide them.' She turns to me. 'An adult man playing with toys. I was going to say that you shouldn't be encouraging such a silly hobby, but at least if they're here, they're not in his house. Small mercies.'

'I think it's a lovely way to honour his father's memory.' I feel myself bristling in a way that I haven't since *he* first arrived. 'I'm lucky that he's let me display them. And look at these beautiful flowers that one of our colleagues has crocheted. Aren't they fantastic?'

I hold a crocheted pansy out on my hand and she takes a step backwards like she might catch something from it.

'Yes. Very nice. Personally, I don't know how people find the time.'

'People around here are happy to dedicate their time to things they love that bring them joy,' I say, and Warren's eyes flit between us and he looks like he's trying to defuse a situation that hasn't started yet.

'They must have more hours in the day than we do then, mustn't they?' The look on her face probably isn't meant to be a sneer, but it definitely resembles one as she looks between us again. 'I came here to see what's got my son so excited, I must say I didn't expect it to be tatty old books and woollen flowers.'

I force myself not to react. Putting everything about the museum aside, I also think I'm dating her son, and I want her to like me. The last thing I should do is rile her up by getting defensive, and I try to focus on the good parts of that sentence, like Warren being excited enough about the museum to share that with his mum. That's a good sign, right?

'You.' She clicks her fingers towards him and makes a gesture that suggests she's telling a trained dog to come to heel, which he does immediately, and she takes his arm. 'You can show me around while we have a catch-up. Delightful to meet you, Miss Carisbrooke.'

It's a formal dismissal, plainly telling me I'm not invited while he gives her a tour of the museum, which is understandable, especially as they haven't seen each other in quite a while.

'Would you like a cup of tea?' I call after them, at a loss for how else to be helpful.

'No, thank you,' she replies.

Warren looks over his shoulder and tries to give me what is probably a reassuring smile, but his eyes look worried. He definitely wasn't expecting her, and there's a tone of condescension in her voice about what she's seen so far.

He takes her into the next room, the one I'd thought about turning into a cinema-style room, and I grab the opportunity to slip past and go back downstairs to Mickey for a gossip.

'Was that his mother?' my best friend hisses from where she's still minding the front desk. 'She of "running the company and pulling all the strings" fame?'

I nod.

'I did try to stop her but she was having none of it. She asked where Warren was and then just started walking up the stairs.'

'It's okay. I get the impression she's the kind of person who can't be stopped.'

Mickey grimaces. 'Was that as painfully awkward as it looked like it was going to be?'

'Yeah. I thought he was exaggerating when he's talked about his mother, but now I'm not so sure. I know you can't judge on first impressions, but she doesn't seem like the type who's going to be influenced by whimsical wishes and handmade beanstalks.' I try to make a joke out of it to cover the nervous restlessness that's taken over me, because I want to be part of their discussion. I want to know what her plans are, if Warren's enthusiasm has swayed her in our favour, and at the same time, they deserve a chance to catch up alone, and I respect that... even when the sound of raised voices filters down from upstairs, and Mickey turns the music player off so we have a better chance of overhearing what's being said.

I climb as many stairs as I dare to without being caught out by creaking floorboards, but they're on the third floor in the kitchen, and their words are too muffled, but it reignites the all-too-familiar pit of dread in my stomach. They're obviously disagreeing about something, and if she was on board with everything Warren and I have got planned for the museum, there would be nothing for them to disagree over, would there?

'Maybe it's about that acquisition in Southampton you said he was late for?' Mickey suggests, being the ever-supportive best friend.

'Maybe,' I reply, but I have a feeling there's a reason for his mother to make the effort of travelling all the way here from her London office, and it has nothing to do with Southampton.

It feels like an eternity before Warren and his mother reappear. He's walking her down the stairs while she clings onto his arm with one hand and has a white-knuckle grip on the banister with the other. Mickey and I were both leaning on the front desk, talking about the film screening idea and which parts actors could act out in real life, and we both quickly stand to attention at the sound of footsteps on the stairs.

'Miss Carisbrooke, walk me back to my car.' Mrs Berrington stops in the lobby and makes a hand gesture towards me that suggests she's calling that well-trained dog over again.

'I will,' he says quickly.

'No, Miss Carisbrooke will.' Her voice is steely and she's clearly not going to be dissuaded from this plan, and I force the nerves down as I go over. She hooks her arm through mine like she did with Warren earlier, and I realise that she's surprisingly frail, and maybe her demand is because she needs the support of something to hold onto, but doesn't want to show the weakness of using a stick or frame.

Warren dashes over to hold the door open for us, and wishes his mother a strangely formal goodbye, and his fingers touch my shoulder as we walk out. 'Liss…'

He hesitates and then shakes his head like he doesn't know

what he wanted to say, and Mrs Berrington is having none of any dilly-dallying, and I have to quicken my pace before one of us falls over as she heads for the steps. I catch his eyes and try to send him an understanding smile. Whatever's going on, and no matter how bothered I am, I don't think he's had an easy couple of hours either.

'There should be a railing on one side of these steps, they're a hazard!' Mrs Berrington barks because I'm still looking at Warren in the doorway and not paying close enough attention as we step down them.

'You're right, I can look into that immediately.' I turn my back on Warren and focus solely on her. 'It really is nice to finally meet you, Mrs Berrington...'

I was hoping she might give me a first name to call her by, but of course, she does nothing so informal, and I continue trying to engage in conversation. 'Are you going back to London tonight?'

'Indeed. My driver is waiting in the car so I can get some work done on the journey. We businesswomen can't waste a minute, can we?' It's a rhetorical question, and her hand is *clinging* onto my arm and she's concentrating on the cobblestones of the street, and despite her abrupt manner, I feel a little bit sorry for her. She's clearly trying to hide her age, and I remember Warren saying she should be thinking about retirement, but refuses to slow down.

'It must've been nice to catch up with Warren after so many months...' I attempt small talk again, even though I already know she isn't the type to appreciate *or* reciprocate it.

'Oh, I think my son has been getting *more* than well enough acquainted around here without my input, don't you?'

I don't know how much he's told her, presumably not *everything* that's been going on between us, so I aim for on-the-fence neutrality. 'It's been a pleasure to have him. He's had some wonderful ideas for the museum going forwards.'

Her cold blue eyes glance up at me. 'Yes, he definitely earns his keep as the company's "fear not, all is not lost" man.'

Like someone's placed an ice cube on the back of my neck and it's slowly sliding all the way down my spine, I get a flash-back to the day he arrived. Those words are exactly what he said to me. *Fear not, all is not lost.*

'Yes, I always send him in before redevelopment so the busi-nesses feel like they've got a fighting chance. He'll "try his best" to save them, but unfortunately, circumstances are such that they can't be saved, but at least they gave it their best try, and he helps to let them down gently. It saves all manner of pesky lawsuits in the future.'

It's a cold early-December day, but the metaphorical ice cube is still sending freezing dismay up my spine. Is *that* what he's been doing here? Has *that* been his job all along? To 'let me down gently' and make me feel like Berrington Developments did all they could while watching the bulldozers level my museum to the ground?

'It helps if the business owners think they've given it their all. I understand that running a business is often a passion and it's not easy to say goodbye to that, but we are businesspeople. It's never personal – we do what's best for business. And for this place...' She wafts her other hand towards the shops of Ever After Street as we walk past them. '...Unfortunately, that's demol-ishing your building and replacing it with a multi-million-pound cinema complex. The construction alone will provide many jobs for local people, and once completed, it will be a beacon of regeneration for the area and bring many extra visitors to this quiet little spot. A triumph for all of us.'

'No.' I struggle to splutter out a response. 'It would be the worst—'

'That's the plan. It always has been, it always will be.' She pats my arm with the hand hooked through it. 'I wouldn't want you to think my son is something he's not.'

'Like on my side?' I say more to myself than to her. Is that what she's getting at? That Warren is not now, and never has been, on the side of the museum? That he's been here solely to make me feel like I had a fighting chance while knowing full well that I did not?

She can tell that I'm biting the inside of my cheek to hold back my emotions. 'He's a businessman. I should surely hope that he is on the side of *our* company, and nothing more. Despite *appearances.*'

There's such an intonation on the word that she definitely knows there's something going on between us, and I find myself *really* prickling at what she's implying. That *this* is all part of Warren's job? Is he tasked with seducing business owners to save them suing his company in the future? That can't be true. What's happened between me and Warren has been... organic. Real. He's been so happy at the museum. Truly happy, not faking it for a job, and I don't know if she's saying this to unbalance me, or to make me question his intentions, but it's impossible to believe.

'What appearances?' I decide to play dumb and see if I can wheedle more of an explanation out of her, because I *cannot* buy that Warren has been anything but genuine lately.

'I came because I see my son making the same mistake I once made – with you.'

Falling in love? She can't really be implying that, can she? I decide to stick up for him and whatever it is I've been feeling in these last couple of weeks. I can't work out if she's deliberately trying to make me second-guess his intentions *because* she knows there's something happening between us, and I'm surprised that Warren has either told her or let it be so obvious that she's worked it out for herself. I didn't think he'd be willing to let her see his professional front slip that much. 'I see someone who's been taught to be ashamed of something he can't control, to hide it rather than seek help, and who thinks that opening his heart is the worst thing he can ever do.'

'It is. Worst thing I ever did.'

'That can't be true. You had love. You have a wonderful son. Things to be so thankful for that would never have happened if you hadn't met your husband, despite the pain his passing brought. That whole "it's better to have loved and lost" thing…?'

'You are young and naïve.'

She was probably going to continue, but I interrupt as politely as I can. 'That's the last thing I am.'

'You believe in magic and love and hope. You believe in making wishes.'

'No, I don't. I believe in my friends, in the street I've worked on for over a decade, in my museum and the people who come here. It's hard work, a business I've poured my heart and soul into because I love it. Because I believe the joy in life comes from the small, unexpected moments, and I love having a chance to help people experience that, as much as I know that I also have to earn money, and enough of it to pay the increased rent along with everything else.'

'The rent will not be increased, Miss Carisbrooke.'

I feel a brief flutter of hope, but it's quickly snuffed out by her tone. 'That was merely an artificial goal for you to focus on. My son has let feelings get involved and now doesn't have the heart to be honest with you. The museum will not be saved. All of your antics, although very amusing, will make no difference. Berrington Developments have weathered many storms, faced much public backlash, but we persist. A large company is unaffected by such trifles. People get their knickers in a knot, and then they move on, because there's nothing they can do about it. I don't care if you've got thousands of signatures on a petition. I don't care if you've got hordes of little kids crying about magical wells and wishes coming true. I don't even care if you've done a number on my son. I acquired this land to build a cinema complex in an idealistic location that will be very profitable for all involved. Public opinion means nothing to me. Money speaks. If you have some way of assuring me that you can earn far more than my cinema complex and create more jobs and do more for the area...'

'Warren suggested... I mean, he said that obviously this place is already in situ. It's already up and running. It might not earn as much, but it also won't cost anything to demolish and build new in its place. That's where savings could be made.' I try not to get emotional at her implications. I push myself to sound unattached and practical, and I wish Warren was here with the right businesslike words to make it sound as logical as it sounded when he said it to me, because I'm struggling to fight the tidal wave of rising panic. This has all been for nothing. And maybe my trust in Warren really has been misplaced too.

When my words make no impact on her, I try again. 'What would you do if someone turned up at your office and told you they were taking over and you had to go? You love your company, you've given it your everything for so many years. How can you think it's okay to do that to other people? How would you react if someone did that to you? Would you not fight back in every way you knew how?'

'I'd have the ability to separate my emotions from common sense. To know if I was flogging a dead horse. Your museum has stood there for ten years. It's never-changing. Just because you get the occasional bright idea or add something new to showcase your papier-mâché talents, it doesn't change the fact that no one comes. A few "moving exhibits" that have captured some young imaginations will make no difference in the long run, you're clever enough to know that.' We've reached the car park and she slows to a stop so she can look at me. 'I'll be honest with you. One of the reasons I came here today is because I've had an investor pull out due to your antics, so I need you to stop. What you and your friends are doing is prolonging the agony and making life more difficult for yourself. Accept that your museum *will* be going by the spring, make peace with it and make your future plans. Otherwise, there will be a lot of children out there who will have their magical hopes and dreams destroyed. We will not be tarred by this, but you will be. Trust me, Miss Carisbrooke, if you stand against us and try to drag our company through any more mud, when this house of cards falls, it will fall on *you*.'

The metaphor makes me shudder, but also shows that they *are* concerned about backlash, and her earlier words about weathering storms were not as assured as they sounded, and it gives me a boost of confidence. 'I'll level with you too. If you've got investors pulling out and you're rattled enough to come all the way here from London, then we're doing exactly what we should be doing, and businesswoman to businesswoman, no, I'm not going to stop. I'm not going to give up on something I love as much as I love Colours of the Wind, and I'm not going to stop falling in love with your son either. No matter what doubts you're trying to instil, I trust Warren.' It's my turn to sound more secure than I feel.

We're approaching an imposing black car, and as soon as we do, a smartly dressed chauffeur jumps out and opens the door, and holds his arm out to help her in.

'That, Miss Carisbrooke, is a grave error.' She dips her head to look out of the car door at me. 'One that, I suspect, you'll come to regret.'

She nods for the chauffeur to close it before I have a chance to respond, and I stand there in silence and watch as they pull away, and then I traipse back towards the museum, feeling both hopeful and defeated.

The company is rattled, but they're also not backing off, and all the doubts that I've overcome about Warren are swirling back around with a vengeance. Were those the words of a mother trying to prevent a beloved son making what she believes is a mistake... or were they the words of a mother who knows him a hell of a lot better than I do?

22

Uh-oh.

Usually, seeing my friends gathered together would be a good thing, but seeing them all waiting outside the museum door as I walk to work the next morning, it looks like there's a dark cloud gathered above them.

Mickey, Marnie, Cleo, and Franca are all waiting for me as I climb the steps. 'What's wrong?'

'Please tell me you've checked social media this morning?' Mickey says.

'I barely have enough time in the mornings to eat breakfast and get in before 9 a.m., I never check it until after I'm here.' I look between the four worried faces. 'Why?'

'Berrington Developments are fighting back.' Mickey sounds grim.

'Okay.' I try not to let worry burble up as I get my keys out and let us all in. 'If they've posted something about the museum, then good, the public *should* know that they're trying to take over the building and turf me out. People love this museum now.

Support will be on our side. None of you have seen Warren, have you?'

When I got back to the museum yesterday afternoon, eager to get the full lowdown from Warren, he'd left, without telling Mickey where he was going. He didn't answer the text I sent him last night, his car isn't in the car park yet this morning, and his uncharacteristic silence has set off a sense of foreboding that I've been trying to stamp down.

Instead of answering, no one says a word. As I shrug my coat off and drop my bag behind the desk, Mickey simply places her phone on the desk in front of me, and then comes round to put an arm around my shoulders and give me a hug.

And that pit of dread I've been trying to ignore since yesterday, coupled with Warren's suspiciously timed disappearance, grows from a seed to a rugby ball. Tentatively I open her phone screen and look at the page she's left it on.

It's the Ever After Street Facebook page, and we've been tagged in a post that's gone up on our timeline so all our followers can see it. MUSEUM OF MARAUDERS is written in capital letters at the beginning, and the poster is... Berrington Developments.

What? I can barely believe what I'm seeing and quickly read the text underneath.

Our company have recently got into business with a little fairytale museum some of you may recognise as the 'Museum of Magic' on Ever After Street where owner Lissa Carisbrooke and her crew claim there are magical wishing wells and exhibits that come to life at night and go out for adventures around the area. However, Berrington Developments are relieved to uncover a fraud that's being run at Colours of the Wind museum. Those 'moving exhibits' are a hoax, every last one of them. Nothing but a money-making marketing ploy run by the street itself, designed to fool your children and take money from your pockets. The wishing well that really grants wishes? Information harvesting – taking your children's names, addresses, and other personal information for marketing purposes, under the guise of making your little ones believe their wishes will come true. Not quite the 'child-friendly day out' they'd have you believe!

'No. No, no, no. "Information harvesting" is exactly the term Warren used on the very first day. This couldn't have come from him. He wouldn't have...'

Mickey's arm tightens around my shoulders. 'It gets worse, Liss.'

'How can it possibly get—' I stop myself. I don't need to ask how it can possibly get any worse, because I scroll further down the page and come to a video. The thumbnail is a black and white photo of us in the museum lobby with the word EXPOSED written across it in big red letters. My fingers are shaking as I press the play symbol.

It takes a moment to work out what I'm seeing. It's camera footage filming... the lobby? It's in night vision, and everything's blank for a few seconds, and then Bram with my model of Remy under his arm comes into view, holding a door open, and Darcy wheels Sleeping Beauty's spinning wheel out. The frame freezes and 'LIARS' gets stamped across it in those big red letters. Then it switches to a different time. There's me, running across the back end of the lobby with the Magic Carpet in my arms. It must've been the night of the stakeout when I was sneaking it to the customer bathroom. Another freezeframe and 'FRAUD' is stamped across the screen. When the video unfreezes, it's Mickey, Sadie, and me, with Cogsworth and Lumière on their way to The Wonderland Teapot. There's another clip of me, Marnie, and Cleo carrying the witch's legs out on the night we placed them under the bookshop walls. The video ends with a still of all of us in the lobby, granting wishes, and the words 'sending unsolicited promotional mail from information gathered via the wishing well' roll across the screen, and then it finishes with the museum logo that Warren drew, but instead of 'museum of fairytales' written around the edge, they've replaced the wording with 'museum of fraudsters'.

There's more writing but tears are blurring my eyes so much that I can barely read it.

Berrington Developments recently acquired this fraudulent museum and we're pleased to announce we will shortly put an end to these underhanded practices once and for all, with demolition commencing in March, and an exciting new cinema and entertainment complex on track to open the following year and bring a much-needed modernisation to Ever After Street. Get in touch and share your stories if you too have been fooled by this so-called 'museum of magic', and help us to continue protecting the public interests, and putting honesty and integrity at the very top of our priority lists.

'This is *all* over social media,' Marnie says gently. 'I wouldn't mind betting that they've hired a publicist to publicise it as much as humanly possible.'

'We've all been tagged too,' Cleo adds. 'Every shop on Ever After Street has, so all our followers will see it too. They're really trying to take us all down with them.'

'The house of cards will fall on you, she said.' I think of Mrs Berrington's visit yesterday. 'This is what she meant. They knew what we've been up to and they were ready to expose it. And I said I wouldn't back down. If I'd been more agreeable, this wouldn't have happened.'

Is this why she came? Nothing to do with wanting to see what Warren was excited about, but as a precursor to *this*? A way of testing the waters, seeing if we were going to go quietly, and when she found out we weren't, the company released this.

'I'm sorry I've got all of you involved too. Everyone's been tarred by my stupid battle.'

'It's not stupid, Liss,' Franca says. 'None of us were going to let Colours of the Wind go without a fight, come what may. And *we* started it. You weren't even involved at the beginning.'

'No, but I've let it continue. I've let us all get caught in the act... I've let a camera film us... Wait...' I play the video again. 'This is all *inside* the lobby. How can someone get this? Mrs Berrington must've installed a hidden camera when she was here yesterday.' Even as I say it, I know I'm wrong. This is footage that was filmed weeks ago, from way up high. I go to the supply cupboard and haul out my stepladder, and then grab Mickey's phone and replay the video, trying to identify where it's been filmed from.

It's a high corner, above the door, from a viewpoint that captures most of the lobby. I drag the ladder into a rough position and clamber up it with one eye on the phone, and at the top, disguised by a nook in the wood panelling, there's an unobtrusive, thin black box with a lens in the centre of it.

A hidden camera. It's stuck up by a Velcro pad, and I rip it off and peer into the lens. Is it still recording now? Is someone from Berrington Developments watching us right *now*? Watching our reaction to their hideous post in real time?

I deliberately throw it *hard* onto the floor to smash it up, and then I climb down and stamp the heel of my winter boot onto it, satisfied with the sound of breaking plastic and the cracks that cover the surface when I pick it up again.

'Someone's installed a hidden camera,' I announce like they haven't just watched me throw it, stamp on it, and kill it dead, dead, dead.

Because it's not 'someone', is it? Some random person hasn't come in and secretly installed a hidden camera without anyone knowing, and then shared the footage with Berrington Developments. There's only one person who could've done this.

One person I trusted, when everyone else in this room told me not to.

'I'm sorry, Lissa.' Marnie gives me a hug as the others all echo her sentiment.

No one needs to say his name.

I feel numb as I put the broken camera behind the counter and then lean on my elbows and drop my head down.

Why would Warren do this? Everything had felt so perfect lately. I had *no* doubt that he was fully on our side until the cryptic warning from his mother yesterday. And now this. He's the only person who could have installed that camera. He must have been filming us all along. He must have known from the very beginning who was responsible for the 'escaped exhibits', and what? Pretended he didn't and bided his time until he could share the footage and make the biggest impact? Cause the biggest amount of harm? I feel violated by the fact someone's been watching me without my knowledge, and the thought of corporate suits sitting around in the Berrington office and spying on us makes my skin crawl.

I look up at the others. 'I'm so sorry. I trusted him. I trusted him *over* you, all of you. Everyone told me that something didn't add up, that something about his reason for being here wasn't quite right, and I got caught up in his eyes, and his smile, and the sense of companionship he gave me. I feel so stupid.'

They all reassure me that no one could've seen *this* coming, but I'm the one who let him in. I'm the one who shared everything with him, who opened myself up to him and truly believed that his intentions were good.

Was he nothing but a corporate plant all along? Sent here to secretly watch us and report insider information back to the company? And there was me, dishing that information out on a nice big dinner plate, like a numpty.

'What are we going to do?' Cleo asks. 'Post a rebuttal?'

'We could claim they've faked the footage?' Franca suggests. 'Say they've used AI to generate it or something – people would be more inclined to trust us than some slimy property developer.'

'Yeah, exactly, we've just got to refute it,' Marnie adds. 'People will always believe the good guys.'

Are we the good guys? We *have* misled people. We've pretended exhibits were moving when they weren't. We've used the interest to further boost our own popularity. We've played up to what was being talked about to increase visitor numbers and benefitted from the increased takings. *We* all know that the information on the wishes was solely to enable us to grant them, but in this world of scammers and fraudsters trying to get your personal information in any way possible, is anyone ever going to believe that?

The only thing I'm certain of is that it's time to be honest. 'No. No more lies. We'll come clean. Tell people exactly why we did it. The only way to fight accusations like these is with absolute truth. I've made enough mistakes with trusting people who clearly had ulterior motives lately, and I don't want to *be* one of them. I'll write something today, figure out how to explain it, tell people about Berrington

Developments and their underhanded tactics and intimidation, but right now, I want to curl up in a hole and never come out.'

I can feel the malaise settling over me like a heavy winter blanket. It was all for nothing, wasn't it? Everything that's happened since September has been a sham. The extra visitors make no difference, the gift shop, the excited kids finding escaped exhibits, the wishes we've granted, the map postcards, the new logo. Every single thing has been for nothing.

We haven't saved the museum... and I haven't fallen in love.

* * *

I have no idea what to write.

When I volunteered for this earlier, it seemed so simple, but now I'm alone, standing at the front desk with the cursor blinking at me from the blank page on my laptop.

It's been a quiet day. The others went to open their shops, and Mickey stayed until I sent her away at lunchtime, but visitors have been few and far between. I suspect the only ones who have come are people who haven't read social media yet, unlike me. I've been torturing myself by reading the comments on Berrington Developments' article all day, despite knowing the cardinal rule of the internet is to never read the comments.

Between that, I've been skulking around and checking every nook and cranny for possible other hidden devices. From their video, it seems like they only had one angle, but you can never be too careful when you've invited a corporate stooge into your life and trusted his every false word.

I don't expect Warren will ever be brave enough to show his face around here again, and yet I can't keep my eyes off the door. I keep watching, *hoping*... no, not hoping... Waiting, maybe.

Thinking he *might* come in. There might be some perfectly reasonable explanation for all this.

Half of me expects him to appear, and half of me is still shocked when there's a soft knock on the museum door and I look up from the laptop screen to see him push it open, come in, close it and turn the sign over to closed behind him.

I look at the clock on the wall and I'm surprised it's reached 4.55 p.m. already. Today has been the draggiest day in the history of draggy days, and I have to appreciate his timing. He must have waited until this exact moment – right before closing time so we'd have some privacy, but before I'd had the chance to lock him out.

'Hi,' he murmurs. At least he has the decency to look ashamed. Very, very ashamed.

I go to say the same but the word gets stuck in my throat and all that comes out is a hoarse gurgle. I'm telling myself that at least something here mattered enough that he'd come back and try to offer an explanation, and even though I don't really want to hear it, I'm desperate to hear it.

He's wearing a suit again, and his shiny shoes squeak on the black and white flooring, and I can't help the pang of seeing him looking as miserable as he did three months ago.

'I believe this is yours.' I bend to get the broken camera from under the counter and slam it onto the wooden desk as he comes over, and I realise I'm *wishing* he'd say, 'Wait, what, I've never seen that before in my life, what is that?'

'I expected it to be in more pieces than that.' He picks it up and leans over the desk until he can drop it into the bin that he knows is underneath. 'I can explain.'

'No, you can't.' I involuntarily take a step backwards at the unexpected closeness of him leaning so far over the desk. 'But *I* can explain it to you, and you jump in and tell me if I've got it wrong, how's that?'

My discomfort must show because he immediately takes a step away again. His bottom teeth pull his upper lip into his mouth and he nods mutely.

'I think Berrington Developments were worried about the public support for the museum. I think they talk the big talk, but in reality, they knew there'd be backlash they wanted to avoid, and they sent you here for insider information. You were supposed to find out about the inner workings of the museum to see what they could exploit and feed it back to them, and you certainly did.'

'No, that's wrong.' He sighs. 'The camera was my misplaced idea. It was personal. I got involved in the living exhibits. I wanted to prove who was behind it. It had nothing to do with them or my job here.'

'If that was true, you would have told me. You would have, at the very least, asked permission to put up the camera. It's illegal to film people without their consent in a private place. It breaks all sorts of privacy and data protection laws. You must've known that.'

'It only ever filmed at night. It was motion-activated between 7 p.m. and 7 a.m., so it only recorded when something moved between those hours. You and I had usually gone by then. I... didn't think of it in those terms. I was just trying to catch out whoever was doing it.'

'By illegally filming them without their consent?' I was trying not to lose my cool, but I snap at him this time, even though the fact it only filmed at night makes me feel better.

A *lot* has happened between us in this lobby and I felt sordid and violated by the idea of a group of lecherous old property developers sitting around and watching *some* of those things, and

I frantically run through anything else they might have seen at night.

'They were breaking into a building that my company owns!'

'They were trying to help me! Which is more than you've ever done!'

'And you were lying to me! I knew you knew who was responsible. You're a terrible liar. When you said no one else had a key, I knew that someone did. The camera was personal curiosity to prove my own theory.'

'You think that's an insult, but I'd prefer to be a terrible liar than a seasoned pro like you.'

'I didn't lie.'

'And yet you're lying now. Because the footage from this "personal curiosity" of yours ends up being used in the most public way to deal us the most damning amount of harm possible. Please, Warren, don't insult me further by pretending that installing a hidden camera and violating our privacy on behalf of your company was somehow above board and an absolutely fine thing for you to do.'

He pushes a hand through his hair, pacing in small widths of the lobby, covering no more than a few black and white squares of the flooring before turning back the other way again. 'I didn't give them that footage. It uploaded automatically to my cloud account and they had access, which I didn't know. I didn't know, Liss. I really didn't know.'

I hate how much that makes me feel just the tiniest bit better. He looks absolutely wretched as he says it, and there's the smallest smidge of relief that maybe it wasn't all as calculated as I thought. 'You knew what they were going to do with it though?'

'I found out yesterday from my mother.'

'And what, your quick disappearing act was because you

went to help? Went to ensure they had the best footage possible?'

'I went back to the office to try and stop them, but I couldn't. The order came from the boss, I didn't have the authority to override it. I'm sorry.'

'Well, that's a nice way of trying to shirk responsibility for this, but nothing you say makes any sense. On the night we stayed here for the stakeout, for example. That camera was already up. You already knew. So what was the point in that?'

'I was trying to catch you out. I knew that either you'd warn the others and nothing would happen, or you'd sneak something out. I was quite impressed that you managed to get an entire carpet out of the bathroom window.'

'Are you seriously trying to make a joke of this?'

'No. I've messed up, I know that. I'm trying to figure out a way to sufficiently apologise but there isn't one, and I'm floundering.'

If nothing else, I appreciate his candidness in this situation, even if it would have been even more welcome in other situations. 'But we got closer after that. At any point, you could have removed the camera or, at the very least, told me it was up there. You could have told me you knew the truth about who was doing it. Because I knew you knew too, and I thought it was because you were emotionally invested enough to have worked it out for yourself, not because you were voyeuristically watching us every night!'

'It was never like that. That makes it sound seedy and sleazy. I honestly didn't think of it from a privacy point of view. I just *liked* seeing the creativity when you lot put your minds together. Every morning, I'd walk down Ever After Street and feel like a kid at Christmas, excited by the possibilities of what you'd come up with next. If you knew I knew, you'd stop, and I could see how much good it was doing for the museum and I didn't want you to stop.'

'Oh, right, because you've *ever* cared about the museum?'

'You know that's not true.' A look passes over his face and he looks utterly crestfallen.

'Do I?' I snap, even though I do, really. There's no way he's been acting all this time. He genuinely *loved* it. I do know that, even though it's a hard belief to cling onto in the midst of everything else.

'I lost my heart to this place – and to *you*. I never intended to, of course I didn't, but you, and your passion and your belief in what you do got under my skin, and I loved the way my life looked with you in it.' He shoves a hand through his hair again, and pushes out a low breath. 'I've never felt as happy as when I was crouching behind a bin with you, watching a child get a teddy he'd wished for. I didn't mean to get involved with any of it, but I couldn't help myself. I fell in love.'

He doesn't specify *what* with, but the admission makes my breath catch in my throat, and the look of devastation on his face gives me an urge to vault over the counter, wrap him in my arms, and tell him I fell in love with him too – but it wasn't *him*, was it? It was who I thought he was, and what I *thought* he was doing here. I have to remember that. 'So what was your real job? Because, according to what your mother said, it was never to save the museum. Be honest with me for once. Everything we're doing, everything we've done, all the viral talk online, the marketing videos *you* filmed... does it make any difference?'

He shakes his head.

'Would it ever have?'

He's biting his lip, and the head shake this time is so small that I could have imagined it, and I clamp the side of my tongue between my teeth to stop a sob escaping. 'It was all for nothing?

And you knew that from day one? So... what was the point? Why were you here at all?'

'What I told you about that is true. This was my chance to prove to my mother that my ideas can work – that there's merit in working with what's already here and using our funds and expertise to improve and revitalise existing properties, rather than just bulldozing and building new.'

'But...?' I prompt because I can hear the bit he's not adding.

'But... the only trade-off was a three-month delay in starting work on the cinema complex.'

And there it is. The real thing he's been hiding all along. He was never, ever here to save the museum, and I should have known that. I should have been more suspicious than I was, like the others were. 'You knew the museum never stood a chance?'

'I did at first, but that was before I came here. Before I met you, saw what you do, felt the magic you create and how much people love this place. Before I realised there was a place where children can make wishes and people come together to grant them for nothing but the sheer joy of it. As time went on, I genuinely thought we could turn things around. I thought my mother would see what we've been doing and reconsider her stance.'

'Right. And you thought nothing of giving me false hope? Outright lies? Bogus promises, pretend goals? Make triple rent and you can stay. And *why* would you bother investing the amount you have? Your time, your artistic talents, the actual real-life money you've invested in things like the gift shop? Why would you do any of that if you knew we'd be gone within months anyway?'

'I thought we could change the trajectory we were on. I thought if Berrington Developments saw the potential in investing and revitalising, for very little output and a lot of extra incoming profit, and if I could show that happening in a real-world scenario and prove that it worked as a business model, then the museum really could be saved.'

I raise an unimpressed eyebrow. If he didn't lie about absolutely everything, he certainly misrepresented it, and it *hurts* to hear him say it like that. 'As usual, everything's about cold-hearted, ruthless business, and humans and feelings don't matter. What was I to you? Just a toy to play with? Something to use for your own benefit and then toss aside when you were done?'

'You were the best thing that's ever happened to me.'

I choke on the lump in my throat at his honesty, because I *believe* he believes that, and it's painful to hear. 'And you're exactly who I thought you were. No, that's not right. You're exactly who I *knew* you were at first, and then let myself be convinced that you weren't, but you were all along. A soulless evil gerbil, and this time, there's no mistake.'

'I'm not, Liss.' There's a wobble in his voice that suggests he's struggling to hold onto his emotions too. 'I've fallen for you so hard, and—'

And I really can't deal with hearing things like that right now. 'So, romantic catfishing too. Great. I'll see if I can work that into my explanation and hope it gains us some public sympathy.'

'It was never...' His eyes flit between my face and the computer in front of me as I type that into my blank document. 'Why *are* you staring at your laptop like it's about to snap shut and take your fingers off?'

'Trying to write something that justifies what we've been doing. A public apology for misleading everyone. An explanation. You turned us into the bad guys. You should see the comments on social media today. People are disgusted with us for trying to do the right thing.'

'Really?' He looks confused. 'Is it really that deep?'

'Yes, it's that deep!' I snarl at him. 'People are angry. We've been painted as scammers and fraudsters because of *you*.'

'You haven't done anything wrong. No adult actually thought the exhibits were coming to life at night and toddling around Ever After Street by themselves. Inanimate objects don't *do* that and everyone knows it. It's like saying that every parent who lets their child believe in Santa Claus is a fraudster. It's nothing like that – it's a harmless white lie that adults go along with to make children's lives a little bit more magical.'

I'm typing things into the computer as he speaks because I suddenly see the right angle to frame our apology. 'And the information harvesting?'

'Tell the truth. You grant wishes from the well – you can't do that without the basic info. Berrington Developments are wrong on that front. They're a seedy, underhanded company who can't see the good in anything, and the only people they've made look bad with their video is themselves.'

I look up in surprise at the contempt in his voice, but he continues. 'And make sure you blame us. The David versus Goliath approach. Heartfelt small business versus big-money bad guys. People will respond to that. They'll understand. Small businesses are being taken over and bought out every day. People will get behind someone who tried to fight back. Don't apologise like you've done anything wrong – apologise like *we* have.'

'Thanks... I think.' I hold his gaze across the lobby and fight the urge to reach out and take his hand. 'What are you going to do now?'

'I'm going back to my real life. Being here has been like living in a fairytale bubble, avoiding reality, but this isn't my world. I don't belong here, even though I wish I did. Since September, life has felt magical, but it's time for me to accept that it isn't.'

'Then you deserve to be as miserable as you are.' It's too harsh and I see him flinch as I say it. I hate what he's done, but I hurt *for* him too. I don't think he's ever been happy in his job and he certainly never will be now, and he's got the look of a man heading for Death Row, never mind a Midlands office.

'Yes, I do, but this isn't over. I'm not going to give up. I'm not good at relationships, but I'm good at corporate stuff. I'm going to continue fighting this from the inside. I know what you think of me, but you weren't wrong to trust me, Liss, and I'm going to prove that, because even if you never speak to me again, I want to be the person I felt like when I was with you.'

'Funnily enough, Warren, I find it difficult to believe a word you say.'

'I deserve that, but can I say one thing?'

I appreciate that he really does wait for me to give him a nod of permission before speaking.

'These past three months have changed my life. I've never felt worthy of being loved. I thought if anyone knew my secret, they'd despise me, distance themselves from me, treat me as less of a person, and you've made me feel accepted and wanted, and that's a point worth proving, so don't give up yet, because I'm not going to.'

I somehow manage to hold it together until he gets outside the door before breaking down in tears. The numbness and anger turns to misery and desolation and pure, unadulterated loneliness. I didn't know how I was going to let him go in good circumstances, and now he's gone forever in *these* circumstances, and despite everything, he's taken a piece of my heart with him, and I don't know how I'll ever get it back.

23

'This is really lovely, Liss.' Mickey reads what I posted online last night. 'That was a nice touch to compare the escaped exhibits to Santa Claus – something that all parents will relate to. And how you've said what everyone's thinking anyway – that all Berrington Developments have done is make themselves look petty and malicious and like they're taking enjoyment from destroying children's belief in magic. They are literally a company who would tell a child that Santa isn't real, whereas anyone with a shred of decency would play along.'

'I don't know if it will make any difference, but it was actually Warren who helped.'

I cut off her gasp of shock before it's halfway out. '*Before* he left for good, never to return.'

She knew he came in last night. I reiterated his explanation for everyone at an Ever After Street meeting this morning, but I hadn't shared every single word we exchanged, and his tips about the apology were actually spot on.

'Why would he do that?'

'Guilt?' I sigh because I'd like to think it was something more than just that. 'I don't know, but he really is surprisingly good at his job. He knows instinctively what people will connect with and how to spark imaginations and reach people's hearts.'

'You didn't have to take full responsibility.' She nudges my arm with her elbow where we're both leaning on the front desk, hoping that a visitor or two might pop in on this otherwise quiet morning. 'We were all in it together.'

'Yes, I did. Have you seen how angry people are? Everything you lot did was to help me. If there's any backlash, I don't want it coming back on you. My time here is up anyway. It doesn't matter what people say about Colours of the Wind now, but the rest of you have got businesses that have to keep going without this sort of negativity directed towards them.'

'Don't say that. We're not letting this place go without a fight. Sadie's ordered some chains. We're all going to chain ourselves to the building before demolition, if it comes to that. And Cleo's got Mr Hastings on the case to see if there's any legal way to intervene in planning permission or anything like that. Witt thinks there may be some objection he can lodge about devaluing the castle or the cinema complex blocking light to the Full Moon Forest or something. He's looking into it. We're not giving up on this and you're certainly not.'

I'm always the one who stands up and fights on Ever After Street, but after everything, for the first time in my life, I'm wondering if it's a fight that isn't worth fighting. I don't think I've ever felt like that about anything before, and my own lack of conviction is what hurts the most because it feels like Warren has changed something deep inside of me, and I keep coming back to what I've heard so many times lately – the museum will not be saved. What's the point in fighting the inevitable? If the past three months hasn't changed anything, nothing will. I have until March to clear out completely. I should spend that time finding storage space for the exhibits and working out my next move, whether it's worth trying to find a new home for the museum, or whether I should give up and look for a nice, normal, stress-free nine-to-five job.

Mickey can tell I'm spiralling into my unknown future. 'Are there any wishes to grant? That always cheers us all up.'

'Yeah, one. An anonymous one – probably because a sensible parent had told their child not to give us fraudsters any personal information – and it simply read "I wish magic was really real".'

She hugs me. 'People will forget. Tomorrow's fish and chip wrapping and all that.'

'Except, in the era of social media, people can keep retweeting and reposting and re-TikToking until the cows come home, and each time it reaches more and more people and earns us more and more cynics.'

'Or supporters.' She taps her phone, the screen still showing the letter that I posted. 'People will understand. You know that. We didn't do anything wrong – *they* did. They made themselves look bad. You've already got comments saying that. And I have a sneaking suspicion that *this* melancholy is far less to do with what people think of you and far more to do with what *you* feel for a certain person...'

'I miss his smile,' I say without thinking it through. 'His real, genuine, happy smile, the one that I didn't see at all at first because he was always so uptight. And not just the big smile, the little smile he got on his face when he was drawing something, the one he didn't even know was there, his contented smile. I shouldn't miss someone who lied and misrepresented *every* single thing from day one.'

'You can miss who you thought he was.' She reaches over to tuck a pink bit of my hair back. 'And it did sound like he truly felt bad and didn't mean for things to go as far as they did. We all make mistakes when feelings are involved.'

I groan at the mention of feelings. I have so many feelings towards Warren that I don't know what to do with them all. In a couple of short months, I thought I'd met someone who'd be in my life for the rest of forever, and having to reconcile that with what's happened in the last few days is something I'm struggling to get my head around. 'I lost my heart to him too, and now I don't trust my own judgement. I ignored the warnings of people who mean the world to me because I was falling for someone who was putting on a front the whole time, and worse still, he was open about it. He *told* me he was putting on a front, and I foolishly thought that meant he wasn't with *me*.'

'On the plus side, at least you can wriggle out of the mandatory plus one at Witt and Sadie's wedding now.' Mickey tries to cheer me up. 'Absolute proof that people should never make plus ones mandatory, ever.'

'I couldn't agree more.' I clink my cup of tea against hers and try to focus on the positives that have come out of this, like how much I love my Ever After Street colleagues and how far they'd go to help me, regardless of the outcome.

* * *

'It's always brave to stand up to adversity, and what a magical way to do so.' A visitor reaches over to pat my hand as she gives me the entry fee for herself and her granddaughter. I recognise her, she's the same one who walked in on me hugging Warren weeks ago.

'Sorry?'

'That rotten company have got a lot to answer for, trying to destroy something that brings joy to children and taking such pleasure in their "exposé".' She does an angry set of air quotes with the hand that's not holding her granddaughter's. 'I'll tell you what, if that cinema complex goes ahead, my entire family have promised to boycott it, and any other building they get their dirty little paws on. Imagine wanting to destroy somewhere as wonderful as this.'

I don't mean to cry, but tears spring to my eyes unbidden at the compassion in her voice, and she apologises for upsetting me, but I've been an emotional wreck in the days since I posted our apology, and the slightest kindness is setting me off.

And people *are* kind. When I posted that apology, I thought it would be dismissed as us having been caught out and trying to cover our backs, but people really do seem to have taken it to heart and heard our point of view. She's not the first visitor to say something similar, and the social media notifications are going mad.

And it all started with one anonymous post...

Re: Colours of the Wind museum on Ever After Street, Here-fordshire. I want to draw attention to this beautiful little place today. A small, independently run museum full of artefacts from fairytales. A place of magic and wonder and imagination. They've recently become entangled in a dispute with a property developer, who are running a smear campaign to discredit them.

The adults among us know those exhibits didn't move by themselves, but we kept up a pretence around children, no different from helping little ones to believe in Santa Claus at Christmas. It's harmless fun, a bit of magic in an otherwise dreary world, and that's all Colours of the Wind was trying to achieve. This didn't start as a marketing ploy, but as a way to make a soulless property developer see what the people of

Ever After Street see – a place where you can leave adult life behind and believe in the impossible, just for a little while. A place where even the most jaded souls can feel wonder again. A place where someone lost, alone, and desperately wishing to find some meaning in life again can find it in every corner.

Warren. The moment I read it, it's like reading the words of a ghost, and I feel the imaginary tingle of phantom fingers up my spine. Is that just a coincidental use of words, the wishing to find some meaning in life and the Santa comparison he said to me, or is he secretly sticking up for us on the internet?

I write this as someone whose wish at the very, very old wishing well was granted, not by magic or fairies, but by a small group of people who put their hearts and souls into everything on Ever After Street. People who love that museum and will do anything in their power to save it, and everybody should be standing shoulder to shoulder with them. Colours of the Wind inspires wonder, sparks creativity, and connects people to stories and to each other. It brings joy to children and adults alike, it ignites the imaginations of all who go there, and it's a vital part of a wonderful community. The world would be a much less interesting place if we let it go without a fight.

It's him. I'm certain of it. It sparked creativity in *him*. Some of those words are exactly the same words I said to him in the early days. And it sounds like Warren, even the businesslike subject line at the beginning.

But if it *is* Warren, that's a hell of a conflict of interests, and I can't work out what he's playing at. If his company know he's writing stuff like this in *our* defence, they'll be the unhappiest bunnies of all time, won't they?

Especially because the tide is turning against Berrington Developments. Warren's suggestion to use the Santa Claus comparison in my apology may well have been our saving grace in getting people to understand the reasons behind what we were trying to do.

Corporate greed!

Someone posts in response to my online letter.

I ran a candle shop for twenty years, and these rotten sods bought one entire side of the street and evicted all of us without a second thought. Six independent shops wiped out, and for what? Yet another cinema-slash-bowling alley! Will never, ever go to anything they've been involved with! Good on you guys for standing up to the pressure from those money-grabbers who think they can own anything!

The museum must stay! How dare they try to ruin childhood magic just to get one up on the owner! Show them where to shove all the colours of the wind!

They granted my daughter's wish too! It was for some colouring books and new pencils. It took me ages to work out where this random parcel had come from until I saw that awful Berrington video! Thank you, Colours of the Wind! Everyone needs to get behind these wonderful humans!

I don't expect it to make any difference to the outcome for the museum, but it's *nice* to think people do see it from our point of view after all, and that everyone can see the damage that developers like Berrington do. The comments I read bring me back to life. So many people are on our side, and it stirs up the fighting spirit in me again. I've never let unbeatable odds deter me before and I'm not about to now either, not when it comes to something I love as much as I love Colours of the Wind. And the thought that Warren's out there somewhere, anonymously supporting us online, makes me think about his true intentions and my mind goes back to something else he said to me last week. It feels like a lifetime ago now, but there was purpose behind it that I didn't understand at the time, but if that post really was him, he's just signposted me in the direction of something that may turn the tide for good...

* * *

It's many never-ending nights spent researching, and a mountain of paperwork that I get Witt to help me with, but this is my last option to save the museum and it has to be *the* one. It *has* to be.

Somehow, the days drag past. It's the seventeenth of December and Ever After Street is busy with Christmas shoppers. The museum visitor numbers have fallen to what they were before September, before the very first pair of glass slippers went to a ballroom all on their own, and it's oddly fitting, like the past three months have been erased from history. If only they could be erased from memory as well.

'Hello, hello!' A cheerful man wearing a festive bowtie and carrying a briefcase comes up to the front desk with a happy smile. 'I'm here about a well? An application has been made to Historic England, suggesting that it might be relevant to us as a site of special historical interest?'

Ahh, finally! I clasp my hands together and try not to get my hopes up. 'Yes, that was me. I have a well in the garden and I've recently come to believe that it pre-dates the building by many years. We're under threat from property developers and if there's anything on this land that they won't be allowed to destroy, I need to find it.'

'I know you, I've been following your story online,' the man says kindly, his bowtie flashing with red and green Christmas lights. 'Trust me, it would be my pleasure.'

I might not have been sure about that first online post, but I *am* sure about this. Warren *asked* me about that well. He knew it was older than everything else here. He told me to look into the well if anything went wrong, but rather than meaning to literally look down it, he was telling me to investigate its age, and in that online post, the specific reference to it being 'very, very old' was a shove in the right direction – one that nobody but me would recognise.

Witt and I have filled in endless forms, taken loads of photos, and sent them off to Historic England with a prayer and a wish, because despite everything, for one final time, I have to put my trust in Warren, and hope that this time, it's not misplaced.

'What would being a site of special historical interest mean?' I ask the man as he sorts paperwork out of his briefcase.

'You've heard of a listed building? Very similar to that, but it includes smaller places, monuments, memorials, and landmarks that demonstrate a connection to an important aspect of the nation's history. In real terms for a building owner, the well would be unable to be changed or altered, it would need to be carefully maintained, and any repair work or modifications will need to be vigilantly managed according to our standards.'

'And developers would be…?'

'No. No developers would be doing anything. The site must be retained, untouched and intact, and if there were to be any development plans in the area, the developers would face an exceedingly complex landscape of regulations. The number one priority is heritage conservation. Planning permission, approval from local authorities and ourselves, and careful monitoring to ensure that no harm comes to the listed landmark.'

'So they couldn't knock down the building and turn it into something new and modern?'

'Good heavens, no!' The man looks like he needs to breathe into a paper bag at the mere suggestion, and he seems like he might be of too much of a nervous disposition for the scream of joy I want to let out.

I close up and take him to the garden where he oohs and ahhs, takes a million photos, and then I show him down to the basement where he gets even more excited about the crumbling stonework and broken remains of what was once the bottom of the well that probably held water once upon a time, many years ago.

'I would estimate that your well was built sometime in the 1600s and pre-dates everything else on this street by quite a few hundred years...'

Or many, *many* years ago, as the case may be.

'I'll be taking this forward with a panel of assessors to make a decision about its listing status, but I would suggest that this is one of the oldest semi-intact wells in Herefordshire, and I can't imagine there would be any objections to designating it a site of historic interest. It's truly a wonder of ancient architecture...'

Instead of re-opening the doors when he leaves with a final flash of his bowtie, I run down the steps and across the street to The Mermaid's Treasure Trove and squeal at Mickey, even though nothing's certain yet, and there are surely all sorts of spanners that Berrington Developments could still throw in the works, but between this and the way their video has backfired on them, it feels like something's finally going in our direction, and my magical wishing well might have been the answer all along.

When Mickey and I have finished dancing around her shop, I tell her everything. 'In a strange, roundabout way, Warren might have done what he said he would. He might have saved the museum.'

'Cryptic clues in a post you don't even know was written by him is hardly cutting down a maze of thorns and slaying Maleficent, is it?'

Like everyone else on Ever After Street, she's still angry with him for the camera transgression, and I am too, but he must've put his job on the line to write that post, and *that* is someone who maybe wasn't so untrue in his intentions after all.

'No, but he gave me the sword to slay my own dragon, and isn't that what every modern-day girl wants in a fairytale? For the main character to be able to save herself... with a little assistance from a handsome prince.'

24

'Oh, come on, there's no way we have to go to the rehearsal dinner,' I moan to Mickey as she forces me to get up off the sofa, where I've spent the remainder of the Christmas holidays since my sisters went home, stuffing my face with chocolate and watching sappy films, and now it's the thirtieth of December, and Sadie and Witt are insisting we all join them for a rehearsal dinner before their big day tomorrow. 'It's not like we're family who need to meet and socialise with other family. I'd rather just stay here. One romance-based outing full of happy couples this week will be quite enough.'

'We're a kind of family. And it's a nice gesture, they want to get everyone together and say thank you before the formality of the big day. Besides, they're not the only ones with something to celebrate this week. Everyone wants to share in your good news too.'

'We haven't got the results of Historic England's decision yet. They might say no.'

'They won't,' she says cheerfully. 'You *know* that's why

Warren mentioned the well weeks ago. He must've guessed what was going to happen and had it as a back-up plan, which he couldn't overtly tell us without betraying his company.'

'I thought you hated him.'

'I do, but keeping my best friend working opposite me makes it marginally easier to un-hate him.'

'I doubt either of us are ever going to see him again,' I mutter, trying to ignore the gaping hole that feels like it's opened in my chest with that thought. So many times this week, with the museum closed for the holidays and nothing to occupy my time, my fingers have hovered over his name in my phone, wondering if I should send him a quick text, an innocent thank you for the shove in the right direction, but nothing changes his actions while he was here, and I've stopped myself giving in to the temptation.

'No, I doubt it, but at least it didn't end on quite such a sour note, hmm?'

'You are disturbingly cheerful today,' I mutter as I go upstairs to change into my red off-the-shoulder tea dress, knowing full well that I was never going to wriggle out of it, no matter how hard I tried. The thought of being surrounded by sickeningly loved-up couples for the next few hours makes me want to hide on the sofa forever, and so does the fact that every single one of them knows what happened to my mandatory plus one, and why I'm going to be the *only* guest on my own.

It's 5 p.m. when Mickey, her partner Ren, his teenage daughter Ava and I walk through the Full Moon Forest and along the stone walkway to the castle gates. It's dark, but the way is lit by streetlamps, and the trees are bare for winter now, their decaying leaves gathered at the edges of the pathways like they've been pushed aside to make way for the guests that will be arriving tomorrow.

'Hello!' Sadie opens the door wearing jogging bottoms and a sauce-splashed top, with her hair tied back in a bandana and a panicked look on her face. 'Oh, God, it's all gone wrong. We've got caterers for the big day and I stupidly thought *I* could cook for everyone tonight, and underestimated both my timings and my cooking ability. Nothing's ready, nothing's set up, and you lot all look lovely and refined and not frazzled at all, so you can help me!'

She hauls us all inside and shuts the cold December night out quickly, and starts barking instructions. 'Mick, set the table! Ren, Ava, you can get the plates from the kitchen! Lissa, chairs! They're stacked in that little terrace! Just outside the patio doors! Quick, go, go, go!'

Before I've had a chance to think, I'm hurried towards a set of glass doors and bundled out into a small garden area, grass and paving stones surrounded by neatly trimmed hedgerow with fairylights winding through it, empty planters that would be full of flowers in the summer, a couple of tables, and... absolutely *no* chairs.

I turn around to go back in because it's obviously the wrong place, but there's a movement in the shadows. 'Hi.'

The scream I let out is not so much a yelp of surprise as a blood-curdling shriek when a familiar silhouette steps forward and I nearly fall over my own feet as I scramble backwards.

'What are you doing here?' I snap, straightening myself out and trying to pretend that my heart *isn't* pounding at a hundred miles an hour, and not just from the shock, but because of *who* it is.

'I've been invited to a wedding but they won't let me in without a plus one. Apparently they're mandatory.' Warren's fiddling with a large brown envelope held between both his hands.

'So you thought skulking by a hedge and scaring me half to death would be the best approach?'

'I thought you might run if you saw me.'

'And there's a very good reason for that, isn't there?' I turn around and try to open the patio doors I just came through, but they're locked from the inside, and I quickly realise that this is not a coincidence. I haven't been sent out here to gather chairs for the dinner. Mickey's suspicious cheerfulness earlier. Sadie's overacting. I know my Ever After Street friends well enough to know a carefully planned conspiracy when I see one. Between them, they've conspired to get me and Warren out here together, and I have a feeling they're not going to let either of us back inside for a while yet.

'So...' I turn around to face Warren and try not to think about how *good* he looks in the black cable-knit winter jumper he's wearing. It's got subtle snowflakes woven throughout it in silver thread, although there are dark circles under his eyes and his face looks pinched with worry in a way that still makes me want to cup his jaw and smooth the lines away. 'Have you been sent to help with the imaginary chairs as well?'

'No, I was waiting for you. This was my fault. I knew they were going to come up with something to send you out here, but no one could have foreseen imaginary chairs.'

It makes me want to snort and he probably hears the burble as I try to hold it back.

'Witt really did invite me. We've met to discuss the well a few times, and we hit it off. The guy who struggles to speak with his stutter and the guy who can't hear, we're a match made in heaven, right?'

I press my lips together and try not to smile. He has no right to be this disarming when I'm trying to hold onto my rightful anger. '*That's* how he knew exactly what to put on those forms, isn't it? I thought it was just part of his old estate agent job, but there was some oddly specific wording that he insisted on. That was you, behind the scenes, right? Even after everything...'

He holds both hands up in a 'guilty as charged' gesture, still clutching the brown envelope in one set of fingers.

We pace around each other, he stays on his side of the terrace in front of the glittering hedge, and I stay on mine, by the patio door, pacing in the light spilling out from inside.

'I wouldn't have run,' I say eventually. He looks so nervous that I can feel my anger towards him dispersing. 'I've nearly texted you so many times this week. Just to say thank you for having a back-up plan. We don't know if it's worked yet, but—'

'It's worked. It's not official yet, but I know old stonework when I see it. So does Witt. That well was built an extremely long time ago, the basement was built to accommodate the well, years later. There's no way it won't go through, and my company knows it too. Liss, I...' He sighs and shakes his head. 'I have something for you.'

He takes a step closer and holds out the envelope, but when I reach for it, he pulls it back. 'I don't expect anything from this. It's not a way of getting you to talk to me. It's simply following through on what I told you I'd come here to do – save the museum and make sure it never ends up in the wrong hands again. I could have sent it in the post, but honestly, I wanted to see you. I wanted a chance to apologise again and...'

'...and you've clearly got the others on your side.' I finish the sentence when he trails off.

He smiles for the first time tonight. 'I had a feeling that to have any chance of winning you back, I'd need a little help from your friends.'

I take the envelope from him and open the top, and pull out... documents. Typed documents full of long, complicated, businessy words that blur in front of my eyes. 'What is this?'

'The title deeds for the museum. It's worthless to Berrington Developments now. They can't touch any part of the wishing well or the basement where it stands. I took it as pay-off to leave the company.'

'What?' This time, the words blur in front of my eyes for a different reason, and I have to hold the pages away so tears don't drip onto them. 'I can't accept this. It's too much. That's a *big* building, it must be worth a fortune.'

'It's literally worthless to anyone except you. No one can touch the building without disturbing the well. No developer will ever be able to do anything with it. No one wants it – except those it matters to. If I keep it, you'll be answerable to me, and I don't want that. The museum belongs to you. It always has done, but now it's official. You will never again have to worry about someone like me coming in and taking over.'

'Warren, you can't do this...'

'It's already done. The paperwork is with the company solicitor, he'll be in touch when everyone's back from the Christmas holidays for you to sign the final agreement. The museum is yours, and there is nothing anyone can do to change that.'

I don't realise how hard I'm crying until a huge sob escapes and tears drip onto my chest.

'I'm sorry.' He takes a tentative step towards me. 'I didn't mean to upset you. I just wanted to do the right thing for once.'

'They're good tears,' I reassure him quickly because he's chewing his lip like he's done something horribly wrong. 'I just can't believe it. You can't have... You can't just *give* me the building. Your company bought it. At least let me pay somet—'

'The company can afford it.' He softly cuts off my protest.

'Between us, we've turned it into a worthless albatross that they were only too pleased to get rid of. You owe nothing. The museum is yours.'

It's like he knows he needs to keep repeating those words so they sink in, and I look up at the night sky, trying to will the tears to stop falling because I cry harder every time he says it. It cannot be real, and yet I'm holding the proof right here in my hand.

'What this bloody garden needs is somewhere to sit down.' I perch against one of the tables and try to breathe through the tears, certain that if I pinch myself, I'll wake up and I really will be out here solely to get some chairs, and this won't be happening in real life. In my wildest dreams, I never expected saving the museum to involve me actually owning it, and I laugh semi-hysterically while still crying, and the resulting noise is enough of a mess that Warren looks alarmed.

'I want to give you a hug but you'd probably wallop me round the head with that bird bath if I tried.'

I glance at the wide bowl on a concrete pedestal. 'Nah. Too heavy to lift.'

He laughs a thick laugh that makes me think he's holding onto his emotions by a thread too.

This is the biggest, most unexpected thing anyone's ever done for me, so big that it obliterates everything that came before. He made mistakes, but he's gone above and beyond to make up for them, and it's increasingly difficult to remember the bad parts, and instead all I can think of is the joy he brought into my life, and how much I've missed him.

'You left the company?' I sniffle and try to compose myself. 'Your own family company that you've worked at for twenty years?'

'Yep. And do you know how many times I've been happy in those twenty years?'

I shake my head.

'Once. It started this September when I arrived here. It was a nice feeling and I wasn't ready to give it up. Berrington Developments is not the company my father wanted to start. It's the company that got all twisted up with my mother's bitterness and grief and her single-minded dedication to ensuring no one ever felt anything deeply enough to get their heart broken again. Nothing has ever been more soul-destroying than going back to that office after being here, and knowing what they'd done with that video. My father wanted to make the world better by bringing new builds to areas that would benefit from them – not by destroying beautiful places that bring charm and magic and light to everyone they touch, and I hadn't realised how caught up I'd got in all that until I came here and saw the real-life impact of what my company wanted to do. I've known I was going to leave for weeks now, but I had to make sure I could take this with me.' He points to the envelope on the table and takes a step towards me. 'I know I messed up, Liss. I should have taken that camera down – or never put it up in the first place – and I definitely should have triple-checked who had access to the footage. I shouldn't have lied about the most likely outcome for the museum and what my job really was. I'm so sorry. There's no excuse and there's no way of truly making up for it.'

'It's not about making up for it. It's about... proving you were who I thought you were.' I tilt my head and try to catch his eyes. 'It *was* you who wrote that first post, wasn't it? The one that mentioned finding meaning in life again?'

His eyes meet mine across the garden. 'So you *did* read my wish after all...'

'Yeah. Sorry, it was so personal that it wasn't easy to tell you.

If I'd known it was going to be something like that, I would have left it well alone.'

'You made it come true, you know. Being with you, seeing everything you do, it showed me what had been missing from my life. Reading those wishes, having the privilege of granting some of them... it made me feel alive again. I meant what I said the other day – I've never been happier than when I was crouching behind a pile of binbags with you. I want to spend the rest of my days hiding behind bins with you, helping people believe in magic and goodness and hope. I know you didn't intend it that way, but your magical wishing well granted the wish I made to appease you, back when I thought this was just another job, that it wouldn't have any impact on me or change my life in any way. I don't deserve it, but can you forgive me?'

I glance at the envelope on the table and then at the windows of the castle, where I can see the silhouettes of multiple shadows, trying not to twitch the curtains and look out. Even my friends must have forgiven him because they've gone to all this trouble to throw us together.

And I missed him. So, so much. Seeing him tonight wasn't just a shock – it was a *relief*. Since he left the other day, all I've wanted is to see him again. I know that I could say no and he'd leave, and I really would never have to see him again, but the thought of letting him go makes my hands start shaking and my stomach turns over and feels like there's a swarm of irate bees buzzing angrily inside it.

I push myself up, walk over on unsteady legs, and wrap my arms around him.

It takes a few seconds for him to react and then his arms slide around me too, uncertainly like he's still reserving judgement on whether this hug is a good thing or a bad thing.

'This seems like a good sign,' he murmurs into my neck, and

it makes me let go of all pretences and cling onto him. My hands slide into his hair and grasp at his arms, desperately inhale his aftershave, and he holds me so close that it's only possible to take shallow breaths, and that's all we do. For long minutes, we just clutch onto each other and breathe, and when he eventually pulls back without taking his arms from around me, I reach up and cup his face.

'Are you okay? You look like you haven't slept since last month.' I rub my thumb over his cheek and look into his emotional blue eyes.

'Yeah, it's pretty hard to sleep when you've lost the best thing that's ever happened to you and you've only got yourself to blame. But I will be... I have a hospital appointment in January to get *this* re-fitted and see if there's anything else I can do to improve it.' He points to his hearing aid and I reach up until I can rub my thumb over his earlobe and he shivers in my arms in a way that's not connected to the cold.

His eyes slowly drift shut. 'Never in a million years did I think I'd let anyone see that, get that close, and just... *trust* them not to treat me differently because of it.'

I lean up and press my lips to his cheek, and the noise he makes is nothing louder than a shivery, shuddery breath, but it's a sound that speaks so many volumes about how much he's struggled, and how different life can be with the right support.

'What will you do now? For work, I mean.' I pull back until I can cup his face again, and I love how reluctant he is to open his eyes and let reality back in to this dreamy closeness.

'I'm actually going cap in hand around all the fairytale museums in the area, looking for a job and a girlfriend...'

I laugh out loud. 'Any specific job?'

His mouth contorts as he gives it some serious thought.

'Museum marketing manager? Gift shop overseer? Chief beanstalk builder?'

'I think one of those could be arranged. Full disclosure though, it does not come with a company car and fancy suits are prohibited. Deal?'

His grin is so wide that his jaw must be aching as he leans down to kiss my cheek. 'Best deal I've ever made.'

'Any specific girlfriend?' I can't stop smiling either as he stands back up again, his arms still around me.

'No, any will do, I'm not fussed.' He laughs when I smack his shoulder. 'Yes, one very, very specific girlfriend, Liss. The woman who got under my skin from day one, with her bright colourful hair and matching attitude, who makes magic and wishes and fairies seem real, and makes me feel like I'm *dancing* in fairydust and floating above the clouds.'

His fingers twist in my hair as he tucks it back and dips his head until his nose can rub against mine, which is either a romantic gesture or an attempt to warm up because both our noses are like ice, and we end up giggling against each other's mouths and losing track of the conversation.

My fingers stroke his hair back as he touches his lips tentatively to mine, soft at first, careful and caring, his fingers running all over me, like he's trying to convince himself that this isn't a dream, and I'm lost in that distant, otherworldly feeling too, still convinced someone's going to wake me up any second and I really am going to be out here alone, having an imaginary-chair-induced fantasy.

The thought makes me grasp at him harder, because if this is some sort of daydream, I want to make the absolute most of it, and he's definitely thinking the same thing because the kiss turns harder and hotter. His stubble grazes across my skin and I gasp against his mouth, nip at his lips, and the noise he makes is a guttural groan crossed with a whimper, and the only thing that stops me from tearing his clothes off right this second is how flipping freezing it is out here, and the vague memory of an audience watching from behind the nearest window.

I force us both to pull back before this gets any more frenzied. Somehow I've ended up sitting on the table again with him pressed against me, and now he leans on the glass surface, gasping for breath, and I rest my forehead against his shoulder and try to remember how to breathe, and we're both shaky, giggly, and completely unable to take our hands off each other, because this still might be a very, *very* vivid dream.

'I come with an investor, by the way,' he murmurs as his fingers run up and down my arm. 'The one who pulled out because his son loved the escaped exhibits so much. I reached out, told him what I was going to do, and he wanted to come on board. He loved the idea of a cinematic room. Told me I was a fool in love when I started talking about you.'

I want to ask if he was right, but he answers before I've plucked up the courage. 'He wasn't wrong. I've been head over heels for you for weeks now, *months* maybe. I didn't mean for it to happen, never even entertained the idea that it *could* happen for me, but then you filled my every thought and I couldn't wait to get to work to see you, and I had this butterfly-ish feeling and found myself with this daft, soppy smile every time I thought about you, and I couldn't stop thinking about you so I couldn't stop smiling, and...' He runs out of words and leans down to kiss me again instead.

'The moment I realised what your secret was and immediately wanted to murder anyone who'd ever said an unkind word to you.' I let my fingers brush over his left ear again when the kiss breaks. 'It made me realise how much of a front you really put on, and how much you'd let me see behind it.

That, and when you admitted you'd started watching Disney movies.'

He laughs and kisses me again, and this time, a cheer goes up from the castle and the patio doors slide open, and I blink in the darkness to see that our audience has grown since we last saw them, and we're now joined by all our Ever After Street colleagues and half of Sadie and Witt's extended families, friends, and people we've never met before.

'I wouldn't be upset if that was locked for a bit longer, would you?' Warren whispers into my hair, holding me tight against him.

'I could happily stay out here all night. It's not cold *at all*.'

He's about to make a joke about ways to stay warm, but Sadie yells from inside. 'Don't make me come and get you! I will haul you both in by your ears if I have to! You've got plenty of time for smooching later!'

'Yes, we do, don't we?'

He rubs his nose against mine. 'We do.'

Life has started to feel like a fairytale since he came here, and it's had nothing to do with wishing wells, fairydust, Disney princes, or escaping exhibits, and everything to do with his smile, his hair that defies gravity, and the way I feel when we're together. Because falling in love is a dizzying real-life version of a fairytale, and like all good stories, I never want it to end.

* * *

'Finally! At first I thought we were going to have to come out there and push your lips together like a pair of dolls,' Witt says.

'Funny, because just now, I thought we were going to have to come out and dissolve the superglue sticking you together,' Mickey adds, amidst a round of whooping and cheering when we get back inside with burning red cheeks that are tingling with embarrassment and not *just* from the chill.

'Let's celebrate.' Sadie clinks a spoon against a champagne flute to make a toast. 'Tomorrow is for wedding jitters, but tonight is for friendship, found family, and absolutely everyone I love being here and being happy. Congratulations to Liss on fighting her own fight for once and winning, and to Liss and Warren, who despite a rocky start, has potential to become a fully fledged member of the Ever After Street community, because the one thing we all trust is Lissa's judgement. Thank you to all of you, everyone in this room, for being a part of our love story, and each other's.'

I look around at all my favourite people, who started off as colleagues, who became friends, who became family. Sadie and Witt, Marnie and Darcy, Cleo and Bram, Franca and Raff, Imogen and Ali, and Mickey, Ren, and Ava. People who mean the world to me and thoroughly deserve every inch of happiness they've found with each other.

Warren squeezes my hand and makes me look over at him with a knowing smile, and leans over to steal another kiss, and it inspires me to raise my glass and make a toast of my own.

'Congratulations to the first Ever After Street happy couple, and to the rest of us who are all going to get married in this castle one day, because there isn't a better place in the world than right here, with all of you. We all bring our own little bit of magic to this beautiful street, and it wouldn't be the same without any of us. Cheers.'

Everyone clinks their glasses and I feel like my heart might burst with happiness. I can't wait to be part of all the stories Ever After Street will get to tell in the future, and to meet all the people who will come here and believe, just for a little while, that the world really can be magical when you're lucky enough to find the right people to make it so.

* * *

MORE FROM JAIMIE ADMANS

A Midnight Kiss on Ever After Street, the first instalment in Jaimie Admans' magical Ever After Street series, is available to order now here:

https://mybook.to/MidnightKissBackAd

ACKNOWLEDGEMENTS

Thank you, Mum. Always my first and most important reader! I'm eternally grateful for your constant patience, support, encouragement, and belief in me. Thank you for always being there for me – I don't know what I'd do without you. Love you lots!

Marie Landry, my best friend and my favourite author all rolled into one. I'm pretty sure this series wouldn't exist without your support and cheerleading. It felt serendipitous that we were both working on our first series at the same time! Thank you, as always, for being the most caring, supportive, and loving best friend I could ever have dreamed of! I love you and I'm so proud – of you *and* of getting to call you my best friend! Team Basketcase all the way! Just remember – the horrors persist, but so do we! And it feels wrong to write this without mentioning Nancy Landry. Even though you're no longer with us, you are always in my thoughts and forever in my heart.

Thank you to Bill, Toby, Cathie, and Bev for your continued love and enthusiasm. Thank you to Jayne Lloyd and Charlotte McFall for being such wonderful friends, and an extra special thank you to Angela Johannes for being the most prolific reader I've ever known and for always giving me something to smile about!

I want to say a massive thank you to everyone who I chat to on social media, who I've connected with thanks to books, and to all of you who show me so much support and kindness on a daily basis. A big shoutout to some Facebook groups who support me tirelessly and are an absolute pleasure to be part of. A huge and heartfelt thank you to all the members and admins of Vintage Vibes and Riveting Reads, especially you, Sue Baker. All the bonkers ladies who try to keep The Friendly Book Community in line. Fiona Jenkins at the PMDD/Severe PMS Support & Information Group, and all the admins of Chick Lit and Prosecco, Book Swap Central, and Fiction Addicts Book Club. If you're a booklover looking for somewhere to brighten your day, lift your spirits, and make you feel like you've found a group of people who understand why we always buy more books even though we need scaffolding to hold up our current to-read pile, please find your way to these groups! You will be glad you did – although your to-read list may not!

Thank you to my fantastic agent, Amanda Preston, and my amazing editor Emily Ruston, along with the rest of the wonderful and hardworking Boldwood team, and everyone who works so tirelessly behind the scenes to bring these books to life. The fantastic copyeditors I've worked with – Candida and Cecily – and my brilliant proofreader, Rachel Sargeant, and the wonderful narrator who has made every audiobook shine, Emma Noakes. Ever After Street would not have been as sparkly as it was without all of you!

And finally, thank *you* for reading! I hope you enjoyed getting lost in Lissa's museum of fairytale magic, along with every other business we've visited on this charming little street. The thing I've heard most of all from readers is how much they wish Ever After Street was real so they could go there – and so do I! I'd never written a series before and I'm so grateful for all the love and support it's received. Hopefully you'll join me again in a future book because there will always be more happily ever afters waiting right around the corner!

ABOUT THE AUTHOR

Jaimie Admans is the bestselling author of several romantic comedies. She lives in South Wales.

Sign up to Jaimie Adman's mailing list for news, competitions and updates on future books.

Visit Jaimie's website: www.jaimieadmans.com

Follow Jaimie on social media:

X x.com/be_the_spark
f facebook.com/jaimieadmansbooks
instagram.com/jaimieadmans1

ALSO BY JAIMIE ADMANS

Standalone Novels

The Gingerbread House in Mistletoe Gardens

The Ever After Street Series

A Midnight Kiss on Ever After Street

An Enchanted Moment on Ever After Street

A Wonderland Wish on Ever After Street

Christmas Ever After

Finding Love at the Magical Curiosity Shop

Dreams Come True at the Fairytale Museum

Boldwood

Boldwood Books is an award-winning fiction publishing company seeking out the best stories from around the world.

Find out more at www.boldwoodbooks.com

Join our reader community for brilliant books, competitions and offers!

Follow us
@BoldwoodBooks
@TheBoldBookClub

Sign up to our weekly deals newsletter

https://bit.ly/BoldwoodBNewsletter